MW00453491

Command and Control

A Joseph Michael Barber Thriller, Book 2

By

Dennis A. Tosh

For Edith Tosh, without whose love and support this project would not have been possible,

For Lexie and Will, the two of you bring boundless joy to my life,

For Warren Maxwell Tosh (1920-2017, United States Navy 1942-1945), who traveled that long and improbable journey from the hills of Fredonia, Kentucky to Launch Complex 39A, Cape Canaveral, Florida, and in doing helped reach for the stars,

For all who served, and in serving gave the last full measure of their devotion – you are not forgotten, and you have created a debt we cannot repay.

Greater love hath no man than this, that a man lay down his life for a friend
John 15:13

Also by Dennis A. Tosh – "The Orion Affair", ©2019, available in Kindle or paperback format on Amazon.com

This book is a work of fiction. Any resemblance to actual persons, living or dead, or actual events, is purely a coincidence.

(*or is it?*)

Command and Control – Summary

In the wake of the collapse of the European Union, sparked by the chaos of Brexit, a new alliance is forged between Germany and France. Their vision – create a superpower on the European continent capable of eclipsing The United States, China, or any nation on Earth. Iran exploits the chaos and devises a plan to settle old scores with a diabolically clever and horrifying twist on cyber warfare. Miscalculations, mistrust, misunderstandings and mistakes push the world to the brink of annihilation as events quickly spin out of control.

Joseph Michael Barber, CEO of his own security firm, Orion Bellicus ("fierce hunter"), is drawn into the swirl of events as he investigates the assassination of an important client, the Chief Executive of an important German defense contractor. What he uncovers is astonishing and beyond his worst fears, and the knowledge makes him an assassination target himself. Barber and his partner, Marcus Day, are drawn deeper and deeper into a web of treason and deceit as they scramble to reveal the truth in an effort to pull the world back from the brink of catastrophe, and it's a race against time.

From the halls of power in Washington D.C. to Silicon Valley in California, from Berlin to Iran, and from China to the desolate northern shores of the Shetland Islands to the mountains of Argentina, Command and Control delivers a horrifying tale of cyber warfare, once again ripped from today's headlines.

The Cast of Characters

The Antecedent:

- **Charles Westborne "Westy" Reynolds III (deceased):** Late Chief Executive Officer of PrinSafe, main protagonist of prequel, "The Orion Affair", murdered by his protégé, Emma Clark

The Principals:

- **Joseph Michael Barber:** Chief protagonist, former SEAL sniper and C.I.A. Special Activities Division, CEO of his own security firm, Orion Bellicus (fierce hunter)
- **General Horst Brandt:** Commander, European Federation Air Force, later acting Chancellor, European Federation
- **Dr. Emma Clark:** Chief antagonist, CEO of the private equity firm, PrinSafe, murderer of Westy Reynolds (in The Orion Affair)
- **Marcus Day:** COO of Orion Bellicus, best friend of Joe Barber
- **Lieutenant General Jean-Baptiste Laurent:** Deputy Commander, European Federation Air Force, come-lately protagonist

The Supporting Cast:

The Americans:

- **Dominick Bastionelli:** Speaker of the House
- **Donald R. Benson:** Executive Assistant Director for National Security, F.B.I.
- **Sarah Einhorn:** President of the United States
- **Charles "Boomer" Ellison**: Vice President of the United States
- **Carleton Espy III:** U.S. Secretary of State

- **General Wilber Forrester:** Commanding General, StratCom (Strategic Command)
- **Burt Hagenlocker:** U.S. Secretary of Defense
- **Radek Malecek:** U.S. National Security Advisor
- **Margaret Shevchenko:** Director, Central Intelligence Agency
- **General John Weatherby:** Chairman, Joint Chiefs of Staff

The English:

- **Jeremy Boren:** Prime Minister, England
- **Simon Davies:** Secretary of State for Defense, England
- **Lord David Herbert:** Chief of the Secret Intelligence Service (MI6)
- **Nigel Worthington:** Foreign Secretary

The French:

- **Gaston Morel:** French President

The Germans:

- **Eric Farhang (Farhang Alipour):** German citizen and Iranian deep plant
- **Dr. Heinrich Krùger:** Chancellor, European Federation
- **Helmut Schiller:** Late CEO of Sternenlicht (in English, "Starlight"), the software company that designed the Federation Command and Control systems
- **Hans-Dieter Zimmerman:** acting CEO of Sternenlicht, post Schiller

The Iranians:

- **Ayatollah Ashtiana:** Iranian Supreme Leader
- **Major General Muhammad Bagheri:** Commander of the Iranian General Staff

- **Dr. Ashkan Ghorbani:** Software wiz, Ph.D.s in math from MIT and Computer Science from Harvard, abducted from the U.S. & forced to work for Iranian Cyber Warfare Command
- **Brigadier General Garshop Hamidi:** Commander of the Iranian Revolutionary Guard Corp

"What was impossible yesterday is only difficult today,
What is difficult today becomes easy tomorrow,

Never ask if, only ask how, and never worry about when – when is now."

The late Charles Westborn "Westy" Reynolds III…………….

Command and Control

Prologue

Hotel Adlon Kempinski, Berlin -- Present Day

His heart raced, and he started to sweat. He could feel his face become flushed, and he imagined that beads of sweat were about to pop on his forehead. A discreet attempt at a couple of deep breaths to slow down his heartbeat and respiration utterly failed to accomplish either. Droplets of perspiration trickled down each side of his torso even though the hotel's reception area was freezing. He was terrified that the woman he was talking to would notice his growing nervousness and all of its biological markers. If she did, it would make him stand out, and given how the evening was likely to unfold, she would remember it. And she would remember him. He couldn't afford to be remembered tonight. The stakes were too high. Bringing attention to himself might invite questions from people to whom he preferred remaining invisible. Questions could lead to discovery, and discovery would be a disaster. Worse, discovery would mean failure.

The irony was, he wasn't even sure what it was he was about to do. He knew the specific actions he was about to take, and he had his suspicions about what they meant, but his handler had told him in no uncertain terms to stop asking questions. When he asked, his handler's countenance had morphed from friendly to menacing. It had scared him, so he quickly shut up, But it only made his suspicions more ominous. Was he about to pass state secrets to someone? That would be easy and present the least risk to him; there was plenty of security at the event, but nobody would be looking for that. Was he passing instructions to somebody else or giving the "go" order for a major terrorist act? It was also low risk for the same reasons. Was he taking a life? This is the one he was worried about, because it would draw an immediate response from the hordes of on-site security personnel so ubiquitous that they were practically tripping over each other. Anyone within the immediate vicinity of anyone killed would automatically be a suspect and might even be gang-tackled. But he didn't know exactly what his mission was, and that was frustrating. The one thing he did know, was the very purpose for his life had built up to whatever act he was about to commit. They HAD told him that. So, whatever the consequences, it had to be big. He almost couldn't believe it. His time was actually here. He could not screw this up.

Having failed to stabilize his composure, Erich Farhang excused himself from the conversation with the woman and started to walk toward the men's room. Once inside, he entered one of the stalls and closed the door. He retrieved the sealed packet from his pocket, opened it and removed what looked like a small square band aid. With extreme caution he affixed the adhesive side of the device to the inside of his right palm. The side facing outward was covered with a thin shield, something he was told to peel off just before he engaged his target. He also was told to be extraordinarily careful. That bolstered his suspicions that he was about to become an assassin. You didn't have to be that careful with just data or a message.

As he exited the stall and walked out the bathroom door, he heard chimes begin to ring, summoning the business people in the cocktail party to make their way to the dining room. He glanced about the room, spotted his target, and began expeditiously closing the gap so as to not lose this opportunity.

Erich Farhang, real name Farhad Alipour, was a child of the Iranian Revolution. He had waited his whole life for this moment. As a young boy, he was selected by the Iranian Ministry of Intelligence for his high intellect and perfect German language skills, being born to an Iranian father and a German mother. The Islamic Republic of Iran had taken a page from the old Soviet Union cold war play book and placed him as a deep cover asset in West Berlin with a family loyal to the Revolution. His instructions were simple -- live the life of a respectable German citizen and excel at everything you do. Someday the Revolution will require something of you. We do not know what and we do not know when, his handlers told him. But when that day arrives and instructions are given, he was to proceed with unquestioned and complete obedience. He would not be told the why. He would not even be told the what. He simply would be given a very specific set of actions to follow and he was to follow them to the letter. After doing so, he was to continue going about his very comfortable life. He may be called upon again someday, he was told, or perhaps he would not. And most importantly, he was never to reveal his mission to anyone on penalty of death. He wondered, if, after fulfilling this mission, he was marked for death anyway. His handlers didn't seem the types who would leave loose ends. He tried to put the thought out of his mind. Better to focus on things you can control, he thought to himself.

He excelled at being a good German citizen. After graduating university with a degree in electrical engineering, he took a job with a German defense contractor. He married a German girl and had two children. His family had no clue as to his real identity. They were a perfect, hardworking German family. And here he stood today, his company's Executive Vice President of Global Operations. His business success is what placed him in the perfect position for a very important task. His business success is why he had received an invitation to this party. And so, he had been chosen to execute a very important mission in service to The Islamic Republic of Iran.

Joseph Michael Barber worked his way through the crowded event center at the famous Hotel Aldon Kempinski in downtown Berlin. The hotel was located right next to the Brandenburg Gate, the cold war icon that had separated the former communist East Berlin from the non-communist West. The hotel's close proximity to such an historic landmark made it a favorite of business guests and well-healed tourists alike. It also made it the obvious choice by the European Federation Defense Ministry as a venue for the second annual gathering of CEOs from major military contractors and senior Defense Ministry officials. The movers and shakers at the event would bond and nurture their relationships over cocktails, the finest wines and an exquisite seven course dinner. More importantly, in the days, weeks and months that followed they would continue to forge the strategy and provide the means to fuel the ascendancy of a new vision for Europe.

The European Federation, or EF as it was called, was born from the rubble of a collapsed European Union, or EU. The opening scene to the tragicomedy was Brexit, or the withdrawal of Great Britain from the EU. Once Britain withdrew, financial markets began rampant speculation about what country would leave next. They had all seen this movie before. The same dynamic occurred over a decade ago with the Greek debt crisis, but cooler heads prevailed then and pulled everyone back from the brink. A cool head was a rare commodity these days. Collapsing stock markets, soaring interest rates and talk by the EU bureaucrats in Brussels of imposing extreme austerity measures on member countries under financial siege led to popular revolts. Spain, Italy and Ireland withdrew. Others soon followed. Then in an act that defied centuries of history, two long-term rivals, Germany and France, forged a new marriage.

They called it a Federation, implying there was a central government but independent control over local issues. This was a clever play on words by astute politicians to soothe a skeptical public, primarily in France. Reality was evident in the name of the EF's new currency. It was called the Deutsche Franc. Franc after the pre-Euro currency in France, the French franc, again to soothe and pacify the French. But no one in the new EF government had any illusions about the significance of the principal modifier, "Deutsche" in the currency's name. The new EF government had no interest in telling the locals in France how to produce or distribute wine. But as for foreign and military policy, as well as fiscal and monetary affairs, the EF spoke with one voice, and that voice emanated from Berlin. Their objective was global hegemony, or dominance, both militarily and economically. They knew they had a long road towards their objective, surpassing both China and the United States, all the while keeping a nuclear Russia placated, but it was their dream.

Barber's security firm, Orion Bellicus, meaning "fierce warrier", was engaged by several defense contractors attending the event to provide the personal protection details for their CEOs. These were no ordinary corporate executives. They were HVCs, or "high value clients", and they all had the highest possible security clearances. Assassination or kidnappings were real risks. Normally, as his firm's CEO he wouldn't personally supervise a protection detail. Given the nature of the protectees, however, his on-site presence and that of his second in command, Marcus Day, were conditions of the contract.

As Barber wandered through the crowded cocktail reception, he had an uneasy feeling. Some people called it a sixth sense. Leroy Jethro Gibbs, the legendary fictional government agent from the hit TV series, NCIS, called it his "gut". Some people just called it indigestion. Whatever it was, he had it in spades. The spacious room was awash with sounds of crowd chatter. With so many people it was almost like white noise. Individual conversations were difficult to discern, even from groups of people right next to him. A string quartet was playing music from a stage, but he could barely make out the individual notes, let alone the melody. Waiters wandered among the crowd with trays of hors d'oeuvres, champagne, single-malt Scotch, and red and white wine. The room was cold. Berlin was in the middle of a brutal heat-wave, and the outside temperature had been 36 degrees Celsius, or 97 degrees Fahrenheit, during the late afternoon just hours before the event. The room's air conditioning was cranked high in what was a deliberate effort at over-kill to offset the massive number of BTUs projected by the party guests. He could feel the AC penetrate his buttoned tuxedo jacket. He wondered what many of the women were thinking, dressed in their strapless or even bare-shouldered evening attire.

As he pushed his way through the crowd, a dark-haired man with a thick athletic build clipped Barber's side and knocked his arm forcefully enough to spill some of the red wine from the glass he was holding. The man turned briefly towards him and said, “excuse me”. As their eyes met, he noticed perspiration on the man’s forehead. Odd, he thought, given the temperature in the room. “No problem,” Barber replied as he watched the man turn away and continue pushing himself through the crowd a little too quickly.

Barber’s senses were on high-alert as he worked his way through the crowd. His eyes scanned the room for potential threats in a disciplined and systematic manner. Although he saw nothing obvious, something still didn’t seem right. He was paid to be cautious, especially when protecting an HVC. But this was way beyond cautious. His senses were at DEFCON 2. In military jargon that meant he was only one step away from an actual fight. Sure, the room was a target-rich environment. The EF Defense Minister was hosting, and there were rumors sweeping the reception that the Chancellor of the EF himself might make a surprise appearance. But virtually every guest had their own protection detail. Barber’s firm was only one of several present at the event. There were probably more armed security in the room than there were actual guests. Security was so omnipresent they were practically tripping over each other. Short of a terrorist bombing, it was hard to imagine that a lone actor could do actual harm. Security against an actual terrorist threat was handled by the EF Defense Ministry itself. The Ministry was neither polite nor politically correct in its threat assessments, taking a lesson from the Israelis. It had quickly garnered a reputation for being extraordinarily effective, even ruthless.

There were HVCs and there were HVCs. Helmut Schiller was definitely one of the later. The firm he presided over as CEO, Sternenlicht, AG, was the software company that designed all the command and control systems for the EF Ministry of Defense weapons systems, from taking “weapons hot” in a jet airplane to launching a strategic missile. Schiller had a security clearance on par with the EF Chancellor, and one that was actually higher than the Defense Minister. It was a position of staggering consequence, given the recent seismic shift the new EF has caused in the strategic status quo. France saw promise from the new Federation as a safe harbor of economic stability in an increasingly tumultuous world. Germany had an entirely different motive. IT could be summed up in two words – nuclear weapons. The union brought France's existing nuclear arsenal under the control of the Federation which as a practical matter meant under the control of Berlin. And many of nukes were now actually being deployed on German soil, since Germany had pulled out of NATO and ordered all Allied forces to withdraw. Sternenlicht, AG company had written the code for the Federation's nuclear permissive actions links and the targeting software. Helmut Schiller smiled as he made his way through the event center and engaged his colleagues in conversation. But deep inside he was a very troubled man. He was a man with a secret.

Barber spoke into his wrist microphone as he hailed his second in Command, Marcus Day. "Hey, Mark I can't shake a bad feeling about this."

"Agreed, boss," Day replied. "I'll be glad when this one's over."

"Me too! All assets, report," Barber barked.

"Alpha 3, clear," an Orion Bellicus security agent announced through their communications network.

"Alpha 4, clear."

"Alpha 5, all clear."

"Alpha 6, clear."

"Bravo 1, all quiet as a church mouse out here."

"Bravo 2, same here."

"Bravo 3, clear."

Alpha was the call sign for the Orion Bellicus security assets inside the event center.

Bravo was the call sign for the assets outside.

Just then a series of chimes started playing over the PA system inviting the guests to make their way from the reception hall to the dining room for dinner. Guests began to file through the double doors towards their assigned tables as the chimes continued to ring every few seconds. Helmut Schiller set his empty champagne glass on a small high-top table and walked through the double doors. He walked towards Table 1, just to the right of the podium. He was pleased to read on his invitation that his nameplate would be positioned at the spot directly to the right of the Defense Minister himself. As he surveyed the room to get his bearings, a distinguished man with dark hair and a neatly trimmed, thick jet-black beard tapped him lightly on the shoulder and said, "Welcome, Herr Schiller," and proffered his hand.

"Thank you, Herr Farhang," Schiller replied, and shook the man's hand almost reflexively. Alpha 3 was the closest asset to Schiller and watched the exchange intently, but the shaking of hands had been occurring literally hundreds of times in the hall over the last 60 minutes. As Shiller continued to walk towards his table there were countless more handshakes among the crowd. Nothing seemed out of the ordinary.

Suddenly Schiller stopped about two tables short of his destination and placed his hand on the back of a chair to brace himself. Alpha 3 began moving quickly towards him and barked into his microphone "Alpha 3, my HVC appears in distress!" Before he could get to Schiller, the German software executive collapsed to the floor. "Alpha 3, HVC down, I repeat HVC down!"

As Erich Farhang arrived at his table all eyes were turned toward the commotion around Schiller. Farhang reached down and carefully pulled the small patch off the palm of his right hand and dropped it on the floor face down, then stepped on it to firmly affix it to the bottom of his shoe. He was now able walk out with it and avoid detection.

He wanted to get away from the scene quickly. He still didn't know exactly what he had done, but he now realized his worst fears -- whatever was on that patch inside his palm, it had likely just killed a man. He had just transmitted 1 milligram of the opioid drug carfentanil, transdermally, meaning through contact with the skin as opposed to being ingested, to Schiller's palm during the handshake. It had come off of the exposed side of the patch he had just dropped to the floor, and it was 50 times the lethal dose. Carfentanil, a Fentanyl analogue drug used for purposes such as tranquilizing elephants, is 100 times more powerful than Fentanyl. The drug is to opioids what nuclear weapons are to explosives. It's lethality to humans is almost instantaneous. By the time anyone figured out what happened, Schiller would be long dead, and Farhang would be long gone.

Farhang had completed his mission flawlessly. Now he waited, although he did not know for what. Safely home to his family? Detained for questioning because of his odd behavior in front of a colleague? Or perhaps a bullet in the back of his head as he walked up towards his home's front door. He thought the latter the most likely. But who knew, maybe he would get lucky.

His Imam called men who died for the cause martyrs and promised them 72 virgins in Paradise. He had believed it most of his life but had always struggled with the logic of it. As he walked out of the room towards the exit, he was suddenly overcome with a sense of remorse and realized the truth, almost an epiphany. The realization was so overpowering he momentarily stopped walking. He wasn't a martyr, he realized. He was a fool, doing the bidding of bearded old men who were far more interested in power than righteousness. He had been a fool his entire life waiting for that call. But what was done, was done.

Chapter 1 – A Clash of Titans

Offices of PrinSafe, Palo Alto California – 3 Years Earlier

It was good to be king, or perhaps more appropriately queen, thought Dr. Emma Clark as she sat behind the large partner's desk she had just purchased to replace the one used by her late mentor, Charles Westborne Reynolds III, or "Westy", to his friends. She was the newly minted Chief Executive Officer of PrinSafe, the private equity firm that was the holding company for the empire built by Reynolds. The empire encompassed an eclectic collection of businesses and was the temporary parking place for countless distressed companies acquired in hostile takeovers then savagely restructured and flipped for huge profits. Reynolds and his team were gifted at it. He had called it "economic Darwinism", a term Emma Clark readily embraced. It left a trail of unemployed, ruined careers and even the occasional suicide. They could have cared less. In reality, Emma Clark found the process of sweeping worthless pawns off a chess board to be almost arousing. Flipping companies was the real profit engine of the empire, and it accrued massive wealth to Reynolds and his inner circle. The wealth allowed Reynolds to purchase enormous political clout. Several Senators and Representatives owed him their careers due to the generous funding of his PAC, or Political Action Committee, Progressive Dawn. Rumors were he had even "owned" the sitting President of the United States and an Associate Justice of the Supreme Court. The wealth also funded the two crown jewels of the organization. They represented the dark side of the business and were enshrouded with security that rivaled the best capabilities of any government on earth. The first, QuarkSpin, was a cyber and digital forensics firm that had capabilities on par with the NSA, or National Security Agency. The second, General Aviation Services, could manufacture things that would make Q from the James Bond movies green with envy.

Dr. Emma Clark's elevation to the role of Chief Executive Officer, on the death of her mentor, was provided for in Reynolds' will. He had judged her intellect and ruthlessness on par with his, and he was actually a bit concerned that she eclipsed him on the latter. She was the only person he ever considered a worthy sucessor. But Clark was not a patient woman, and Westy Reynolds was a robust man with a long runway left. So, she had hastened his demise with a dose of radioactive isotope Polonium 210 in a Starbuck coffee cup. It had cooked his insides in a slow and painful death as he lingered for several days. That coffee cup would never be found. There was much speculation as to the culprit, but the investigation led to nothing but cold trails and dead ends. It was the perfect murder. She would miss Westy, she thought, but not very much.

The morning sun beamed through the large windows behind her desk chair, and she could feel its warmth on the back of her neck. Cool air conditioning, falling gently from a ceiling vent, bathed her face and provided an interesting contrast. The room was brightly lit with can lighting from the ceiling supplementing the bright sunshine flooding the office from the windows. She liked the fact that the back wall faced East. It was the reason she conducted most of her important meetings in the mornings. The bright sunlight would shine in the eyes of anyone sitting across from her desk and throw them off guard. She reserved the chairs at her desk for adversaries. Friends would be invited to the more neutral spaces occupied by several comfortable sofas and easy chairs.

She was prepping for what she considered to be an interesting meeting that afternoon. The fact that she considered it interesting, and not important, was a measure of both her confidence and her arrogance. The meeting was with the President of the United States. President Sarah Einhorn had called her several weeks ago and said she thought it appropriate for them to have a chat. Having a chat with the President was, of course, far more complicated than it sounded. They couldn't simply talk on the phone. There were White House phone logs, taping systems, and other security measures that virtually guaranteed any conversation from the Oval Office would be heard by somebody other than the direct participants. Einhorn couldn't simply walk into Clark's office on the opposite coast either, as there would be travel plans, press briefings, and potentially uncomfortable questions as to why the President would be meeting with the CEO of a private equity firm. So, President Einhorn decided it was time to pay a visit to the Governor of California and tour the repairs being done to the Golden Gate Bridge after the terrorist attack of three years ago. Since she was there anyway, she would meet with several of her major donors at a luncheon held at a donor's estate in Napa Valley. It just so happened to be one of the favorite vineyards of a certain private equity executive who routinely made large purchases of their signature and very expensive Cabernet Sauvignon. Dr. Emma Clark picked up her invitation, looked at it, and smiled. She could kill two birds with one stone at this meeting, as her wine cellar was getting low on that particular label. A discreet conversation with the Vineyard's owner had secured a private 15-minute meeting between Clark and Einhorn, and Clark would have a device in her purse that would block all electronic signals coming from the Vineyard's library, the location of the meeting.

The room was paneled in dark mahogany and had two-story tall book walls from floor to ceiling. Books occupied every available bit of shelf space, and many of them were bound in leather. There was a walkway about 4 feet wide around the walls where the second story would normally be, and each wall had two ladders, on rollers, providing access to the books towards the top. A giant oriental rug adorned the middle of the space, flanked by sofas. In between the sofas was a large carved coffee table adorned with a Remington Wild West sculpture, a cowboy on a horse with the horse reared up on its back legs. The two women sat next to each other on one of the sofas to facilitate an easy and quiet conversation. As she sat down, Clark reached into her purse and turned on the jamming device. "OK, madam President, this room is now sterile. What's on your mind?"

"Well first, let's skip the pleasantries," the President almost barked. "We're in the last stages of our damage control over this epic screwup engineered by Bill," referring to her late Chief of Staff, "and Westy," she said testily. The screwup was the clandestine anti-terrorism program that engaged in widespread domestic spying, broke countless laws and resulted in the deaths of several innocent people. "The press won't let go of this bloody 'deep state' angle, but we've managed to firewall it around the small group we had arrested. We'll be taking some heat for a while and there will be an investigation, blah blah blah, but I've got the Speaker and the House Chair of the Government Oversight Committee in my back-pocket, so there will be enough noise to make it look credible, but it won't go anywhere. I have it on good authority that the three folks we arrested will not be doing any talking -- ever."

Wow, Clark thought to herself. This woman is essentially telling me she is aware of a plan to murder the Attorney General, The Secretary of Homeland Security and the Director of the FBI.

"There's a plan in place to make the Boy Scout the ringleader and the fall guy," the President said.

Clark decided to interrupt, if for no other reason than to demonstrate she was not intimidated by the woman. "The Boy Scout?" Clark asked.

"Yeah, Erby," the President responded, referring to the late Admiral Mark Erby, the President's former National Security Advisor who was killed in one of the related apparent terrorist attacks.

"Got it," Clark replied. A good fall guy, Clark thought, although that was ironic, she reflected, given that Erby was probably the only one of the gang who had a conscience and actually tried to shut the thing down.

President Einhorn bristled momentarily at the interruption, then continued. "So, bottom line I am confident things are contained on my end, but I am worried about security on yours. Westy was the prime contractor on software analytics and, shall we say, the rather exotic hardware that was the centerpiece of this clusterfuck. Your organization is in a mess right now, and I fear too many weaker hands know too many things they shouldn't. How do we fix that little problem Dr. Clark?"

Wow, Clark thought, as she reflected on the President's opening salvo. She thinks we're the weak hands? She should know that real bullies don't bark, they just bite. After the moment's hesitation to process what the President just said, she responded, "This organization remains rock solid, Madam President, and frankly my security is better than yours."

Einhorn bristled again. "I respected Westy," the President thought, but it really sucks to have to put up with this insufferable bitch. "OK," she continued, "but let's consider this official notice that I'm going to hold you accountable."

"Let's understand, Madam President, that we will hold each other accountable."

Einhorn's back arched and her face flushed. Who the hell did this woman think she was, talking to the President of the United States like that? Her anger momentarily clouded her judgement and she blurted out a comment she instantly regretted. "I'm not just talking about the use of incriminating files," she said, barely able to restrain the fury about to erupt in her voice.

"Neither am I, Madam President."

Einhorn's anger immediately morphed into fear and a cold chill shot up her spine. This woman and her resources could make good on that threat, she thought. Einhorn knew that Clark could strategically leak information about Einhorn in a way that could damage her politically, but she never expected a physical threat. The conversation was getting out of hand, and they had strayed way off topic as well. This was not the point of the meeting.

Emotions had gotten away from her and she had to regain control and a positive track.

"All right, Emma," the President said using Dr. Clark's first name in an effort to reflect a friendlier tone. "Let's both dispense with the theatrics. It's counterproductive. I trusted a handful of men who had watched too many James Bond movies and were too enamored with high-tech toys to find a workable solution to complex problems. That included Westy, by the way. It was my mistake, and I don't intend to let it happen again. I have another idea. That was the real reason I wanted us to talk."

"Let's hear it," Clark responded.

Meanwhile, over 7,600 miles away, a frightening plan was about to be given birth.

Chapter 2 – There is Another Way

House of Leadership, Office of the Supreme Leader, Tehran – Present Day

Dr. Ashkan Ghorbani was terrified. "What am I doing in this place" he asked himself. He was about to have an audience with the Supreme Leader. Such hallowed ground was not for a mere mortal such as he, he thought. If his idea ultimately worked, he would receive the gratitude of a grateful Imam. If it didn't, well he didn't want to think about that. He was trained as a mathematician at M.I.T. and then earned a Ph.D. in computer science from Harvard. Both universities loved foreign students. Admitting an Iranian to elite doctoral programs over American applicants was seen as a way by some in university administration as giving the middle finger to what they regarded as American cultural snobbishness. He was prospering as an assistant Professor of Mathematics at Cal Berkley before he found himself back in his native Iran. The events of 9/11 changed everything. He felt constantly under suspicion. He hated the looks he would get as he was out in public outside the welcoming confines of the University. He longed for his extended family back in Tehran and his Persian culture. But he knew life back home would be far more difficult than the comforts and freedoms he enjoyed in California, and he regarded whatever subtle prejudice he encountered as a small price to pay for that freedom.

Then there was that day undercover agents from Savak, the Iranian secret police, took him for a ride and suggested his skills could be of considerable use to his home country. His fields of expertise were advanced encryption mathematics and cyber security. He woke on an airplane headed to Iran, and here he stood today.

The downside of not performing well was driven home by the man standing next to him. Brigadier General Garshasp Hamidi, of the Revolutionary Guard, was six foot three inches tall and about 240 pounds of solid muscle. His neck was as big around as Ghorbani's thighs. He had a head of thick black hair and a neatly trimmed beard that looked as dense as black steel wool. His eyes were narrow and appeared set halfway back into his head. There was a thick scar on his right cheek. Legend was the scar resulted from a knife wound inflicted by an angry subordinate who attacked him just after being verbally disemboweled by the General in front of his troops. The General had been caught off guard, so the story went, and the soldier had landed a lucky blow. In the flash of an eye, the General responded by severing the soldier's head with a swift swing of his ceremonial sword, right in front of his astonished and terrified men. These physical characteristics added to his sinister appearance. At 43 years old he was young for such a senior officer. Many believe his rapid ascension was due in no small part to his reputation for savagery in dealing with subordinates who didn't live up to his expectations or otherwise disappointed him. Ghorbani trembled at the prospect of finding himself on the General's bad side.

Iran was being crushed by the West's economic sanctions. Sanctions had been reintroduced when the former American President had pulled out of the Joint Comprehensive Plan of Action, more commonly known as the Iran nuclear deal. Iran ultimately responded by restarting their uranium enrichment program. The Supreme Leader was convinced the only way to move beyond the sanctions and a foreign policy of crisis management was to acquire nuclear weapons as quickly as possible. It would finally force the world to treat them as peers. He saw little downside, given that American sanctions had already been put back in place, and saw little risk from the Europeans responding in kind given the economic benefits Europe was experiencing from renewed business with Tehran. He greatly miscalculated. Restarting enrichment had galvanized Europe into what seemed like the only thing the disparate countries could agree on against a background of the growing fervor towards breaking up the European Union.

Then Dr. Ghorbani's research had stumbled onto something. The implications were astonishing. The breakthrough had quickly come to the attention of General Hamidi, who seized on it as potentially being Iran's ultimate solution. The General provided almost unlimited resources to take the theory to a proof of concept. He now wanted to take it to operational readiness. They wouldn't dare take it to that step, however, without the Supreme Leader's approval. So here they were, in the outer offices of the Supreme Leader himself.

Both men sat quietly in the outer office awaiting an audience. It was not unusual for supplicants to wait for hours before being ushered into the inner sanctum. General Hamidi found this tedious, but his outsized ambition gave him the self-control to hold his tongue. He did not share the reverence of his colleagues for the Imam. He was outwardly religious, as was essential for any senior official in the Islamic Republic, but in reality he regarded religion as a narcotic for the masses. He believed in himself, he believed in his ambition, he believed in his destiny, and he believed in his right to destroy anyone who got in his way. Beyond that, he believed in little else.

The General stood up and started to pace. He looked down at the slightly built scientist. His gaze was derisive. The man nauseated him. He respected the scientist's intellect, and was extraordinarily pleased with the breakthrough that brought them to this place, but such people were an anathema to him. He regarded them as weak; weak physically and weak of will. They were a servant class to be used in the service of the strong. They were to be treated just kindly enough to ensure their continued creativity and cooperation, but also treated in a manner that left clear the downside of displaying an uncooperative spirit. The General had to constantly guard himself to control his bark when confronted with modest disappointments such as slow progress or the inevitable challenges that were natural parts of any scientific or engineering endeavor. And everybody knew his bite was far worse than his bark.

"Sit up straight!" the General barked at the scientist, then softened his tone ever so slightly and said "Remember where you are. It is a privilege to be in this place."

"Yes General," Dr. Ghorbani replied with an expressionless voice. He had no doubts about the General's reputation but still found the man irritating. The General was a brute, born of large body controlled by an average mind. He regarded the General's strategic mindset as limited to matters regarding the application of force, and little else. The General was a bully, and Ghorbani was frightened of him the way a person would be frightened at being in the same cage as a hungry tiger. But a person would not regard a hungry tiger as his better; the tiger would simply be an animal with a temporary tactical advantage given an unfortunate set of circumstances. And so, this was the manner in which he regarded the General. It galled him to have to serve such a limited intellect, but he understood his downside. They had made that clear to him during the rendition flight from the United States. At the moment the General was the tiger. Braun trumped brains in the short term. In the long term we shall see, he thought.

The Supreme Leader's Chief of Staff walked out the door of the inner sanctum and approached the two men. "Ayatollah Ashtiana will see you now," he said. They were ushered into a small room. Sitting across from them on folded knees was the Imam. This was his formal meeting place, and the room's appointments appeared spartan for a man of his enormous power and status, except for the large Persian rug that covered most of the floor and was no doubt priceless.

"Salām Alaykum," the General said, as the scientist kept his head bowed and remained silent.

"Alaykum Salām," the Supreme Leader said as the two men faced him and bowed.

"I trust you bring me good news today, General. I am growing impatient with the slow progress on our advanced weapons programs. Our nuclear program is essential to our continued independence and our pursuit of justice and self-sufficiency. Our enemies will not respect us until we have achieved parity with the West. What is the status of our enrichment program?"

Parity, the General thought? What did this old fool expect of him when Iran was being crushed by economic sanctions and treated as a pariah. The enrichment program had fallen victim to a cyber-attack. The Imam knew this. He asking the question just to humiliate him. He controlled his frustration and answered in a calm, measured voice. "Our enrichment programs are in shambles. As you know, the West, we believe the United States, successfully penetrated our centrifuge labs with a computer worm that rendered the individual units highly unstable. The instability at high revolutions caused them to self-destruct. The sanctions have made it impossible to purchase parts needed for the repairs, and we estimate it could take two to three years before we have a fully operational enrichment process again. We have solved all of the engineering problems related to manufacture and miniaturization, but without the fissionable material, it is not possible to assemble a device ourselves."

"I am sure, General, you did not come here to brief me on something I already know. What do you and your colleague have to tell me?"

The General now smiled. "We have made an unexpected, and quite unusual breakthrough. My colleague is here to explain it to you. We are here to tell you there is another way. And this fig tree will bear its fruit quickly. We call it Allah's Sword."

The Grand Ayatollah smiled. "Allah-u Akbar," he said with a pleasant but less than zealous voice. "Tell me what is on your minds, my sons. Tell me about this sword."

Chapter 3 – The Dream

Home of Joseph Michael Barber – Present Day

Shades of dawn broke through the bedroom window as the sun rose early on the East Coast. The room was cold for a mid-July day, about 69 degrees thanks to the air conditioning that was cranking full blast. It had been a sweltering 97 degrees the previous day and warm, humid air had kept a cooler night at bay. Their Golden Retriever had slept on the foot of the bed with its head and shoulders draped over Barber's feet, forcing him to lay flat on his back. The dog stirred as a flickering light danced across its face from the morning sun gently shining through tree branches and leaves swaying in a gentle, but hot morning breeze. The animal let out a sigh and laid its head back down as if to say, "Just five more minutes please." A cold room generally fostered a much deeper and restful sleep. The human body needed to lower its core temperature a bit to achieve a sleep that was truly regenerative. But during the wee hours of this particular morning it was failing to deliver that outcome for one of the bedroom's occupants.

In spite of the chilly temperature in the room, Joe Barber was soaked with sweat and the sheets beneath him were drenched. He was having the dream again. There he was, sitting in the rear passenger seat of a vehicle parked in a deserted stand of woods. His hands were bound behind him with zip ties. His heart was pounding, both in the dream and in his chest as he lay there in bed on the edge of consciousness. He sensed danger, but it was not clear from whom or what. Then a dark figure, faceless but sinister looking, opened the car door and reached in to pull him out. Two hands grabbed his shirt collar and began to lift him to his feet. The sense of danger was now acute, and he felt a fear like he had never experienced. It was a fear born of a certainty of impending death. This is what it must feel like to be walked to the electric chair he thought. He didn't know why, but he knew the man wanted to kill him. Visions of his family flashed before his eyes – his wife Diana and his children Allyson, Joe Jr. and Murphy, and he was overcome with sadness as he realized he would never see them again. He had to do something. But what could he do? He was unarmed and couldn't use his arms or his hands. He was bathed in a seemingly unshakable hopelessness.

Then his training kicked in. Somewhere deep in the lizard portion of his brain an instinct took hold that eliminated all rules of normalcy and replaced them with a powerful desire and determination to do whatever it would take to survive. As he swung one foot out the door and planted it on the ground, he could feel himself launch his body towards the stranger. His forehead hit the man's cheek as his mouth opened widely in an exaggerated fashion and locked on the bottom portion of his assailant's neck. His teeth clamped firmly around a large portion of flesh. In one fluid motion he could feel his teeth come together as he severed muscle, tendons and arteries, then his head started twisting wildly from right to left and broke free. He could feel and taste a large chunk of the man's flesh still in his mouth. His face and upper body were now saturated in blood from an arterial spray, and he could sense the taste of bitter, copper blood as he saw the man fall to the ground in slow motion.

Suddenly his eyes opened wide and he let out a large gasp like that of a drowning man whose head had just breached the surface and sucked in a desperately needed gulp of air. He cried out loudly the word "No!" then sat up straight in bed. He was almost hyperventilating, then his eyes surveyed his surroundings and his bedroom dresser came into focus, then the Golden Retriever at his feet, the TV on the wall and the large reading chair in the corner. His breathing started to normalize as the powerful surge of adrenaline that had been pumping into his veins at last started to dissipate.

His wife suddenly awoke and cried out "What's wrong?" in an alarmed voice. "Are you OK?"

"Yes," he replied in a calmer voice now. "I'm fine, and sorry."

"The dream again?" she asked.

"Yes," he answered. "I'm ok," he said again to reassure her.

"You're a stubborn man, Joseph. A doctor could help you come to terms with that if you would only trust someone and give it a try."

"I know, I know," he replied. She had offered the same advice several times before.

"I'm going to go ahead and get up. We have a busy day ahead of us trying to figure out how we lost that protectee in Germany. Go back to sleep for a while. Maybe we could have dinner at the Club tonight."

"OK," she said sleepily, then rolled back over.

Barber climbed out of bed and walked towards the bathroom. He was profoundly thankful it was just the dream again and not the real thing. He had no intention of following his wife's advice about seeing a psychiatrist. He had never told her the dream itself was from something that actually happened.

Chapter 4 – The Test

Islamic Revolutionary Guard Corps, Cyber Command, Tehran

"Ready missile drill," called out the Iranian Revolutionary Guard Captain as he stood at his console in the CnC, or Command and Control Center. There were two rows of consoles arranged in a semi-circle in front of a large screen that displayed a map spanning most of Europe all the way to the East coast of Iran. Behind the two rows was a desk that was the VIP station. Today it would normally be occupied by General Hamidi had he not been standing menacingly next to the young captain who was supervising the drill. The exercise was a simulated launch of a missile aimed at the Wailing Wall in Jerusalem. The software would track the simulated launch from its source to target and provide a BDA, or battle damage assessment, based on the accuracy of the hit and the payload of the missile.

"I confirm targeting coordinates of 31 degrees, 77 minutes 67 seconds north; 35 degrees, 20 minutes, 45 seconds east," the Captain announced as he read the data from the computer screen in front of him.

"Targeting coordinates are correct as entered and are locked," a lieutenant replied from a station immediately to the captain's right.

"General we will now confirm authentication codes," the captain said as he and the general each pulled a plastic encased card hanging from lanyards around their necks. The cards were called "biscuits" after a similar device used by the United States to authenticate permission to release nuclear weapons. The Iranians hate the Great Satan, but they admired their adversary's security protocols and emulated them.

Each man cracked the plastic casing and pulled the two halves apart, providing access to their individual authentication cards. The General read the code on his card. The captain then did the same and announced, "I concur, Sir, we have a valid launch order." Such an order could only come from the Supreme Leader himself.

"Proceed, captain," the General said.

"Release of nuclear weapons has been authorized," the captain announced over the intercom through the boom mike he was wearing. "Insert keys into launch consoles and prepare to take weapons hot."

The Captain and another Lieutenant who was sitting at a console at the opposite end of the second row each retrieved a key from a small 4-digit combination lock safe at their desk and placed the keys into a rotating lock at the upper right-hand corner of their consoles. The keys had to be turned at the same time for the weapon to arm, and the physical separation between the two men prevented no individual from arming and firing a missile by himself. "Rotate keys on my command," said the Captain. "Five, four, three, two, one, rotate." Both men turned their keys 90 degrees, or a quarter turn to the right. The weapon's status light on every console in the room switched from red to green, indicating the missile was armed and ready to fire.

The captain turned to Hamidi and said, "We are ready, General."

"Fire," the General responded.

The captain reached to his console and flipped up a switch cover. He placed his thumb and index finger on a metal sleeve around a button that was located just below the flipped up cover and rotated it one half turn to the left. The weapons status light on each console now started blinking green. He placed his index finger on the button and depressed it. After depressing the button, the weapons status light turned blue, indicating a successful launch.

Then they all waited.

Even though this was only a simulation, the tension in the room was extraordinarily high. Everybody knew the stakes. This was the first operational readiness test of a new weapons system. It was common practice in virtually every military after an important readiness test to conduct what was called a "post-mortem." Everyone in the room knew that any failure ensured the term would take on a literal meaning.

They continued to wait and watch the path of the simulated launch track towards its target. Then the missile icon on the screen and the target icon merged and the screen displayed a yellow flash as the two icons came together.

"Detonation confirmed," the captain called out. "Zoom in for damage assessment," Everyone held their breath as they waited for the picture to display a closeup of ground zero. As the picture came into focus the Captain's hands started to tremble.

"What is the meaning of this?" barked the General?

The picture of the simulated detonation was not the Wailing Wall. They had missed the target.

"Run analytics," the Captain said with a voice that almost broke. The General was now in the Captain's personal space and fuming. Everyone noticed the commander had his hand on his sidearm. Nobody was sure if this was based on instinct or if something really bad was about to happen.

A voice began speaking over the intercom. It was coming from the simulation supervisor who was monitoring the software from another room. "Stand by," the man said. "Running diagnostics."

Several seconds elapsed. As they waited for the answer, the captain feared his heart was going to explode out of his chest.

"Detonation was not a miss," the disembodied voice continued. Detonation occurred precisely at targeted coordinates of 31 degrees, 77 minutes 67 seconds north and 35 degrees, 20 minutes, 45 seconds east. The Wailing Wall is located at longitude of 35 degrees, 23 minutes and 45 seconds east," he said with an emphasis on the 23 minutes. "Target coordinates were wrong. Simulated detonation occurred precisely as programed but 3 miles west of intended target."

"What is the meaning of this?" the General screamed. "Do you fools not understand that if this had been an actual launch we would have expended our one precious shot and failed?"

Everyone in the room remained silent.

"Who programmed the coordinates?" the General barked.

The Captain stood silent. He was afraid for himself, but he was terrified for the young technician who made the mistake. He knew he had to say something, anything, or the General's rage would soon become uncontrollable. "General, sir, we, we will, we will ... conduct ... a thorough ... investigation and...."

"Shut up you idiot!" the General barked again. "The only thing I want to hear coming out of your mouth is the name of the man who programed those coordinates!"

"But ... sir ..." the Captain was stammering.

The General was skilled at intimidation and forcing the reaction he needed from people. He was also smart enough to know that the Captain was not responsible, and the man's continued service was needed to prevent unacceptable delays in the program. He also knew that a good leader would often respond more quickly to a threat to one of his men than a threat to himself. He unsnapped the cover to his holster and retrieved his 45-caliber sidearm. He then reached across the Captain to the lieutenant sitting at the station to the right and grabbed him by the scruff of the collar and slammed his head so hard into the top of the console that he broke the man's nose. Blood started pouring from the man's face as the General took his sidearm and pressed the barrel to the man's temple. "I will give you 5 seconds to tell me the name of the idiot who programmed that missile before I shoot this man in the head."

The Captain still hesitated. The entire room was now locked in that no-man's land between trying to figure out if a threat was real or just a bluff. Then the General started counting back from 5 and the uncertainty all but vanished. By the time he got to the number 2 a weak voice spoke up from the back row. It was a Sergeant. "It was me, sir," the man said. "I will personally oversee the establishment of safeguards to ensure it doesn't happen again." He knew his comments were little more than an act of desperation.

"That won't be necessary," the General sneered as he turned to face the man. He then raised the pistol and fired a round into the man's face. The General was confident he would not have to deal with another such act of abject stupidity.

Chapter 5 – Angels

300 Block of Hyde Street, San Francisco California

It is a city of staggering contrasts. Home to some of the wealthiest people in the world and real estate prices that make it all but unaffordable to anyone but a "one-percenter", it is also a place where its growing squalor rivals some of the worst third-world slums. Restaurants like Saison offer a menu with multi-course meals costing over $400 a person and a wine list with selections priced in the thousands. Just blocks away the streets are littered with homeless, the mentally ill, drug addicts, prostitutes and various other expressions of human destitution. Nobody walks around with "flowers in their hair" as the popular song from the 60's once proclaimed. Decades of political corruption have left the once-proud city practically in ruins as the political class welcomed and pursued every popular and avant-garde social justice theme proffered while ignoring the basic needs of its residents. It is a place where the downtrodden can become virtually lost and invisible in a sea of human depravity.

A man lay on the sidewalk nestled up against a building and shivered in the cold morning air. He was 30-something but looked more like a man in his fifties. He had a beard of several weeks' growth embedded with numerous remnants of whatever food he was able to find, and his hair was matted and disheveled. The early dawn temperature was in the high 40s as the city was shrouded with fog. Curled up in a fetal position helped him keep himself warm, but not very much. Yesterday he was hungry, but today he was just numb. Ernesto Valesquez had fought in the second Gulf War, Operation Iraqi Freedom. Joining the Army had been his salvation in many ways, but after the war he was discharged. With no skills, he wandered from one day labor job to another. His sense of disappointment in himself led to a sense of desperation, then depression. A sympathetic physician at a Veteran's Affairs clinic diagnosed him with mild schizophrenia but could offer little in the way of treatment since his illness wasn't a war injury and the diagnosis came years after his discharge. So, he lay in the mean streets of San Francisco without hope.

Then a non-descript white paneled van pulled up and stopped just a few feet from where he lay. Two men got out, one holding a quilted jacket, and walked to him.

"You look cold and hungry my friend," one of the men said. "We are part of a local rescue mission and we'd like to try and help you. Is that ok?"

The man's voice was friendly and sounded caring. Ernesto's eyes fluttered as he tried to process what he was hearing. "Was this a dream?" he thought. He forced his eyes to focus on the two men and tried to sit up. The combination of the concrete and his uncomfortable sleeping position made his back hurt and he struggled to get his torso off the ground.

One of the men gently grabbed his upper arm and lifted him to a sitting position. "We have a warm jacket here for you and we would like to take you to our shelter and give you something to eat. Would that be ok?" the stranger asked.

Ernesto continued to struggle to process what he was hearing. Was the man an angel that had been sent to help him? He didn't know. The one thing he did know is that these were the very best words he had heard in as long as he could remember.

"That would be very nice," Ernesto responded in a shaky and barely audible voice.

The strangers gently took ahold of each of his arms and now lifted him to his feet. One man held him upright as the other helped him put on the jacket, then zipped it closed. They walked him to the van, opened the sliding door and helped him into one of the seats then buckled him in. Ernesto didn't notice it, but after the seat belt snapped into place, one of the men reached down to a key just below the seat belt mechanism and discretely turned, then removed it.

"There we go my friend," one of the strangers said. "We'll have you to our shelter in no time and get you some warm food to eat. Let me lean this seat back for you so you can be more comfortable."

The captain's chair in the paneled van was the most comfortable thing Ernesto Valesquez had experienced in a very long time. As he felt the van begin to pull away from the curb, he couldn't believe his luck. "If these two strangers were not angels, they were the closest thing to angels I have ever encountered," he thought. Within minutes he was sound asleep. He was indeed going to a place where he would get a warm bed, warm food, a hot shower and modern sanitation. The strangers, however, were about as far from angels as one could get.

Experimental Laboratory, QuarkSpin Corporation, Undisclosed Location

Ernesto Valesquez awoke in a comfortable bed in a small but nicely appointed room. One of the men who had picked him up from the streets of San Francisco entered the room with a tray of food. It smelled incredible to him. It was scrambled eggs and bacon, a large bowl of oatmeal, fresh fruit and a large glass of milk. The man offered to help him get into a chair next to the bed, but Ernesto had regained considerable strength after almost two weeks in the facility and insisted on getting up and into the chair himself. He was showering every day, was clean shaven and his hair was clean and neatly trimmed. In spite of the kindness of these strangers he was becoming increasingly uncomfortable with the lack of information about where he was or what their plans for him might be.

"How long will I be staying here?" he asked.

"You are likely to be discharged in a day or two," the stranger responded. "We are working on placing you in a halfway house and arranging for a job for you at a local Starbucks. Last night's shot of antibiotics was your last. Your health is much improved, and you've gained almost 10 pounds. You were quite a mess when we brought you in. Congratulations. This is a brand-new program and it's so good for us to see such an early success in you. After you are placed back into the community we are going to continue to follow up and make sure you stay on track. It's such a tragedy that we can't help more, but we do what we can. Our slogan is 'solving poverty, one life at a time.'"

Ernesto's eyes almost watered at the kind words from the stranger. His sense of discomfort subsided a bit as he reflected on his amazing good fortune. 'Of all the people suffering on the streets,' he asked himself, 'why me ?'

In a room next door, a person in a white lab coat was sitting at a station with multiple controls and monitors, including a closed-circuit TV with an audio and video feed from Ernesto's room. Several people were standing behind the person, including Dr. Emma Clark, CEO of QuarkSpin.

"I can confirm device migration is complete," the seated person said. "We are ready to begin the test."

"Commence the memory test," Dr. Clark said.

"Commencing now," responded the seated technician. "Subject has been ablated," the tech spoke into a microphone.

Inside Ernesto's room the attendant received the message through an ear piece. He then opened a chart and began asking Ernesto a series of questions.

"What is your name?"

"Ernesto....uh, er, Ernesto."

"What is your last name?"

"Uh, ummm, uh, I can't remember."

"Where are you?"

"I can't remember."

"Who brought you here?"

"I don't know."

"Where do you live?"

Ernesto's eyes started to water. "I can't remember," he responded with a slightly broken voice.

"What do you do for a living?"

"I don't know. I think, I think I might be in the Army"

"Which Army?"

"I don't know."

"What are the names of your parents?"

"I don't know." He was now starting to cry.

"Take ablation to level 2," Emma Clark said.

The tech reached up to the control panel and turned a dial one more notch to the right. "Ablated at level 2," he responded, as a larger portion of his brain's hippocampus was fried with a small electrical pulse.

The stranger in the room now continued his interrogation.

"What is your name?" There was no response.

"Where do you live?" There was no response. Ernesto stared at the stranger with a confused look.

"What do you do for a living?" There was no response.

"Where are you right now?" No response.

"Commence the cognition test," Clark said.

"Commencing cognition test," responded the tech as he reached up to the to control panel and rotated a different dial to the right. "Cognition ablated," as the implanted device now fried a portion of his brain's frontal lobe.

Ernesto's head started to bob, and his expression went from confused to blank. The stranger now lightly slapped him in the face. There was no response. Ernesto slumped to the right side of the chair and lost control of his bladder. He then started to babble unintelligible noises.

"Congratulations team," Dr. Emma Clark announced. "It looks like we've solved the last of the technical issues with the software. I would say this test has been a complete success. Initiate deletion. Put him down."

The tech reached up and turned a third dial to the right. With that Ernesto's heart stopped beating. "Confirm deletion of subject Delta is complete," the tech announced.

Ernesto was subject Delta because he was the fourth in a series of test victims. Subjects Alpha, Bravo and Charlie had met similar fates, but after less than successful tests.

Emma Clark smiled. She felt nothing for the victim in the other room. She had just committed murder without the slightest pang of remorse or guilt. After all, it was hardly her first time. The most important lesson she learned from her mentor, Westy Reynolds, she reflected, was that rules don't apply to people like her. It was liberating, even exhilarating. There was nothing she couldn't accomplish, and there were no limits to the things she could do in pursuit of those accomplishments. There were only two requirements – be effective and be smart. It was the latter that drove her real sense of empowerment. She was fully aware that there were weaker persons in that room, but she would motivate them with wealth. And if money didn't work, she had insurance policies in place for each of them.

Dr. Emma Clark turned and headed for the door. "Congratulations again team. Very nice work." She was now prepared for her meeting with President Einhorn.

Chapter 6 – I Don't Think So, Madam President

Palo Alto Museum of Modern Art

"What a beautiful building," President Sara Einhorn commented as they walked through the glass atrium. On one of the interior walls hung an oil portrait of Charles Westbourne Reynolds III. Reynolds' estate had funded the recently completed museum in his honor, and his personal art collection was displayed along with donations from other members of silicon valley's uber wealthy. Dr. Emma Clark walked next to the President as the entourage made its way down the hallway towards a small conference room.

"Ouch!" the President almost shouted and grabbed the back of her neck as an excited Secret Service agent immediately leaped towards her to assess what just happened.

Clark swatted her hand close to the back of the President's neck and knocked something to the floor then stepped on it. "I'm so sorry Madam President!" she exclaimed as she bent down to the floor with a piece of Kleenex and scooped up the offending object and briefly showed it to the President. "I was told we had a wasp problem in this building and maintenance has been eradicating several nests. I am so sorry. Are you ok?"

"I'm fine," the President said with more than a hint of irritation. "Fortunately, I'm not allergic. Let's get on with this." The Secret Service agent was not looking intently at the back of her neck. "I said I'm fine, John," she said to the nervous agent standing next to her. "And John, I'd like you and the detail to stand guard right outside the room please. This is probably one of the safest places in the city." The agent fought back a slight frown. He didn't like leaving the President alone, but he knew she was not a person to be crossed. Protesting would be an exercise in futility and likely to summon the woman's wrath, which was legendary.

President Einhorn, Emma Clark and two of Clark's assistants entered the room and closed the door. The conference room seemed very ordinary, but it was not. Once the door was closed and everyone sat down, Clark reached across the large table to a control pad, punched a 6-digit code into a keypad and pushed a button. A light on the panel changed from red to green. "The room is secure now Madam President," Clark said. The room had just become a large Faraday cage. A special energized wire mesh lined all four walls and the floor and ceiling and shielded the room from any electromagnetic signals going in or out. Nobody outside of the conference room would ever hear what was about to transpire inside.

"Before we address the scheduled topic, I need to brief you on an important recent development," Clark said. "Madam President, I must ask your indulgence to allow me to finish the entire briefing before you comment. On the whole what I have to say I believe is very good news. However, some of what I am about to say will certainly surprise you. Some of what I say may shock you. It is important to hear the entire briefing to put everything in its proper context."

The President shuffled in her chair slightly giving away body language of a modest discomfort. "OK, Emma, I'm listening," she responded.

"We have made some recent major breakthroughs in three separate technologies that have facilitated a remarkable new device," Clark continued. "We have succeeded at developing and testing a third generation of the original Sparrow nano-drone listening device and given it an entirely new mission." The term 'Sparrow' was a reference to the device deployed three years ago to covertly capture personal conversations so they could be fed into a 'big-data' threat detection system run by the now defunct National Security Agency Department of Special Activities.

First, we have been able to take miniaturization to a whole new level. The new device is smaller than 1/200th of the original Sparrow. Let that number sink in a bit. In technical terms it is 6.2 nanometers. That's about 2.4 to the negative seven inches. To put it in perspective, it's small enough to easily transit most of the human vascular system. That size presented major engineering challenges in both its control and power supply, but we solved both. Second, we have succeeded in developing circuit boards with hard-wired software at a size that is just slightly greater than the molecular level. The potential applications for this are astounding, but that's a topic for another time. Without boring you with the technical details, let me just say that solving the software problem doesn't just enable a rudimentary level of control, it enables complex tasking and device maneuverability through a fluid medium. Finally, we had to figure out how to power it. Breakthroughs in miniaturization and software allowed us to develop a nano-Seebeck, or thermoelectric generator. To put it in layman's terms, the device can create electrical power from any proximity heat source, such as body heat."

President Einhorn was starting to become impatient. "Ok, that's great, blah, blah, blah, but how is it relevant? Why do I need to know all of this? This is not what I came here for, and frankly I thought I made it clear quite some time ago that I was done with allowing my people to play with your toys. How is all of this connected to me?"

"Bear with me Madam President," Clark responded. "That will all be very clear in just a few minutes."

"The human brain is probably the most complex thing in the known universe. Science suggests that at the present state of the art it would take a super computer the size of a Manhattan skyscraper to approximate the capability of the human brain, and an entire dedicated nuclear plant to power it. And there's still no assurance that such a device could replicate the self-awareness, complex problem-solving ability or abstract thinking of a person of even average intelligence. Yet the three-pound mass of grey matter every person walks around with between their ears does all of that and more and is powered by an occasional cheeseburger. But the brain also has some distinct, and frankly quite useful, vulnerabilities. It is supported by an almost 400-mile vascular system. Our device has the ability to fire a small electrical charge and oblate the walls of whatever blood vessel or capillary it happens to occupy, and it can be maneuvered to any portion of the brain, or the body for that matter, we wish. By firing rapid pulses, it can literally tear a blood vessel open for as much as one or two centimeters. Leakage from the blood vessel can create damage that can do anything from mildly altering a person's personality, to destroying their memory, to even death. We can literally alter the personality of any person we implant with the device. Think about the possibilities. We can make our enemies more compliant, or absent that, render them babbling fools or render them, well, frankly dead. The only limitation to use right now is how to get it into the desired target. It has to be injected. Ingesting it won't work because stomach acids destroy it. It can't be administered trans dermally either. But once we get it into a human's bloodstream we will be able to eliminate our enemies and control our friends. We are working on a more granular software sub-routine to selectively oblate memory which could be of enormous benefit. The applications are almost endless. The subject will have no idea they have been administered the device and it is too small to be detected post mortem, with x-ray or even MRI . We have tested the device on primates and human subjects and have confirmed that all tasks are now online and fully functional. We have named the device the Raptor."

President Einhorn sat expressionless as Emma Clark completed her initial comments. She then cleared her throat and began to speak. "This is madness. Do you mean to tell me that you have actually injected human subjects with this thing, this Raptor, or whatever it is you call it? Do you have any idea of the number of laws you have broken? And what do you mean you have confirmed all tasks are now fully functionable? Mother of God, have you actually murdered people with this thing as part of your tests?" The President was almost out of her chair now and nearly apoplectic. She now started to shout, "I didn't bargain for this insanity. This meeting is over. I am going to relay all of this to Justice and shut down your entire operation!"

Emma Clark just smiled and waited for the President to complete her rant. "I don't think so Madam President. We are disappointed in your response; we hoped you would see the potential of this system. We did, however, anticipate the possibility of this kind of a reaction, as disappointing as it is. The wasp sting you believe you sustained while walking through the atrium was actually the injection of a Raptor from another drone cleverly disguised to look exactly like a wasp. Our telemetry confirms the Raptor has successfully migrated to an alert station in proximity to your hippocampus, the portion of your brain that controls emotion, memory and stimulation, including arousal. We have several programs hard-wired in the software that could generate, shall we say, interesting results. Let me assure you we have no intention of using them except in an emergency. We all sincerely hope that will not be necessary. All we ask is that you think about the potential benefits. Once you are fully vested in the project and have skin in the game, the device can be disabled and instructed to purge itself from your system." She was lying about the possibility of purging the device. There was no such capability and there was no 'kill-switch' so to speak to disable it. Nevertheless, better to give the President a glimmer of hope.

President Einhorn looked almost catatonic. She rose from the table and said, "I guess this meeting is over."

"This meeting? OK ma'am, if you wish. I will follow up with you in a few days to discuss next steps. Please keep an open mind."

The President of the United States stood and began to exit the room. For the first time in as long as she could remember she had nothing to say and no idea what to do. It was the worst feeling of her entire life. She had been had, and was helpless to fight it. She thought for a minute she was getting a headache and wondered if that bitch had turned some dial on a remote control to cause it just to prove a point. Now that's real paranoia, she thought. As she exited the room, she was deeply depressed. But she was still the President of the United States, she reminded herself. She was going to get this woman, no matter what it took.

Chapter 7 – A Growing Sense of Foreboding

Executive Offices, Sternenllcht A.G., Koln (Colonge) Germany

Neither one of them expected it to be a pleasant meeting. In fact, this meeting was likely to be a real ass-chewing they thought. Their security firm, Orion Bellicus, provided the protective detail for Helmut Schiller, the Chief Executive Officer, or CEO, Sternenlicht A.G. while he attended the European Federation's Ministry of Defense supplier's conference. Sternenlicht is a major German defense contractor and he was a man with many secrets. The conference itself was a target rich environment of senior executives from both suppliers and the EF Defense Ministry. The authorities were on high alert for terrorists or anti-EF extremists unhappy with the new direction of central Europe under the heavy hands of Germany and France, but the authorities used all of their resources to cover Defense Ministry officials and had nothing left for corporate attendees. Private security firms were ubiquitous as executives spared no expense in supplementing their own protection. Orion Bellicus had a superb reputation, but nevertheless they had lost Schiller. Helmut Schiller was assassinated as he walked towards his table in the dining hall in full view of everyone in the room.

Protecting clients who were high value targets was a tricky business, and this certainly wasn't the first time the firm experienced a mishap. Two previous protectees had been injured in attempted abductions, although their injuries were minor, and they emerged from the experience profoundly thankful to their security detail for escaping with their lives. One client had actually been kidnapped, but she was recovered unharmed within several hours. The Albanian gang of human traffickers responsible for the abduction of the woman was sent a 'message' by Orion Bellicus' special operators who cast doubt on the gang's reputation as the most savage players in Eastern Europe's dark underworld of human misery. But this was the first time a client had actually been killed while under their watch. It was about as total a mission failure as one could imagine. And worse, they had no clue as to who did it or even how it was done.

The first responders had initially believed that Herr Schiller had succumbed to a fatal heart attack. He had been under a cardiologist's treatment for high blood pressure for years and had previously undergone two angioplasties, or "balloon treatments" to open up clogged arteries. However, in a stunning revelation the autopsy results concluded that the cause of death was an overdose of an extremely powerful Fentanyl derivative, several times the fatal dose. Medical examiners quickly ruled out an accidental overdose from recreational use. There were no needle marks anywhere on the body suggesting the drug was self-administered, and it was inconceivable that a man of his intelligence and responsibility would be so reckless with was known to be an extraordinarily dangerous drug. Suicide was quickly ruled out as well. Many of his colleagues had noticed he seemed a bit off his game recently, but nothing in his life suggested he was despondent and inclined to the extreme measure of taking his life. Besides, mood swings were hardly uncommon among senior executives. So, it was now a murder investigation.

The German authorities and Interpol were leading the investigation into Schiller's death. So far, their efforts had resulted in nothing but dead ends. Joe Barber and Marcus Day had been interviewed extensively about the events of that night and were cooperating with authorities in any way they could, but their testimonies shed little additional light.

No one had claimed credit for the assassination, which likely ruled out an act of terrorism. Besides, terrorists generally liked massive casualties and the accompanying big headlines so it seemed unlikely that any terrorist cell would be satisfied with the death of a single executive. Schiller had enemies, as any senior executive would, but it was highly unlikely that any of his enemies would have the motive to commit murder.

The most puzzling aspect of the investigation was how the deadly dose of the drug had been administered. Numerous eyes had viewed the security camera recordings of the events that night and nothing stood out. There were countless handshakes, pats on the shoulders and other seemingly benign interactions throughout the pre-dinner cocktail party right up to the moment Schiller started to collapse. Every interaction within five minutes of his demise was examined extra closely frame by frame. Still nothing. And how would such a dangerous drug be transported to the crime scene. Even touching a small amount of the stuff could be fatal, which made administering the drug all the more complicated.

Joe Barber and Marcus Day had tacit approval from the authorities to use the extensive resources of their firm to see what they could uncover, along with a strict warning not to interfere with or in any compromise the official investigation. Of course, it wasn't as if a lack of approval was going to stop them. They had walked up to the edge of a legal line more than once while building their company and occasionally stepped over it. Neither man took their first serious failure particularly well and they would do whatever they had to do to get to the truth.

The two men sat in the CEO's conference room and waited for what seemed like an exceptionally long time. Barber was pretty certain the extended wait was a deliberate effort convey a clear pecking order for the meeting. Finally, the Senior Managing Director and acting CEO of Sternenlicht, A,G,, Hans-Dieter Zimmerman, opened the door, walked into the conference room and sat down at the head of the table. Two of his aides, a man and a woman, followed close behind him and took a seat on each side of the table with the woman sitting down next to Barber. All three were expensively dressed and exuded an air of arrogance. Neither casual dress nor casual attitude had found its way into Sternelicht's executive suite, Barber silently mused.

Zimmerman sat stone-faced. He opened the folder he carried and placed in front of him on the conference table. He then appeared to start reading its contents as if neither Barber or Day were in the room. He held his silence for an uncomfortably long time as he flipped several pages in the folder back and forth; giving the impression that he was studying them. It was a sophomoric act, like pretending to be the alpha predator toying with its prey for amusement before attacking it. This guy was massively full of himself, but he was no alpha predator, Barber thought. Barber's and Day's eyes briefly met as Day cracked a slight smile in response to the act and then lightly shrugged his shoulders.

"Herr Barber," Zimmerman finally began, "the best detective minds in Europe have so far been unable to shed any light on the antecedents to your failure. Why are you here wasting my time? What can you possibly contribute to this investigation? This business is best left to the professionals, don't you think?" he asked deliberately conveying an insult. He continued to look down at the folder while making his comments then slowly turned his gaze towards Barber and stared at him intently for dramatic effect. "We paid you a handsome sum for your protective services and you failed miserably."

"As you know, Herr Zimmerman," Barber responded, "we are supplementing the investigation. As the lead security team on site at the dinner we had a unique perspective on the events of that night. Forensics teams from the EF's Federal Criminal Investigation Office and Interpol have extensively examined the entire venue and uncovered nothing. Extensive reviews of security camera footage have been equally unrewarding. We believe a less conventional approach is necessary."

"What exactly do you mean by less conventional?" Zimmerman asked with almost a dismissive tone.

"For starters we need to pay more attention to context – the context of Schiller's mood, or mental state, or whatever you want to call it," Barber responded.

Zimmerman's nostrils flared slightly, and his face became flushed, betraying a flash of anger. "And you think our National Investigative Service and Interpol haven't thought of that?" Are the two of you amateurs?"

Barber just smiled, ignoring the second such insult within just minutes. "As you know we have provided the security detail for Herr Schiller several times in the past. Part of our protocol for client engagement is an interview prior to any event. Our interview team includes a psychologist who evaluates the client's mental state and profiles them. This helps us develop a more robust threat assessment by identifying potential concerns the client may have. It also helps us detect behavioral patterns that enable a more bespoke security plan tailored to the client's individual needs and peculiarities. We are completely transparent about this process and maintain strict confidentiality of the assessments."

Zimmerman's ice-cold countenance was momentarily broken when Barber made the comment about the role of the psychologist. The executive looked stunned.

"You profiled Schiller?" he asked.

"Yes. Standard protocol and completely transparent. Our clients are thoroughly briefed on all of our preparations including the psych assessment and all sign an acknowledgement form prior to the process."

Zimmerman's countenance immediately changed as he looked Barber in the eyes with a slightly furrowed brow then glanced back and forth between Barber, Day and his two aides. His reaction to Barber's revelation bordered on the defensive. As his eyes met Day's he briefly paused as Day betrayed a slight smile. "Gotcha," Day thought, although he suspected Zimmerman's reaction was more likely that of an alpha wannabe whose arrogance had just been broken than someone trying to hide something. Zimmerman cleared his throat then refocused on Barber as he attempted to regain control of the room.

"Go on," Zimmerman said, now with a firm voice.

"As I said," Barber continued, "we've previously been engaged as Herr Schiller's security detail, four times to be exact. The EF Defense Conference dinner was the highest-profile event by far. That gives us three previous assessments of him to compare with the present. That's a context neither the German authorities nor Interpol have."

"And you didn't bother to share that with them?" Zimmerman asked with his arrogance again in full bloom.

"We offered," Barber responded, "but they were dismissive."

"So, the brightest police minds Europe think your little process is meaningless, but you think it's important, eh? Please, by all means continue," Zimmerman said with a mocking tone.

"Comparison among the different assessments clearly suggests that Herr Schiller was a decidedly different man going in to that dinner. We have a proprietary algorithm and rating scale to measure a client's mental state. A rating of one suggests virtually no stress whereas a ten suggests the highest possible stress and prominent suicidal thoughts. Schiller was an eight. The average of the three previous ratings was a 3.4. Something was troubling him, and it was something that he was unwilling to reveal during our interview. We also have a similar metric for deceit, and he scored nine. He was definitely hiding something, likely whatever was troubling him. If we can determine what that something was it could add considerable insight into the 'why' and perhaps even the 'who'."

Zimmerman's tone softened a bit. "I agree he seemed a bit pre-occupied of late, but that is hardly uncommon for a man with his responsibilities."

"The problem," Barber continued, "is the stark difference between the most recent and the three pervious assessments. Such a sudden and stark decline in his state of mind suggests a recent dramatic event. Prominent people can be talented at hiding things – it's part of the 'poker-face' skill. It's not uncommon for colleagues or even spouses of our clients to miss the signals. But our people are trained to look through the veneer. I have no doubt whatsoever he was a man with a recently acquired secret, and one that greatly troubled him."

There was a long silence, then the woman spoke up. "How should we proceed?"

"We will need a list of the people he spent the most time with over the last several months. We'll need to interview them. Also, we will need to know which aspect of your business he recently spent most of his time on, and especially if he was spending an unusual amount of time in the weeds."

"In the weeds?" the woman asked with a puzzled look.

"I'm sorry," Barber responded. "It's an American expression. Was there anything he was working on in greater detail than would be typical for a Chief Executive."

The CEO and his two aides reflexively looked at each other as Barber's comment seemed to hit a nerve.

"You will have our cooperation, Herr Barber, at least initially. My two assistants here will arrange interview times with the appropriate individuals, and we should be able to make them available within the next couple of days if that works for you."

"We'll make it work," Barber replied.

"I should caution you, however, that Herr Schiller was the Chief Executive Officer of a major European Federation Defense contractor and details on many of the things within his remit are, as you Americans say, 'above your pay grade.'" You do not have EF top security clearances and there are simply many things we are not going to be able to legally reveal to you."

"I understand, Herr Zimmerman. Let's proceed and see what, if anything, we can find. If there are roadblocks, we will deal with them as they arise."

"Very well," Zimmerman responded. "Now if you will forgive us, we need to go back to work. Frau Schmidt here will contact you no later than tomorrow morning with a list of names and an interview schedule. I suggest you plan on spending most of the day with us and perhaps the next."

"Thank you, sir," Barber responded.

As Zimmerman walked back to his office he fought back a growing sense of foreboding. A series of thoughts started flowing through his mind. At first they were somewhat random, but then they started swirling together with an increased cohesion until a spontaneous realization flashed before his consciousness that momentarily stopped him in his tracks. His foreboding morphed into terror as he pondered the implications of where his mind had just taken him. "The code," he whispered to himself. "Oh my God, was if it was the code?"

Chapter 8 – Poodles and Pit-Bulls

Offices of the European Federation Defense Ministry, Berlin

The morning sun beamed through the large windows of the sixth-floor office and illuminated a broad room paneled in dark oak and lined with bookcases full of serious works on military history and biographies of prominent leaders from the pre-Roman era to the present. A large crystal sculpture of Otto von Bismarck sat atop a five-foot tall pedestal just to the left of the center of the room. Sunlight penetrated the sculpture's clear face and with a prism-like effect projected various colors of the rainbow across the room, painting the back wall. A massive desk sat just off the window facing the countless books, projecting the gravitas and power of its occupant, General Horst Brandt, Commander of the Europaische Bundesluftwaffe, or EBL.

The EBL, or European Federation Air Force as it was called in the English translation, was the fusion of the legacy German and French Air Forces. Most importantly it was the service that maintained command and control of the European Federation's stock of nuclear weapons and that made Brandt the second most powerful man in the EF, eclipsed only by the Chancellor. In theory he reported to the civilian Defense Minister, but nobody in the government had doubt about his ability or willingness to do whatever was necessary to protect the EF and its ascendant ambitions. As the top EF Air Force Officer, he had direct operational command of all Air Force assets, unlike the top officers in each of the American uniformed services, who under law were primarily advisors to the President and did not command troops in the field. He had been a three-star and Deputy Commander of the German Luftwaffe at the time of the birth of the Federation. His exceptional intellect, the ability to think quickly on his feet and his gift of a golden tongue empowered him to deftly outmaneuver his boss, Lieutenant General Ingo Gerhartz for the top prize. It didn't hurt that he also held a doctorate in theoretical physics. His ascension brought a fourth star and overall command of the most lethal military force on the European Continent.

Horst Brandt was a voracious reader, especially of military history and biographies. He believed the power of his mind and the force of his will destined him to lead and achieve great things, and he saw many similarities between himself and the great military minds of the past. But he also believed that fueling his mind with the lessons of the past was necessary to transform a powerful intellect into something capable of formidable strategic thinking. So, he read, and he studied, and he learned in an effort to keep his mind's fuel tank full. Without that fuel, he constantly told himself, he would never achieve his ambitions or his destiny.

Classical music was being piped into his office, providing the perfect background noise to foster creative thinking. He loved Wagner, and the irony of that didn't escape him, given he hated almost everything about Wagner's other prominent German admirer, Adolf Hitler. His hatred of Hitler, however, was not borne out of moral repugnance but from disgust with what he regarded as the man's epic stupidity. A tiny man, with a tiny mind who nevertheless was that siren whose song charmed the frightened masses into submission and even hero worship. Brandt was fond of a comment used by the American Comedian George Carlin, spoken as a joke but something Brandt regarded as a brilliant political observation – "Beware the power of stupid people in large groups." He had contempt for garden variety democracy. It was little more than mob rule, he told himself. People needed to be led, and by a ruling class. Intelligence, education, vision and will were all essential in leaders, and he was convinced he had an outsized measure of each. The key, however, was being clever in how you used them. The masses had to be convinced they were following their own free will and desires. He believed the ability to impart that sense is what defined a great leader.

Brandt closed the book on his desk and set it aside. Short of a national emergency he spent the first two hours in his office every morning reading and thinking. He believed that discipline allowed him to maintain a strategic focus and avoid the trap of spending most of his time just reacting to problems. He had been reading a biography of Hermann Goering that morning, one of Hitler's closest confidants and Commander of the Luftwaffe during most of the Second World War. The biography had been written by a German Professor who admired Goering's intellect and bravery. The author was an idiot, Brandt mused, who completely missed the General's countless strategic blunders. Goering, for example, made a fateful decision on September 7, 1940 during the Battle of Britain which altered the course of the war. He decided to switch from the air superiority battles with British fighters to massive nighttime bombings. At the moment of that decision, the British fighter force was on the ropes and almost destroyed. Had Goering pressed the attack, the fighter aircraft could have been obliterated and Germany would have achieved complete air superiority, likely guaranteeing victory. Instead, the British fighter forces were given time to recover, and the rest, as they say, is history. It was one of the most important lessons he carried throughout his career: When the enemy is on the ropes, don't disengage – destroy with overwhelming force. Mercy and grace have no place in warfare.

His thoughts were interrupted by a buzz on the intercom. He reached across the desk to press the button and said, "Yes?"

"Sir, General Laurent is here," his assistant responded.

"Send him in."

Jean-Baptiste Laurent was a Lieutenant General, or General de corps d'armee in the French military, and Second in Command in the EF Air Force, or EBL. In a concession to political expediency, it was decided the position needed to be occupied by a French national. Both Germany and France maintained their separate military identities, and officers of their respective uniformed services kept their individual uniforms and titles, although the EF maintained a robust consolidated command structure. Because of the extraordinary importance and power of the EBL, however, the selection of

Laurent was as rigorous as the selection of Brandt, and Laurent was every bit as ruthless as his boss. He was disciplined by his superiors during the second Gulf War, Operation Iraqi Freedom, for criticizing the decision of France to oppose the invasion and sit on the sidelines. Truth be told he could have cared less about Saddam Hussein or the risk of WMDs; he was just itching for a fight. Brandt enthusiastically endorsed his nomination knowing he would have a number two who never backed down from a fight.

Laurent walked into Brandt's office with two cups of coffee and sat one down on his boss's desk. "Good morning, sir," Laurent said.

"Jean-Baptiste," Brandt replied, "a fine morning indeed." He picked up the coffee and took a large sip of the black liquid not realizing it was blistering hot. He felt a searing pain on his tongue as if he had just licked a hot poker. After briefly turning the air blue by uttering a series of unintelligible curses, he sat the cup of steaming liquid back on his desk and regained his composure. "I should have known you would be the one to have weaponized a cup of coffee."

"It's just in beta test, Herr Général," he said with a smile. "I plan to test it next on the Americans."

"Excellent!" Brandt exclaimed, now smiling himself. "A real stealth weapon – I love it!. Could I perhaps persuade you to test it on our British friends first?" Both men chuckled at the response.

"You have British friends, mon General?"

"A figure of speech, Jean-Baptiste," Brandt chuckled. "Simply a figure of speech. Besides, you should not be so hard on those poor souls across the Channel. After all, it was their rejection of greater Europe and the hissy-fit they called Brexit that laid the foundation for our Federation today, was it not?"

"Indeed, mon Général Laurent said with a broad smile. "However, I think their current problems with the Republic of Scotland across their northern border present sufficient punishment for the time being, so I will focus this new weapon on the British colonies and not the Brits themselves. Besides, the Americans are far more addicted to coffee than the Brits, who continue to display this odd cultural preference for tea," he said tongue in cheek.

"I hear rumors of very positive results from our recent tests of Project Dart," Brandt said, adopting a more serious tone as he changed the subject.

"Yes, General," Laurent replied. "We field tested a prototype on a Mirage 2000. The new battery systems developed by BMW from their electric automobile division were a real breakthrough. We were able to cut battery weight by 60% while still delivering enough energy to accelerate a 300-gram projectile to Mach 15 in the lab and Mach 12.5 from the aircraft. The effect on target was devastating, and that's at only 40% of system potential. The biggest challenge to increased velocity is the atmospheric resistance. Our engineers are working on a new projectile design we believe will result in significant improvements."

General Brandt leaned back in his chair and smiled. Project Dart was a code name for a new type of kinetic weapon that was his brainchild. The concept itself was not all that new. It was essentially an airborne railgun. A series of magnets placed along a long tube attached to the bottom of the aircraft accelerates a projectile to hypersonic speed thus delivers an astounding amount of energy to a target and, consequently, an astounding amount of destruction. It was based on a simple principle of physics embedded in Einstein's famous equation $E=MC^2$ which defines the relationship between energy, mass and velocity. A derivative of this famous equation, $F=M/2V^2$, converts the concept of energy, or E in Einstein's equation, to the concept of force delivered to a target. (F)orce= one half of the projectile's mass (M/2) times the square of the projectile's velocity (V^2). Potential energy, or destructive force, increases at a rate equal to the square of the increase in its speed. In simple terms, changing the speed of a projectile has a much larger impact on its destructive force than just making it bigger.

This discovery has staggering implications. Throughout the annals of military history increased firepower was achieved primarily by increased throw weight – the bigger the projectile fired at a target the greater the destruction. One of the most prominent examples of this was the growth in breach size of naval guns on warships during the early 20th century; the 16-inch monsters on U.S. World War 2 battleships to the 18-inch behemoths on the Japanese battleship Yamato. But increasing throw weight resulted in essentially a linear increase in destructive power. Because velocity is squared in Einstein's equation, increasing a projectile's speed results in an exponential increase in its" bang". Taken to its extreme, if you could get a projectile moving fast enough, you could give a sewing needle the destructive power of a 16-inch naval projectile. As a weapon it has the potential to occupy a very useful space between the EF's conventional and nuclear capabilities, and successful deployment would vault the EF military to the status of global leader in weapons technology and innovation.

There were two major constraints, however, in taking the theory to practical application. First, you need a lot of electrical power to accelerate a projectile down a rail to hypersonic speed. Second, batteries are very heavy. The new battery design by BMW solved both. It was ironic, Brandt thought, that BMW's research was built on the concepts the automobile company Tesla freely shared with competitors based on their aspirations of fostering a green world free of fossil-fuels; especially ironic given it was an American company. "Give me an enemy of good intentions and a bleeding heart and I will rule the world," he often told himself. It was also ironic that BMW's subcontractor for battery development was a little-known company in Palo Alto, California called QuarkSpin, now led by a woman who projected herself as a bleeding heart, anti-war progressive. The research and development were conducted by QuarkSpin's German subsidiary, called CWR Industries, itself a company buried in a corporate ownership network so complex it would be all but impossible to unscramble.

Laurent continued, "The next milestones are three sequential tests of systems capability at ten percentage point increments in power – 50, 60 and 70 percent. Once we validate operational suitability at 70%, we will upgrade the permissive action links to level two, one step below nuclear authorization. That will require confirmed authorization from you before taking weapons hot. Sternenlicht is working on the codes, although I will confess I am a bit concerned about the company right now given the apparent assassination of Schiller."

"I share your concern, Jean-Baptiste. Nobody had a more comprehensive and deeper understanding of our command and control systems than Schiller. I want to believe such knowledge and his murder are not related, but as our American friends like to say, "I don't believe in coincidences."

"You have American friends, mon Général?" Laurent said with a smirk and deliberately exaggerating the French accent to his German.

"Well I like to think I am at least good at making them think so, Jean-Baptiste," the General said with a grin.

"I would like to caution you, mon Général," Laurent continued with a heavy dose of sarcasm, "what is it that the Americans say.....something about laying down with dogs."

General Brandt let out a hearty laugh at the comment. "Indeed, Jean-Baptist. Indeed. But it depends on the dog, does it not? There is a difference between a poodle and a pitbull. Most Americans think they are pit-bulls but are really poodles. Emma Clark of QuarkSpin sells herself as a poodle but is a Pitbull on steroids."

"The investigation into Schiller's death is at a standstill. The authorities have no motive, no suspects and from what I understand virtually no leads," the French General said, steering the conversation back on point.

"Yes, and very unfortunate," Brandt replied. "I understand a couple of civilians are also involved; the two men who led Schiller's protection team."

"That's correct, Sir."

"I especially don't like civilians poking their noses around Schiller's work, Jean-Baptiste."

"I'm not comfortable with it either. They have a good reputation, but I don't see what they can contribute. I actually know one of them from his military days, and he's smart. The problem is any breakthrough in the investigation is likely to come from uncovering a motive related to Schiller's professional responsibilities, and that's something we don't want civilians poking their noses in. "

"I completely agree. Have our military Criminal Investigative Service assign a couple of agents to follow these guys and keep tabs on what they are doing. I also want our own people to conduct a parallel investigation of the entire incident and maintain the strictest confidentiality in doing so. I am fed up with the lack of results from our civilian authorities, but I don't want the Federal authorities thinking we are second guessing them."

"Yes, mon Général. You know of course that such action on our part is prohibited by law?"

"I don't care. If we run into trouble I will simply go to the Chancellor and he will back me, but I don't want to play that card unless necessary. Let me be clear. I want you to supervise this personally. My gut tells me factions inside of Sternenlicht itself are likely responsible; possibly some pacifist group that is unhappy with the ambitions of the European Federation or our ownership of nuclear weapons. We cannot allow malcontents to compromise our command and control systems. Too much is at stake. This is your highest priority and you are authorized to use any means necessary. Time to release a few pit-bulls ourselves. Just keep all actions off the radar. I want results, and I want them quickly."

"Yes sir," Laurent said as he stood, saluted his boss and started to walk out of the office.

"Jean-Baptiste," Brandt called out as the French General was within two meters of the office door.

"Yes, mon Général."

"Let me be clear. I said by any means necessary."

"Yes sir, I understand. And with my pleasure."

Brandt's mind flashed back to the countless jokes he had heard over the years at the expense of the French military, such as "How many Frenchmen does it take to defend Paris? Nobody knows, it's never been tried." It was a colossally misplaced sentiment, and anyone who had ever told that joke had obviously not met Jean-Baptiste Laurent. Brandt smiled, then focused his attention on the two folders from the Ministry of Defense Intelligence Command sitting his desk. As the classical music continued to play in the background, now Bach, he looked at the folder labels. One was titled Joseph Michael Barber, the other one Marcus Day. He opened the folder labeled Barber and started to read.

Chapter 9 – Things are not as they Appear

Berlin, Germany

It was an exceptionally beautiful Summer morning as the City of Berlin came to life. The temperature was a mild 17 degrees Celsius, and the air was awash with a gentle breeze and low humidity foretelling the coming of a glorious day. Joggers started to populate the streets, each with their minds engrossed in their music or audiobooks or whatever it was they had piping through their ubiquitous white headphones. A few couples walked their dogs, mostly elderly ones who had the time for such an indulgence, and mothers pushed their babies in strollers. Business people scurried about in full battle dress headed to their places of work. There was a decidedly upbeat mood hanging in the air, characteristic of a people who were enjoying considerable economic prosperity and a resurgence of their nation's importance and pride in Europe and on the broader world stage.

A man emerged from a luxury private residence in the heart of the city right off the intersection of Rosa Luxemburg Strasse and Munz Strasse. It was an impressive home at over 290 square meters, or over 3,000 square feet, in American terms. It had five bedrooms and 3 baths and came into the possession of its present occupant at a price of over 3.7 million Euros. A Mercedes S-Class sedan sat out front patiently awaiting the arrival of its owner. This was the home of someone important, the home of a successful businessman.

Eric Farhang, or Farhad Alipour as he was known to his handlers, emerged from his expensive home with a countenance that was distinctly different from the carefree people populating the streets. He didn't feel either successful or important at the moment. He felt afraid. It had been several days since he had successfully completed his mission on that fateful night of the dinner party. He was still alive, and frankly that astounded him. But he was too smart not to know he and his family were still in grave danger.

If he was to be dispatched, he knew his handlers were patient. So, every time he stepped outside, every time he turned the lights off in his house at night, and every time he pushed the start button on the dashboard of his automobile he trembled at the prospect of it being the last instant of his life.

He was a realist and he knew he was much more of a liability than an asset to his handlers now that he completed his assignment and passed the Fentanyl-based drug to his target. But he wanted to hold on to some hope. After all, his handlers had not threatened him. In fact, they told him to go back to living his life. But then there was that dreadful complication. He had bumped into the man who was in charge of his target's security team as he was pressing his way through the crowd. Their eyes had met. He had briefly offered an apology. In the process the man had noticed the stress on his face, his perspiration, and his hurry, all things that were out of context. He stood out, exactly what he did not wanted to do. And when the guy reviewed the security camera footage he remembered him, pointed him out to the investigators. The federal police had brought him in for questioning. The police had nothing on him, and they had been very polite, as befitting a man of his professional prominence. That trait was in the German DNA. He was released with nothing being said that even remotely suggested he was regarded as a suspect. But he had been noticed and interviewed and was certain his handlers would be aware of it. If he had any small ray of hope of getting through this experience with his life, that hope was now gone. It was only a matter of when.

He closed his front door, locked it, and keyed in the security code to the alarm system as he prepared to leave. Lot of good that would do he thought. As he started walking towards his car, a tall, muscular male jogger appeared running left to right and just a few seconds away from crossing his path. The man was wearing summer jogging clothes, a pair of blue-tinted sunglasses and earbuds and had a smartphone in a sleeve affixed around his upper arm. Alipour's senses were all transmitting a maximum threat warning, but he relaxed a little as he regarded the man's clothing and realized it would be difficult to hide a weapon given the way the man was dressed. He relaxed, that is, until he noticed the oversized fanny pack affixed to the man's side. As the jogger approached he froze with fear, unable to command his legs to do anything but hold his present position. The man was now just about ten feet to his left and still running. "So, I guess this is it. This is how I die," he thought. Things seemed to shift into slow motion, but jogger's legs maintained an aggressive gate. The man was now in front of him. Nothing happened. Alipour was now holding his breath. He followed the man with his eyes as he continued to run. But now the jogger was running away and not towards him. His eyes, now in tunnel vision, shifted to another figure that had just come into his view. It was a young woman, a mother pushing a stroller. He stopped holding his breath and exhaled, then gasped as if he had just broken the surface of water after a long and difficult assent. The woman smiled then looked ahead again. She was clearly not a threat. He was overwhelmed with a sense of gratitude at still being alive. His knees started to buckle at the relief, and he steadied himself to keep from falling.

Then Farhang saw it. The woman reached into a diaper bag that was hanging over the handle of the stroller. It was her movement that caught his attention. She was in the process of pulling something out of the bag. His sense of relief was replaced with confusion as events once again shifted into slow motion. His brain could not process the sensory input fast enough. The object was black. His confusion began to morph back into fear. The lizard part of his brain took over as the fight or flight response started to blossom and his heartrate accelerated in response to the subconscious detection of a threat. He had no idea what the item was, but her arm was moving too far backwards to be consistent with retrieving something that would normally reside in a diaper bag. Whatever it was it was long. Then the item came into full view. It was a medium-sized pistol with a long suppressor attached to the end of the barrel. For the second time in just a few seconds his brain told him he was in mortal jeopardy and about to die. Their eyes met. Her eyes were still smiling. And not a sadistic, killer's smile but a gentle smile. A mother's smile. He then heard a muffled 'thwack' and felt his face hit the ground.

Chapter 10 – To the Gates of Hell and Back

Berlin, Germany

All he could feel was the pain. It felt like his body was being crushed under something terribly heavy, but somehow he felt distant from it as though he was disembodied and viewing things from a distance. He had heard of people experiencing similar sensations. They were usually associated with something called a 'near-death' experience. His brain was engulfed in a dense fog that seemed to keep reality at bay. Was he in Paradise as the Prophet had promised? He couldn't be. There was no pain in paradise, or so he had been taught. Where were the 72 virgins he was promised as a reward for faithful service? There were no virgins, only the pain. Was he even dead? He had seen the pistol in the woman's hand and heard it's report as she pulled the trigger just before everything had gone blank. He had to be dead. That was the way his death was destined to arrive. He knew this in his heart from the moment he saw his target slump in that dining room several evenings ago and realized what he had done. They couldn't possibly let him live, and his hopes to the contrary were just wishful engagement in fantasy.

He felt a powerful pair of hands grip him by the back of his shirt and lift him off the ground as if he was a rag doll. "Allah be praised," he thought, "I am not dead!" He sensed himself upright, almost on his feet, and then perceived motion as the powerful hands were now forcing him to walk. His feet barely seemed to be touching the ground as if he were a marionette pushed along by some unknown force. But then his relief at being alive started to morph back into fear. Was he really alive he wondered, or Dear Allah no, was it possible he was being roughly escorted to that other place? His fear became terror. He cried out, "No! Allah u Akbar! There is no God but Allah and Muhammad is his messenger!"

"Be quiet," a voice commanded. It was a deep baritone that dripped with power and authority. He immediately thought of the character Darth Vader from the Star Wars movies. It was the voice of death itself, he thought.

His body began to convulse with fear. He was dead and this frightful being was ushering him to the gates of Hell.

After several seconds under the aberration's power, he felt himself being shoved forward as powerful hands released their grip on the back of his shirt. He now braced himself for the heat, the fire that he now knew was to be his punishment for all eternity. A plethora of thoughts raced through his mind. He did not understand. He believed he had lived a good life. He was faithful to the five pillars. He faithfully rendered his service and did everything asked of him. He expected the physical death of his mortal life. That was a price he was willing to pay in service to Allah. But he could not imagine his fate was about to be eternal damnation. He cried out to Allah again, but as he did so, he felt the side of his torso crash against something hard. His shoulder and ribs seared with pain.

"Be quiet, I said." That dreadful voice again. "You are not dead, and you are not in Hell, although you may wish you were before this is over." He heard a grinding sound, then something that sounded like a door slamming shut. A short distance away he heard a commotion. There were other people close by. He then felt movement and sound; a struggle of some sort. He could hear voices outside. They were the voices of the street; ordinary people going about their ordinary tasks. He was in a vehicle of some sort. A Van! The sound he just heard must have been its sliding door being closed. He was overwhelmed with relief to realize he was not in Hell. But his relief was short lived again as he started to wonder who his captors were, where he was being taken, and what they wanted from him. So many rapid back-and-forths between a mental state of terror and hope had his heart beating out of his chest. He feared he was about to have a heart attack. He felt the powerful hands again as they pulled his arms behind his back and affixed his wrists together with what felt like a zip tie.

"Who are you and want do you want?" he called out in terror.

"I said to be quiet," the voice responded.

Then he felt a prick in his shoulder, and everything went black.

90 seconds earlier

"Joe!" Day's shout blasted in Barber's earpiece. "We have a tango at target's 2 o'clock!"

"Copy," Barber replied. "Male jogger has just passed the front walk and has not displayed any threat. What's the tango?"

"Behind him!"

"What?" Barber replied. I don't see anything."

"The stroller!"

"What? Marc, it's a freaking mother pushing her baby! What's the threat?"

"I've got eyes on the stroller; it's not a real baby. It's a doll! She's starting to move her hands!"

"Got it! Do I need to tap her?"

"Yes!" Day shouted into his mic. "I'm not close enough. She just put her hand in the diaper bag and is starting to pull something out. I think it's the butt of a pistol – tap her now!"

"Got it! You secure the target!" In one lightning fast and fluid motion Barber pulled a small device out of his jacket, leveled it, then pointed it at the woman. It looked like a cell phone but was slightly thicker and much heavier. A camera on the device captured the woman's image and displayed it on a screen centered in a pair of cross hairs. He pressed what looked like the home button of a cell-phone and there was a loud crack as an underpowered 22-caliber ballistic round propelled a small tranquilizer dart through her clothing and deep into a muscle in her back. The round was designed to be powerful enough to penetrate muscle but not burrow deep enough to damage vital organs, provided the user had a good aim. As he did so, Marcus Day sprinted towards Farhang.

Barber's shot with the tranquilizer device was a fraction of a second too late to stop the woman's shot, but still he got lucky. As the woman retrieved the pistol, leveled it towards Farhang and started squeezing the trigger the dart sunk into her back. It caused a sharp pain about a nano-second before the trigger-squeeze was completed. The sudden and unexpected pain made her right arm flail ever so slightly. It also prevented her from processing the fact that Marcus Day had just started to tackle Farhang thereby altering the position of her target. It was enough. She got off the shot, but it missed its mark. As the quick-acting sedative began to take effect, the would-be assassin first became unstable and started to slump. As she did so, Barber grabbed her by the arm, propped her up and led her to his van parked just a few meters away. The drug was designed to make its target compliant but not unconscious. This allowed Barber to get her to the vehicle under her own power. Shortly after the woman was secured, Day shoved Farhang into the van behind her, closed the door, then walked calmly around the front of the van, climbed into the driver's seat and proceeded to "Get out of Dodge". Several onlookers continued to stare at the scene in confusion and one even pulled out his cell phone out to make a call, presumably to the police. But before any of the authorities could arrive on site the van would be long gone.

Chapter 11 – An Unpleasant Lifting of the Fog

Undisclosed Location – Present time

The fog enshrouding his consciousness was beginning to lift as he felt a harsh slap across his face.

"Wake up!" a voice commanded, but not Darth Vader's voice this time.

His eyes fluttered as he shook his head back and forth in an effort to clear it. He noticed the room felt freezing. He was shivering and covered with goose bumps. The cold metal seat pressing against the back of his legs added to the effect as he realized he was only wearing his boxers. His shoulders hurt. As the fog continued to lift, he could tell his arms were wrapped around the back of the chair and tightly bound. His wrestled his hands against the restraints, accomplishing nothing, then again went slack. He gradually opened his eyes and looked into the face staring at him from less than a foot away. He recognized the man's eyes. He had seen those eyes before. But whose? He concentrated and forced the scene before him to come into focus. As his vision cleared, he suddenly knew who the man was. "It's you," he said weakly. You were the man I bumped into at the hotel."

"Correct," the voice replied.

"You….," he hesitated, then continued "you were the man in charge of Schiller's private security. You were the one who identified me to the police in the security camera footage."

"Correct again. Joseph Michael Barber at your service."

"Where am I?" he said in a weak voice. "I thought I was dead. The woman. Where is the woman? She had a gun. How did you get me? Wait, I'm confused. Where did you come from? How did you stop her? How…….."

"Shut up," Barber barked. "You and I both got lucky. My colleague and I were waiting for you this morning. We planned to intercept you as you left your home and have you join us for a little conversation. Apparently your colleagues had other plans for you this morning, but their timing sucked. We noticed the threat, the woman, so we neutralized her."

"But I heard a gunshot."

"That was a bit of luck too. We intervened just in time to screw up her aim. One second of hesitation and you would be dead. Now shut up. I'll ask the questions from here out."

"What do you want from me? I was questioned by the authorities then released. I don't know anything," he said. "Your name is Barber. Joseph Barber. You have kidnapped a German citizen and I will file charges if you don't release me immediately."

"Wrong, right, and wrong," Barber replied. "First, you obviously know a great deal, or they, whoever *they* are, would not have tried to kill you. More about that in a moment. Second, yes I am Joe Barber, and right now I am the only thing standing between you and certain death. Third, I doubt you are in a position to file charges against anyone, now that I have you cold on murder. Now like I said, your job here is to answer questions, not ask them."

As the fog engulfing his brain continued to lift, he was able to regain a little more control over his ability to think. "That is nonsense," he said summoning a tone of indignation. "I was leaving my home for work. You kidnapped me. I have no idea why anyone would try to kill me," he lied.

"Well, we'll have to ask the lady in the next room about that, won't we?" Barber asked sarcastically.

Farhang's brief effort at bravado quickly faded and he literally turned white. "What lady in the next room?"

"The assassin who tried to kill you. Yes, we have her as well. We picked up both packages at the same time and brought the two of you here together. In the same van. Isn't that ironic?" Barber chuckled for effect. "The assassin and her target together in the same vehicle. In case it hasn't dawned on you yet, asshole, we saved your life back there. You're welcome.

On second thought, save the 'thank yous' for now as we don't know yet how this day is going to end, do we?"

Farhang was clearly shaken at the revelations and tried to regain some control over the conversation. "The German authorities questioned me and concluded nothing. There were dozens of people who came in contact with Schiller that night. All I did was say hello."

"My colleague is in the next room questioning the assassin as we speak. He can be, well, very persuasive. I am confident that shortly he will persuade her to confirm you were her target. That will provide proof positive that you were the person to administer the fatal dose of fentanyl, or whatever it was, to Schiller. So, if you insist on wasting our time, you can hang on to that little act for a bit longer. You should realize, however, that wasting my time makes me very grumpy. You would not like me grumpy."

"I don't know anything about Schiller's death," he said almost pleading.

"How did you administer the lethal dose of that drug?" Barber asked.

"I don't know what you are talking about!"

"I asked, how did you deliver the carfentinal?"

"I am a German citizen and a senior executive of a major defense industry supplier, and this is outrageous! I demand to be released at once!" he shouted.

"Yes, I will say that senior executive bit has me very intrigued," Barber responded in a calm, almost patronizing voice. "We are going to have to discuss that in a bit more detail I'm afraid. But for the moment let me ask you again. How did you give Schiller the drug?" Barber slapped Farhang across the face again, this time much harder. Blood flowed from his split lip and he started sobbing.

"I don't know any……"

Before he could complete the comment Barber used the heel of his boot to kick the man in the groin so hard the chair moved backwards several inches. “I’m starting to get grumpy now dumb-dumb. Can you tell? This is nothing. I promise you will not leave this place alive until and unless you answer my questions – who gave you the orders, and how did you give Schiller the narcotics. Every time you insult my intelligence by denying that knowledge your punishment is going to become a little bit worse.”

Farhang gasped as the pain from the kick flooded his field of vision with a display of starbursts like it was a major German holiday. He couldn’t breathe and briefly entertained the thought that Hell might have been a better outcome than where he sat. His heart was racing as his fear turned to terror again. He tried hard to take in a lung full of air and failed. After feeling like he had been suffocating for an eternity he managed to capture a small breath and said in almost a whisper, “I don’t know who they are. I honestly don’t know.”

“You don’t know who your handlers are?”

“No, I have no idea”

Barber sensed a resignation in the man’s voice which imparted a credibility to his answers. “Well, you just as much admitted to me that you were the assassin, didn’t you? You told me with a very convincing voice that you don’t know who your patrons are. That’s progress! Problem is by doing so you essentially told me that you do indeed have patrons, and by inference, that confirms you were given instructions to carry out the assassination.”

“I didn’t know it was going to be an assassination,” he replied. “All I knew was that I was to pass something to him with a handshake. I assumed it was data or instructions of some sort or whatever. I didn’t know it was going to kill him,” he said with a clearly shaky voice.

“You administered the narcotics with a handshake?” Barber asked in surprise. “How did you avoid killing yourself while you carried it?”

Farhang was sobbing again. He remained mute.

"Take a look at this!" Barber commanded. He picked up a folder, retrieved a photograph from it then placed it in front of Farhang's face. "I didn't want to have to play this card, but you have left me no choice.

Farhang was horrified. It was his family. "You wouldn't," he said, clearly pleading.

"Ah, that is entirely up to you, lad. I wouldn't if you honestly answer my questions. Remember where we retrieved you. It was in front of your home. I know where you live – sorry I know that is such an overused line but is an accurate one."

Farhang hung his head and started to weep again. "Please, no, not my family. Kill me, but don't hurt my family." His entire being was gripped tightly in a vice of despair. He now longed for the return of the fog that had enveloped his consciousness immediately after the assassination attempt. The present reality was just too painful.

"I have no intention of killing you my friend; after all, if you are dead, you can't answer my questions, can you? But consider this, my colleague in the next room will soon get the answers we need from that woman as to who sent her to dispose of you. Those answers will enable us to verify the veracity of what you tell us. The well-being of your family depends on you telling the truth." Barber was lying of course. He had no intention of harming the man's family, but the guy believing it was a powerful motivator.

"Who were your handlers?" Barber repeated the question.

He was now a broken man. "I don't know their names," he said almost pleading, "But they are Revolutionary Guard Corp."

"Iran?" Barber asked. "Revolutionary Guard?"

"Yes. The Islamic Republic of Iran," Farhang said meekly through his sobs.

"Say that again," Barber commanded.

"I said the Islamic Republic of Iran. My handlers work for the Revolutionary Guard Corps. They only tell me what I need to know to carry out my mission. Nobody is ever given the full picture. And nobody is ever given names. They confirm their identities with validation codes."

"How does a senior executive of a major defense contractor become involved in something like this?" Barber asked with a sense of astonishment.

"I was placed in this country at a young age but was raised to believe in and never question the Revolution. I was told that someday something might be asked of me and that I was to follow instructions precisely without asking questions."

"Are there more like you?"

"Yes. All over the world, even the United States. But I don't know who they are. None of us knows who the others are."

"And you were told to kill Schiller?"

"No. I was told to deliver something to him with a handshake. I had my suspicions, but I did not know my actions would kill him until I saw him collapse in the ballroom."

"You did not know you were carrying carfentinal?"

"No, but I suspected it was something dangerous. The patch I placed on my palm had a cover on it and I was told not to remove it until the last minute. I was also told under no circumstances to touch the side facing outwards once the cover was removed."

"Why did the RGC want Schiller killed?" Barber asked.

"I have no idea. We are never given the why, only the what. I doubt even my RGC handlers knew the why. General Hamidi would never allow people in the country, in Germany, with that knowledge. He is far too cautious. He would be concerned that if captured they would reveal the knowledge."

It made sense. Barber believed him and decided there was no point in asking any more questions. The implications of what he just learned were staggering. He was going to have to do some creative thinking on how to convey this new intelligence to the authorities without compromising his own actions or getting himself and Marcus Day in trouble.

"What are you going to do with me?" Farhang asked.

"We're going to let you get yourself cleaned up and dressed again then drop you off a couple of blocks from your home."

"You're not going to kill me?"

"You and I both know we don't need to do that. You know you were a dead man the minute you shook Schiller's hand. I'm afraid that woman will not be the only person to pay you an unwelcomed visit."

Farhang hung his head and said, "I know" in a voice of resignation.

"We reap what we sow," Barber said without the slightest sense of empathy, then left the room.

Barber walked down the hall to where Day was still working on the woman. He poked his head into the room and said, "Pay dirt. The Iranians – RGC."

"Why am I not surprised?" Day responded.

"Where are you with her?" Barber asked.

"Nowhere, other than she's an independent who is engaged by a third party. No way to trace her back to the owner of the contract."

"Yeah, that's what I suspected," Barber replied.

"Yup. It's the way her business works."

"Exactly. So, what do you think we should do with her?"

"This," Day responded, as he casually pulled a suppressed Glock out of his jacket and put one round in her chest and one in her head. "Sorry, but just cutting her trigger finger off doesn't work for me." It was a reference to the time three years ago when Barber disabled an assassin by cutting off her trigger finger instead of killing her.

"OK, I get it," Barber replied. "After all, she was an assassin. You probably just saved a whole lot of lives."

"What are you going to do with our friend next door?" Day asked.

"Kill him," Barber responded.

"That's a tad harsh, don't you think?"

"What, you're the voice of restraint now?" Barber responded. "You shouldn't be the only one having the fun."

"Joe?" Day asked with a puzzled look.

"Relax. I'm not going to put a round in him. I'm just going to let him go. He was a dead man the minute the RGC gave him his marching orders. And besides, it's not exactly like he can go to the police and ask for protection. I suspect he was told by the RGC that if he refused to sacrifice himself like a good soldier then an ugly fate was likely to befall his family. All we did by stopping the woman was delay the inevitable, and I would guess not by very long."

"You're right," Day replied. "I give him less than 48 hours."

"I give him less than 24," Barber responded.

"Did he know why Schiller was a target?" Day asked.

"No. He didn't think his handlers knew either. That's 'need to know' information and kept very tight to the vest."

"Makes sense. Too bad his knowledge was so compartmentalized. Our problem, partner, is we've now solved the who, but we still don't know the why, and sounds like we are at a dead end," Day responded.

"I still think it has to be something related to what Schiller was working on."

"Agreed. But for now, you go cut him loose and I'll summon the clean-up crew."

Barber started walking back towards Farhang's room. He kept asking himself, "Why would the Iranians want to kill a German defense industry executive? What do you gain by killing a German defense industry executive? What can possibly be the motive for offing a German defense industry executive responsible for development of command and control systems? Why would you.......," he then stopped dead in his tracks. He suddenly remembered a scene from one of his favorite movies, "The Hunt for Red October." Alec Baldwin is shaving in front of the mirror in a bathroom aboard the aircraft carrier asking himself "How do you get a bunch of sailors off a Russian nuclear submarine?"

He suddenly turned and started running back towards Marcus Day. "Marc!" he shouted.

Chapter 12 – "There's an App for That"

Biotech Lab Annex, QuarkSpin Corp, California – Undisclosed Location

A young homeless man sat on the side of a clean hospital-type bed and waited. He didn't look homeless, however. He was freshly showered and clean-shaven. Next to his bed was a table and a food tray that contained the remnants of a fairly nice breakfast – scrambled eggs, bacon, rye toast and fried potatoes. Next to the tray was a coffee cup, now completely empty, and a half-consumed glass of orange juice. He couldn't believe his luck. He had been scooped up from the mean streets of San Francisco and whisked away to this beautiful place and promised a second chance – food, shelter, medical care and a government-sponsored jobs program for the indigent and mentally ill. They told him he was about to be placed in a halfway-house back in the community. Just a few more days to make sure he was healthy enough to be released. Yesterday they had given him a shot of antibiotics and told him he had to remain isolated in his room for just another 48 hours until the medicine made its way into his system. The doors to the room were locked, but that didn't bother him. They actually made him feel safe. Besides, he had everything he needed here. There was even an on-suite bathroom that was the nicest he had ever used. So, test subject Echo sat and he waited.

Dr. Emma Clark stood in a spacious observation room and looked through the two-way mirror. "Very compliant," she observed.

"That's been our consistent experience with these homeless subjects. Good food, a comfortable bed and a little kindness makes them very cooperative," responded Dr. Vihaan Acharya, dual PhDs in Neuroscience and Biomechanics.

Dr. Acharya had come a long way in life. He was born to the 'Untouchables' cast in India. Although officially outlawed, the Asian Indian caste system remained a strong cultural force. A century ago they were the ones who scooped out the open latrines and could never aspire to more than menial tasks. Marriage between castes was forbidden, and anyone who violated that rule was ostracized by their families. Even today they could be the subjects of a prejudice that in many ways resembled the racism that still existed in pockets of the United States. He felt the prejudice every day.

But an IQ north of 165 was his ticket out of the miserable life and the status of his low birth. His promise was detected at an early age, and he soared through the elite schools in his home country, ultimately capturing the prize of graduate school in the United States at M.I.T. and Cal Tech. Several years ago, he caught the attention of the late Charles Westborne Reynolds III with his doctoral dissertation at Cal Tech in neuroscience, "Neuropathological Perspectives on the Intersection of Biomechanics and Neurotransmitter Interruptions as a Method for Behavioral Modifications – a Forensics Approach." His protégé, Dr. Emma Clark, would review titles of dissertations from several prestigious graduate programs and refer promising titles to Reynolds. When she read it she was stunned, and immediately passed it on to her boss. Both she and Reynolds thought Acharya's was one of the best they had ever read. In fact, after reading it, Reynolds told Clark it was the only one he ever read that was better was hers.

So, after passing an extensive vetting process Acharya was offered a salary that was three times greater than his next best alternative. He excelled at the work. He displayed an enthusiasm that never abated even as the ethical lines of his remit became increasingly gray. There was never the slightest bit of moral hesitation at what he did. In fact, it seemed the darker the task, the more he enjoyed it. He had dispatched four people in fatal tests of QuarkSpin's new hardware without the slightest bit of remorse, and even smiled when the tests were successful. He was minutes away from dispatching the fifth, subject "Echo".

In just four years he had been selected as Clark's heir apparent to the CEO job at QuarkSpin. When Clark was elevated to the Chief Executive job at PrinSafe, the top job was his.

He reminded Clark in many ways of herself. She wondered if his ambitions were as big as hers. The prospect of her being in the same position as Westy just before his demise hadn't escaped her. She would keep a close eye on this guy. In the meantime, however, she was going to enjoy this test.

Dr. Acharya held an iPhone 10X Max and looked at the screen. "This will also be a test of the new controller app," he said. "You actually download the software to your iPhone from the Apple App Store."

"You're kidding!" Clark exclaimed with astonishment.

"Not at all. We named it 'Brainiak'." He replied with a grin. "The app itself will appear to be a low-skill game. We designed it low skill to ensure there wouldn't be a lot of interest in actually playing it. Let me show you how it works."

He stood next to Clark and showed her the screen of his iPhone, then began to explain. "Under the game's settings tab there is an option called screen saver. You open the option and touch the copyright symbol icon and then it launches a retinal scan," he explained as he navigated the small screen with his thumb. "It just scanned my retina to confirm my identity. The scan happens in the background and isn't even noticed by the iPhone owner."

"Right," Clark responded. "I didn't see a thing."

"Precisely. There are only two authorized retinal configurations in the system, yours and mine. If an unauthorized user happens to stumble on the functionality they will only see the four screen saver options. When an authorized retinal scan is validated, as just happened with mine, the app will display this secondary validation screen that asks for a 9-digit code. The code will be a mix of alpha, numeric and special characters so the number of combinations is in the millions. You and I will each have a validation code and the team will change it at random intervals as an additional security enhancement."

"How do we receive the code?" Clark asked.

"Good question. The answer of course is any way you want, but my thinking is each of us gets a card with the code on it."

"Ok. We can talk about that later."

"Of course."

"Once the correct code is entered," Acharya said as he started to tap in a code with his thumb, "the screen will display a list of names of the people who are implanted with the device." He then touched the name 'Test Subject Echo'. "You can see here there is ample space between the names to reduce the risk of accidently selecting the wrong person. Once you select your target, the device will ask you to place your thumb on the screen and read the thumbprint as a second confirmation measure. If the thumbprint is verified, a slider bar will be displayed. This is the master controller and it controls the amount of damage inflicted. Sliding the icon from left to right increases the effect from a severe headache to death by stroke."

"Impressive, Vihaan," Clark responded. "So, the device you injected into Test Subject Echo has the new software code for the severe headache option?"

"Yes."

"Do we need to somehow get a new device into the President if we want to just give her a headache?"

"No, that's the good news. All that's needed is a firmware update. It's already done. We are good to go."

"You're a genius, Vihann. Great work!"

"Thank you. Now, shall we proceed with our test?" he asked with a smile.

"Please do," she said, as she smiled back.

Dr. Acharya placed his thumb on the screen and began to move the icon to the right along the slider. As he did so the homeless man behind the two-way mirror grabbed the sides of his head and cried out in agony. Acharya left the slider in position for several seconds then returned it to full-left. The man seemed to recover somewhat but cried out for help. Another man in a long white physician's coat quickly entered the room accompanied by a woman dressed as a nurse. Neither one of them were the medical professionals as each pretended to be. "What's the matter?" the man dressed as a doctor said in a voice dripping with compassion and empathy.

"My head," the man cried out, "My head hurt so bad I thought it was going to explode!"

"Are you still in pain?" asked the woman dressed as a nurse.

"No, but I don't know what happened!"

The woman took the man's blood pressure and called it out, as if reporting it to the doctor but it was really intended for Clark and Achaya in the observation room. "One fifty over ninety-five," she said.

"High," Clark observed, but not dangerous. "Take it again in a couple of minutes," conveying an instruction through the earpiece of the woman pretending to be the nurse.

The man in the doctor's coat looked into the subject's eyes and listened to his heart as if he was performing a medical exam. A few seconds later the subject cried out in pain again as Acharya pushed the slider back to the right for several seconds then backed off.

"I'm going to go get you something for the pain," the imposter doctor said, then he and the woman left the room.

Acharya looked at Clark and said "This next test will be an extended one. I want to verify that a substantially longer exposure to the stimuli doesn't decrease the subject's functionality. The objective is to hurt them, not to damage them." As he pushed the slider to the right for the third time, Test Subject Echo was subjected to a massive headache that lasted for 10 minutes. It wasn't pretty. The poor homeless man writhed on the floor in agony as the device pulsed his parietal lobe, the part of the brain that interprets pain. He was kept under close observation for about two hours after the test. The test was declared a success. The lab technician then entered his room with a syringe that purported to be for his pain. Five minutes after the injection, the man was dead.

Chapter 13 – Of Revelations and Abductions

Undisclosed Location, Berlin

"Marc!" Barber shouted as he ran back towards the room where Day had just shot the assassin, forcefully opening the door with his shoulder.

"Joe?"

"How do you get a bunch of sailors to want to abandon a Russian nuclear sub?"

"What?" Day responded, with a look of confusion.

"How do you get a bunch of sailors to want to abandon a Russian nuclear sub?" Barber all but shouted the question again.

"You're not making sense!" Day exclaimed.

"'The Hunt for Red October.' The scene where Alec Baldwin is standing in front of the mirror shaving and keeps repeating the question then suddenly realizes the answer was in front of his face all the time!"

"What?"

"Word association!" Barber shouted. "He spontaneously realized the association with 'want to abandon' and 'nuclear'!"

"OK I'm still not following you," Day replied.

"Why would you want to assassinate a German defense industry executive?" Barber shouted again.

"Huh?"

"Why would you want to assassinate a German defense industry executive whose background is in software development. Why would you want to assassinate a German defense industry executive whose background is in software development and whose company developed a whole new command and control system for, among other things, the EF's newly acquired nuclear weapons?"

Day's eyes lit up with recognition. "Right! The Iranians have figured out something about that code and maybe Schiller caught on and was about to confront them. Or maybe the Iranians have a plant in his company like our clown next door and Schiller was on to that."

"Exactly! The European Federation, AKA the Germans, never trusted the French. And the French and the Germans are engaged in a lot of high-tech commerce after that disastrous Iranian Nuclear Deal," replied Barber.

"Right. Thank you, John 'effin Kerry!"

"Yeah. And we know the EF rolled out that new CNC (command and control) system just 6 months ago. That was part of their PR blitz when they took over the French nuclear arsenal and started moving part of it to German soil. They thought a new and more secure system would buy them some credibility with the UN."

"Right," said Day. "Schiller's death has to be connected somehow to his involvement with that new system."

"Exactly. And whatever it is the Iranians know, or think they know, they want to make sure nobody else knows that they know. I think Schiller was on to them and they concluded he had to be silenced,"

"Now we just need to figure out what that 'something' is."

"And somehow get our hands on whoever Farhang's handlers were."

The sound was faint, but it was unmistakable. A muffled 'thwack' came from the direction of the room holding Farhang. Barber and Day stopped talking and looked at each other with recognition.

"Sounds like we've got company," Day whispered.

"Right," Barber replied. "And they're armed. I'd swear it sounds like somebody just put a round into Farhang."

"Yup," Day said as he drew his Glock 19 from his side. "My guess is whoever was after Farhang had eyes on their assassin to make sure the job got done. When they saw our takedown they probably called a tactical team, which is why there was a delay before they got here."

"Right," Barber replied, "Makes sense. Get outside, Marc, and see what's there. Maybe we'll get lucky and get a license number or at least a vehicle description. I'm going to go pay our company a visit."

"On my way," Day replied. "Be careful, partner."

"Always," Barber replied.

Both men quietly walked out of the room, silenced Glocks at the ready. Day turned to his left and started to walk towards the exterior door. Barber turned right and started walking back towards the room where Farhang was, in the opposite direction of Day. Both proceeded in a crouched position, almost crawling, and were barely breathing to stay as quiet as possible.

Day reached the exterior door, or doors, more precisely. They were floor to ceiling glass panes inside aluminum frames which latched in the middle. Given the position of the sun, sunlight poured through the glass from the left and brightly illuminated the right-hand side of the entryway. Fortunately for Day, the left wall was still buried in shadows which provided an opportunity for partial concealment from anyone who might be looking into the doorway from the street or a parked car. He flattened his back to the left wall to minimize his profile then inched his way closer to the entrance. Hiding himself was no easy task, given his size. With his back against the wall he peered out the window to his right. Nothing. There was no foot traffic which was normal he figured given the location of the building was not in a crowded area, and he couldn't see any vehicles either. He then stretched his neck to see out the left-hand side of the doors. It was then he noticed a Range Rover parked just a few meters down the street to his left. It was occupied by a driver but nobody else. That vehicle had to belong to their company, and the driver was no doubt at the ready to whisk them away.

Barber headed in the opposite direction from Day and slowly approached the room where they held Farhang. He gently pushed open the door to the room by about an inch. Then, all hell broke loose. He felt a powerful blow to his kidney, which seemed more like it came from a knee than a fist. The blow took its toll and his body started towards the floor. He silently cursed himself for the mistake of ignoring potential threats from behind. He felt a large boot slam his wrist to the floor as the Glock was wrenched from his grip. He was disarmed and in great pain but not yet out of the fight. He forced his mind to ignore the pain and started to twist his body to the side to gain access to a large knife sheathed to his right ankle. A swift kick to his stomach forced him to reflexively curl into the fetal position. As he curled up he felt two men push his hands and feet together and secure them with zip ties. He was now exhausted, riddled with pain and completely helpless. He was grabbed under each arm and lifted to his feet. As he became upright, he got a brief glimpse of Farhang before two men dragged him out of the room. Farhang was slumped in the chair with his head leaning to one side. There was an ugly scene of blood and brain matter on the wall behind him. Farhang was dead.

Day continued to stand as tight to the wall as possible, stretching his neck as he looked for an opportunity to exit the building and find a better vantage point to catch the license number of the Range Rover. He concluded there was no way he could exit the building without being seen and would be a sitting duck given the open space between the doors and the Range Rover. He knew his best course of action was to wait and watch. After a few minutes he saw four men appear in his field of view. Two of the men were forcibly walking a third, while a fourth man walked a few feet behind. They were headed towards the Range Rover. There was no mistaking the man's identity. It was Barber, and it was decision time.

Every fiber of his being was screaming at him to charge out of the building and help his friend, but his training and discipline overrode his instincts. There was too much distance between himself and Barber's assailants, and there were three of them. He could put down one, no problem, and would even make the charge against two. But to charge three, he realized, was a suicide mission. No way could he take down three. And he knew that such a cowboy act, while brave, carried too much risk of Barber being collateral damage. So, he stood concealed against the wall as best as possible, and he watched.

Arriving at the vehicle, one of the men opened the rear door Barber was shoved into the back seat. One of the assailants sat next to Barber and the other walked around and entered from the opposite side. The third man climbed into the passenger side front seat. As the vehicle started to pull away, Day moved away from the wall and looked directly out the window. At this point he no longer cared about concealment. He could see the license number as the vehicle passed in front of him. That was one small consolation, he told himself. At least with the license number they would have an easier job identifying the car. He stood there and watched the Range Rover drive away.

Chapter 14 – The Chase

Undisclosed Location

Marcus Day watched the Range Rover speed away with Barber inside. He pulled a cell phone out of his pocket, unlocked it, accessed his contact list and touched a name to initiate a phone call. "This is Alpha 2," he announced, using his call sign of Alpha 2 instead of his given name. Joe Barber was Alpha 1. "I need a tac team deployed immediately just to the east of my cell phone GPS location. Target is a late model silver Range Rover, License number Bravo Papa X-ray seven four two niner. Repeat, Bravo Papa X-ray seven four two niner. Alpha 1 has been abducted and is in the vehicle. Subject vehicle contains three armed Tangos, repeat, three armed Tangos. Maintain eyes on vehicle but do not intercept except as last resort. Follow vehicle and determine destination. I also need a pick up at my cell phone GPS location and a sweeper team to sanitize the site."

As the Range Rover continued down the road, Barber laid on his side and reeled from the groin kick. The pain was excruciating. Just as he was about to catch a full lung of air one of his assailants kicked him in the side again. He was pretty sure he felt a rib crack and his pain became ever more severe. One of the men in the vehicle started yelling at him. The guy wasn't speaking either German or English. Barber thought he recognized it as Farsi, but he wasn't familiar enough with the language to make out what the man was saying. At least it confirmed his suspicions that his abductors were Iranian.

He could tell the van was proceeding at a measured pace as if they were just driving to work, a shopping mall or some other routine destination. He assumed his abductors didn't want to draw attention to themselves with excessive speed or erratic driving. The sounds outside were the normal sounds of the streets; unintelligible pedestrian chatter, vehicles on the roads and the occasional car horn. It was obvious they were taking him someplace where their real work would begin. He felt helpless. Helpless was not a sensation he was accustomed to. He was an alpha predator, a former Navy Seal and CIA Paramilitary Operations Officer. He was the one who was supposed to be rendering a person of interest to a black site for questioning. He was not supposed to be the person laying on the floor of an SUV with hands and feet zip-tied. He remembered his recurrent dream and imagined biting into the neck of the man who just kicked him, but he knew it was pointless. There were three of them in the vehicle, and they were powerfully built and on high alert.

Eric Hill, Orion Bellicus' Special Operator code-named 'Bravo 1', stood in the safe house looking out the window as he felt the cell phone in his pocket buzz. He retrieved the phone, pressed a virtual button on the screen to activate the call and a single word emanated from the phone: "Authenticate," triggering Orion Bellicus' process for validating orders in the field.

"Sunrise," he replied, using the authentication code for the day.

"You are authenticated," the voice replied.

"Authenticate," he then said in return, repeating the process from his end.

"Thunderstorm," came the voice of Marcus Day on the phone, providing the reciprocal code.

"You are authenticated," Hill replied in kind.

Day then spoke, "Deploy immediately to coordinates just transmitted to your phone. Instructions will be conveyed in route. Expect high probability of hostile response. Full weapons complement authorized."

"Roger that," he replied.

Three minutes later a deep blue BMW X5M progressed rapidly down the road towards a set of GPS coordinates programmed into a specialized navigation system. The vehicle contained five men, each of whom were easily over two hundred pounds. Two of the occupants were former Navy SEALs, two were former Army Combat Applications Group, formerly known as Delta, and one was a former Force RECON Marine. Hill, one of the former SEALs, was the group's Commander. They were part of Orion Bellicus' SOF, or Special Operations Force, individually recruited, vetted and trained by Marcus Day himself. These men comprised the Orion Bellicus Tactical Team Bravo.

Each man was armed with a suppressed Sig Sauer P226 pistol chambered in 9-millimeter parabellum rounds and a Sig P239 backup pistol in a sleeve holster at the small of their backs. They also carried a Heckler and Koch MP7 4.6 by 30-millimeter machine pistol in a side sling and a Zero Tolerance 0223 folding knife in a forearm sleeve which allowed for quick draw in close quarters combat. Their torsos were protected by ultra-lightweight Kevlar vests capable of stopping most small arms rounds. Each man wore a lightweight Spring jacket which concealed most of their firepower, at least to casual observers. Hill also carried a low-tech version of the sedation gun that Barber had used on the would-be assassin in front of Farhang's house. It looked more like a conventional pistol than a cell phone and was intended for a tactical situation where simplicity of operation was more important than deception.

As the BMW X5M progressed towards their target's last known coordinates, Bravo 1 spoke to the team. "This is a hostage rescue op. Alpha 1 was abducted approximately 10 minutes ago. He is in a silver Ranger Rover with license plate Bravo Papa X-Ray seven four two niner. We are not to engage while vehicle is in route. Mission Is to intercept, identify and follow vehicle to its intended location. Extraction of Alpha 1 to be executed at destination. After Alpha 1 is secure, all tangos are to be rendered to the safe house for interrogation. There is a high priority to capturing Tangos alive. Use of deadly force authorized only as a last resort. Any questions?"

Nobody said anything.

"Weapons check." Each man examined the three firearms they were carrying and verified the chambers were charged. They also withdrew the folding knives and verified they could easily deploy the blades.

"Bravo 3 and 4, the two of you carry the smoke and concussion grenades. Do not deploy except on my command." Both men acknowledged and attached the devices to loops on the inside of their jackets.

"I don't need to tell you that there cannot be any collateral damage on this op. We are operating on German soil, make that European Federation soil and our presence is not sanctioned. If this goes South and the authorities have to intervene or in any way become aware of our presence, each of us individually will be in a world of hurt. A successful op is one where not a single shot is fired. Regard your clubs as your primary weapons. Understood?"

Each man acknowledged with either a nod of the head or a "Roger that."

"GPS says subject vehicle is approximately 35 meters ahead of us," the driver announced.

Hill retrieved a pair of high-power Leopold binoculars from the center console and scanned out the front window. "Got it!" he exclaimed. "Silver Range Rover. We are too far back to make out a license plate number, but it has to be our target. Let's get around two of the vehicles in front of us to close the gap a bit but no closer."

"Roger that," replied the driver.

Back where Marcus Day was waiting for his pick-up, a late-model BMW sedan pulled in front of the building. As he saw the vehicle, he ran out the door and jumped into the passenger front passenger seat and the driver quickly drove the vehicle away. "Sit rep," he barked as he fastened his seat belt.

"Tac Team Bravo is in pursuit right now about 25 yards behind the target vehicle. They are headed west on Shildhorn Strasse and just past the 103.

"Wait a minute," Day replied with a worried voice. "Give me a map!"

The driver reached down to a pocket on the driver's side door and retrieved a map of the city. Day quickly opened it and found where Shildhorn Strasse and the 103 crossed. He traced his finger westward along Shildhorn to determine possible destinations. Something caught his eye. He felt like his heart stopped. "Shit!" he yelled. "Do we have comms with Bravo?"

"Of course," the driver responded, handing Day an encrypted walkie talkie.

"Bravo 1 this is Alpha 2," Day said in an urgent voice.

"Bravo 1 here boss."

"Are you still following target west on Shildhorn Strasse?"

"Negative. Target just turned left on Schlo Strasse."

Day found the intersection on his map, then replied, "This is critical. Let me know if he makes a right turn on Grunewald Strasse. It should be about 4 blocks from your last turn."

"Copy," replied Bravo 1. "He's signaling a right-hand turn. Vehicle is slowing down. Vehicle is turning right!" Eric Hill exclaimed. "What's up, boss? Where do you think he's headed?"

Day was overcome with a sense of dread. He threw the map at the inside of the BMWs window in a fit of rage and turned the air inside the vehicle blue in a string of profanities that even stunned the driver. He quickly regained his composure. "Sorry. I think he's headed for the Iranian Embassy. If he turns right at Altenstein Strasse that will confirm it."

"Well that would be a great big bucket of bad, wouldn't it?" Bravo 1 replied.

"No kidding."

"Wait, target signaling a right turn. Turning right on Altenstein. Now signaling a left turn. Turning left on Pobdielskaillee."

"That confirms it," Day replied. "He's less than a block from the Embassy right now."

"Roger that. I can see the flags. What are our instructions? Are we to engage?"

"Negative," Day replied. "Break off pursuit. We can't afford to get into a firefight in front of the Iranian Embassy. Even if we win, we lose because of the exposure, and I can assure you we will not win.

"We can still intercept the vehicle!" Hill shouted. "We can't abandon Alpha 1!" He regretted the words the minute they came out of his mouth. He knew the tactical situation was a "no-win," and there was nothing they could do.

"Did you copy my instructions, Bravo 1?" Day queried in his most authoritative command voice.

"Yes, we copy," Bravo 1 replied. "Breaking off pursuit. Sorry, boss."

"Rendezvous at the safe house," Day ordered.

"Copy that. See you at the safe house. Tac Team Bravo headed to safe house. Bravo 1 out."

Barber could feel the vehicle start to slow down then make a left-hand turn. It came to a stop. He heard the window role down and there was an exchange between two men, again in Farsi. He felt the vehicle slowly proceed and after several seconds a horn lightly beeped. The sound of its echo suggested they were in a garage. As the vehicle came to a stop, he felt a pair of strong hands affix a blindfold around his entire face. Two sets of arms then lifted him from his prone position and started to drag him out of the van. He continued to hear men speaking in Farsi as he was forcefully moved along. He had no idea of where he was or where they were taking him, but he had a pretty good clue as to what for. This was not going to be good, he thought, as his world went black.

Chapter 15 – The Consummate Fixer

PrinSafe HQ, Palo Alto, California

Emma Clark's intercom buzzed. "Ms. Clark, General Brandt is on the line," her administrative assistant announced.

"Thank you," Clark responded. She picked up the receiver and pushed an icon on her desk to connect the call. "Good morning, General. Nice to hear from you."

"Nice to hear your voice, Dr. Clark," the General replied. "I very much enjoyed our dinner in Cologne last month."

"As did I, General. How can we be of service?"

Being of service to the commanding general of the European Federation Air Force was becoming increasingly problematic for U.S. domiciled companies, including a private equity firm like PrinSafe. Since the formation of the EF three years ago tension had continuously escalated between "New Europe", as it was called, and the much of the rest of the world. The U.S. Congress was openly pushing the Einhorn administration to consider economic sanctions. The U.S. Department of Defense was imposing restrictions on transfers of technology from its suppliers to the EF military. Trade tensions were exacerbated as the EF worked to develop strong economic ties with countries considered hostile to the interests of the West, including Iran, North Korea and China. The Middle East was even in play as the Saudis were becoming increasingly skeptical of the U.S. commitment to their royal family. PrinSafe operated a subsidiary in Germany, CWR Industries, that supplied technology and hardware to the EF's rail gun project, Dart, and consulted Sternenlicht on cyber security protocols to protect the new command and control system.

"Emma, I have been advised that your President is being pushed by the Chairman of the House Foreign Relations Committee to stop the work CWR is doing for Sternenlicht on Dart and for us directly on cyber."

"Is that so?" Clark asked. She was stunned, and frankly furious. She couldn't believe the President hadn't given her a heads-up on that push. Why did she have to hear this from a German General?

"I'm afraid it is. Our sources tell us she is looking favorably on the request and plans to issue an executive order within the week. Such a development would be a major setback for us. CWR could be replaced, but we would lose considerable momentum and face unacceptable delays in finding someone else. Besides, we trust you. And trust is not a commodity that is easily replaced, is it?"

"No, it is not. You have very good intelligence, Helmut," Clark replied. "My people in D.C. have heard rumors but nothing that definitive," she lied, not wanting the General to know she was actually in the dark and was hearing this for the first time. "I am going to have to talk to them about that. What do you want me to do?" she asked, but she already knew the answer to that question.

"Well I am aware of two things, Emma. First, you have a personal relationship with the President. I am sure you can leverage that relationship, right?"

"And second?" Clark asked.

"Second?" he asked almost as a rhetorical question. "Second, of course, is you are a consummate fixer, are you not?"

"Let me go to work, Helmut. I'll get back to you."

"Thank you Emma. A pleasure, as always."

"A pleasure indeed," she responded, then disconnected the call.

Clark was angry. She opened her top right-hand side desk drawer and took out two cell phones. They looked identical but had very different functions. She picked one of them up and powered it on. When the home screen appeared, she touched a game icon named 'Brainiak', opened settings, the screen saver option, and in less than a second a page appeared asking for a code. She retrieved a laminated card with five numbers, two letters and two special characters from her suit jacket and carefully entered each on the screen, which then prompted her to place her thumb on a small circle. As she did so, a slider bar appeared.

Clark picked up the second phone, already on and highly encrypted, and placed a phone call to the personal cell of the President of the United States. After several seconds her call went to voice mail. She then sent a text, "Imperative we speak immediately." Three minutes passed. There was still no answer, so she sent another text, "Am sending a different kind of message this time. Please answer the phone immediately!" She then touched the slider bar on the first phone and moved it one hash mark to the right for three seconds, then returned it to its original position.

President Einhorn sat in her private study next to the Oval Office, reviewing a series of polling results with her Director of Political Affairs. She had felt her personal cell phone vibrate in her jacket pocket but ignored it. Suddenly she was struck by a blinding headache. It felt as if the top of her head was going to explode. Her field of vision was flooded with starbursts as waves of excruciating pain pulsed back and forth between her temples. She was overcome with a massive wave of nausea then, just as suddenly as it appeared, the headache vanished. She then realized what had happened.

Her Chief of Staff was stunned at what he had just witnessed. "Are you all right, Madam President? Should I call for the doctor?"

"No, I think I'm fine. I just got really sick to my stomach, but it seems to have passed. I'll be alright, but give me a few minutes will you?"

"Yes ma'am. I'll be in my office. Just call when you are ready to continue."

"Thanks," the President said, as the man walked out of the office. She retrieved the cell phone from her jacket, looked at the screen and immediately recognized the number.

The phone buzzed again as another text appeared. "Hope you got my message. Calling back now. Suggest you answer the phone. Promptly."

About five seconds later the phone rang. "What the hell do you think you're doing?" the President asked in a shaky but clearly angry voice.

"Getting your attention ma'am," the voice responded.

"I am not going to be played like a puppet!" the President shouted. "You know I can just walk into a Faraday cage to shield me from your signal then order a Secret Service assault on your offices and take you and your entire organization down!"

"That would be unwise on so many levels Madam President. First, an 'assault' on our office, as you characterized it, would reveal a great deal of information you would not like in the public domain. For instance, your involvement in the Sparrow program. And you shouldn't take comfort in the notion that the Service could destroy records during such an attack. A parallel set of records is stored at an undisclosed location, and we have a fail-safe that if there is any such attack on us they will be immediately be released. And speaking of fail-safes, I have some additional bad news. The device we implanted in you also has a fail-safe. The details aren't important. Just suffice it to say that any action against us will trigger a signal to the device that will cause you to experience a stroke severe enough to render you a vegetable."

Clark then paused and waited for a response. She waited several seconds. None came. She then continued, "Madam President, I don't like this unpleasantness. You and our organization have enjoyed a relationship over the last several years that has yielded enormous mutual benefits. You wouldn't be President if it weren't for the support of Westy, and I have continued that suport. Once you leave office you will become extraordinarily wealthy. I don't want to be heavy-handed. I want our relationship to continue. I want us to be friends. Can we be friends, Madam President?"

"If you want to be my friend why did you do this to me?" Sarah Einhorn said with a shaky voice that was almost pleading.

"Because your recent behavior has been, how shall I say, unpredictable. And there have been times when I have felt, well, unappreciated. Even caught off guard. That is the reason for the urgency of my phone call."

"So, what is it you want," the President said with a tone of resignation in her voice.

"It has come to our attention that you are contemplating additional restrictions on subsidiaries of American companies providing products and services to the European Federation military. I might add that I am very disappointed that I had to hear that from someone else and not you."

"You're not ignorant of the news, Emma. Congress is up in arms about what they consider German sabre rattling. Their economic ties with Iran were bad enough, but now they are making noise about sponsoring meetings between their defense ministries to discuss 'issues of mutual interest', whatever the hell that means. Increased trade sanctions are a proportional and measured response to that. And I don't consult you on foreign policy. Besides, how does this impact you?"

"One of the companies on the sanction list is CWR Industries. It is one of our subsidiaries headquartered in Cologne – a German company. It is very important to us."

"I'm not given that level of detail. I have no idea who the companies are."

"The Congress is still deadlocked on the issue," Clark said, "and we understand the Chairman of the House Foreign Relations Committee has channeled you privately to consider an executive order for the sanctions. We are also told you are favorably disposed to such an order."

"How did you become aware of that?" the President responded in astonishment.

"That's not important. What is important is no such order be issued."

"Emma we'll throw a few more government contracts at you to make up the economic loss, but I have to issue that order. I was just going over polling results when you called. Additional sanctions poll 65 percent positive.

The Congress is up in arms because the American people are up in arms. It would be political suicide not to do so."

"Frankly Madam President, it could be literal suicide to do so," Clark responded with a naked threat.

The President became angry again. "Don't you threaten me! I want our mutually beneficial relationship, as you call it, to continue as much as you do, but you are not running this nation's foreign policy from Palo Alto," she shouted into the phone.

Clark wasn't going to waste time indulging the President's tantrum. She picked up the other phone and put her finger on the slider, then moved it to the first has mark again. This time she left it in place for several extra seconds.

Sarah Einhorn summoned every bit of self-control she had to keep from crying out in pain. She couldn't afford to let anyone to see her in this state. The pain finally passed.

"Sarah?" Clark said softly. "Are you there?"

"Yes," the President replied weakly.

"No executive order, Sarah."

"I understand."

Chapter 16 – Escape

Inside the Embassy, The Islamic Republic of Iran, Berlin

The sensation was surreal, like an out of body experience. He felt like he was hovering several feet above his head looking down at himself. Through the dense fog he experienced a sensation akin to a poke in the arm which didn't make any sense. None of it made sense. But gradually the dense fog started to lift, and his vision slowly cleared. He was no longer floating up above. His body and spirit seemed to merge, and he was starting to view things through his eyes. The scene before him came into focus. He was sitting at a table. Two men sat across from him. Finally, one of them spoke.

"Welcome to the Islamic Republic of Iran." The man spoke perfect English, although with a mild accent, middle-eastern perhaps.

"What?" Barber replied. His head was clear, but he was still confused.

"I said welcome to the Islamic Republic of Iran. At the moment you are in the Iranian Embassy to the European Federation. We are in Berlin. Don't worry about your confusion. It will pass in just a few minutes and your head will be perfectly clear." The man spoke in a non-threatening, almost pleasant voice.

It was starting to come back to him; going to the ground just outside the door to the room where they held Farhang. It was in the safe house, he remembered. The vicious kicks. The pain. He looked around the room. It didn't seem particularly threatening. The two men who sat across from him had dark hair and thick beards. They appeared to have stocky, muscular builds and were dressed in normal casual street clothes – solid colored button-down shirts, one blue and one black, and cotton slacks. No neckties and no sport or suit coats. On the table in front of him sat several yellow legal-style writing pads and several inexpensive retractable ball-point pens. In front of each of them sat an unopened bottle of water. The man doing the talking was nursing what appeared to be a cup of hot tea. There were no security guards in the room, which struck him as odd. Perhaps they were stationed outside.

"Where am I and how did I get here?" Barber asked. "And what do you want?"

"Ah, a man who likes to get down to business," said one of the men as he then paused for a minute to take a sip of his tea.

"Well perhaps we should start by explaining your circumstances," the man said. "First, you need to know that escape from here is simply impossible. You will notice the room has no additional security guards. We find such overt displays of force not to be conducive to constructive conversations, and frankly, unnecessary. Trust me, even if you managed to get past both of us, which you will not, you will not get very far. Even if you managed to get outside of this building, which you most certainly will not, you would be shot on your way to the front gates, which are, in any event, also locked."

"Second, you are in a conference room in the basement of our Embassy. It sits directly below our intelligence directorate. We do all kinds of fun things here. From the floors above we plan the theft of weapons purchased by the Germans from the Americans which we in turn give to our friends in Hezbollah to kill Israelis. We make sure some of those weapons even find their way to Afghanistan to kill you Americans. Delicious, isn't it?" he said with a smile.

"Once you arrived in our compound, we drugged you with a fast-acting sedative to make you, well, more 'pliable' I believe is the word you Americans would use, and also to prevent you from seeing much while you were en route to this location. You were then given a shot of counter-sedative to speed up the recovery process."

"Third, you will remain our guest here in the Embassy while we interrogate you. Such an unpleasant word, isn't it? I would much prefer we simply have a conversation. Wouldn't you agree? Don't answer that now, but think about it please, as the nature of your stay here with us will depend heavily on how good of a conversationalist you are."

"Fourth, once we conclude additional dialogue with you will prove unproductive you will be flown to Tehran for incarceration. The nature and the length of your incarceration will entirely depend on how cooperative you are here."

"The length of my incarceration?" Barber interrupted. "Like you are going to let me go."

"Oh, I don't use the word length in terms of how long you will be imprisoned. I use the word to define how long you will be allowed to be incarcerated until you are executed."

"I see," Barber replied.

"The one thing you must understand is the life you had when you woke this morning is now over. It ended the moment you passed those gates outside. You now belong to us, and you will never see freedom, your country or your family again."

"And that brings me to my fifth point. We have an asset back in Connecticut on station near your home, and she is waiting for my directions. She is following your wife. Don't worry we will shortly show you proof. If you disappoint us, you will not be the only one to suffer. I haven't decided, by the way, exactly what those instructions might entail. I am considering, however, the view that a conventional headshot may be too merciful an action, and something more exotic may provide better motivation. Don't worry. If we go down that road, I promise you will have a front row seat. Now, I have just a few simple questions. Let's start with how you knew we were targeting Herr Farhang this morning?"

Barber was reeling, but it was a mental state he would not allow himself to indulge for very long. No harm in humoring this guy as long as he could get away with it. His interrogator's guard would be down, and he might accidently reveal something.

"We didn't know," Barber replied. "We wanted to talk to him ourselves and were there to ask him some questions. When we saw the hit going down we figured we had no choice but to intervene."

"Oh Mr. Barber, must you really disappoint me so early in our conversation? If all you wanted to do was ask him some questions, he would not have been delivered to, what do you call it, ah yes, your 'safe house' with hands and feet zip-tied, now would he? You were planning to abduct him, weren't you?"

"Our hope was to simply question him," Barber lied, "but he proved very uncooperative and left us no choice."

"What did you learn from him at your safe house?" his interrogator asked.

"Nothing," Barber lied again. "Your team arrived before we got very far."

The man took another sip of his tea and sat in the chair with a contemplative look as if he were considering the next move on a chess board. Just then, his cell phone rang. He picked it up, touched the screen to answer the call then placed the phone to his ear. After several seconds, he touched the screen again and put the phone down. "You'll have to excuse me for a few minutes, but no worries I'll return shortly." He then turned to his colleague at the table and said, "Keep our friend here company until I get back. And Mr. Barber, please don't be foolish. It will not be in your best interests, or the best interests of you family to attempt an escape, which I assure you will certainly fail."

The man then got up and left the room. As he opened the door to leave, Barber could see there were no guards in the hallway either. "Boy these guys must really be cocky," he thought, "or maybe right." Then his training started to kick in.

Most people thought that SEAL training was all about acquiring crazy ninja combat skills and learning to perform superhuman feats. They were wrong. As any special operator would confirm, it was not so much about the physical as it was about the mental. Sure, you had to learn how to do crazy-hard things but what mattered was mental toughness. Many an epic jock washed out because he didn't have the mental toughness and discipline to get through the training. In BUDS, or Basic Underwater Demolition training, SEAL, they learned to focus on one task at a time and to build on small successes. Just survive this evolution. Just get to the next meal. Just make it to the next sleep cycle and everything will be ok. It was how you turned the impossible into the possible and how you made it to the end. In advanced training they learned how to improvise and pull those small successes out of a hat in circumstances that were constantly changing in the worst ways possible. They were lessons learned that Barber took with him throughout his life.

It was Barber and one man in the room now. Joe knew if he was going to seize this opportunity he would have to act fast. He looked around and surveyed what he had at his disposal. It wasn't much, but it would have to be enough. He noticed the stack of yellow legal pads on the table. He then noticed the three ball-point pens. Suddenly the idea struck him. He gently grabbed the bottom of one of the legal pads and slid it in front of him. He then casually picked up a ball-point pen and placed one end in his mouth as he stared at the legal pad as if he was about to write something. The man glanced at him, and in the lizard part of the Iranian's brain it must have registered as a series of non-threatening actions as he glanced away and continued to look bored.

Then Barber made his move. He launched out of his chair over the table. The Iranian's brain wasn't able to process the input fast enough to register it as a threat, so he froze for just a split second. It was enough. In one fluid and lightning-fast move Barber reached across the desk with pen, writing end out, and in a large arch rammed the pen into the Iranian's neck. He must have hit a major artery because blood started squirting like a pulsing fountain. Before the man could react, Barber grabbed both sides of his head, twisting it violently to the sound of a loud "crack", then gently lowered his torso to the table to avoid the sound of the guy falling out of his chair. He rifled through the man's pockets to see if there was anything useful. Unfortunately, the man was not armed, but he did find a cigarette lighter in the guy's pocket and placed it in his. Small success number one achieved, now on to the next.

He gently opened the door to reveal a dimly lit hallway. He must indeed be in the basement, he thought. He quickly walked down the hall praying he would not encounter anyone. As he passed a door he heard a low-pitched hum and concluded it must be the entrance to a utility closet. He needed to get out of that hallway and figure his next move before he encountered someone else, so he quietly opened the door and stepped in.

He felt a quick flash of despair as he remembered the man's words about how difficult it would be to get out of the compound even if he managed to get out of the building. This was an exercise in futility, he concluded. He started to worry that his actions would accelerate an action against his wife. Then the training kicked in again. He pushed the naysayer out of his mind. Focus, he self-admonished. It was then he smelled it. A faint whiff of natural gas. He looked back into the room and noticed piping running all over the place. He turned to the source of the steady hum that attracted him to the room. It was the HVAC system. The fans. Then the idea hit him. A fire! If he could start a fire, or even better make that gas explode it would summon the first responders from the City of Berlin. The Iranians would have to allow them access to the compound to do their work. Access points would have to open to provide access, and he could get out that way. But this fire had to be big, really big, like headline big.

He looked around the room for anything that might break one of those pipes free. He was in luck! It looked like a tool chest was positioned at the opposite side of the room against the wall. He noticed several oxygen masks next to the tool chest. They must be pre-positioned for first responders. He grabbed one and put it on, then pushed it up to his forehead until he figured he really needed it. He looked again for the source of the noise and found a large rectangular aluminum box that was humming. It had to be the HVAC fan. Each side was screwed to a frame with a number of sheet metal screws. He found an electric screwdriver in the toolbox and began to loosen the screws on one of the side panels. His actions were overwhelmed with a sense of urgency. He knew his interrogator would soon return to the room and find a grizzly scene. He had precious little time. He held the screwdriver up to the panel, but as he tried to insert the device into the screw head he dropped it. His fine motor skills were off because of his injuries. He picked up the screw driver and tried again. This time he managed to get the panel off in short order. Air was now being drawn into the air-conditioning system from the room as well as the outside feeder pipe. He located the furnace. It was massive. He started looking around the sides of the furnace towards the bottom and found what he believed was the natural gas line. "OK," he thought, "Before I actually do this, how am I going to trigger this thing without killing myself? I can't exactly light a match after filling the room with gas, can I?"

He looked around the room again. "Think!" he admonished himself. There were several rags on the floor by the workbench. He opened a cabinet above the bench and found a can of WD40 oil. "Bingo!" he thought. He retrieved the can, removed its cap and proceeded to soak about two-thirds of the rag with oil. An adjustable crescent wrench sat atop the workbench. He retrieved it and walked back to where the gas line was connected to the furnace. "Here goes nothing," he thought. Pulling the oxygen mask over his face and starting its flow, he began to unscrew the coupling for the gas line. Suddenly he started to hear a hiss. "That's great!" he thought, "the thing's under pressure. This might just work." Within a minute the line was free, and gas was pouring into the fan intake which fed the upper floors. He briefly thought about the fate of people upstairs. Recalling what he was told they did, he quickly purged his conscience. Diplomatic niceties were a luxury he couldn't afford right now. As far as he was concerned, this place was now a military target. "Oh crap!" he said out loud as he realized natural gas was being sucked into close proximity of a high-speed fan; an electric high-speed fan. "Can't control that," he told himself, "so let's get out of here and light this fuse."

Barber exited the utility room and closed the door. The sounds coming from the room were no different than when he arrived, but that was about to change in a big way. He knelt down and stuffed the dry end of the rag under the door. He uttered the words, "Ok Marcus, hold my beer and watch this," then used the lighter to ignite the end of the rag soaked with the oil. He knew all kinds of things could go very wrong at this point. It could detonate prematurely without enough force to summon municipal first responders. Or it could detonate prematurely with massive force and kill him. He had absolutely no way to gauge how big the bang was going to be or whether his makeshift fuse would do the trick. He also knew he couldn't control any of that, so he let it go. It would be what it would be. He just ran as fast as he could.

It took longer than he expected. That was good news, as it allowed him to put a fair amount of distance between himself and the explosion. He only encountered one embassy employee in the hallway as he was running. The guy appeared to be a maintenance worker who was confused at seeing a stranger running down the hall. He allowed Barber to pass without trying to intervene.

The effect of the explosion was epic. Enormous fireballs erupted out of several windows on the upper floors, caused by the gas pumped upstairs by the HVAC fans. More importantly, a fire at least fifteen feet tall blazed from the top of the building. It was spectacular. The explosion and resulting fires would get maximum visibility and likely draw dozens of first responders.

Barber had placed a fair amount of distance between himself and the HVAC room, but the concussive effect of the explosion still propelled him fifteen feet down the hall before he skidded to a stop. He lay there stunned but still conscious. "I'm still breathing," he thought. "That's good sign number one." He started moving his feet up and down and opening and closing his fists. They worked; "good sign number two." He then moved his arms and his legs. No bones broken; "good sign number three." Now up on all fours like a dog, he took inventory. He sustained several serious abrasions but there was no serious bleeding; "good sign number four." He had survived.

He stood up by sheer force of will and commanded his legs to walk down the hall. Nobody was approaching him from behind. He figured anyone much further back was likely dead. He could now hear sirens approaching. First responders were already on their way. "Gotta love that German efficiency," he thought.

His next objective was to get out of the building. He had no idea where he was, so he just ran like a rat running a maze. A burst of adrenaline was returning his body to full function, at least for the moment. He came to an intersection in the hallway and turned left. As he continued to run two people, also wearing gas masks, passed him headed in the opposite direction. The logical assumption was those men were trying to run out of the building. He assumed he made a wrong turn at the hallway intersection. Those guys would know the way, so he turned around and followed them. As he progressed down the hall the crowd was growing. Most had on gas masks, but a few didn't. Several of the ones who didn't were now laying on the floor choking on smoke that was rapidly pouring into the space. He then saw it. A door. They were all running for that open door. He could see daylight! Add another small success!

He exited the building in the middle of the crowd of runners. It was a scene of mass confusion. Numerous fire trucks were now on site and one of them had already connected their hoses to the water supply and was spraying the fire. Several first responders were opening gates or cutting through them and moving people to safety. Nobody seemed to notice Barber as he pushed his way through the crowd. The gas mask he was wearing made him look like everyone else trying to get out. It was almost like a rugby scrum moving across the courtyard towards safety.

His scrum managed to get to an open gate, and he was soon out of the Embassy compound. Nobody challenged him. As he passed the gate he removed his mask and tossed it aside. He continued to walk down the street towards freedom as the intelligence wing of the embassy remained engulfed in flames. His cell phone had been confiscated. There would be no calling Day for a pickup, so he just walked. He knew the minute his team saw the news reports of the Embassy explosion they would know it was him. They would come looking for him. They would find him. He was safe. And he now had a score to settle.

Chapter 17 – A Lesson in Motivation

Pyongyang International Airport, Democratic People's Republic of Korea (DPRK)

Iran Air flight 407 touched down at Pyongyang international airport at 2:48 in the afternoon local time. The aircraft sat on the tarmac for over two hours in 90-degree heat. The pilot had been ordered to shut down his engines by Pyongyang ground control, and auxiliary power was not offered during the wait. As a result, there was no air conditioning, and they couldn't even circulate outside air. To make matters worse, they were ordered to keep the doors closed until KPRK Customs arrived.

Finally, Dr. Ashkan Ghorbani was allowed to deplane alongside his travel partner Colonel Kamran Arabi of the Revolutionary Guard, both men soaked with sweat from the interminable wait. He had no idea why he was on the trip. General Humidi had ordered him to accompany the Colonel. When Ghorbani tried to inquire as to why, he was subjected to a blistering rebuke by the General. He was told he did not have the prerogative to question the General's orders. He was there to watch, to listen, and to learn, and that was all he needed to know. To watch what? To listen to what? To learn what?

Colonel Arabi appeared circumspect, almost depressed, during the flight to Pyongyang. Ghorbani asked him the purpose of the trip. He said he was there for a briefing. That was all he was told. The Colonel wouldn't say much else and sat mostly mute through the flight. What in the world could be the purpose of them travelling to the DPRK, especially just before Ghorbani's upcoming test? What kind of briefing? What could he, Ghorbani, possibly learn from the North Koreans? He didn't want to contemplate the answers to any of those questions. After their miserable reception at the airport, he was certain this was not going to be a pleasant trip.

The two men walked down a moveable stairway was pushed up to the airplane door. Ghorbani noticed was they were at least one hundred yards away from the terminal. That struck him as odd. The second thing he noticed was the sunshine. He looked around and reflected that almost any other place on earth this would be considered a beautiful day, but the scene looked depressing. Depression was a defining characteristic of this place, he thought.

As he continued down the steps, he noticed a car was parked adjacent to the aircraft. There were two guards standing by it. They weren't smiling and didn't appear to be high level officials. This had to be another bad sign, he reflected. As the two Iranians got to the bottom of the ladder one of the guards held out his wand and snapped it back and forth between them and the vehicle in a motion that looked like he was directing traffic. He was telling them to get into the car. They both obliged. The scene unfolded without the Koreans uttering a single word.

Once inside the vehicle, the driver pulled away and exited the apron where the aircraft was parked, then proceeded onto a road that appeared to go nowhere. The vehicle was cramped and hot, although not quite as bad as the parked plane. The men were pressed up against each other in too little space, and their Korean escorts, or whoever those guys were, had rotten breath. Each exhale from them smelled like the result of a lifetime without dental work and an over-sized portion of kimchi for lunch. Ghorbani could hardly breath.

Ghorbani took note of the orientation of the sun and concluded they appeared to be headed northwest. This was another bad sign. They were headed away from the city. They continued in the vehicle for over an hour. The trip was made even more miserable by the guards' continuous chain smoking. "I guess North Koreans don't worry much about lung cancer," he though. No point; there's a long list of things likely to kill them long before a build-up of tar and nicotine. He was starting to actually appreciate the oppression he was subjected to in Tehran.

In the distance he could see some kind of a compound. There were several buildings surrounded by barbed-wired fence. His heart sank even further. Were they about to be imprisoned here? But that didn't make sense. Why not just throw them in jail in Iran, or execute them, for that matter? That seemed more Hamidi's style. The General liked to experience the misery he doled out first hand.

As they approached the compound, a guard was waiting at the gate. He had a brief conversation with the driver, which Ghorgbani couldn't understand, then passed the vehicle through. As they proceeded through the gate and into the yard, they could hear dogs barking in the distance. The vehicle approached a building that appeared to be in slightly better condition than the others, then pulled up beside it and stopped. The guards got out of the vehicle and the one with the baton repeated the snapping motion, ordering the men to enter the building. There wasn't the slightest sign of friendliness from anyone they encountered. Once inside they were met by a DPRK Colonel with an interpreter. He told them through the interpreter that they would be separated temporarily. A large guard grabbed the Iranian Colonel by the arm and ushered him down a hall with far more force that was necessary. Ghorbani couldn't help but notice that Colonel Arabi did not resist and had a look of resignation on his face.

Ghorbani was led to a room and told to wait. He was terrified. He had heard rumors of what happened in the DPRK but had never given them much thought. He looked around the room. It was empty. It didn't even have a chair. He waited until he lost track of the time. What the hell was happening in this place? Finally, a guard entered the room and announced that he would be re-united with his travel mate. He didn't know whether to be relieved or terrified. He quickly concluded relief was foolish.

A guard took him by the arm, much more gently than the treatment Arabi had received, and led him down a hall. The smell was terrible. As they approached the end they came to another door. The guard opened the door and led him in. His knees immediately became weak. He doubled over and vomited on the floor. The guards laughed, but they did not strike him. Standing in front of him was Colonel Arabi. His face was a bloody pulp, and his arm was obviously broken.

"Come with us," the interpreter said.

They walked out the door into some kind of yard. He heard dogs barking. His heart was now beating out of his chest, and he was sweating profusely. He had never experienced fear like this before. He watched as a guard opened a tall gate and led Colonel Arabi into some kind of animal pen. The guard then walked out, turned and locked it. Ghorbani now noticed the dogs. They were in a pen next to the one that held Arabi. They looked emaciated. They were obviously hungry. Canine teeth were bared with saliva dripping from the sides of their snouts. One of the guards then pressed a button and an electric motor opened a small gate separating the two pens. The dogs rushed through the opening, leapt for Arabi and began tearing him to shreds. His screams were like nothing Ghorbani had ever heard. He lost control of his bladder and the guards started laughing at him again. He tried to turn away, but two guards forced him to face the carnage. He tried to resist until a third guard forced him to watch with a knife to his throat. The interpreter had made the instructions clear.

After what seemed like an eternity, Arabi was finally dead. The interpreter told him he was to follow the guard back into the building and not to worry, that this fate was not to be his. Once inside he was led into the same conference room he had been in earlier and handed an envelope. "You are to read this," the interpreter said. The envelope simply had the word, "Lesson" on it. He opened the envelope and unfolded a single page. It read:

From: Commanding General, Garshasp Hamidi, Islamic Revolutionary Guard Corp

To: Dr. Asjkan Ghorbani, Project Lead

Subject: Today's Lesson

This is the reward for failure. I thought it useful for you to witness it first-hand. You are about to conduct a very important test. Do not fail. Failure will not bring this outcome initially to you, for we realize your continued services are essential to achieving the glorious goals of our Islamic Revolution. But to ensure you remain sufficiently motivated, we will visit this outcome first on your wife then each of your children and other members of your family each time you fail, until you do succeed.

Ghorbani sobbed uncontrollably. This man, Hamidi, was a monster. What did this Colonel do to deserve such a fate? He couldn't imagine. He had no idea that Arabi had been the man tasked with assassinating Farhang, and that he failed.

Chapter 18 – Equivocation

Office of the Prime Minister, 10 Downing Street, London England

Jeremy Boren's rise from a backbencher MP to England's Prime Minister was improbable. The Constituency of Altershot lies at the extreme northeast corner of the County of Hampshire and is about 50 kilometers south east of London, and in May of 2010 it sent Jeremy Boren to Parliament as a newly elected MP. Boren had been a barrister prior to his election. He built a law practice that provided a comfortable living, but he found the work unfulfilling. A restless spirit led him to leave his practice and try his hand at politics. He loved the history of his new profession and its rich symbolism. For months he felt chills every time he walked into the Parliament Building and thought of the people who proceeded him. What an honor, he believed, to walk the same halls as Churchill, Balfour, Disraeli, and England's Kings and Queens. But the daily grind of politics wore him down. He began to feel like a ship adrift in a storm and his spirit again became restless. The storm was the countless fools he was forced to deal with on a daily basis, the massive egos, countless arguments with other MPs incapable of seeing the people's needs and the greater good. The restlessness was driven by the inability to accomplish anything meaningful and, worse yet, realizing it was because no one cared. His frustrations soared. So, he began to withdraw and assume the role of a back-bencher in a safe constituency while he thought about where the next tack of his sails should take him. Then one day his issue arrived.

Brexit. He understood it like no other member of Parliament. It was a colossally stupid idea but born of understandable frustrations. The Nation's political and business leadership didn't "get it." They regarded Brexit as a temper tantrum by the lesser-educated and lesser informed, and nobody thought it would pass. But it did pass, and worse, it gave birth to a contagion that caused the unravelling of the United Kingdom into its separate constituents. The contagion then metastasized and jumped the English

Channel, tearing apart a large swath of the remaining European Union and, in an even more sinister development, giving birth to a union of German and France as the new European Federation. Once the new European Federation was born, "All the King's Horses and All the King's men couldn't put" the status quo ante back together again.

In the wake of ensuing chaos, Boren became the voice of reason, a voice of wisdom and even a voice of hope. He spoke to the people and to his colleagues in Parliament in terms they understood. People were weary of Continental overreach and were susceptible to the rise of populism and nationalism as a reaction to it. But the vast majority weren't racist, they didn't fear 'the other', as immigrants were called, and they didn't hate government. They were offended by and tired of those labels. They just didn't want to be ignored. And they just wanted their government to work. Boren was a prophet calling from the wilderness, and on so many points he proved to be correct. This was no truer than his impassioned warnings that Britain's ruling class had no plan and no ideas on how to manage their divorce from the EU, and there would be dire and unintended consequences as a result. His soaring oratory skills, honed as a barrister, served him well as he became England's 21st Century's "Pied Piper". Soon he was center stage as head of the Conservative Party, then elected PM.

So here he sat, as PM, and expecting a phone call from the President of the United States. Rain was pelting the windows in PM Boren's office at Number 10. It was another dreary day in London, and the weather matched his mood. It had been a difficult week. The ugliness of divisive politics was in full bloom as Boren worked hard to forge a consensus for heightened trade sanctions against the European Federation. He was a skeptic at first, and not anxious to exposure English business interests to further harm in the wake of their nation's deepening recession. But the American President had made it a hard sell, citing the increased militaristic rhetoric coming from Berlin and the

EF's move towards a friendlier relationship with Iran in spite of increased warnings from the international community.

The American President cited the "special relationship" between the United States and England and the need to present a united front. Boren understood the importance of that "special relationship" England had with the United States and did his best to honor it. The relationship was especially important as England became increasingly isolated with the breakup of the United Kingdom and an ascendant Continental Europe charting its own path through the EF. But he detested Sarah Einhorn. He found her arrogant, heavy handed and unreliable. He regarded her view of the "Special Relationship" was entirely one-sided. The United States could not act unilaterally, she argued. Unilateral action would not only greatly diminish the impact of additional sanctions, it would invite constant criticism and perhaps even political censure against the U.S. in the United Nations. In the end Boren had relented and done the difficult work of forging a consensus among an even more skeptical Parliament. Then two days ago he had been briefed on new intelligence about an exotic, new EF weapons system that was in the testing phase. It was something called a rail gun, and that changed everything. His perspective on additional sanctions changed from skepticism to full-throated support.

Nigel Worthington, the English Foreign Secretary, a position comparable to the American Secretary of State, sat across from Boren's desk in a wing-backed Churchill chair. Lord David Herbert, Chief of the Secret Intelligence Service, more commonly known as MI6, sat in a similar chair immediately to Worthington's left.

"Well, she's now thirty minutes late," Worthington commented, looking at his watch, a gold Rolex President.

"I'm sure she regards us as her poodles," the MI6 man commented.

"Well chaps, Madam Sarah has never been one big on punctuality, has she? I don't know what this phone call is about, but I am anxious to share with her your intelligence, David. It's an absolute game changer. I intend to ask their C.I.A. to take a look at it and independently verify, and if validated suggest we jointly announce it at the U.N. So, this call is not a total waste of time. Let's indulge her a bit."

"What troubles me is the circumstances of this call are more than a bit odd," Worthington said. "We have absolutely no idea what she is up to, and I don't like it!" The phone call from President Einhorn had been arranged by her Chief of Staff through back channels, something he regarded as very odd. Her chief of staff stressed the importance of discretion, and that the call and its subject matter be kept out of official diplomatic channels and held strictly between the participants. The British Foreign Secretary was even asked not to speak to the U.S. Secretary of State or his ambassador about it.

Boren found the apparent subterfuge annoying. "Why back channels? Why such secrecy?" he asked himself. Such tactics and the drama that enviably accompanied them were tedious, he thought. "Just pick up the bloody phone and call me Sarah. No need for the cloak and dagger." Her recent behavior was becoming more and more unpredictable. Whatever this call was about, it couldn't be good. It was not yet five o'clock in the afternoon, yet Boren had a half-consumed glass of Scotch on his desk.

The intercom on the PM's desk finally buzzed.

"Excuse me sir," his secretary said.

"Yes?" the PM replied.

"It's your call, sir. The President of the United States is on the line."

"Thank you. We are ready."

"Jeremy?" the voice on the other end queried.

"Good morning, Sarah. Secretary Worthington and Director Herbert with me."

There was a long pause. "David my stated desire was to have this conversation between just you and me."

"Would you like me to ask them to leave?" he responded, as he smiled and shook his head "no" at the two men sitting across from him, signaling he had no intention of actually asking them to leave.

"No, that won't be necessary," the President replied, in a tone that reflected her her irritation.

"Sarah, I would like to speak first and offer some comments I believe you will welcome. May I do so?"

There was a long pause again. She then responded, "If you must."

Boren hit the mute button on his intercom and commented "Well she seems to be in another jolly-good mood, doesn't she?" while rolling his eyes. He took his finger off the mute button and continued, "I am pleased to report that after a great deal of arm-twisting I have convinced the MPs to support additional restrictions on exports of military technology by British industry to the EF. I will also say that I did not make a lot of friends in the process, and the consensus for additional sanctions is fragile. It is important for us to act quickly before the consensus falters. In addition, I believe we should to call the EF Chancellor on a joint line about an hour before our announcement. That will give him an appropriate heads-up as a diplomatic courtesy, but not sufficient time to orchestrate any kind of pre-emptive rebuttal before we announce. I must also inform you that we are in possession of new intelligence was crucial to achieving consensus. I would like to share it with you after you tell us what's on your mind, and that is why I invited Lord Herbert to join us. So please, Sarah, the floor is yours."

The three men heard the President clear her throat, and in a voice that actually betrayed a slight nervousness said, "Jeremy, I have come to believe our actions may be a bit premature, and I am actually having serious second thoughts about moving so quickly. My preference would be to take a little more time to study the impact on U.S. companies before we act."

Boren, Worthington and Herbert sat silent with looks of complete astonishment. It was the last thing they expected. Boren pushed the mute button again, looked at Herbert and asked, "What the bloody hell is going on here?"

"Jeremy?" the President queried, in response to the long pause.

"Yes, Sarah, we are still here. Sorry we were trying to process what you just said. Did I hear you correctly, that you want to hold off on additional sanctions now?"

"Yes," she said, this time tersely.

"Madam President," he replied taking a more formal tone, "We have some intelligence that is highly relevant to this discussion. May I share it with you?"

"Of course," she replied.

"Lord Herbert, please proceed," the PM said.

Lord Herbert began to speak. "Madam President, we believe we have definitive proof that the EF Air Force has operationally tested an airborne railgun. Such a sophisticated weapon is massively destabilizing. We cannot allow Europe to be caught up in a new arms race."

"A rail gun?" the President asked.

"Yes, Ma'am," Lord Herbert replied.

"Aren't you being overly dramatic?" she asked. "Isn't that just a fancy type of rifle?"

"No, Madam, it is not." Herbert replied in a tone of irritation and disbelief at the comment. PM Boren gave him a stern look. It was a clear signal to tone down his reactions to avoid making her angry. "No, Ma'am. I won't bore you with the physics now, but it's a system that can deliver incrementally greater destructive energy to a target than conventional weapons. If successfully deployed, it would be a massive game-changer. Our militaries have been working on such a system for years and it's not an exaggeration to say we are literally years behind the EF on this."

"Again, Jeremy," she said, responding to the PM and not Lord Herbert in a thinly-veiled insult to the latter, "Aren't you being a bit overly dramatic?"

"No Sarah, we are not," Prime Minister Boren responded in a terse tone. "And there is another complication. The bloody Russians. Both CIA and MI6 have been following their work on a similar weapons system. Like us, they have been pursuing a similar technology. We do not know where they are on it, and consequently do not have a clear sense of what the Russian response will be. There are two possibilities. One, is they regard it as a threat and act as a counterforce. That's the best possible outcome, believe it or not. Alternatively, and far more ominous, they are working with the EF on joint development. That has diplomatic implications I don't even want to contemplate. I fear reality may lay with the second hypothesis. It is crucially important that we send a strong message and that we do so with all deliberate haste. With respect, the implications of this are way beyond any near-term economic impact increased sanctions may have on either of us. That cannot be the focus right now."

"You're overreacting, Jeremy. I'm simply not convinced yet."

"No, we most certainly are not!" the Prime Minister exclaimed. "And further, Ma'am, we are concerned about the EF's closer ties to Iran. They've even bloody floated the idea of joint military exercises in the Persian Gulf. Germany may be preparing to share the new weapons tech with the Islamic Republic. We cannot allow this to happen, and increased sanctions on the EF is the only way to pursue that goal short of actual military action. Nobody has the stomach for that right now! And further, I just told you it was a very difficult to get a consensus on this. If we back away, I will lose all credibility and the likelihood of achieving that consensus again effectively goes to zero!" He was almost shouting. "Sarah, this is not the time to go wobbly!"

"Oh please, Jeremy, spare me the Margaret Thatcher quotes," the President said, referring to the time Thatcher used the same words to stiffen the backbone of George H.W. Bush just before the first Gulf War in 1991.

"Sarah, I am at a complete loss to understand your position here. Do you have any idea how much personal political capital I have invested to achieve consensus for these sanctions? As I told you, the consensus here is very fragile. Your participation is key to retaining it. If you equivocate I will look like a fool and you will be labeled a 'flip-flopper.' I can assure you there is almost no scenario at present where I can convince our Government to go it alone. Once the consensus folds, it folds, and I fear it will take a disaster of some type to resurrect it."

"I'm sorry Mr. Prime Minister but you have my decision, at least for now. The United States will not be imposing any additional sanctions at this time. You are free, of course, to do as you wish. I'd like you to send Margaret at C.I.A. what you have on these rail gun tests. And send her the raw intelligence. I want our people to independently analyze it. Thank you for your time, Jeremy. Now I must go," and with that, she abruptly hung up.

The three men looked at each other in utter astonishment. Lord Herbert was the first to speak, "Well, I'd say she buggered that up to a fare-thee-well, didn't she?"

"Yes, she did," Boren responded. "Bloody Americans. I'd love to go back in history and kick Cornwalllis' fat ass."

Oval Office, White House, Washington D.C.

President Einhorn sat at the Resolute Desk and rubbed both her temples. She had a headache. It was bad, but not nearly as bad as the ones Emma Clark caused, so she assumed it was from natural causes and not another gift from the West Coast.

This decision was going to be a hard sell. The responses to her sanctions delay from the Secretaries of State and Defense were going to dwarf that of the English PM.

Chapter 19 – A Necessary Detour

Orion Bellicus Headquarters, Rye, New York

The jet landed at 4 A.M. Eastern Daylight Time at Westchester County Airport with Barber on board. Joe Barber loved flying his King Air 90 twin-engine turbine powered airplane up and down the East Coast whenever circumstances allowed it, but it didn't have the range or the speed for intercontinental flight. The ever-widening remit of his security company, Orion Bellicus, and its extensive international business required the purchase of a Gulfstream G550 jet with transcontinental range to support his extensive long-distance travel. He learned to fly the Gulfstream and was type-rated in it, but growing demands on his time often made flying it impractical. Most of his time in the air was now spent working. On this trip, however, he was in no condition to fly the plane or to work. He was recovering from his recent abduction by the Iranians and the dramatic escape from their Embassy. His ribs were killing him from the beating he took when he was captured at the safe house and his 15-foot flight down the hallway of the Embassy after the explosion. The ribs were likely cracked, but at least not seriously broken. His team had offered him Vicodin on the flight home, but he wanted a clear head. Being able to think clearly was important right now, so large doses of ibuprofen had to suffice. It hurt to breathe, but he just sucked it up. Fortunately, his physical wounds were superficial. He would recover, but it would be a while before he was back at the top of his game.

The flight back home was an inconvenient but necessary detour. Inconvenient because the last 72 hours had been productive in getting some of the answers to questions about the who and why of Schiller's death, and the flight back to the States would break that momentum. There were still many questions that needed answers. The flight was necessary because one of his abductors had threatened his family if he didn't cooperate. He not only didn't cooperate, he escaped. Threats were a pretty common thing in his business, but threats against family members were rare. And they knew his identity, his address, and the names of his wife and children. Most troubling of all was his captor's assertion that they had an asset already deployed close to his home ready to murder his wife on a "go" order. That was not the kind of threat Barber could ignore. He knew the threat could have been an idle one, but his instincts told him it was real. In matters of family, he would never take the risk, even though he knew the Iranian who made the threat likely died in the embassy explosion. There were others who could give the kill order, and there was no persuading him not to fly back to the States and personally supervise the take-down of that assassin himself. So, he left Marcus Day in charge in Berlin and got on that airplane.

They arrived at Orion Bellicus headquarters about 5:15 A.M. Barber walked into the conference room adjacent to his office and met his team. Several members of his operations team were waiting for him. They were shocked at his appearance. Their boss had clearly taken a beating.

"Give me a sitrep," Barber commanded in a weary sounding voice.

His new Director of Security Operations, Alexa Hemmingway, call sign "Alpha 3", stood next to him. She was five feet eight inches and weighed in at one hundred thirty pounds of solid muscle. A retired Army Lieutenant Colonel and African-American, she left the military when it became apparent that she would never receive a coveted combat command to spite graduating at the top of her Ranger class. Her job at Orion made her effectively the Commanding Officer of the Company's "tac", or tactical teams. The teams were listed in the Company register as security officers. In reality they were a special operations group recruited from the ranks of Navy SEALs, Army Rangers, and Marine Force Recon. Some of them had previous experience as C.I.A. paramilitary officers.

She began to speak, "Family remains in the sub-basement panic suite," referring to the 2,000 square foot space beneath the basement that provided a secure location in case of a threat. Many homes in Barber's neighborhood had "safe rooms" or "panic rooms" as many preferred to call them, but his was the only one with essentially an entire apartment with food supplies that could last for weeks in an emergency. She continued, "Everything is quiet. Tac team Delta is deployed throughout the inside of the home and Team Echo is patrolling the grounds."

"What's the situation on the ground right now, Alex?" Barber asked as someone handed him a very strong cup of coffee.

"All is quiet. We had our people show up dressed as gardeners to keep the neighbors from getting suspicious. They deployed infrared cameras and motion sensors all over the property and there's been nothing but a bunch of white-tail deer and a few smaller animals. We've also launched three of the ultra-quiet drones and have them systematically roaming the property at five hundred feet. Also, nothing. We've kept the family in the sub-basement suite since your phone call. Family is a little shaken, but otherwise doing well. Both teams report no activity."

"Thanks. I talked to Diana while I was in the air and again when we landed. She's a bit angry, but otherwise seems to be holding up well."

"Yes sir, we noticed that," Hemmingway said with the hint of a smile.

"I'll bet you did," Barber responded. "Any sense on the nature of the threat? A sniper?"

"That's likely," she responded. "Problem is If we are dealing with a sniper that person could be deployed beyond our perimeter, and we don't have enough people to secure the entire neighborhood. Too many people in the area would likely draw the attention of neighbors and possibly the police. We want to keep this off the books."

"My guess is a sniper was their 'Plan A', but we have to assume that they know we are on to them. There's no way they would not have noticed our deployment at my house. That really complicates their attack plan. So, our target may be a sniper, but I don't think a sniper shot is the biggest risk right now. You've taken that off the table with the security measures.

Whoever is out there is aware there is no way they could take a bead from the grounds without being noticed. Also, this is a residential neighborhood and not some isolated estate. There's no way for them to get a good line of sight from anyplace other than the grounds. It's not exactly like they can climb up a tree in a neighbor's front yard and take aim," Barber said.

"Agreed," Hemmingway responded. "He is going to have to improvise."

"Correct," Barber replied. "If the contract is still active, and we have to assume it is, my guess is our target is lying in wait someplace. He is going to need some kind of intel to let him know when Diana or a family member is vulnerable. Have you combed the area for surveillance devices that are not ours?" Barber asked.

"No, we haven't, at least not systematically. We've been trying to keep a low profile and not appear to be a bunch of guys snooping around, but I agree. We need to do it."

"Put somebody on it, now."

"Done," Hemmingway responded. "We need think through what a plan B might look like."

"Right," Barber replied, "a bomb of some sort?"

""Team Delta thoroughly searched the house and it's clean. If they haven't positioned a bomb already I think that's a low probability. Also, it's too high profile, too messy."

"I agree," Barber replied.

"Do you think there is any way the asset knows there's a panic suite below the basement?"

"No. He would have been given a file on me." Barber answered. "Given my background he would assume I have a panic room in the house, but I can't believe he would suspect there is a 2,000 square foot secure suite under the basement, and no way would he assume it's blast proof. My guess is he would suspect a panic room next to the master bedroom."

"Right," Hemmingway replied.

"Well, it won't be with a sniper rifle for the reasons we have already discussed," commented one of the operators in the conference room, "but he could us an automatic weapon of some sort in a drive by."

"Like a Mac10 or fully auto AR 15?," Hemmingway asked.

"Yeah," the operator replied.

"I don't think so," Barber said. "That would be a 'spray and pray' attack. Too low a probability of success unless she walks outside the door and presents herself as an easy target. He will know we are armed, and unless he gets all of us on the first pass he will be in serious trouble when we respond. Maybe he goes for the big gun, like an AR10. It would give him the firepower to penetrate the walls of the house and the bullet-proof glass and aim wouldn't be as vital. Delivering that much extra energy to his target will up the likelihood of it working. All he would need is confirmation that his target left the panic room."

"Right," Hemmingway agreed, "but I'm not sure it would up the likelihood enough. And it's a much heavier weapon. It would be very difficult to accurately shoot it with one hand."

"Exactly," Joe said.

"What about an RPG?" asked another one of the operators.

"Not likely," Barber replied. "Much more difficult to conceal than an AR15, and it provides only one shot."

"Way too high profile too, boss" the first operator responded. "He'd never get into position to fire before we would see him. And he'd never get away, either, because he would hit the house but none of us deployed around it. Also, absolutely no way a sniper is going to carry a reserve weapon like that to carry out a hit in this neck of the woods. I think our speculation is taking us a bit over our skis. This isn't Afghanistan. I think we're going to have to flush out this guy. That's the only thing that will work. We can't allow a stand-off to last indefinitely, and he has more time than we do. Like you said, this is a residential neighborhood and we can't have Tac Teams walking around geared-up with weapons. My guess is we'll have less than 30 minutes of time on the property once we show up before neighbors start to get suspicious and call the police. Anything longer than that draws way too much attention."

"You're right, and thanks for the reality check," Barber replied.

Hemmingway forced back a smile. "This kid showed guts talking to the boss that way," she thought.

Barber replied. "To flush him out we are going to need bait. One of two possibilities. First, we stage some kind of movement in the house to make it look like the family is being moved out of a second-story panic room. Problem is now that he knows we are here it's way too difficult to do that without it looking like an obvious set-up. This guy' no amateur and he'll figure that out."

"I agree," Hemmingway responded.

"That leaves option two," Barber replied. "The bait is me. I show up and walk right through the front door."

"That will certainly get their attention." Hemmingway said.

"I think that's the best shot we've got for a quick resolution to this," the second operator spoke up again. "Whoever out there will see you pull up in the Lexus and assume you are there to move the family."

"How do we get him to think I'm going to move the family?" Barber asked. "Maybe he thinks I am just checking on them, or plan to stay there myself for a while."

"We pull up in the Expedition 15 minutes later," the operator spoke again. Two of us get out, stand by the vehicle and act like bodyguards. We look around like we're checking for threats, which will be easy because, duh, we are. We pull the coiled cable to our earpieces out of our shirt collars a bit to make sure they can be seen, and we act like we are talking into the wrist mics. That should convince him we are about to move the family."

"I think that works, boss," Hemmingway responded. "We have Jennifer assigned to Delta right now," she said, referring to Jennifer Alontonio, one of Orion Bellicus' female operators, "We send her out in a raincoat, a large hat and sunglasses. He'll think she is Diana."

"Great plan," Barber responded, "except for the part where we all get sprayed with AR15 rounds, or whatever weapon he's got, the minute she shows herself."

"Hold on, boss," the first operator said. "It won't come to that. Whoever is out there is going to have to position himself very quickly after we show up in the Expedition. If he doesn't, he knows he will likely lose the opportunity. I think he starts to move as soon as the two of us get out of the Expedition, before Jenn ever walks out."

"We have Echo deployed in vehicles patrolling the perimeter." Hemmingway said. "We don't really need Delta in the house anymore, except for Jennifer. Let's pull them out and put them in vehicles also. The minute the asset starts to prep for the attack we should see him. We simply hold Jenn in reserve as a backup plan in case he doesn't get flushed by these lads."

"OK, it's not perfect, Alex, but I think it's probably the best we've got," Barber replied. "How do we take the asset down? I don't want to use lethal force unless absolutely necessary."

"Agreed, but unless this guy walks right into us we may not have a choice," Hemmingway responded. "I hope he shows early enough to avoid it, but hope is not a strategy, boss."

"You're right," Barber replied. "But let's try and avoid lethal force if we can."

"I agree," Hemmingway said. Just then her phone rang. She pulled it out of her pocket and answered. "What's up?" She put the caller on speaker phone.

"This is Echo 1. We have found seven small video cameras buried in the grass in a circle around the house, all facing inwards. There are two additional cameras in the front lawn facing outwards. Shall I disable?"

"Disable the cameras facing the house," Barber replied, "but leave the ones facing outward from the front lawn in place. We want them there so he can see us arrive. He'll just think we didn't spot them."

"Roger that," the man said.

"Anything in the woods?" Barber asked.

"We've not found anything yet, but I'll have the team take another sweep."

"Good," Hemmingway replied. "What about local vehicle traffic?"

"We've had at least a half dozen vehicles drive by the house in the last 45 minutes. None of them appeared suspicious but I would guess our target has to be in one of them. They were photographed as they passed and input to the surveillance software. If there is a repeat drive-by we will be alerted. Also, there was a female jogger who ran by the house about 30 minutes ago. Based on the way she was dressed I doubt she's a threat. No place to hide a weapon."

"You don't know squat about women's running gear," Hemmingway retorted with a faux-mocking tone in her voice. "You'd be surprised at what we can hide in those shorts. Maybe you should do a little more research."

"Roger that," the operator said, with his face in the process of turning crimson.

"OK, enough talk," Barber said. "Let's roll. I'll grab the LC 500 from the garage."

"Saddle up people," replied Hemmingway. She then picked up her phone and pressed the speed dial for Delta 1, the commander of the Tac Team deployed around the perimeter of Barber's house. "We are inbound in the Expedition with Alpha 1 in the Lexus. I'll brief you on the plan enroute. Pull all vehicles out of the immediate area. I don't want this guy spooked before he's flushed."

"Delta 1, roger that," responded the leader of Tac Team Delta.

"Echo 1, roger that.

Chapter 20 – Takedown

Rye, New York, In a Garage 75 Meters Away from the Barber Residence

It's amazing what people post on Facebook and how little thought they give to unintended consequences. The sniper who owned the hit on the Barber family casually drove though Barber's neighborhood and took pictures of the mailboxes along the street with an iPhone. Back in the hotel, the sniper opened a laptop and entered each address into reverse lookup function on the Whitepages web site. Soon there was a list of names matching the addresses. The Whitepages site then was closed and Facebook was opened. Each name was entered into the search line at the top right-hand side of the website to determine if the resident had an account. The hit rate was over 80%. The asset then "creeped the resident's Facebook page", as young people would say, looking for personal information. The process yielded a treasure-trove of intel. The sniper was looking for one thing in particular – who was on vacation. There were three families. One family posted pictures of an out of town wedding they were attending. That family would likely be home within 24-48 hours the sniper concluded. One family was posted pictures from the Magic Kingdom in Florida that were date-stamped two days ago. It was a possibility, but not knowing exactly when they might return made that option risky. But one was perfect. A wealthy, retired couple left two weeks ago for a three-month trip to Europe. They posted pictures of their travels several times a week, and a post yesterday showed them in Oslo, Norway. Their home was only 75 meters down the street from Barber's front door with a direct line of sight. The garage door of the house even had a couple of small windows. It was perfect.

The sniper next clicked on the family's list of Facebook "likes". One of them was the Brinks Home Security Corporation. "Thank you," the sniper thought, as that little bit of information made the circumvention of the home's security system far easier. With the name of the system in hand, the sniper then searched Google for on-line user manuals. Several detailed manuals were found. After reading them, it was easy to detect weaknesses in the system and figure out how to circumvent it, keeping the planned intrusion confidential. Each time the vacationers checked the security app on their phones, all would appear quiet and normal.

The sniper set up shop in the garage, and even hacked into their home wifi system. In less than 4 hours the entire surveillance network was in place, and the Barber's house was being watched from the obscurity of the nearby garage. Now it was just necessary to wait for the right opportunity. "Plan A" was back in play.

The sniper noticed the arrival of the Tac Teams from Orion Bellicus immediately. Their arrival was strange, the sniper thought. The most likely reason would be that the target, Barber's wife, was now aware of the threat and had called for help, but the briefing package for the hit specifically mentioned she would be unaware of the contract. It was supposed to be, literally, like shooting fish in a barrel. There was another odd thing. The instructions specified no action was to be taken until a "kill" order was conveyed via the burner phone that was included in the briefing envelop. So, if the target knew of the threat, why hadn't that kill order been given? The longer the sniper waited, the less likelihood of a successful hit. Why wait? None of it made sense. Had the client been compromised? The sniper had no way of knowing. All the communication with the client was one way, and the burner phone had yet to ring. Fortunately, the contract had a provision that it was to be cancelled if the kill order wasn't delivered within 5 days, with payment still made in full. Maybe it was only necessary to wait it out.

Lexus LC500 with Barber on Board, inbound to his residence

"We're eleven minutes out now," Barber announced to the speaker phone in the vehicle.

"Roger that," Echo 1 replied from inside the residence.

"Echo 1, I need you to ask Diana a question right away."

"Yes, boss," the man replied.

"Ask her if she is aware of any of our neighbor's being on vacation right now."

"Roger that."

"What are you thinking, Joe?" Hemmingway asked.

"Maybe our target is smart enough to figure out who's not home," he replied.

"And is using an empty house as a base. Good thought boss."

"Yah, or maybe not the house, but the garage," Barber replied.

"Alpha 1 this is Echo 1."

"Go ahead Echo 1," Barber replied.

"Diana says the only vacationers she is aware of are the Gardners. They live across the street and two houses down."

"Hmm," Barber thought. "If I had the contract I would consider that a pretty good place to set up shop." He then spoke into his mic, "OK, I'm calling an audible, team. Here's what we are going to do. Do not proceed to my home yet. Meet me one street over and park the Expedition next to my Lexus. Do not leave the vehicle. Stay put as backup unless I call for help.   Before we try using me as bait I am going to take a look at that house, starting with the garage. I think there is a chance our sniper is using it as an overwatch. Give the address to Lauren and have her hack into the security system and disable it. I don't want to set off an alarm or get my picture taken by triggering a motion detector." He was referring to Dr. Lauren Cartwright, the Orion Bellicus Director of Forensics.   She held Ph.D.s in applied physics from M.I.T. and forensic science from Cal Tech, in addition to being a computer hacker extraordinaire.

"Roger that," Hemmingway responded.

Back Yard of Home Serving as Sniper's Surveillance Post

The sniper was a careful planner, but nevertheless missed an important step. Numerous surveillance cameras had been placed around the Gardner's home to alert the sniper if anyone approached from the front, which was regarded as most likely, but there was nothing placed at the back of the house. As a consequence, there was no warning as the shadowy figure approached the house from the rear.

As Barber surveyed the property, he started to recall vague details of the home's layout. He attended a party hosted by the homeowners the previous Fall which included a brief tour of the garage to see his neighbor's prized Lamborghini. He remembered that the only entrance, other than the garage door itself, was a door on the side, towards the front. There was no way to use that door without being seen by someone inside the garage. There was, however, an inside entrance to the garage from the home's mudroom. He also remembered that there were several floor-to-ceiling cabinets just inside the garage, to the right of that door, that would make it difficult to see it being opened unless you were standing close by.

Barber approached the rear door wall to the family room, and spoke into his mike, "Any word from Lauren about the security system?" he asked.

"Hang on, Joe," Hemmingway said, "Just getting a call from her now. Wow. Ok, Lauren says the system has already been disabled. Happened two days ago, and it's a sophisticated hack. Apparently there are several indoor cameras to monitor the residence, and a false video stream is being broadcast to suggest to the owners that all is well."

"OK, team, as far as I am concerned that is proof-positive. Our target is in that garage. I'm going to into the house and will enter the garage via the mudroom."

"Do you want company, boss?" Hemmingway asked.

"No, stay in the Expedition unless I get into trouble. The fewer people walking around the outside of this place, the better. I don't want a firefight and I want to take this assassin alive. I'll call if I need help, or obviously come running if you hear gunfire."

"Roger that."

Barber pulled a tight-fitting pair of latex gloves from his pocket and stretched them over his hands. He then pulled out a small device and picked the lock to the door wall faster than the owner could have unlocked it with a key. As he walked inside, all was quiet. "Good," he thought. "The alarm system really is off, or at least the audible siren wasn't triggered."

"I'm in," Barber announced over his communications network, or "ComNet."

He quietly made his way through the family room and past the kitchen. To the left of refrigerator was a hallway that he remembered led to the mudroom. As he crept down the hallway he saw the door to the garage. Arriving at the door, he tried to turn the handle and found it was locked. He expected that. Picking that lock had to be done with a great deal of care to avoid any noise that might alert anyone inside. There were two locks to open, the door knob and the deadbolt. I took him almost 90 seconds, but both locks were finally, and silently, breached. With his gloved hand he very slowly turned the door knob to verify it was unlocked, as he held a silenced Glock 19 in the other.

He then remembered the problem with opening doors is they tend to creak if not properly lubricated. He stopped turning the doorknob. Fortunately, the door hinges were on the house side, and not the garage side, of the door. The gloved hand slid into his pocket and retrieved a small bottle of WD40 oil. He lubricated all three hinges and then waited several seconds to allow the oil to soak in. He gently closed his grip around the doorknob again, silently turned it and started to pull the door open. The door silently gave way and he could feel the heat from the garage start to pour into the air-conditioned house. He continued to slowly pull to widen the gap just enough to squeeze through, then slowly closed the door behind him. He didn't want too much air conditioning to pour into the garage, fearful that the cold air could alert whoever was inside. He kept his body pressed tightly against the side of one of the cabinets and peeked around the corner.

When he saw the silhouette, Barber was a surprised. Standing about twelve feet away from him and staring out a garage door window with a pair of binoculars was the unmistakable figure of a woman. Next to her was an open laptop computer on an adjacent table. Barber guessed she was about five foot-six, give or take an inch, and solidly built. She had blond hair that draped over her shoulders and was banded in a pony-tail. "Clever," he thought, and effective. A five-and-a-half foot blond likely would not be viewed as a threat, even by his highly-trained team. Good choice of a sniper, although seeing a woman in that role brought back some dark memories from about three years ago.

He quietly stepped away from the cabinets and pointed the pistol at her, then spoke. "I have a suppressed 9 mil pointed at your head," he announced as a red laser dot painted the back of her skull. "Slowly turn around."

As the woman turned her face came into view. He was stunned. "It's you," he said, astonished. The red dot was now directly in the middle of her forehead.

She smiled in response to his comment. "So, we meet again."

She was dressed in joggers clothing -- short shorts and a tank top. Barber looked at her right hand. It looked slightly deformed, and her index finger was missing.

"How is this possible?" he asked. "With that injury? You should be done with this profession."

"The small 22-caliber round you fired into my hand went in between my second and third metacarpal. It shaved the third a bit but didn't damage the second at all. There was very little muscle damage and the wound healed nicely. Turns out with enough practice you can still pull a trigger with your middle finger. Voila! You should have used your nine mil."

Barber stood in front of her in stunned silence trying to process what she had just said. After she had tried to kill him three years ago, he had tracked her down to her home in Fredericksburg, Virginia. Instead of killing her, he decided to "retire" her from her profession by destroying her trigger-pulling hand. Or so he thought. It was supposed to be an act of mercy. The fact that she was now the asset with the contract to kill his wife was inconceivable. "I guess no good deed goes unpunished", he thought.

"How did you get the contract on my family?" he asked.

"Oh, that was pure luck. I've done some work in Europe for the European Federation and was somehow referred by them. You know the way this business works. Same as last time we met. I never know who my actual client is, although I occasionally have suspicions. I honestly didn't know the targets were your family until I opened the briefing file. I can assure you it then became a labor of love, given our history."

Barber walked several feet closer to her while keeping the red laser dot trained on her forehead. "Well maybe instead of your hand this time I should just put a round into your forehead."

"Oh, I don't think you're going to do that. It's against your 'code', isn't it?"

"Screw the code," Barber said with a cold fury in his voice.

Unfortunately, his ordeal of the last several days had left him weakened and just a tad careless. He took another step towards the woman. It was all she needed. He had closed the distance just enough.

She turned her head and looked at her laptop with a puzzled expression. It was a ruse to draw Barber off-guard. It worked, and he looked at the computer as well. In a lightning fast move she leapt forward and with a sweeping kick that knocked the Glock out of his hand. Following through with the momentum, she landed a knife-like strike to his throat with her left hand.

He was spared a broken windpipe only because the force of the first kick pushed him backwards slightly, thereby lessening the force of the second blow. But it still caused a spasm that tightened his throat making it difficult to breath. A third kick landed center mass, driving the air out of his lungs. The pain in his already damaged ribs was incredible. He staggered backwards, almost passing out. He was in serious trouble and he knew it.

He fell backwards into a workbench but managed to remain on his feet. She saw him struggle to fill his lungs with air, but something was wrong. Her blow to his throat should have dropped him, but it didn't. She withdrew an automatic knife from the inside of her jogging shorts and deployed the blade. He managed to look up and saw her coming at him. As she closed the gap, he noticed her eyes. She appeared dispassionate, in control, and clearly not overtaken by a rage. Her eyes were neutral, as if she was simply about to take out the trash. She was a professional, and this was business.

She was intent on the kill, something that simply had to be done. Her calling the contract a "labor of love" wasn't true. It was simply a thing designed to make him angry and thereby throw him off balance to increase her advantage. It worked. He was close to going down, almost finished, and she could see it. One more blow with a knife this time and he would be done, bleeding out on the floor of the garage like a gutted fish.

But not quite. As Barber's right arm flailed backwards on top of the bench he felt something cold and hard. It was a wrench. He weakly grabbed it and swung it towards her arm holding the knife. His strength was diminished, but the wrench was heavy, like the kind used by pipefitters. As it made contact there was a loud "pop" that signaled her arm just broke. The break was ugly, with the two halves of her forearm now at an angle to each other not intended by nature. The knife flew out of her hand as the damaged arm fell useless at her side. She screamed in pain and staggered backwards, now off balance.

Barber braced himself against the top of the workbench with his elbows and tried to stand again and prepare another strike. As he did so, he once more swept his hand over the top of the bench trying to feel for something that could be used a weapon. He felt what seemed like a large screwdriver and picked it up, holding it behind his back and out of sight. Try as he might, he could not command his legs to move his body forward. He continued to prop himself against the workbench, willing his legs to keep him off the floor as he and readied himself for her next strike. She was damaged now, but he wasn't foolish enough to think she was out of the fight. At least the broken arm evened the odds a bit he thought. He stood there, vulnerable, but he had a plan.

Her eyes were no longer dispassionate. This wasn't "just business" to her anymore. Overcoming her sudden change of fortunes required every bit of adrenaline her system could produce, and she fueled it with a building rage. She had been seriously wounded and realized she was about to go down herself, but she summoned every bit of strength to prevent it. He appeared almost spent, struggling to breath, so she knew she still had a chance. She had to finish him.

She commanded her legs to move her forward. They complied. As she got closer to him he slumped a bit, signaling he didn't have enough energy left for another round. Perfect, she thought; I am going to win this. But it was his turn for a ruse, and he waited for her to take the bait. With her good arm she picked up the wrench that had damaged her and staggered two additional steps forward before raising it to ready a swing, this time at his head. She took another step, longer this time, to close the distance between the two of them and bring him back into her range. She then allowed herself to fall forward towards Barber to accelerate her blow with the momentum of her body as she prepared to bring the large wrench down in a wide arch to crush his skull.

As she did so, Barber swept his right arm out from behind his back and fell towards her before she could begin the downward arch of her weapon. As their bodies merged he drove the long shaft of the screwdriver deep into the center of her chest. Her face immediately morphed from an expression of rage into one of shock. She hadn't seen him grab the screwdriver. Her good arm went limp and the wrench fell onto the concrete floor of the garage with a loud "clang." His counterattack caught her totally by surprise. She let out the guttural sound of a mortally wounded animal as the two of them fell to the ground together. Barber was now laying almost on top of her. He was finally able to get a bit more air into his lungs, but he was still in great pain. He ignored it and forced himself to breath. The handle of the screwdriver remained in his grip, and he twisted its shaft in a circular manner to further tear up her internal organs. He could see her eyes flutter as the life now began to exit her body. He leaned over her and whispered into her ear, "You come after me like you did three years ago, that's business. You come after my family, that's personal." Several seconds later Emilee Magnesson was dead.

"So much for the virtues of being a tough guy with a heart," he thought, reflecting on the break he had given her after their previous encounter three years ago. He rolled over onto his back and tried to catch his breath. As the spasm in his throat finally passed, he felt like a drowning man who had just broken the surface of the water. He tried to sit up, but as he did so the pain in his chest felt like a bolt of lightning. He laid on the garage floor for several seconds trying to summon the energy to speak again, still in considerable pain. He closed his eyes and concentrated, willing his vocal cords to respond to his demand for sound. He finally keyed his mic and said, "I could use a little help here."

Chapter 21 – An Important Discovery

Rye, New York, Neighbor's Garage used as Sniper Overwatch

Barber was still laying on the floor of the garage as Alex Hemmingway and another of the operators entered to render assistance. Hemmingway immediately leaned down to assess his condition.

"How badly are you hurt?"

"Not as bad as I look. Got kicked in the chest and it hurts like a son of a bitch thanks to my broken ribs, but I don't think she did any additional damage."

"Can you stand?" Hemmingway asked.

"I think so," Barber responded. "Let's see."

Hemmingway and the other operator grabbed him under each shoulder and slowly lifted him to his feet. They carefully let go, and he managed to remain standing. He then took a couple of tentative steps to gauge his ability to walk. He was successful.

"Looks like I am still among the realm of the living."

"That's more than I can say for your friend here," the other operator said.

"Looks like you've made a bit of a mess, boss," Hemmingway replied.

"I know," Barber replied. "Wasn't my intent, but she got the drop on me. That was almost me laying there on the floor."

Hemmingway spoke into her wrist mike, "This is Alpha 3. Alpha one is secure and ambulatory. We will evac within 5 minutes. We are going to need a cleanup crew in here immediately."

"Take a look over there," Barber said. "It's her laptop. Let's make sure we take it. Lauren can look at it and see if it tells us anything."

"Hey, I see there's a USB key still in it," Hemmingway responded. "Let me take a quick look before we bug out."

Hemingway clicked the space bar on the laptop and, as expected, a screensaver immediately appeared. She closed the laptop, pulled the USB key out, then looked at the operator standing next to her and said, "Go get me your MacBook Air." In less than two minutes he was standing next to her again and handing her the small laptop with the screen booted up. She clicked on the device, opened a file that appeared in its window and started reading the contents. "There's only one file on this USB key, and it's encrypted, which I expected. I'll bet it's the mission brief from whomever her client is. This could be a huge score. The U.S. infected all of Iran's defense systems with a virus that puts a digital fingerprint on every computer file or email they create. It should allow us to trace any email or data file right to its specific source. Her client had to be the Iranians. This means it's almost certain, once Lauren does her magic, that we should be able to trace the contract to the specific organization within the Iranian government that prepared this file. I'm betting it has to be the same source as the hit on Schiller."

"That's great," Barber said as he took a few more tentative steps and gradually brought his legs back to life. "I suggest we gather it up and get out of here. Somebody alert Lauren to be ready to look at that key fob."

"Will do," said Hemmingway as she pulled out her phone to call Dr. Lauren Cartwright.

"And let's keep my family in the safe suite for another 24 hours, and keep security deployed inside the house. If all remains clear I would say we are out of the woods."

"Roger that."

Forensics Lab, Orion Bellicus HQ, Rye, New York, Late that Evening

Back at Orion Bellicus headquarters, Dr. Lauren Cartwright stared into the flat-paneled computer screen as the software continued to digitally interrogate the USB drive Alex Hemmingway retrieved from the laptop of the late Emilee Magnesson. It took hours to break the encryption on the key fob, but there were few encryption algorithms Cartwright was incapable of breaking, and the file eventually yielded its contents. The next step was more straightforward. The NSA had infected Iran's governmental and defense systems with a virus that added a digital "fingerprint" to any file or email. The "fingerprint" positively identified the source, and even the specific individual in the case of an email..

As the Orion Bellicus computers worked their magic, the computer screen showed the circle of flashing hashmarks made famous by Apple's operation systems. The circle had been spinning for almost three minutes when suddenly it disappeared. It was replaced by a simple message:

Source: Defense Ministry, Islamic Republic of Iran, Cyber Warfare Division

Their suspicions had just been confirmed, and Lauren Cartwright had a phone call to make.

Chapter 22 – Existential Fear

House of Leadership, Office of the Supreme Leader, Tehran

General Hamidi stood and waited. He hated to wait. He shot people who made him wait and could ordinarily do so with impunity. Today he had no choice. Today he could not shoot the person forcing him to wait, although he wanted to badly. He wanted to for a long list of reasons that went beyond his extreme consternation with the moment. Today the person forcing him to wait was Grand Ayatollah Ashtiana, the Supreme Leader of Iran. So General Hamidi sat and he waited, his anger building by the moment and made worse because it was an anger without an outlet. Fortunately for him, he was smart enough to know that. One word from the old man behind the doors and he could be the one led to a nearby courtyard and shot. So, he sat and simmered like a pressure cooker dangerously close to exploding. But he knew this pressure cooker would not explode. Exploding would result in his swift demise. Exploding would be no different than him swallowing poison with the expectation that it would kill the old man behind the doors and not himself. So, he sat there, and he waited.

Although a monster, Hamidi was nevertheless an educated man and well-read. As he sat there, he recalled a quote from English history that he found himself repeating countless times over the last several years. It was a quote attributed to the English King Henry II regarding his frustration with a religious leader, Sir Thomas Beckett, "Will no one rid me of this meddlesome priest?" Translation: "Will no one rid me of this meddlesome Imam?" But that was England, and this was Iran. And he was no king.

An aid to the Supreme Leader passed through the doors from the inner sanctum into the waiting room and approached the General, then spoke, "The Imam will see you now. You have five minutes."

"Five minutes," Hamidi thought, "only five minutes for the single most daring and consequential action ever taken by the Islamic Republic." The five-minute limit made him even more furious, if that was possible. He stood without saying a word and allowed the aid to lead him into the Supreme Leader's reception room. By protocol, it was General Hamidi's responsibility to initiate the greeting, given his lower status, so he bowed his head and said "Salām Alaykum." He did not use the prefix "al", as most in the West were accustomed to hearing, because that was the Arabic form of the greeting. General Hamidi hated Arabs.

"Alaykum Salām, my son." The Supreme Leader responded. "Be seated," he said as more of a command than an invitation.

Hamidi walked to a mat on the floor and sat down, legs folded. He remained silent until the Imam invited him to speak. The wait seemed interminable and wasted at least one of his precious five minutes. He wondered how real the time constraint was, but he was experienced enough with the Imam not to test it.

Finally, the Supreme Leader spoke. "I am disappointed in you, General Hamidi. I would have expected more progress by now, but instead I hear you are devoting your time to acts of vengeance on those who disappoint you."

Hamidi was stunned by so sharp a rebuke at the beginning of their meeting. He cleared his throat, steeled himself, then spoke, "It is important to provide lessons to those who do not deliver results, Your Excellency. It keeps others motivated."

"Oh, I agree. Lessons are very useful in motivating people, General." Another long wait. At least another minute gone, then he spoke again. "Delivering results requires us to remain motivated, as you put it, does it not?"

"Yes, your Excellency," Hamidi said, then swallowed hard.

"And proper motivation includes a focus on the proper priorities, does it not?"

"Yes, your Excellency," Hamidi said, bowing lower this time.

"Do I need to motivate you, General? Perhaps provide you a lesson, as you call it?"

Hamidi was not easily intimidated, but a cold chill shot up his spine at the Imam's words. First a rebuke, then a threat. The Supreme Leader had shown impatience with him in the past, but he had never voiced such an overt threat. Hamidi felt beads of sweat break out on his forehead. He experienced an emotion almost completely foreign to him. He experienced fear. His heart was racing, his breathing rapid and shallow. His mind flashed back to when he was a young Lieutenant and was savagely admonished by his Commanding Officer when he couldn't answer a question. He was fearful he was going to die that day. The knot grinding in his stomach felt the same as the knot he experienced back then. He finally cleared his throat and spoke, "My life exists for no reason other than to serve the will of Allah, as he reveals his will to me through you, your Excellency." It was a lie of course, an act of self-preservation, but he was smart enough to know what had to be said. He hoped it was enough. He sat before this man so many times in the past and felt himself in the presence of an old fool. This old fool had just reduced him to a quivering child, just as that Commanding Officer had done to that young Lieutenant so many years ago, and just as the General himself had done to so many men under his command.

The Supreme Leader allowed Hamidi's words to hang in the air for some time. It was another brilliant act at intimidation and caused Hamidi to momentarily wonder whether his words were enough. Finally, the Ayatollah spoke, "Good," he said. "Now tell me about our progress. Tell me about Allah's sword."

"You Excellency, as you know our first test did not provide results to my satisfaction. We successfully simulated a missile launch, but the targeting software was imprecise. We missed the intended target by almost five kilometers. We are planning a second test shortly, one that should prove far more realistic. Dr. Ghorbani, the scientist responsible for the software, has been working on improving its accuracy. We are optimistic the next test will provide much better results."

"Dr. Ghorbani? You mean the scientist you sent to North Korea for two days to witness the execution of Colonel Arabi instead of keeping him back here working on the problem? That Dr. Ghorbani?"

Bile rose in his throat at the Imam's words. He had been in the Supreme Leader's office for less than four minutes and this was already his second rebuke. His throat tightened and he was fearful he would now be unable to speak.

The Supreme Leader noticed the General's face turn ashen. The Imam was gratified to realize that he was likely the only person on the face of the Earth who could elicit such a reaction from the proud and arrogant General, but he also concluded it was time to lighten up a bit. "Relax," he said, "you are one of my most dependable Generals and I believe this glorious task would not be possible without your leadership. Just make sure your theatrics remain efficient. A bullet can convey motivation in much less time than a plane ride."

"Yes, your Excellency," Hamidi replied as he exhaled, realizing he had been holding his breath.

"Now tell me of your plans. Take whatever time you need."

The last comment put Hamidi much more at ease. After the most terrifying four minutes he could remember, he now believed he might actually survive the encounter. He steeled himself again and began to speak. "The scientist I recently brought into your presence, Dr.Ghorbani, has refined the accuracy of the software. We are now confident in our ability to alter a missile's trajectory to a high degree of precision. We have reliable intelligence that the European Federation test a solid fuel missile the day after tomorrow. We plan to alter its targeting coordinates by 7.3 kilometers. We are using such a precise number to verify the software is highly accurate. It's enough of a change in target coordinates to validate our capabilities, but not enough to make the European Federation Military suspicious that someone is playing with their missiles. If this test is successful, we will conduct a final test the following day by remote firing one of North Korea's short-range ballistic missiles. It will be unarmed, of course."

"The North Korean Supreme Leader will not be pleased, and I suspect that at least one of his Generals is not long for this world," the Imam said with a bit of a chuckle.

"May it be as Allah wills it, Your Excellency," Hamidi said. "If all goes well, we will regard the system as operational. It will then simply be a matter of you giving your blessing."

"Very good, General. Your report pleases me."

"Thank you. You are most kind Your Excellency. May I have your permission to conduct the next two tests as I have just described them?"

"Go do your work, General. May Allah guard your heart and bless your efforts."

General Hamidi rose from his seated position, bowed before the Imam and began to walk backwards towards the exit door carefully avoiding turning his back towards the old man. The meeting had started off terribly, but it seemed to end exceptionally well. When almost at the door, he turned and reached out to the handle to open it. As he did so, the Supreme Leader spoke again.

"General."

Hamidi turned his head towards the voice and queried, "Yes, Your Excellency?"

"Do not fail me, General."

"Yes, Your Excellency."

"And General," the Supreme Leader said yet again. Hamidi's recently found optimism evaporated. He did not speak this time, but locked eyes with the man and braced himself for what he feared was about to follow. He felt his hand on the door handle begin to tremble. The Supreme Leader then conveyed the most direct threat of all.

"Lessons await those who fail."

Hamidi again said nothing as he bowed his head a bit lower and walked through the door into the reception area. He couldn't get out of that room or that building fast enough.

Hamidi exited the building and briskly walked to the automobile waiting to take him back to his headquarters. As he approached the vehicle, his driver quickly dropped the cigarette from his hand and stepped on it to put out the ember then opened the rear door for Hamidi to get in. He got into the vehicle without saying a word. As the driver began to pull away from the House of Leadership Hamidi looked out the window at the throngs of people crowding the streets and thought about his last 15 minutes. The Supreme Leader was a dangerous man, and Hamidi had been shaken badly by the encounter. But as the vehicle steadily increased the distance between the two of them his rapid respiration and heartbeat finally started to slow, and he began to relax. If Allah's Sword was successful he would be untouchable. Even this fool, the Supreme Leader, would regard him as a hero of the Islamic Revolution. Then a fear crept into his consciousness that gave his optimism momentary pause. He had instructed his agent in their Berlin Embassy to capture the American, Joe Barber, who was still asking too many questions about Schiller's death. But his agent had been killed in the Embassy explosion and Barber had escaped. Hamidi had been the one to arrange for a sniper to kill Barber's family, but he had not received confirmation yet that the deed was done. If the hit on Barber's family had gone off as planned, Barber would be consumed with their death and not focused on Schiller's. That would keep Barber busy until long after Allah's Sword struck its fatal blow. But while the sniper was supposed to be untraceable, Barber had already connected a lot of dots that were supposed to be impossible to connect. If Barber somehow was able to link the sniper to Hamidi, it would be a disaster. It would raise questions about whether Hamidi was complicit in Schiller's death, and that would bring unwanted attention to Iran's interest in the European Federation's Command and Control system. It could completely derail the project, Allah's Sword. "But that's impossible," he thought. "Nobody will ever make that connection. Even if they figured it out, there was no way they would irrefutable proof." Hamidi tried to put such an absurd notion out of his mind. Nevertheless, he would not sleep well that night.

Chapter 23 – A Shiny New Toy

Office of the Chancellor, European Federation HQ, Berlin

The office was over 185 square meters, or about 2,000 square feet in English terms. Soft classical music by Johannes Brahms was piped into the space by a Bang & Olufsen sound system. The outside wall was floor to ceiling bullet-proof glass, capable of stopping most sniper rounds yet still appearing thin as a filament to the casual observer. In front of the window sat a massive bespoke desk, resplendent with intricate carvings, atop a platform raised 12 inches off the floor, 25 feet wide by 20 feet deep, intended to fuel a more elevated perception of the desk's occupant, almost as if it were a throne. The office was curated with antiques on loan from the Louvre, valued at over 100 million Deutsche Franks, or more than $120 million U.S. dollars. The walls were covered with art work that rendered the space one of the most impressive art galleries in all of Germany and included works by two of the occupant's favorite German painters, Stormy Sea (1930) by Emil Nolde, and Wanderer Above the Sea of Fog (1819) by Casper David Friedrich. It was a space intended to project two essential attributes – gravitas and power, and it made the American's Oval Office look like a cubicle. It was the office of the Chancellor of the European Federation, Dr. Heinrich Krüger.

Krüger was blessed with the handsome, chiseled good looks of someone right out of central casting. At fifty-two years old he still retained a full head of yellow blond hair, contrasted by vivid blue eyes. He stood six feet two inches, which was tall, but not imposing. He appeared fit, thanks mostly to a lifetime on the tennis courts after advancing to the quarter finals at the French Open while at University, but he did not have the physique of a weight-lifter. He projected an out-sized presence through his charisma, lightning-quick intellect, and oratory skills that many believed had not been witnessed since Sir Winston Churchill.

His father was an academic in the field of theoretical physics, and his mother was a concert violinist who had mentored the now famous German violinist Anne-Sophie Mutter when the child was just a young musical prodigy. His upper middle-class childhood brought him the privilege of private schools. It was at the boarding school Schloss Neubeuern in Bavaria that he first heard stories of Germany's sins during World War 2. He was no Nazi sympathizer and believed the intellectual foundation of National Socialism was repugnant, but he tired quickly of how the world seemed to blame Germany for so much while ignoring the sins of others. His teachers hammered it into him and the other students at the prestigious academy. Most of all he became resentful at how the international community just wouldn't let it go, even seven or eight decades after the conclusion of the World War II. The nation he knew was industrious, hard-working and creative. He entered university as a proud German intent on changing his nation's place in the world. After completing studies at Oxford in mathematics and economics, he entered a doctoral program in economics at Universität Mannheim where he earned a Ph.D. in only four years. Prior to launching his political career, he became the youngest full Professor of Economics in his alma matter's history and was even once regarded as a finalist for the Nobel in his field.

Krüger's political aspirations were not so much personal as they were ideological. He regarded personal power and wealth as merely the bi-products of success and not ends in and of themselves. His destiny was to change the world and to change his nation's place in it. He longed for a resurgent Germany free from living under the thumb of NATO and free to provide for its own defense as it saw fit. He fervently believed his calling was to lead Germany to its true destiny as a superpower, both economically and militarily. He saw Brexit and the collapse of the EU as a blessing; a once in a generation opportunity and the perfect antecedent that created a power vacuum he would lead his nation to fill. The formation of the European Federation with France provided the way to project a resurgent Germany in a slightly less worrisome light to the rest of the world, had Germany simply "gone it alone." He believed he was born for this time, this place and this destiny, and he would do anything to fulfill it. He bore no particular ill will towards anyone, but woe to anyone who would try to get in his way.

Krüger leaned back in his chair and closed his eyes as he listened to a particular favorite passage from Brahms Piano Concerto Number 1 in D minor, the Adagio, or second movement. The movement is introduced by bassoons, and is played in D major, providing a bright contrast to the rest of the work. The music enveloped him and took his consciousness to a place far away from his responsibilities as Chancellor, but his concentration was interrupted as his secretary buzzed his intercom to announce the arrival of Generals Horst Brant and Jean-Baptiste Laurent from the EF Air Force.

"Send them in," he barked, irritated by the interruption to his trance-like bliss.

Brandt entered the expansive office first, as was the custom for the senior officer. Following him was Lt. General Jean-Baptist Laurent, his Deputy Commander. Their immediate boss, the Defense Minister, was at a conference in London, but he had been previously briefed. Laurent found his meetings with Krüger intriguing, reinforcing his perception that the marriage of Germany and France in the EF was not the marriage of equals, at least in the minds of the Germans.

"Please, Generals, come in," Krüger said as he remained sitting at his desk and waved his hand to invite both men to take seats across from him.

Both men walked across the office and climbed the two steps to the raised platform then took the seats opposite Krüger, as directed. It was not lost on Laurent that the discussion would take place atop the formal platform and across Krüger's massive desk, and not on the sofas in the more informal sitting area on the right side of the office. It was rumored that Krüger did this every time a meeting involved a Frenchman as a way to subtly reinforce his sense of German superiority. Laurent was convinced the rumor was correct.

"Good morning, Generals," Brandt began, "I have been looking forward to this briefing. Tell me about our Project Dart."

Brandt took the lead. "As you will remember, Chancellor, the last time we met about Project Dart, the rail gun had been successfully tested onboard an aircraft, albeit at a much lower destructive power than required to make it operationally successful. There were two issues: attaining the speed necessary to achieve the required force on target, and the energy necessary to accelerate the projectile to that speed. Our initial airborne test achieved an acceleration of Mach 12.5. We engaged the services of a subsidiary of an American firm to solve the engineering issues and the results have been spectacular."

"An American firm?" the Chancellor queried with an expression of astonishment.

"Yes, Chancellor, the subsidiary of the American firm QuarkSpin, which is headquartered in California."

"Emma Clark's company?"

"Yes sir. Again, a German subsidiary of her company, CWR Industries, located here in Berlin. The ownership structure is deliberately opaque to reduce the risk of scrutiny. Nobody knows they are the subsidiary of a U.S. company. It is buried within a nest of several Limited Liability Companies, with nonsensical names, that makes its provenance very difficult to establish." Brandt replied.

"Our intelligence directorate believes we are at risk of increased sanctions against American and English companies doing defense work for us," Krüger replied. "The American Congress, in particular, seems to be insistent. I'm sure you are not unaware of these things. I'm happy the engagement has produced results, but what if sanctions cause us to lose them as a supplier?" the Chancellor asked. "We need access to technology that is sustainable."

"Yes sir, we are aware. First, it would take quite some time before anyone would uncover that the Company has U.S. connections. Second, and more importantly," he said with a smile, "I have it on the highest authority that the move towards sanctions has been killed, at least for now." Brandt replied.

"How is that possible?" Krüger asked.

"Let's just say Dr. Clark is a consummate fixer."

Krüger looked astonished again. "What does she have, compromising pictures of the leaders of Congress and the President?" he said, laughing.

"I don't know her leverage sir. All I know is I placed a phone call and the problem went away."

"Amazing," the Chancellor replied. "Remind me to arrange a private dinner with her the next time she is in Berlin. Anyway, we are a bit off point. What is the breakthrough you alluded to? Where are we?"

"The subsidiary, CWR Industries, developed a generator that is integral to the engine turbine of the Mirage 2000. It provides an exponential increase in power output compared to the previous geared system design and is much more reliable. Their power storage solution is ingenious. Much of the weight of the old battery design relates to retaining the energy in the battery once it is charged. But that energy is only needed at time of firing the projectile. They developed a series of light-weight capacitors that are only capable of retaining the generated energy for a few seconds, but that is enough. Reducing the energy storage time greatly reduced the weight requirements of the system by eliminating the heavy batteries. The projectile's atmospheric drag was greatly reduced by drilling a series of precision ports, or holes in the projectile itself. The elongated holes in the projectile are angled in such a way to make it spin in route to target, with a dramatic increase in accuracy. The net effect is we are now capable of a muzzle velocity up to Mach 40 and reduction in velocity of no more than Mach 5 on a target at 10 miles."

Krüger smiled and exclaimed, "Impressive! I must confess I have very little training in physics. What exactly do these numbers mean?"

"The projectile has a mass, or weight, of 400 grams. A 400-gram projectile travelling at Mach 35 places a force on target of almost 58 billion Newtons."

"Again, I'm not a physicist, General. I concede that 58 billion is a large amount of anything, except perhaps Marks during the Weimar Republic. What does it mean, in layman's terms, please? Are we talking a firecracker or a nuclear weapon?"

"Let me describe it this way," Brandt responded. "The largest non-nuclear weapon in the American arsenal is the GBU-43/b fuel-air bomb, or MOAB, called the 'Mother of All Bombs." It is over ten meters long and weighs over 8,500 kilograms. It has a destructive force equivalent to about 11 tons of TNT. Our projectile is only 23 centimeters long and weighs only 400 grams. At a speed of Mach 35, five Mach numbers below the system potential, it delivers a destructive force equivalent to 137 tons of TNT, or 12 times more than the MOAB."

Krüger's expression went blank for several seconds as he tried to process what he had just heard. "Mother of God," he replied. "With that much force you could obliterate an aircraft carrier with a single shot."

"You could obliterate a lot more than an aircraft carrier, Herr Chancellor," Brandt replied.

"What is your proposal, General? What are our next steps?"

"Five of our Dassault Rafale fighters are now equipped with the systems and are fully operational. Any use of the system, of course, will require your prior approval. The systems are locked with Permissive Action Links similar to how we control the release of our nuclear weapons."

"Good, of course," the Chancellor replied.

Brandt took a breath and chose his next words carefully. He was about to propose something that was bold and would change the status quo ante. "As our next step, Chancellor, we need to make the world aware of this capability. We need to announce this in a way that leaves no doubt that it is a quantum leap. This is a technology no other nation has perfected as yet. It will be a tremendous boost to our national pride."

"Yes sir, most definitely. The Paris Air Show is next month. That could be an effective forum for our unveiling," the Chancellor said.

"We were thinking of something far more dramatic, Chancellor."

Krüger's eyebrows raised in a reflexive response to the comment. "What, General, do you have in mind?" he asked, trying to hold back the hint of a smile.

"To achieve maximum credibility, the world needs to see the system function. Since I assume that you do not contemplate destroying a French air base at the unveiling, we recommend firing the weapon on a target not on EF soil."

Krüger leaned back in his chair and remained quiet for several seconds as he stared into the eyes of both men sitting in front of him, processing what Brandt just said. "I would very much like to demonstrate this capability, Generals, but I would prefer not to start World War 3 by attacking a neighbor or former ally,"

"Neither do we, Chancellor. We were thinking of a defensive action."

Krüger was starting to become a bit irritated. "A defensive action? A defensive action against, perhaps, England or Russia, or I know, even better, an American air base. Of course, what could be more effective than poking a nuclear power in the face? What could possibly go wrong?"

"We were thinking Sweden," Brandt replied.

The Chancellor's expression turned from annoyance to puzzlement. "Sweden? Well, that's certainly novel. Perhaps Lichtenstein would be a more convincing target. Perhaps we could sink one of Lichtenstein's aircraft carriers, defensively, of course," he said sarcastically.

Brandt remained expressionless at the intentional snub and began his closing arguments. "We believe, sir, Sweden actually provides the perfect opportunity."

"I'm listening."

"You will recall sir, as part of our defense preparedness exercises we tested Swedish airspace several times over the last couple of months with our Mirages. Our initial incursions were simply met with complaints, but the last three times our aircraft were painted with their air-to-air and ground-based fire control radar. The last such event they even continued after we left Swedish air space. We lodged formal complaints and warned them in the future we were prepared to take defensive measures, if necessary."

"Yes, I recall," the Chancellor replied. "We followed the Chinese model of dealing with the Americans in the South China Sea."

"Exactly. We suggest a trap. We fly the Dart-equipped squadron of Mirages towards Ronneby airbase in southern Sweden until they sortie a response. We are confident that both the aircraft and ground radar will paint us. We then turn our jets around and fly towards open water. If they continue to paint us, which I believe they will, one of the jets turns back and fires a dart at the ground radar installation. We dial the power back to something short of Mach 20 so it doesn't look like a nuclear detonation. We claim it was a defensive action and point out that these 'routine training flights' have taken place several times over the last two months without incident and remind them that Sweden was warned not to paint our aircraft with radar. We claim self-defense. Neither the Americans nor Russians are going to respond with anything other than the normal diplomatic handwringing. Even at the reduced power, the illustration of our capabilities will be abundantly clear."

"What if the Swedes fire back?" Krüger asked. It seems to me a heroic assumption to believe we are going to fire a highly destructive weapon at one of their bases and they are going to just allow our aircraft to just fly away without responding."

"Ronneby Air Base will be heavily damaged, if not obliterated. They will certainly loose communications for at least several minutes until their backup systems go online. The Swedes will not fire on us without clearance, and by the time comms are restored or re-routed, we will be long gone. In fact, they probably won't even realize what happened until we are back in international airspace. We will be essentially retreating under a cloud of massive confusion, so I am confident they will not fire. Painting us with fire control radar is only an intimidation technique."

"I don't share your confidence, General Brandt," Krüger replied. "General Laurent, you have been conspicuously quiet during this conversation. Do you support General Brandt's proposal?"

"Mon Chancellor," Laurent replied, "there is a time for debate, a time for consensus, and a time to act. There was much spirited debate between me and General Brandt prior to this meeting, but we arrived at a decision. As Deputy Commander, yes, I support the proposal. As for the risk of the Swedes returning fire, I am not quite as sanguine as General Brandt, but I do regard it as unlikely."

"But I take it you regard it as a higher risk that General Brandt?"

"Yes sir, I do."

"And the diplomatic response, do you regard that as a higher risk as well?"

"Yes, Chancellor, I do. My instincts tell me we are underestimating the response from both the Americans and Russians. I do not believe their response will be a military strike, but I believe the diplomatic blowback could be considerable. We shall see. As I said, these decisions are the result of debate and consensus. I claim no veto."

"I share your concerns, General Laurent," the Chancellor responded, "but as a pragmatist I also believe the risk needs to be weighed in light of the opportunity and not viewed in isolation."

"Point taken," Laurent replied.

Krüger sat back in his chair and stared reflectively at the painting Wanderer Above a Sea of Fog for several seconds. As he did so, it occurred to him that at present he was immersed in that sea of fog and not wandering above it. Such was the nature of leadership at the highest levels. He had to make momentous decisions with far less than complete information, then manage the consequences. He believed Brandt was naive in downplaying the likely diplomatic response to entrapping Sweden. But he also realized the enormous boost the revelation would give to Germany's, the European Federation's gravitas by displaying an operational technology nobody else had. Even when the other superpowers developed it in response, as surely they would, it would never change the fact that Germany had done it first. It was like winning their own mini space race. He would not achieve Germany's destiny by being timid. The decision was obvious. He shifted his gaze from the painting to the two men sitting in front of him. "Very well, Generals. Let's go test our shiny new toy. We will blame Sweden, then fall all over ourselves apologizing, suggest a joint military commission to find procedures to avoid such an incident in the future, perhaps even offer reparations. The world will squawk, but if we feign contrition they will soon get over it. Just make sure you find a way to do this with minimal loss of life."

"Absolutely, Chancellor," Brandt said. The two generals rose from their chairs and started to exit the office. As they came close to the door, the Chancellor called out again, "General Laurent."

"Yes sir?"

"After the test, see to it that somebody sends Emma Clark a dozen roses anonymously, with a simple 'Thank You'. You French are so much better at that sort of thing than us Germans."

"Of course, sir," Laurent responded, bristling at the closet insult.

Chapter 24 – The Announcement

Büchel Air Base, State of Reinland Pfalz, Germany

Afterburners glowed as the three Dassault Rafale jets began their take-off roll down runway 21 at Büchel Airbase in Western Germany. Soon they were climbing out at a rate of 250 meters per second towards a cruising altitude of 10,000 feet in route to the southwest Swedish coast. The aircraft were arrayed in what is called a "vic" formation, with the lead aircraft in front and the two wingmen positioned one on each side, equal-distance and slightly behind the lead. The formation resembled the tip of a spear. All three aircraft were equipped with the new Project Dart rail gun, mounted underneath the aircraft's belly, along with a magazine of 6 projectiles.

The early evening sun lit up their cockpits. A few wispy strands of stratocumulus clouds, backlit by the sitting sun burning a bright orange and yellow, decorated the western sky on the horizon. After their initial climb out, the three pilots moved their control yokes slightly to the right as they steered the aircraft towards an initial course of 20 degrees on the compass and headed out of Germany towards the North Sea. The forecast was for thunderstorms over Sweden's Ronneby Air Base, and while it wouldn't deter their mission, it could make a precise battle damage assessment difficult if cloud cover prevented the onboard cameras from having a clear view of the ground.

The flight over Germany was non-eventful. In about 45 minutes the jets went "feet wet", crossing the north German coast and flying out over the North Sea. With their PGS navigations systems and autopilots now engaged, their course was adjusted to 340 degrees to ensure they didn't encroach Denmark's airspace. In another 35 minutes they adjusted course again to about 45 degrees, or more northeasterly, to cut a path in between Denmark and Norway towards Sweden. After just another 7 minutes, they made a final turn towards a southeast heading of 160 degrees into the Kattegate Strait, towards the Southeast coast of Sweden, and locked on to their final destination of Ronneby Air Base.

The jets had been ordered to maintain strict radio silence to this point, but as they approached their target, the lead pilot broke silence to hail Büchel Air Base in Germany and request an important clearance, "Ok, we are about 5 minutes from coastal radar range. Request weapons arming sequence. Request permission to take weapons hot."

Office of the Chancellor, European Federation HQ, Berlin

Dr. Heinrich Krüger sat at the conference table in his office with Generals Brandt and Laurent flanking him. An EF Colonel stood next to the Chancellor with a briefcase handcuffed to his wrist. It was the EF's "Football", or codes and instructions for arming the rail gun systems as well as their nuclear weapons, and it was modelled on the American system. Krüger retrieved a thin plastic case from his pocket as the Colonel unlocked the briefcase and powered up the secured laptop affixed to the inside of it. Krüger bent the case sharply until there was an audible "snap", then pulled the two halves apart and retrieved the card inside. On the card were four random letters, four random numbers, and three random characters. Krüger placed his thumb on the laptop's digital fingerprint reader. As he did so, a light on a panel next to the laptop changed from red to green. He then retrieved a small cup attached to the laptop by an electrical cable and placed it over his right eye. A second light on the panel turned from red to green, indicating a successful retinal scan. Only one red light remained. He then entered the 11-digit code from the card into the laptop's keyboard and hit "enter". The final red light turned green, and at the same moment an encrypted electronic code was transmitted to the aircraft releasing the lock on the rail gun weapons system.

50 Miles Northwest of Ronneby Air Base, Sweden

The lead pilot spoke again for only the second time. "I confirm weapon enabled. Arming weapon now," he said as he flipped up a plastic guard over a weapons-select touch screen and touched an icon with the special material stitched to the tip of the index finger on his right-hand glove. As he did so, the color of the icon on the touch screen turned from red to green. "Weapon is hot."

"Flight 2 confirms weapon hot," the second pilot, announced.

"Flight 3 confirms weapon hot," the third responded in kind.

"Set rail muzzle velocity to Mach 28," the lead pilot instructed.

"Roger that," came the response from the two wingmen.

"Two minutes from radar range, 5 minutes to target," said the lead pilot.

Suddenly a voice sounded excited: "I am being painted!" one of the wingmen exclaimed.

"So am I!" responded the lead.

"Me too!" reported the other wingman.

"Radar acquisition is from the ground, but I also make out three bogies climbing out from target. I am not being painted by air-to-air, at least not yet. Time of intercept with bogies is less than one minute!"

"Ok, drop altitude to 6,000 feet and prepare for a pass over the airbase," the lead pilot instructed, as the three jets dropped their noses and quickly bled off 4,000 feet of altitude.

"I am now being painted by air-to-air," the lead announced. "But no missile lock."

The six high-performance jets in two groups, one group German and the opposing Swedish, closed towards each other at a rate of twelve hundred knots. Within seconds, the three Swedish JAS 39 Gripen fighter jets flew past the oncoming Dassault Rafales. The lead Swedish Gripen fighter jet flew over top the three EF fighters at a distance of only 2 or 3 meters, while the other two Swedish jets passed beneath at a similar distance.

"Wow, that was close!" the lead pilot exclaimed.

As the three Gripens passed the Euro Federation pilots, they turned their aircraft into a wide arch to the right, coming around to a position just behind the intruders, or their "six", meaning "Six o'clock position.

The three Euro fighters' headsets crackled with a new voice: "Unidentified aircraft, you are in Swedish airspace. Reverse course immediately and exit. Our aircraft will escort you to the coast," said a voice likely from Ronneby Air Base in heavily Swedish-accented German.

The lead EF pilot hailed the Swedish jets over the radio and followed a script he was provided before taking off. "We are European Federation aircraft on a routine training mission. We do not have hostile intent. We will reverse course shortly,"

"Reverse course immediately!" the voice commanded. "Reverse course or we will take defensive action. You are in violation of Swedish airspace."

The three Federation pilots ignored the second warning and continued towards their target. The mission plan was to fly 15 kilometers deeper into Sweden beyond the base, then reverse course. It would allow additional time for the Swedes to decide to try and scare them by painting the aircraft with a missile lock, and it would put Dassaults in better firing position. The tactic worked.

"One of the bogies has me in missile lock!" a wingman exclaimed.

"I'm now in air-to-air and ground-based missile lock as well!" the lead pilot shouted. "Ronneby Air Base controller, instruct your forces to drop missile lock or we will be forced to take defensive action!"

There was no response. The lead pilot toggled the weapons select dial on his control yoke and selected the rail gun as the final step prior to firing the new weapon. He then reached up to the control panel and selected a rail gun speed of Mach 23. He centered the aiming radar on the base and depressed the firing trigger on the yoke. He aimed at the middle of the base's runway. There was a loud whirr and a slight shutter as the magnets were energized with a massive but short-lived burst of electrical power, and the projectile exited the front of the aircraft heading towards its target. At Mach 23 the effect was almost instantaneous. There was a massive explosion as the equivalent power of almost six tons of TNT engulfed the base in a huge fireball. The weather had cleared somewhat and the lead aircraft's camera captured the impact. As the three Dassaults now raced towards the coast, the rear-facing cameras continued to capture the imagery as the destructive power unfolded.

"One of those aircraft just placed me in missile lock again!" shouted the lead pilot, as he dove the aircraft and executed a 6-g turn to try and evade. "They just launched!"

An AIM-120 advanced, radar guided missile dropped off the rail of one of the Swedish jets and began racing towards the flight leader's aircraft at Mach 4. The missile had been fired at a distance of only three and a half kilometers. The lead pilot ejected a cloud of thousands of strips of aluminum to try and confuse the missile's guidance system, then put the aircraft through several abrupt and violent maneuvers in an effort to avoid being hit. It wasn't enough, The missile had been fired from too close a range, and it remained solidly locked onto its target. The AIM-120 struck the Dassault jet in the fuselage just behind the left wing. There was a large explosion, and the plane erupted in a fireball. The lead pilot never knew what hit him. The two wingmen pushed their throttles forward to full afterburner to hasten their exit to the coast.

The Swedish pilot never received clearance to fire on the European Federation intruder. But she saw the aircraft fire at her air base and saw the massive destruction unfold from the impact, so she wasn't about to let the culprit escape, clearance or not. Neither of the other two EuroFed aircraft had fired, so they would be allowed to return home.

General Horst Brandt's desire to showcase to the world the capabilities of the European Federation's newly developed advanced weapon system was successful beyond what he could have imagined, but General Laurent's instincts were correct. They greatly underestimated the diplomatic fallout that was about to ensue. And even worse, a series of events were about to transpire that would convince the world the rail-gun strike was just the first step in an EuroFed march towards a militaristic aggression not seen since the Second World War.

Chapter 25 – A Startling Revelation

Aboard the Orion Bellicus Gulfstream G550

It was going to be a long flight from Rye, New York back to Berlin. It would take a little over 8 hours, but the comfort and attentive service he was anticipating aboard the Orion Bellicus Gulfstream G550 would at least make it somewhat tolerable. As Barber gently settled himself into one of the aircraft's seats, a sharp pain from his battered ribs momentarily made it difficult to breathe. He reached down towards his right side and grasped the seat belt, then pulled it over his lap and fastened it. As he did so, his shoulder cried out in protest. Barber still hurt like hell from his abuse at the hands of the Iranians and the fight, just yesterday, with the blond female assassin the Iranians sent to kill his family. He was hoping that the two Vicodin and three fingers of Macallan 25-year old Scotch he was about to indulge would provide a modicum of relief. "I'm getting too old for this," he thought.

Once airborne, and after completing his self-administered anesthesia, he reclined the plush leather cabin chair to about a 45-degree angle, closed his eyes and tried to go to sleep. The sound of the aircraft engines bathed the cabin in a white noise, and he found the mild turbulence encountered during climb-out to be almost soothing, almost like being rocked in a cradle. The cabin lights were now dimmed enough to make eyeshades unnecessary, and a Bach violin concerto was quietly playing over the aircrafts sound system. The Vicodin and alcohol were starting to numb his pain. As his eyes grew heavy, he allowed his consciousness to slowly slip away. But instead of rest, dreams embroiled him again in a horror. He suddenly imagined being pulled out of the back seat of an automobile. He sensed his body deliberately thrusting upwards towards an assailant, then felt his jaws clamp into the man's neck in a desperate and last-ditch act of self-defense, overwhelming his consciousness with the wet and coppery taste of the assailant's blood. The dream had returned. He was once again reliving his near brush with death of just three years ago and the unspeakable method he had used to cheat it. He awoke with a startled jump, as his body launched out of the chair, as far as the loose-fitting seatbelt would allow.

"Are you OK, sir," the flight attendant queried.

"Yes, I'm fine. I must have been dreaming."

"is there anything I can get you?"

"No thanks," Barber replied.

'You're sure you are ok?" the attendant repeated the question.

"Yes, I'm sure," he replied.

His heart was pounding. As he looked around to reinforce where he was, his pulse and respiration began to slowly return to normal. He closed his eyes and tried again, but in spite of what would ordinarily be a perfect set of conditions, sleep eluded him. It was active mind syndrome. He could shut his body down, but his brain was now running at full throttle off the adrenaline spike from the dream.

After about 2 hours, Barber concluded sleep was not going to happen and resolved not to waste the rest of the trip trying. He returned his chair to full upright, then politely asked the flight attendant to bring him a glass of water and the satellite phone. The flight attendant was in reality former Delta Special Forces and now an Orion Bellicus special operator, and he attended to Barber's request with his usual crisp efficiency. As he handed Barber the phone, he sat down a small tray that proffered not just the water but, anticipating his boss' need, another two fingers of the Macallan 25. Barber smiled at the gesture and said, "Thank you."

Barber quickly downed the entire glass of water, then took a small sip of the amber liquid and punched the number for Marcus Day's cell into the satellite phone. He had left Day in charge in Berlin while he made a detour to the United States to deal with the threat to his family. Day answered the phone on the second ring.

"Hey, Joe. How are you feeling?" Day asked. "Didn't expect to hear from you again so soon."

"Couldn't sleep, and I feel like I just went 15 rounds with Mike Tyson," Barber replied.

"Wrong," Day responded. "First, you wouldn't last 15 seconds with Mike Tyson, let alone 15 rounds. And second, if you did go 15 seconds with Tyson you wouldn't be feeling anything at all, because you'd be dead."

"Ok," Barber replied, "point taken. I feel like I wish I were dead. How's that? I'm getting too old for this shit, Marc."

"Aren't we both, pal?" Day responded.

"Indeed. I'll survive, but I plan on trying to avoid any altercations for a while. I need to heal a bit or I won't be so lucky next time. I barely survived the little dance I had with the blond assassin."

"That's what I'm told," Day responded. "My wristwatch says you have over five hours of flying time left, and it's the middle of the night. What's so urgent to justify a phone call? You should be working on that rest you said you need."

"Can't sleep, in spite of a generous dose of pain meds and the plane being stocked with the Macallan. Have you heard anything from Lauren about that thumb drive?" Barber asked.

"Not yet. I talked to her a few hours ago and she told me she was close. I don't think she's going home tonight until she's cracked it," Day said.

"I don't imagine she will," Barber responded. "So, I think it's pretty clear Schiller's death had something to do with the Sternenlicht's software used in the EF's strategic weapons command and control systems. What I can't figure out is what. Iran has practically become an EF ally in the last two years, and their commercial contacts have become huge and worth a fortune. Germany and France have essentially become Iran's economic lifeline against the rest of the civilized world's sanctions. Why would they want to screw with that?"

"Agreed," Day responded. "The EF certainly doesn't represent a threat to them."

"And what does killing Schiller accomplish?" Barber asked.

"Exactly. Their acting CEO, Hans-Dieter Zimmerman, told us that Schiller liked to stay close to the software project's development – it was his baby before his elevation to the top job. Zimmerman even said Schiller would sometimes review the code late at night and test it himself for flaws, but I don't see how that made him a threat to Iran," Day responded.

"Right," Barber replied, "unless maybe somehow the Iranian's hacked it."

"But what would be the motive for that? I doubt they even have the capability. And if they did, why hack an ally? Why not hack Israel, the Saudis, or even the United States?"

"Exactly," Barber replied again. "Although they are allies, they are hardly friends. Do you suppose the Iranians could have had an asset in Sternenlicht or in the EF Ministry of Defense that Schiller somehow uncovered?"

"That sounds more credible that uncovering a hack, but for it to be a motive the Iranians would have to believe Schiller hadn't outed the asset yet to the authorities. How could they know that?" Day responded.

"You're right. Just a thought."

"Hey Joe, let me put you on hold for a minute. I've got a call coming through from Lauren. Hopefully she can shed a little light for us."

"Roger that." Barber replied.

Hotel Adlon Kempinski, Berlin, Marcus Day's Room

"Lauren," Day responded as he answered her call. "What have you got?"

"Where have you been?" Lauren Cartwright asked. "I've been trying to reach you for over two hours."

"I've been here," Day responded. "Cell coverage isn't great in my hotel room, so I just went down to the lobby. I've actually got Joe on hold; he just called me from the Gulfstream. Do you have something yet?"

"It took longer than I expected," she replied. "Their encryption was pretty good, but I've got a fingerprint for the source of that briefing file."

"And......?" Day queried.

"Are you sitting down?" She asked.

"No but go ahead."

"The source of the assassin's briefing file is the Iranian Revolutionary Guard Corp Cyber Warfare Division."

"Wow," Day responded. "The Cyber Warfare Division?"

"Yup," she replied.

"Any way you can hack them?"

"We've looked at that, but I don't think so, at least without a lot of work and a lot of time. Hacking into a system is taking the game to a whole different level than simply decrypting a digital fingerprint. With enough time I could do it, but it would take a sustained effort and a lot of resources, and I doubt I could complete the task in enough time to do you much good. But, do you and Joe want me to try?"

"No, not yet at least. I take your point. Uncovering that source has been very helpful Lauren. Great work. Now go and get what I suspect is some badly needed sleep."

"Will do."

Aboard the Orion Bellicus Gulfstream G550

Barber sat patiently on hold, hoping Day would come back with something helpful. After several minutes, he heard a click on the line and Day's voice returned."

"You're not going to believe this," Day said.

"Waddaya got, Mark?"

"Lauren was able to decrypt the source of the document. It came from the IRGC, get this, its Cyber Warfare Division."

"Woah!" Barber exclaimed. "You know what this means?" he asked rhetorically.

"Yes. It means Schiller must have uncovered some kind of hack, and the Iranians must have believed Schiller hadn't outed them yet."

"Yup. It's the only explanation now that makes sense," Barber responded.

"I agree, but what kind of a hack, and what could possibly have been their motive?" Day asked.

"I have no earthly idea Marc," Barber replied. "I have no earthly idea."

Chapter 26 – A Strange Death

Schönefeld Airport, Berlin

The morning sun peeked brightly above the eastern horizon as the aircraft closed on its destination, Schönefeld Airport, about 18 kilometers southwest of central Berlin. A moderate temperature of 20 degrees Celsius, or about 70 degrees Fahrenheit, along with light and variable winds, made for a smooth approach as the airport grew ever closer. The Orion Gulfstream G550 made a standard bank to final approach and settled into the glidepath for runway 25 left, a massive stretch of concrete almost 13,000 feet long that provided more than four and a half times the distance required for the aircraft's return to terra firma. Barber sat upright in his seat and reflexively gave his seatbelt another yank to confirm it was tight as he waited patiently for the aircraft to land. The Vicodin and alcohol had largely worn off by now, and the pain in his ribs was becoming a little more pronounced, but all in all, given what he had been through the last several days, he felt reasonably good and glad to be alive.

As a pilot himself, Barber was acutely tuned to the sounds of an airplane during transitional phases of flight, like take-offs and landings, climb outs and descents. As the aircraft crossed the runway's threshold, he noticed the sounds of the two jet engines quickly diminishing as the pilot reduced power to idle, then heard a light "chip" of the tires as the plane made contact with the runway, the modest sound foretelling a smooth and uneventful landing. After a short landing roll and the loud whine of thrust reversers, the Gulfstream slowed sufficiently to turn onto a taxiway and towards the Executive terminal run by the local Fixed Base Operator, or "FBO", Jet Aviation Services. As the plane came to a full stop just outside the terminal building, his flight attendant/bodyguard deployed the staircase towards the front of the aircraft, just behind the cockpit. Barber grabbed his duffle, exited the plane and walked towards the terminal building to clear customs and meet his ride.

As Barber walked out of the terminal, he spotted the BMW M5 waiting for him. It was a beast of a sedan, with a 617-horsepower motor capable of propelling the vehicle from 0 to 60 miles per hour in a mere 2.8 seconds. Orion Bellicus always provided very fast cars for their senior employees, not just as toys, but as a security measure. The second thing he spotted was Marcus Day emerging from the driver's seat.

"Good morning Marc. Why the personal greeting?"

"Have you seen any news?" Day replied.

"No, what's up?"

"It's too recent to have made the papers, but it's all over the networks here and on the net," Day responded as he handed Barber an iPad displaying the home page of The Financial Times of London.

Barber took the tablet and read the headline as he stood by the BMW:

Stockholm: ***The Swedish government has accused the European Federation of a massive attack on Ronneby Airbase in the southwest of the country.*** *The following is a statement from the Prime Minister:*

For Immediate Release: "Yesterday evening, at 2100 Central European Summer Time (1900 GMT), The Kingdom of Sweden was suddenly and deliberately attacked by air forces of the European Federation. Massive ordnance was dropped on Ronneby Air Base, resulting in catastrophic damage and massive casualties. Three European Federation Dassault attack aircraft were observed by radar violating Swedish airspace and were subsequently ordered to retreat. Swedish aircraft were sortied to provide escort out of our sovereign airspace. The European Federation jets responded to our instructions with aggressive maneuvers, endangering our aircraft. Subsequent to the encounter, one of the Federation jets fired its ordnance at Swedish soil. The nature of the ordnance is unknown at this time and is under investigation. Early battle damage estimates confirm enormous destructive power and suggest the ordnance was not conventional. One of the Federation jets was shot down by air-to-air missile, and our forces are in the process of recovering the wreckage. The Government will hold a press conference once more details of the attack are known.

The Kingdom of Sweden was at peace with the European Federation and is unaware of any conceivable motive for the attack. A full diplomatic response is being prepared, including invoking the NATO charter and pursuing diplomatic action at the United Nations. Swedish forces are on high aler,t and any additional violation of Swedish airspace will be met with the full sound and fury of our defense forces.

"I just read the words, but I still can't process what I am reading!" Barber exclaimed. "What on Earth could be their motive? And what's this about it being a 'non-conventional' weapon?"

"I have no idea," Day responded. "The EuroFed attacking Sweden is about the stupidest and most nonsensical thing I have ever heard."

Office of the Chancellor, European Federation HQ, Berlin

"What the hell happened?" Chancellor Krüger, standing behind his desk, literally screamed at Generals Brandt and Laurent as they walked into his office. "They shot down one of our aircraft? And they are recovering the wreckage?"

"We did not anticipate them scrambling jets in response to our incursion. It was the first time they have responded with such an aggressive move," General Brandt replied. "We are certain their rules of engagement would have required confirmation from their national command authority prior to firing on our jets, and we are equally certain it would not have been possible to obtain such confirmation by the time their aircraft attacked our jets. One of the Swedish pilots must have shown unexpected initiative."

"Unexpected initiative?" the Chancellor barked. "You have mastered the understatement, General. And by spreading our aircraft's wreckage all over Swedish soil we likely have handed them the technology of our weapon, and soon thereafter the British and the Americans. A little reverse engineering and we will be facing a wrath of our own making."

"No, sir," General Laurent responded this time. "The weapon system was encased in a number of magnesium flares designed to ignite on any sudden impact, either from air-to-air missile or a ground crash. The weapon system will be nothing more than a pile of unrecognizable melted metal when it's recovered."

The Chancellor stared at Brandt for several seconds before saying, "Good. One thing is proving to be fairly certain. Your instincts, General Laurent, about the potential for diplomatic blowback I believe will prove well-founded. I suspect we are about to face a shitstorm beyond our worst fears. In the meantime, keep our forces on high alert but well within the European Federation borders. I don't want to give anyone an excuse for escalating this," the Chancellor ordered.

"Yes, sir," General Brandt responded.

Capital Building, Office of the Speaker of the House, Washington, D.C.

Dominick Bastionelli, Speaker of the House of Representative and Congressional Representative from New Jersey's 9th Congressional district, sat in his ceremonial office inside the Speaker's Suite, 1233 Longworth Congressional Office Building, at the Nation's Capital. The son of second-generation Italian immigrants, his grandparents had arrived in New York City in 1949 from the city of Brindisi on Italy's east coast. Raised in Bensonhurst, Brooklyn, young Dominick learned his survival skills on the mean streets of his neighborhood. Tall but wiry, he developed a quick temper that often got him in trouble with his contemporaries. He never shied away from confrontation and displayed an out-sized tenacity once engaged. He became an excellent scrapper, mostly from getting a lot of experience at it, and soon garnered the nickname, "the PitBull". He never let a verbal insult go, and he never conceded a fight. Once he clamped on, he wouldn't let go until either he or his opponent was on the ground and bleeding. His father was a proud man, especially of his immigration documents, or "papers" as he called them. He would tell young Dominick, "Don't ever let anyone call you a WOP," an ethnic slur common on the streets of New York, which means "without papers". "Cuz I got papers!" his father would proudly announce. One day after school, a classmate called him a "WOP". Dominick decked him.

Once Dominick hit his early teens, his parents were worried about him becoming involved with the local gangs, so they moved the family to Northeast New Jersey into a community where fighting skills weren't so highly prized. His parents, like all parents, wanted a better life for him, and Dominick had another attribute that could help make a better life a reality – he was highly intelligent. His aptitude scores at school constantly placed him towards the top of his class. Collage at Rutgers on a wrestling scholarship, then law school at NYU, including law review his third year, confirmed his parent's assessment.

After graduation, he worked in the State Prosecutors office, then as a congressional aid, then ultimately as the Chief of Staff for the Congressman for New Jersey 9th District. When his boss decided to retire, he was the logical choice as a successor, and he ran unopposed. He proved to be a consummate politician, and the experience of his youth made him a highly successful infighter in the cutthroat world of Congressional politics. He quickly rose through the ranks of House Leadership, instilling discipline in a diverse and bickering caucus, admiration in his friends, and fear in his enemies. So here he sat, Speaker of the House of Representatives, still harboring ambitions yet to be fulfilled.

Bastionelli was a staunch critic of the new European Federation and saw it as a real threat to global stability. He was leading the House movement to impose a new and more restrictive round of sanctions on the EF, and he saw the attack on Sweden as a confirmation of his judgement. The Speaker was stunned, and furious, when President Einhorn had reneged on their agreement and at the last minute stopped the new round of sanctions being led by the U.S. and England. He sat in his office with the Chairman of the House Foreign Affairs Committee and his Chief of Staff and waited for his secretary to place the call to the President of the United States.

"I have the White House on the line, Mr. Speaker," his secretary announced.

"Thanks," he responded, then after hearing a click said, "Good morning, Madam President. Shocking news, this morning!" he exclaimed. "Have you talked to the Swedish Prime Minister yet?"

"Good morning, Dom, and no, I have not. They are a bit busy now. Her office tells me she will return my call as soon as they finish with their press conference. I understand they are still struggling to understand the facts."

"Has she talked to Chancellor Krüger? Have you?"

"No to both questions. Krüger is not returning calls at the moment either."

"What about back channels, Madam President?" Bastionelli asked with growing irritation. "Has SecState or SecDef reached out," he asked, using the shorthand titles for the American Secretary of State and Secretary of Defense. "Have they talked to their counterparts?"

"No. I directed both of them to reach out, but their phone calls are not being returned either. Our ambassador in Berlin talked to several people in their Foreign Ministry and they claimed to be completely in the dark. He said they sounded genuinely upset and that he believed them. We are dealing with a real information vacuum at the moment."

"Do you think that is because this was some kind of an accident, or some rogue operation Krüger wasn't aware of?" The Speaker asked.

"I doubt very much the first," the President responded, "and I sure as hell hope it's the second. I'm afraid that's about our best-case scenario for now. The whole thing just doesn't make sense."

"Agreed. Madam President. It is absolutely essential that we elevate the sanctions and do so as quickly as possible. The Western alliance must show a quick and unequivocal response. Have you talked to Prime Minister Boren?" he asked, referring to the English Prime Minister.

"No, but he has a call into me. I haven't had the chance to return it yet."

"I am confident the PM will recommend the same. Frankly we are all a bit confused by your recent reluctance to act. It is essential that we act now," the Speaker said.

"I understand the sentiment, Dom, but I am reluctant to act until we have a better sense of the facts," the President responded. "I am not going to be pushed into something premature, so don't go there. You won't like my response," she said, clearly implying a threat.

Bastionelli couldn't believe what he was hearing. The woman had come to power with a reputation of being decisive and lethal, metaphorically, to anyone who crossed her. Yet now she seemed seized with indecision and reluctant to act. He took a deep breath to quell his rising anger, then responded, "Our view here on the Hill remains that we have to do something immediately, even if we aren't agreed on the entire package. Frankly, I don't see any set of facts here that would not require action. Also, in light of current events I don't believe our previous plans go far enough. They aren't sufficiently punitive given this attack. An immediate response would demonstrate resolve. It doesn't have to be the whole smash. We could announce something and say we are in the process of drafting additional measures, but we must announce something, and we must announce it today. You are going to have a real problem with your own party's caucus if you don't act," the Speaker said, figuring it was now his turn to lay down a threat.

President Einhorn kept thinking about her recent conversations about the sanctions with Emma Clark. She agreed with the Speaker completely, but all she could do was think about the headaches and the threats from Clark. Surely that crazy woman, whatever her motive, would see the obvious need to act considering what had just happened. Here she was, the President of the United States, sitting in the Oval Office, yet fearful for her life if she didn't consult with Clark before doing something that clearly needed to be done. And she couldn't tell a single soul about her predicament. Anyone hearing her story would think she was crazy. Her thoughts were interrupted by the sound of Bastionelli's voice again.

"Madam President, are you still there?"

"Yes, sorry, I was thinking. I understand your perspective. I am inclined to agree, but I am not prepared to do anything until we have a better understanding of the facts. Waiting twenty-four hours won't make a difference."

"Are you going to hold a news conference on this?" the Speaker asked.

"Yes, of course, but not until after we have a clearer picture and I get a few phone calls returned. My best guess is mid-to-late afternoon."

"You know that you are going to be asked about a response," the Speaker replied.

"I know, and I hope I will have a better idea of what it should be once we know what actually happened."

"OK, Madam President, it's obviously your call, but I think you are making a mistake on this. Everyone will be looking for a swift and decisive action."

"Acknowledged, Dominick, but you have my decision. I will call you later today. Right now, I need to go; as you can imagine I've got a bit to do."

"Thank you, Madam President, and good luck," and with that, the Speaker of the House pushed a button and disconnected the call.

The three men sitting in the Speakers office looked at each other in disbelief. "I don't understand her reaction," his Chief of Staff responded.

"Neither do I," said the Chairman of the House Foreign Affairs Committee.

"I'd swear that woman's either getting senile or somebody has dirt on her," the Speaker responded. "That's not the Sarah Einhorn I know."

"It most certainly is not," his Chief of Staff replied.

"Ok, here's what we are going to do," Bastionelli announced. "I want you..........," he paused mid-sentence. "Oh," he uttered, almost as if he were crying out in pain. His eyes shifted from the Committee Chairman back to his Chief of Staff. He cocked his head slightly to the left, then his eyes seem to go blank, expressionless. His right cheek started to twitch, then his eyes rolled back into his head.

"Boss?" His Chief of Staff said. "Mr. Speaker, are you ok?"

Bastionelli didn't respond. Instead his head started to wobble a bit as the two men noticed a small amount of spittle drool out of the corner of his mouth. His head fell forward on the desk with a loud "crack" as he let out a faint guttural sound.

The Speaker of the House was dead.

Chapter 27 – Existential Fear, Redux

Oval Office, The White House, Washington D.C.

President Einhorn's thoughts were interrupted by the voice of her secretary. "Madam President, Prime Minister Boren is on the line."

"Jeremy, what a mess!" she exclaimed. "What do you know? Nobody senior in the EF is returning our phone calls right now. We've only had some mid-level conversations with their Foreign Ministry and those people seem to be as much in the dark as we are."

"They are not returning my phone calls either, Madam President, although I did manage to talk to the PM of Sweden. Evidently, they are getting a better picture of the damage, but they have no clue as to the motive. As of yet, the PM has not spoken to Krüger. She tells me the damage to Ronneby Air Base is massive. It wasn't a small tactical nuke because there was no radiation signature. But the damage is way beyond conventional ordnance. I am told it appears to be on the level with a fuel air bomb, actually several fuel air bombs, but those things are massively heavy and could not possibly have been delivered by fighter aircraft."

"How did it play out?"

"Apparently there have been numerous incursions into their airspace recently EuroFed fighter jets, likely on missions to test their coastal radar capabilities."

"Why on Earth would the EF want to do that? It's not exactly like they were enemies, at least not before this morning."

"Sweden's theory is the EF has developed some kind of new threat detection radar and were testing it. Better to test against the Swedes than the Russians, so to speak."

"Agree with that!" the President exclaimed, "But it's still highly provocative."

"Agreed. The previous incursions were considered a diplomatic nuisance and more than a bit arrogant, but otherwise not particularly threatening. They would paint the EF aircraft with their missile defense radar, the jets would bug out. Diplomatic complaints would be filed, then everyone would get on with their lives, as you say."

"So, what happened?"

"Started off the same as the other incursions, but when the EF jets refused to turn back after being painted, the Swedes sortied several interceptors to escort them out. Sounded like they were getting a bit fed up and wanted to demonstrate a bit more resolve. The EF jets maneuvered aggressively with the Swedes, continued deeper into Swedish airspace than before, and when they turned around, one of them fired on the Air Base. She is at a complete loss as to motive, and frankly so am I."

"Yeah, me too, Jeremy. We need to get through to Krüger before we're going to have much of a chance of solving this puzzle," the President said.

"Agreed," the Prime Minister responded. "But one thing is absolutely certain, Madam President, going back to our recent conversation. We must announce a new round of sanctions against the EF, and we must do so by the end of the day. We must announce something, at least as a start. I would like your permission to put our Chancellor of the Exchequer in touch with your Secretary of the Treasury to work out the details."

"I'm fine with them drafting something, but I don't want to announce until we have a better sense of the overall picture."

"Sarah, I believe we are very likely to have that before the end of the day, but regardless, I believe we must demonstrate swift and decisive action."

"Let's have our people talk and circle back with each other later in the day," she said to buy herself time. "I will need to consult with Congress, of course, before doing anything."

"I understand. Let's talk once our lads have a draft of something. Hopefully by then we will have talked to Herr Krüger and better understand why the hell he decided to bugger things up."

"Sounds good, Jeremy. Talk to you later." With that, she hung up.

Einhorn was becoming increasingly uncomfortable from the pressure to act, not knowing what the implications were for her personal safety. Just then she was struck by a another one of the blinding headaches. She closed her eyes tightly, placed her head in her hands and summoned every bit of self-control she had to keep from crying out in pain, fearing it would bring several aides running into the Oval Office to see what was wrong. She didn't want anyone to see her in this condition and question her ability to carry out her duties. Then just as quickly as the headache appeared, it vanished.

Then, almost as if on cue, her private cell phone vibrated. She retrieved it from her jacket pocket, looked at the screen and immediately recognized the number.

"Madam President. Good morning. How are you feeling?" The voice was Dr. Emma Clark's.

"You insufferable bitch," she retorted in a whisper. "You don't need to put my head in a vise to announce a phone call."

"Of course not, Madam President, but I suspect my little calling card provides a bit of extra motivation to be attentive."

"What do you know about what happened in Sweden?" The President demanded.

"Actually, probably not as much as you do. The EF is an important client of ours, but they do not consult us on their foreign policy."

"I'm sure you realize I am under enormous pressure to impose even more onerous sanctions on your 'client state', as you call them. Given what just happened, I have no conceivable excuse not to do so."

"Precisely the reason for my call. Under no circumstances are you to agree to additional sanctions at this time. I believe with a little patience, things are going to work out quite nicely."

"I just got off the phone with the Prime Minister of England!" the President exclaimed. "He is insisting on announcing additional sanctions by the end of the day! I'm going to have to hold a press conference of some sort and every member of the press is going to push me on that subject as well! I'm going to look like a doddering fool if I don't rattle a sanction saber or two!"

"You are the leader of the free world, Madam President. You can hold the Prime Minister of England at bay. As for the press, it's simply a 'no comment at this time'"

"It's not that simple!" She almost shouted, then lowered her voice to avoid being heard. "My previous conversation was with the Speaker of the House. I know you know the man. You've held fund raisers for him. They call him the 'Pit Bull'. The entire caucus, my party's caucus, is also insisting on new sanctions and I can't just put them off without appearing as though I've been bought!"

"Yes, you can," Clark said calmly.

"Why is this so important to you?" The President asked.

"My reasons are not your concern, and you are being too dramatic. It's time to think with our minds and not with our glands, Madam President. Cooler heads and all that, right? I can also assure you the Speaker will be no problem, and I can also assure you the Congress will have their attention diverted to something more important for a while."

"What are you talking about?" The President asked.

"Just trust me, and remember, under no circumstances are there to be additional sanctions. You have the authority to prevent it, and I expect you to use whatever authority is necessary."

"You're crazy!" The President shouted.

"Goodbye, Sarah. And good luck. You are going to have a very busy day."

With that, the line went dead. Sarah Einhorn, President of the United States, couldn't believe the nightmare she found herself in. The nightmare was about to get worse. Her secretary buzzed her again.

"Yes?" She queried.

"Your Director of Legislative Affairs is here to see you. He says it's extremely urgent."

She stood as the man entered the Oval Office, obviously out of breath from running. He had a look of extreme concern across his face. Sara Einhorn's heart felt like it was beating out of her chest. She was terrified at what the man was about to say.

"Madam President, I'm so sorry. The Speaker of the House is dead."

She stood in front of him now with her mouth gaping open. "How?" she asked, her voice starting to break.

"We don't have the medical examiner's report yet, but all signs point to a stroke."

"When?" She asked.

"Within the last 20 minutes."

She placed her hand, trembling now, over her mouth. As her knees began to buckle, she braced herself with the other arm against the top of the Resolute Desk checking her near collapse. Her eyes welled with tears. "Oh my God," she cried, as her lower lip quivered uncontrollably. But she wasn't grieving for the Speaker; she couldn't have cared less about Dominick Bastionelli. She was grieving for herself, and she had never been so frightened in her life.

Chapter 28 – An Interesting Twist

PrinSafe HQ, Palo Alto, California

Emma Clark was in a really good mood. "Westy would be proud," she thought, referring to her one-time mentor and former boss. In three short years at the helm of PrinSafe, she acquired power Westy had only been able to dream of. She was likely the only person on Earth who could order the President of the United States to do something, or in this case, not to do something: not recommend it, not even demand it, as politicians usually bristle at demands and ignore them, but actually order it, as if she were a Drill Sergeant scaring a new recruit to death over the consequences of disobedience. It was heady stuff, even for her uber-disciplined mind. It almost made her high, like a rush of endorphin after a long run.

She was brought down from the high by the ring of a very special phone. It was one of the most secure communication lines in the world. The signal was masked by an encryption algorithm better than anything possessed by the NSA, or National Security Agency. Calls to and from the phone went through so many different and obscure connections, changed daily, that its provenance was impossible to establish. There wasn't a nation on Earth that could trace it. Additionally, voices on both ends were digitally altered and rendered impossible to identify, even with state-of-the-art voice recognition software. And she loved the fact that the phone was hiding in plain sight, as a very ordinary looking device sitting on her desk just to the right of her laptop. Only her most important calls, requiring absolute confidentiality, were conducted over that line.

She lifted the receiver and simply said, "Hello." She knew who the caller would be. She was expecting the call.

"Good morning, Dr. Clark," the altered voice on the other end of the line said. "I trust things are well."

"Good morning. They are very well. I have firewalled any additional sanctions for the time being. I suspect those firewalls will remain in place for at least a week or two. Our German affiliate will continue to provide you with the code you need during that time, but I suggest you proceed with all deliberate speed. Even I can't delay sanctions indefinitely."

"That window should be more than sufficient. Recent events have been fortuitous, providing very useful distractions, as you would say. We expect to move forward within the week."

"Excellent," Clark said.

"Per our agreement, we have wired five hundred million U.S. dollars to the account you specified, the same one as before."

"Excellent. Thank you."

"Thank you, Dr. Clark."

"Here's to a growing and mutually beneficial relationship, my friend," she said.

There was a long pause on the other end of the line, as if the caller was doing it for effect. The man finally began to speak, and even through the digitally altered voice Clark could make out a distinct change in his tone: "You are not my friend, Dr. Clark. But you are, of course, a most useful acquaintance. My hope is that you will remain so. It is certainly in your interest. Let us not delude ourselves, however. While I find liaisons such as ours to be necessary, I also find them frankly distasteful. I am most confident you do as well. Our relationship is based on mutual interests, not mutual values, and it is certainly not based on friendship."

She paused a couple of seconds herself, not for drama, but trying to process what she had just heard. She was momentarily stunned, but then she spoke: "As you wish," Clark said.

"It is as I wish, and as it is meant to be. We are useful to each other so long as we are useful to each other. You have been very useful to us, and for that you have our money and our gratitude. I hope things remain as such. Those who are not useful to us receive our wrath instead. Good day," the voice replied, then the line went dead.

Emma Clark paused again for a moment, then reached across her desk and placed the phone back into its cradle. She turned her chair around and stared out the window as she thought about the five hundred million dollars, and her mood improved. She then thought about the way the conversation had ended. It was odd. No, it was much more than just odd. The man was cold, clinical, and almost disrespectful. Did he actually threaten her, she wondered? She was not used to that. As she thought about his parting comment, the good mood was replaced with a slight flash of anger. She was not used to being talked to that way, and realized her anger was a confirmation that her motivation in almost everything was not money, but power. She had just wielded it against the President, to her great satisfaction. But she sensed it had just been wielded against her, at least in some small way. Or was it really in such a small way? After thinking a few more seconds, her anger was replaced by another emotion, one that was mostly foreign to her. Emma Clark felt fear.

Chapter 29 – A Change of Plans

Hotel Adlon Kempinski, Berlin

The ride from the airport to the Hotel Adlon was uneventful, except for the weather. Severe thunderstorms rolled in about 20 minutes after the Gulfstream landed, and the drive along the motorway was punctuated with dramatic displays of lightning and explosions of thunder so intense they could feel the Mercedes shake. Traffic was moving at a crawl, as rain was pounding the windshield so hard it was difficult to see.

"I'll be happy to get out of this mess," said the driver, the man who had been the Gulfstream's flight attendant and now served as Barber's driver/bodyguard.

"So will I," Barber replied from the front seat. "This feels like a northern Virginia thunderstorm. I didn't think Germany had storms this bad."

"You guys are a couple of wusses," the pilot joked from the back seat. "Try flying through this on climb out."

"Yeah, but we're not blowing through this at 200 knots and this Benz doesn't have an autopilot," the driver retorted. "And you don't have traffic just a few feet from you in all directions."

"Stop your whining," the pilot joked again. "It's just a little rain, boys."

"We must be getting close," Barber commented, trying to change the conversation from the miserable weather.

"Nav says we're about ten minutes from the hotel now, but at this crawl I'm not so sure," the driver related.

"Just try and get us there in one piece," Barber replied, then winced in pain as he shifted his position in the front seat.

"You still look miserable, boss," the driver stated as he noticed Barber's expression. "You take anything more for pain?"

"I popped four Advil before we deplaned. What I need is the Vicodin and Scotch, but I'd like to have a clear head for a while. We've got a lot to do when we get to the hotel."

"Marc has some sandwiches and beer waiting for us in his room," the driver replied.

"Good, I'm starving," Barber said

The storm was starting to break as they pulled up to the hotel. The driver handed the valet the keys to the Mercedes, the three men exited the vehicle, entered the lobby and walked towards the elevator that would take them up five floors to Marcus Day's room.

Day had his room door open and was standing in the hall as the three men emerged from the elevator. "This way, lads," he said in a mock English accent. "You look terrible, Joe, but then again you never looked that good in the first place," he joked.

"Thanks for the encouragement," Barber replied. "I needed that."

"Always here to give you my best," Day said. "Come on in and get something to eat."

All four men filled their plates with inch-thick corned-beef sandwiches and helped themselves to Weihenstephen Hefe Weissbier, a popular Bavarian wheat beer, then took seats on the hotel room's sofa and chairs. Day sat on the side of the bed.

"Where are we, Marc?" Barber asked, to start the conversation.

"While you guys were in route I managed to get us a meeting at 3 o'clock with Zimmerman at Stenenlicht."

"That's great. Have you talked to him since I left for the States?" Barber asked.

"No. I tried several times, but he didn't return my calls," Day replied.

"How did you manage to get a meeting?" Barber questioned.

"Last time I called, which was earlier this morning, I asked his secretary to give him a message. I told her it was very important, and that he was expecting it. The 'expecting' part, of course, wasn't true, but I figured it would increase the odds she would actually deliver it. I told her to tell him, 'it's the code', and said he would understand what it meant," Day said.

"Good work."

"The attack on Sweden changes everything," Barber said. "The Administration and Congress are going to have the European Federation in their cross-hairs. That presents us with two big problems. First, I don't think our own government is going to look too kindly on an American security firm continuing to do business with the EF. In fact, I think it's likely that there is a very short window before Orion falls under a new round of sanctions and we are forbidden to even be here. Second, the EF is going to be angry about the sanctions and whatever modest level of trust we enjoyed here is going to disappear like a vapor in the wind. They might kick us out before our own government orders us home."

"Exactly," Day responded. "This business with Sweden must be the only thing anyone who is anybody is working on right now. Schiller's death just became number 687 on their list of 686 priorities."

"Agreed," Barber said.

"So, what's our objective, then?" Day asked. "Why are we still here? We've certainly solved Schiller's murder, at least to our satisfaction. And given the circumstances, we've vindicated our firm; there was no way anyone could have prevented the kind of assassination the Iranian's managed to pull off. What we're left with now is a possibility the EF has a security breach on their command and control system. That's unfortunate, and maybe even destabilizing, but how is it our problem?"

"That's the right question," Barber responded, "And I agree, but we have to think bigger than that."

"How so?" Day asked, believing he already knew the answer.

"Let's start by discussing where we are on the facts," Barber said.

"OK," Day responded.

"Given Iran's involvement in this," Barber continued, "and especially the involvement of their cyber warfare group, I think there's way more than just a possibility of a breach: I believe the odds are overwhelming that the EF's command and control systems have in fact been compromised. This might even explain what happened in Sweden."

"So, you believe that attack could have been a rogue operation of some sort?" Day asked.

"I'm certainly hoping so, and I'm sure there are a lot of people here who are hoping so as well. It's the least bad in a list of very bad explanations," Barber said.

"Agreed," Day responded, "but I'm a skeptic. You haven't read all the morning's press yet. I'm convinced what happened over Sweden was deliberate. If not, they're doing one hell of a cover up job, and what would be their motive for that? You've also got the fact that the EuroFeds are not denying the attack, which makes you theory about Iranian involvement unlikely."

"Look, we're getting off track," Barber said. "Whether the attack on Sweden was rogue or deliberate isn't the point. It's much bigger than that. I'm afraid whatever the Iranians are up to is just getting started, and I'll concede the evidence for their involvement in the Swedish attack is thin. My point is this is way beyond us vindicating Orion over our lost protectee, or even getting back at the bastards going after me and my family. I'm afraid those nutcases in Iran may be planning something dramatic, even possibly an attack of some sort."

"Ok, so again I ask, what's the plan? What do you want to do?"

"Two things. First, at a minimum, I think we need to float this theory with Zimmerman and try and get him to take it seriously."

"I agree, Joe, but you know the evidence is thin."

"That's why we need to be completely candid with this guy and tell him everything. Remember Zimmerman doesn't know yet it was the Iranians who killed Schiller. The fact that the Iranian military is involved is going to get his attention. I know our evidence is circumstantial, but it's pretty bloody dramatic circumstantial – my being renditioned to the Iranian embassy in Berlin, Farhang's murder, the attempted murder of my family, and a solid connection to their cyber warfare group. It's not a smoking gun for a compromised defense system, but it's a jigsaw puzzle with a lot of pretty tightly fitting pieces, enough to see the picture."

"Tell him everything?" Day asked, sounding a bit skeptical.

"Yes, absolutely everything. I'm talking the whole smash."

"Do you have any ideas of how many German laws we have broken in the last several days? I have no desire to spend the rest of my life in a German prison, and I'm sure neither do you. What's to stop Zimmerman from taking everything we say to the authorities?" Day asked.

"His company's reputation," Barber answered. "If he goes to law enforcement or the military with the suspicion of a security problem but doesn't know exactly what it is and doesn't have a fix, he and Sternenlicht are finished. If he goes with a problem and a solution, he's a hero. We're going to help him find the truth, and if our suspicions are correct and they've been compromised, we'll have Lauren and her team work their magic build a patch. German senior executives are, if nothing else, survivors.""

"What if the guy thinks we're full of it, or panics?" Day asked.

"John," Barber said, turning to John Cunningham, the Orion Bellicus pilot, "I want you to have a charter jet standing by to get both of us out of Dodge quickly if that happens. Rent it with your alias passport so it won't be traceable to us. If we try and use the Gulfstream, they'll never let us off the ground, and even if we somehow manage to get into the air, we'd be escorted back to Berlin by a couple of Mirage's."

"That works," Day said. "It's still a big risk, but that's a reasonable plan."

"What if, after spilling our guts, the guy is still a skeptic?" Cunningham asked.

"Good question, but I don't see how he can be," Barber responded. "We have proof it's Iran, we have proof it's their cyber warfare group, we know Iran's behaved badly, and he certainly knows that Schiller was the architect of their command and control system and knew it better than anyone. I think the conclusion is indisputable."

"I just had a very chilling thought," Day said.

Both men sat there and locked eyes silently for several seconds as they each contemplated the same possibility.

"You and I are on the same wavelength, pal," Barber finally responded.

"I don't think believing we're lying is the real risk," Day said. "I think the real risk is he already knows we are telling the truth."

"The risk is that Zimmerman himself is somehow personally involved."

"Exactly," replied Day.

"Think about it," Barber asked. "For the Iranians to be on to Schiller, somebody must have told them."

"Right," Day responded, "and for that to be true, Schiller would have to have shared his concerns with whomever that person is."

"Right," Barber said, "and there's no way that Schiller would have shared his suspicions with some mid-level employee. He would have shared it with someone very senior," Barber replied.

"Like Zimmerman," Day said.

"Exactly. Like Zimmerman."

"I agree that Zimmerman is the most likely, but he wouldn't be the only person in the company to fit that bill," Day observed.

"I agree," Barber replied. "I'm hoping his reaction to what we tell him gives us some insight on that. In case it doesn't, I think I have an idea on how to make it a little more definitive."

"I'm listening," Day responded.

"We tell him we think there is a mole in his company, somebody who has been working with the Iranians for some time now, and we tell him we have a pretty good idea of who the mole is."

"But we pretend we think it's somebody else, and not him," Day said.

"Precisely. If the mole is Zimmerman, his only conceivable motive would be money. If he's dirty, I think he'll run."

"I think you're right," Day said.

"I called Lauren during the flight here and asked her to hack into his wealth management account at Deutsche Bank and see if there is anything that looks suspicious. She said she'd get to it as soon as she finished the digital fingerprint analysis. I expect an answer shortly, hopefully before we go see the guy."

"That would be very helpful."

"There's one more thing, Marc. I have to take this to Maggie," Barber said, referring to Dr. Margaret Schevenko, his former mentor and present Director of the C.I.A.

"C.I.A.?" Day asked, .

"Yes."

"I know you trust her like your mother or your older sister, whatever; but you realize that is going to take things to a whole new level, right?" Day asked. "She's not going to sit on it. She can't."

"Yes, I understand that," Barber responded, "and I don't want her to. That's the whole point of telling her."

"Why?" Day asked.

"She's the only one I trust to navigate this through the system without serving some political motive," Barber responded. "And she's in the best position to figure out the threat. If we take it to someone else, it will eventually find its way to her anyway. Besides, she's the most senior person in government service I have a direct line to; I think that personal connection is critical. Otherwise there's too big a risk it will just be ignored."

"I think that makes great sense," Day said.

"I'm going to have John here fly me back to D.C., provided the German authorities aren't on our tales, and I'm going to tell her everything in person. The trip will give me a little more time to heal. You still have the best tactical awareness here on the ground so I'm going to leave you in charge again."

"Roger that. I assume we are going to keep the Germans in the dark about our intention to brief C.I.A.?" Day asked.

"Absolutely!" Barber exclaimed.

The conversation was interrupted by a buzz on Barber's cell phone. He winced again in pain as he stretched to the side to get access to his jeans pocket, retrieved the bulky iPhone, watched it unlock in recognition of his face, and placed it to his ear.

"Hey, Lauren. Did you find out anything?

"Yes, I did." Dr. Lauren Cartwright responded.

"Let me put you on speaker," Joe said. He touched the speaker icon, then laid the phone on the arm of his hotel chair. "Go ahead."

"This is interesting. First, there was nothing unusual about Zimmerman's account at Deutsche Bank. He has a little less than a couple million euros in it, which isn't out of line for a senior executive like him."

"I agree," Barber replied."

"However, I thought about another angle. We still have a back door to the NSA's big data archives from that episode of three years ago with the crazies who were running the domestic spying program." She was referring to the now defunct rogue organization, formally embedded in the National Security Agency, that Orion Bellicus had uncovered. "Anyway, we did a search on calls from Zimmerman's personal cell phone. Long story short, after running a giga-bite of phone calls through our evaluation software, we uncovered 17 incidences of him entering the same 17-digit sequence of numbers into this phone over the last three years. That's too long of a sequence to be a phone number, so I guessed a bank account, like in a 'numbered' bank account, like in a numbered 'Swiss bank account."

"Brilliant," Barber responded.

"Anyway," she continued, "I'll spare you the hacker mumbo-jumbo, but we managed to trace the account back to the United Bank of Switzerland and determined there is a 47 million euro balance in the account."

"Wow. That's no small chunk of change. Obviously, a payoff," Barber said. "No German exec below a CEO would have that kind of wealth, and there would be no reason to keep that much in a numbered Swiss account unless he was hiding something."

"Exactly," Dr. Lauren Cartwright replied.

"Can you tell where it came from?" Barber asked.

"Yes, but it's complicated. It appears as though the funds travelled a long and winding road, and we worked hard to trace it backwards. Wire transfers were made to the account in odd amounts, down to a fraction of a euro, through about a dozen banks in Europe and Asia. Those transfers originated from a consolidated account in Singapore, which in turn were funded by banks in South Africa and Zimbabwe, both of which appeared to have taken a 10% cut. The transfers from the African banks were funded by banks in Hong Kong, North Korea, and get this, the Ukraine. Those transfers were funded from two banks in Iran: Bank Saderat and Bank Melli. Both Iranian banks are on the sanctions list. And this is the most interesting part: A recent, major source of the Iranian banks' cash came from the funds that were unfrozen after the Joint Comprehensive Plan of Action was signed."

"The Iranian nuclear deal," Barber observed.

"Exactly," Cartwright replied. "So, in short, we unfreeze Iran's funds which wind up in the two Iranian banks, and a small chunk travels from Iran to Asia, from Asia to Africa, from Africa to Singapore, from Singapore to a dozen highly respectable banks in Europe and Asia, and from them to the United Bank of Switzerland into a confidential numbered account controlled by one Hans-Dieter Zimmerman. Voila!"

"You're a genius, Lauren!" Barber exclaimed.

"Yes, of course I am," she said.

"And insufferable," Barber replied, "but most definitely worth it."

"Yes, I am, and yes I am. Now if we can table this delightful repartee for a second, there are a couple of important points I still need to make."

"Go ahead," Barber said.

"This was a very sophisticated piece of money laundering. That's the first point. Second, the Iranian's couldn't have done it without help."

"I was wondering about that," Barber responded. "Why the need for help?"

"They're certainly smart enough to come up with a plan like this, but they could never have gotten the cooperation needed from most of those banks. They had to have somebody, or some organization, that on the surface appeared clean to help facilitate it."

"Any idea who?" Day asked.

"No earthly idea, but we could keep pushing, especially on the last couple of rounds of transfers and see if we could figure out the senders. Just so you know, that's a lot more difficult than it sounds, but with enough time I'm sure we could at least gain a hint or two."

"Do it," Barber replied.

"Roger that, boss. Now if you boys will excuse me, I have some more work to do. Good luck."

"Before you go, send a copy of the paper trail to our encrypted message board," Barber said.

"Will do, boss. Be careful out there, boys."

"Thanks, Lauren. And good work. Really good work." With that, Barber closed the call.

"So, our objectives for the day obviously have just changed," Day observed.

"You got that right," Barber replied. "A change of plans. Cancel the meeting with Zimmerman. I've got to get on a plane and see Maggie, and we've got to get this intel to someone in the EF, but it can't be Zimmerman."

"Nope," Day responded. "But it just so happens that I know a certain French General."

Chapter 30 – The Briefing

House of Leadership, Military Office of the Supreme Leader, Tehran

Ayatollah Ashtiana sat on a cushion with crossed legs as the senior government officials entered the room. Major General Muhammad Bagheri, Commander of the Iranian General Staff and the nominal head of the Iranian military, sat immediately to the Supreme Leader's right in recognition of his status, but nobody in the room was under any illusion that Bagheri was the one in charge. Brigadier General Gashasp Hamidi, Commander of the Iranian Revolutionary Guard Corps, took a place immediately to the Supreme Leader's left. On paper Hamidi was one of General Bagheri's direct reports, but Hamidi was the one doing the briefing today, and Project "Allah's Sword" was his creation. As Hamidi contemplated the brief he was about to deliver, he reflected on the binary nature of his fate; the success or failure of the Project would either put him solidly in the seat to the right of the Supreme Leader, or otherwise result in his death before one of General Bagheri's firing squads. Hamidi was the master of his brief and knew how to deal with adversaries; one did not rise to the head of the Revolutionary Guard Corps without being ruthless and skilled in the quick dispatch of one's enemies, domestic or foreign. But he was still a man who knew fear. He had experienced it, somewhat to his surprise, during his last visit to the Supreme Leader. The man had threatened him. Even though Hamidi held the man in contempt and regarded his religious fanaticism as the product of a simple and narrow mind, an entire political infrastructure existed to ensure the will of the Supreme Leader was carried out ruthlessly, without hesitation or mercy. The cleric could make people disappear with a simple whisper and subject anyone he wished to imprisonment, torture or death. The decision of the Cleric suffered no recourse. His authority was absolute. So Hamidi, while not intimidated, was wary, and he would deliver the brief with great care.

Hamidi looked around the room and considered his audience. Sitting to the right of General Bagheri, one additional seat removed from the Supreme Leader, was the President of the Republic, Amin Agassi. The position of his seat, subordinate to General Bagheri's, was a clear symbol that Iran, while a Republic in name, was in truth ruled not by a civilian authority but by Oracle of Shia Islam, the Grand Ayatollah, and the military that kept the Revolution alive and the Ayatollah in power. Also present was Ahmad Moghadam, the Chief of the Supreme Court. It was an irony, Hamidi thought, as this meeting hardly would be guided by the rule of law, and the Supreme Court would have no say whatsoever in the matter. Akbar Rafsanjani, Chairman of the Expediency Discernment Counsel, sat next to Hamidi. Of all the people in the room, Hamidi mused, this man likely knew much of what Hamidi was about to say because of his role as a close advisor and confidant to the Supreme Leader.

The room was uncomfortably warm, as evidenced by Hamidi's observation that several of the men appeared to be sweating. In spite of the oppressive heat of a Tehran summer, the air conditioning was barely running, with the thermostat set to 29 degrees Celsius, or about 84 degrees Fahrenheit. The Grand Ayatollah, like most men his age who suffer from thinning blood and a variety of ailments, struggled to keep warm, and the comfort of others was rarely his concern. Hamidi liked the room hot. Decades of military service outdoors conditioned him to the heat, and he regarded the discomfort of others to be a tactical advantage.

As Hamidi waited for the Supreme Leader to begin the meeting, he quickly reflected on what he was about to say. His brief would be a major surprise to almost everyone in the room except the Supreme Leader himself. More significantly, it would be more audacious and consequential than anything they could have imagined. If successful, he was about to change the status quo ante forever and likely redraw national boundaries all over the Middle East and beyond. It would give Iran, Persia, the unquestionable right to unite Islam under a single Shia banner. And while in the midst of celebration, he would do everything in his power to dispatch the old man in flowing robes and take his place as the new leader of the Revolution. Not that he cared about the Revolution; it would simply be his banner. His lust was for power.

Hamidi's thoughts were interrupted as Ayatollah Ashtiana raised his hand as a symbol that he was about to speak. Hamidi remained calm in the knowledge that this meeting was a simple formality. There would be a variety of reactions to what he was about to present, and possibly strong objections, but the decision had already been made. The purpose of the meeting was not to ask for permission to deploy Allah's Sword; it was to inform those in the room of what was about to be done.

The Grand Ayatollah began to speak. "Welcome, my brothers. May Allah be praised; peace be upon him. I have asked you here to inform you of a glorious journey we are about to begin together. But before I begin I must first command from you a pledge of silence. Nothing you are about to hear today is to be discussed outside of this room, even among yourselves. The attainment of our glorious quest depends on absolute secrecy. Anyone who breaks the pledge will be regarded as guilty of apostasy and will be subject to the consequent punishment. Do any of you have a question or regard yourself as unable to be faithful to this pledge?"

There was absolute silence in the room. Nobody even dared clear their throat. Everyone knew the punishment for apostasy: it was death. And everyone understood that an inappropriate question or expression of reticence would quickly result in the same fate.

The Ayatollah spoke, "What I give you today is Allah's Sword," he said in a tone that was not the rousing voice of a master orator but was barely above a whisper. The quiet nature of his words was deliberate. It was a common technique of his and forced everyone in the room to direct a laser-like attention to what he was about to say. He continued: "It is a weapon that we will plunge into the bosom of our enemies, and it will light a flame of Islam that cannot be extinguished. Its success will forever be a testament that we, the Shia, are the true followers of the Prophet. It will settle for all time the apostasy of the Sunni, as Allah has shown His favor and bestowed this mighty weapon upon us, and not the Arab, and those whom the Arab has led down the path of darkness. Prepare the way for the 12th Imam as he prepares himself to be revealed. I will now ask General Hamidi to brief you on the glorious journey we are about to begin."

The room sat in stunned silence. What could possibly bring about what the Supreme Leader had just said? The 12th Imam? General Hamidi surveyed his audience again, looking into the eyes of each man. He saw a variety of emotions. Some suggested confusion, as though what was just said was too much to process. Many eyes remained stone-cold, not showing any emotion at all. Some showed anticipation, even excitement, and a few betrayed fear. Hamidi struggled to hold back a slight smile. The Supreme Leader had done a masterful job of setting the stage.

Hamidi began to speak. As he did so, he spoke in a business-like tone and demeaner. "Before I begin, I want to encourage you to ask questions. As the Imam has stated, this is not a debate, and we will not be making a decision today. The Imam has already made the decision on the matters I am about to reveal. But, it is important that each of you understand what is about to be done. If you seek clarification, we encourage you to ask. I assure you that any comment made in the form of a question will not be regarded as disrespectful. Are there any questions, so far?"

Nobody spoke. Most were trying to figure out whether the invitation to ask questions was sincere.

Hamidi continued, "Today I can tell you that Iran is a nuclear power." He then paused to let it sink in.

General Bagheri, Commander of the Iranian General Staff, suddenly sat more upright and snapped his head towards Hamidi. "How is this possible?" he asked, with an expression of utter astonishment. "Where did we get the fissionable materials? We have not enriched uranium to more than five percent, thanks to the sanctions. Where are the weapons stored? How is it possible that this could happen with such secrecy that even I was not aware of it?"

Hamidi smiled. "There are no nuclear weapons stored on Iranian soil, General, and we have not enriched uranium to weapons grade," he said, pausing to allow General Bagheri's confusion to further fester.

Bagheri managed to regain his composure as he commented in a more business-like voice, "Well. General Hamidi, I am sure we are all fascinated to hear your explanation."

"Thank you, General Bagheri. Now, allow me to explain. As you are all aware, Iran has been nurturing stronger commercial ties to the new European Federation, especially Germany. Parallel to this, there have been exchanges between our militaries under the guise of enticing the EF with the prospect of weapons sales and a role as mediator in the Islamic world. Such things would greatly enhance their prestige. As you know, these overtures are made under the guise of exploring best practices for military command and control systems with an objectives of reducing the risk of miscalculations and accidents. As part of this, we were introduced to the German firm, Sternenlicht, which is a computer engineering firm responsible for the design and deployment of the EFs command and control systems, including those used for their strategic weapons."

"By that, do you mean nuclear weapons?" the President of the Islamic Republic asked.

"Yes sir, the EF's nuclear weapons. The EF has three classes of nuclear weapons: high-yield warheads on long-range delivery systems with hypergolic propellants, liquid rocket fuels such as kerosene or hydrazine with liquid oxygen as an oxidizer; low to medium yield on short to intermediate-range delivery systems, often mobile, using solid propellants such as nitramine, and submarine-based medium to high yield weapons also delivered with solid fuel rockets. May I continue?"

"Yes, of course," the President said.

"Our conversations with Sternenlicht gave birth to an idea. What if, instead of devoting our resources to developing atomic weapons, we were simply to 'borrow' them from another country?" Hamidi asked. He paused again to allow the preposterous notion to sink in.

"And exactly what nation is to be so gracious as to loan us something virtually the entire world has been working tirelessly to deny us?" asked the President again, this time with a thinly-veiled sarcasm.

"Germany," he responded, then again waited for comment.

"That's preposterous. You're playing games," Bagheri said, growing impatient. "They would obviously never do that. What, exactly, are you talking about?"

"About 18 months ago we began a project in the Cyber Warfare Group to hack into the European Federation's command and control system. It has been wildly successful. We now have the capability to fire one of the EF's nuclear missiles at any target within its range, and they will have no idea what is happening until the rocket motor ignites."

There were audible gasps at this revelation.

"Any target we wish?" General Bagheri asked. "Isn't every one of those missiles pre-programed with a target package."

"Yes," Hamidi answered, "but we also have the capability to retarget the missile as if we were sitting in their command and control center ourselves."

"How was all of this done?" The President asked, with a tone of astonishment.

"We have a talented group of computer engineers in Cyber Warfare, but they kept running into roadblocks. We became aware of a young Iranian national, educated at the American MIT and Harvard Universities who was doing ground-breaking work in IT systems security, and we convinced him to help us."

"You convinced him to help you?" Bagheri asked incredulously. "And he came back to Iran just like that?"

"Well, General, we did provide him with some motivation," Hamidi said, smiling.

"What kind of motivation?" Bagheri asked.

"I threatened to kill his family if he didn't cooperate, so cooperate he did. His work was essential in breaking through their firewalls while remaining invisible. As some of you know, hacking into a system is not all that difficult, but hacking into a system without being detected, playing around inside the system and re-tasking it without being discovered, now that is the skill of geniuses, and this young man qualifies. We have attempted several times to measure his IQ and have been unable. He scores 100% on every test we give him."

"So, this computer engineer," Bagheri started to say, before being cut off by Hamidi.

"More accurately a mathematician," Hamidi corrected.

"This mathematician," Bagheri said, irritated at the interruption, "was the key to our breakthrough?"

"One of the keys, perhaps the most important key, but there were others."

"Who were the other key individuals, and if this mathematician is such a genius, why were they needed?" The President asked.

"The issue of retargeting the missiles proved even more daunting than hacking the system. It was not just a matter of manipulating code, the targeting data itself was encrypted. We had to break that encryption. Fortunately, I have a contact in the west who, for a fee, was willing to offer the services of the sub-contractor to Sternenlicht which wrote the encryption software."

"Who was that, and what is the sub-contractor's name?" General Bagheri demanded.

"The name of my contact is not important. The name of the company is CWR Industries."

"What did this cost us?" The President asked.

"Five Hundred Million Dollars to my contact, and about five million Euros to a senior executive in Sternenlicht to look the other way."

"That is a staggering amount of money," the President said, struggling to hold back anger.

"Yes it is, but it was a staggering task. And without the ability to retarget the missiles, the successful hacking of the system is useless. Look at it this way, how much would it cost us to develop a warhead and delivery system ourselves. What we spent would constitute only a small fraction of that cost. And besides, it was a decision made by the Supreme Leader. Are you questioning his judgement?" Hamidi asked.

The Iranian President's face became ghost white as he realized the implications of his question.

"How did you acquire the acquaintance of a senior executive of Sternenlicht?" Bagheri demanded.

"That, General, is beyond the scope of this meeting," Hamidi said as his stomach churned at the realization of where the General's question might lead. Nobody in the room, except for the Supreme Leader himself, was aware that Sternenlicht's CEO, Schiller, had become suspicious of Hamidi's plot and that Hamidi had ordered the man's execution. Nor was anyone aware that there was an American, Joe Barber, who had figured out that the Iranians were behind Schiller's death, or that Hamidi's agents had failed to capture Barber and neutralize the threat. The entire Iranian diplomatic corps bought the story that the explosion at their Berlin embassy was the result of a faulty HVAC system. Fortunately for Hamidi, the handful of people who had known the truth were killed in the explosion. But would the Supreme Leader reveal this truth and throw the meeting into turmoil, Hamidi wondered. The man was an old fool, after all, and Hamidi didn't rule out him doing something that stupid. Fortunately, General Hamidi was pleasantly surprised by what happened next.

The Supreme Leader raised his hand again to stop the conversation and make a point. "I find these details to be tedious." It was clear he was becoming impatient. "General Hamidi, would you please now share the most relevant details of Allah's Sword."

Hamidi spoke. "Each and every one of the EF's missiles potentially represents Allah's Sword. But we must choose carefully which we fire, because we will likely be able to do it only once, at most twice, before the EF enacts countermeasures to block our access. In addition, to avoid the attribution of events pointing to us, the code we implanted includes a termination option, in essence a 'kill switch', that will erase everything we have embedded in their systems and remove any evidence of our presence. Even if they figure out it was us, which I believe is unlikely, they will be unable to offer proof."

"The plan," the Supreme Leader said, with a tone of impatience again, "will you be so kind as to share the plan."

"Day after tomorrow," Hamidi continued, "we will fire one of their missiles with a 10-kiloton warhead."

"At what target?" Bagheri asked impatiently.

"At Tel Aviv. And the true Genius of this plan is that the world will believe Germany is guilty of another effort at their 'final solution'.

The room remained silent for several seconds. Oddly enough, Hamidi noticed, nobody seemed to be smiling. He assumed his revelation would be met with a chorus of "May Allah be praised," but no one uttered a word. Was his government going soft, he wondered, now that the prospect of turning their rhetoric into action was a reality?

"The timing is very propitious," Hamidi continued. "Germany is mired in chaos at the moment due to their little adventure over Sweden. The attack on Tel Aviv will appear to be a second attack by Germany on another nation."

"Did we have anything to do with the attack on Sweden?" Bagheri asked.

"No, we did not," Hamidi replied. "I have no idea why they would do that."

"Which kind of missile do you intend to fire?" Bagheri asked.

"We will fire one of their short-to-intermediate missiles that uses a mobile launcher as a platform."

"Why?"

"We do not have confidence in our ability to successfully communicate commands to their submarine forces, and submarine platforms have the highest level of safeguards of any of their systems. We will not launch a long-range weapon because the warheads they carry would be overkill, and we don't need that much range, given our target. Also, the long-range rockets are liquid fueled, and initiating the fueling sequence would alert them that something is about to happen. Our success is not a forgone conclusion until the rocket actually takes flight. As I have said, their short-to-intermediate range missiles use solid rocket fuel. The European strategic forces will have no idea anything has happened until it is too late."

"Won't they see their systems display the firing commands?" Bagheri asked.

"No, our software masks all indications of the launch. Their command stations will appear as though everything is normal and that nothing is happening. The only indication they will have is the launch itself."

"Why wouldn't they simply abort the launch, destroy the missile that is, shortly after they detect launch? Surely their systems have an abort capability, don't they?" Bagheri asked.

"Yes, they do; however, our software is designed to detect an abort command and to jam it. Once the missile is launched, Sir Isaac Newton is in the driver's seat and there is nothing anyone can do. It will hit its target."

"You mean Allah is in the driver's seat, don't you, General Hamidi?" The Supreme Leader corrected.

"Yes of course, your Excellency. Forgive me," Hamidi said, with a penitent expression, but seething with internal rage at the comment.

"Is there anything else you wish to say, General Hamidi?" the Supreme Leader asked, signaling he was impatient for the meeting to conclude.

"Just one more thing. It is important for everyone in this room to understand that other nations are going to see Germany as the guilty party responsible for this attack. We have taken great diligence to ensure our efforts contain nothing that can link what happens to our Islamic Republic. That is why it is so important to maintain absolute secrecy of these matters. The only thing that could link the launch to us is an indiscretion from somebody in this room."

"Or your soldiers that push the button, correct?" General Bagheri observed.

"There are only a handful of people who will man our launch room. They will become martyrs after the launch, except for the scientist." Hamidi responded, sending a chill across the room with his words. Most everyone in the room immediately wondered if they would be chosen as a martyr as well.

The Supreme Leader once again held up his hand to forestall any further discussion, then began to speak, "I believe General Hamidi's explanations have been sufficient. We must all go back to our daily activities as though nothing is different. Remember the oath of silence I commanded of each of you, and the consequences for breaking it. Let us now go back to our duties. May Allah bless this mighty and historic endeavor."

As people began to stand and walk out, Hamidi took a deep breath and let it out slowly. He survived the meeting, and there was no pushback, whatsoever. General Bagheri was a pompous ass, as he expected, but he handled the man well. Now all he had to do was pull off the most momentous and consequential deception in the history of warfare. He stood up and began to exit the room himself. As he did so, there was a slight increase to the spring in his step.

Chapter 31 – The Meeting

Madame Claude Pub, Wrangelkiez District, Berlin, Germany

The atmosphere was surreal. The Pub was housed at the bottom of a narrow stairwell in a former brothel on one of the district's quieter side streets. Red lights glowed from the entrance as passers-by were embraced by the almost gothic lyrics of Dark Night of the Soul by David Lynch. The arrangement of the furniture was disorienting, by design. It was not the sort of place normally frequented by high government officials, and it was seen rarely by tourists, except those with an exceptionally adventurous and brave guide. To call it eclectic would be an understatement. It was a gathering place for those who fancied themselves as living on the edge of society, whether such a fantasy was true or not. Nobody came there to be noticed; it was anonymous. It was perfect.

Marcus Day sat by himself at a corner at a table and waited. Nobody noticed him, which was remarkable, especially in Berlin. People tended to notice a six-foot seven inch black man north of 250 pounds with the build of an NFL linebacker. He wore a pair of Barbell Apparel-brand blue jeans, the only brand that simultaneously fit his massive thighs and 34-inch waste, along with a simple black t-shirt that stretched tightly around his large chest and arms, sculptured to betray a single-digit percentage of body fat. A pair of Maui-Jim sunglasses, aviator-style with a blue-mirror finish, framed a face that focused on a newspaper and occasionally sipped a German beer. Yet nobody paid any attention to him. The place was perfect.

Marcus Day and Jean-Baptiste Laurent had crossed paths in a previous life. When Day was a young Marine First Lieutenant, he was deployed to Somalia as part of a clandestine multinational mission to capture a Somali Warlord with a fetish for slaughtering remote villages. It was there he met a much younger Capitaine Jean-Baptiste Laurent, a helicopter pilot in the French Air Force, responsible for ferrying the Marines into and out of their downrange LZ. The two of them had hit it off, and for a while would have even considered themselves friends. They kept touch with each other for several years, and when Barber formed Orion Bellicus, Day had even offered Laurent a job, but the Frenchman politely declined, expressing his thanks but affirming his desire to continue his a career in the French Military. Over the years, as is often the case with friendships forged in youth, the two men lost touch. But Day still considered Laurent an honorable man and someone he could trust. So, he reached out to his old friend simply telling him he was in Berlin and would like to catch up over a beer before he flew back to the States. Day had told him nothing over the phone about the matters at hand. It wasn't the sort of thing that should be shared over an unsecured phone line. He had to share it face to face.

As Day picked up his pint of beer, his peripheral vision processed a familiar image. He looked up and noticed a man approaching his table. Laurent was dressed in civilian clothes and looked older than Day remembered him. The Frenchman was balding slightly with his remaining hair mostly grey. He still looked fit, but more fit in the sense of a man who spends a reasonable amount of time in a gym; not the fitness of a man who retained the sharp skills of combat. As he approached the table, Day stood up and the two men shook hands, then hugged.

"Good to see you, my old friend," Laurent said.

"It has been way too long, Jean-Baptiste," Day responded.

"Indeed, it has," Laurent said as both men sat down. "What are you drinking?"

"A Spaten Oktoberfest," Day replied, as a waitress walked up to the table.

"I'll have the same as my friend, here," Laurent said to the waitress. "So, how is life treating you? Is your security firm doing well? Orion Bellicus, if I remember correctly."

"I would say very well, and you remember correctly. I am now the Chief Operating Officer. I work with friends and very smart people and the pay is excellent. I would say you missed a great opportunity, but I see you are now a Lieutenant General. That is quite an accomplishment. Congratulations," Day said as the waitress placed Laurent's beer on the table.

Laurent picked up his glass and raised it as in a toast and said, "Here's to old friendships and to whatever brought you here."

The two men clinked glasses, and each took a long drink. Laurent continued: "So, Marcus, I am intrigued by your choice of pubs. This place is more than just a bit off the beaten path, and I would think not exactly to your style. What brings you to Berlin, and why is it I feel suspicious that this is not strictly a social visit?"

"I'm afraid it isn't, Jean-Baptiste. I have some unsettling news to share with you. I reached out to you because it is critical that this news receive the most serious attention from your military, and you are the only one I can trust. I should also tell you that as soon as our conversation concludes, I have a car waiting for me that will take me to the airport and a flight back to the United States. I am asking for the sake of our friendship that you do nothing that will stop me from getting on that flight."

"Why would I do that?" Laurent asked. "Are you in trouble? Have you broken German laws? Are the police or Federal authorities looking for you?"

"I am not in trouble, at least as of yet, and no, there are no German authorities looking for me. And this isn't about me. I have certain information that you will find very disturbing. There are forces in this country that would like to detain me if they were aware of what I know, including, I am sure, your superiors. You will understand that in a few minutes. But I also want to assure you that I will continue to cooperate with you, and you alone, once I am back home. What I am about to tell you is not for my benefit. It is vital information, of a national security bearing, that the European Federation very much needs to know."

"I assume this must have to do with Sweden, correct? You know that as a French Officer and a senior military leader in the EF, I am not at liberty to discuss any of that with you, regardless of whatever personal opinions on the matter I may have."

"It has nothing to do with Sweden, Jean-Baptiste. It's bigger than that, potentially much bigger."

Laurent sat back in his chair and stared at the giant man sitting across from him for several seconds without saying anything, as if to size him up. The smile and friendly expression on his face were now gone, replaced by a look almost quizzical. He spoke, "Well you certainly have my attention," Laurent said in a serious tone. "I will say, Marcus, I have never known you to be a man prone to an excessive or inappropriate use of hyperbole. By all means, share with me what is on your mind."

"It should come as no surprise to you that the remit of part of Orion Bellicus includes personal protection engagements for senior executives both in the United States and broader Europe."

"Yes, that is what I have heard. I did a little research on your firm after your phone call."

"We had the personal protection contract for Helmut Schiller of Sternenlicht," Day said.

"Well, my condolences on that, my friend. I presume that outcome won't find its way into your marketing brochure. I knew the man and liked him."

"No, it won't. We investigated his death with the cooperation of the Sternenlict, at least initially, before this Swedish business started closing doors to U.S. firms. And here's where I have to lay the unthinkable on you," Barber said.

"Ok, please proceed."

"My firm is in possession of irrefutable evidence that Schiller was assassinated on orders of the Iranian Revolutionary Guard Corps. They used a deep cover asset to carry out the attack and used a fatal transdermal dose of a narcotic, a fast-acting Fentanyl derivative, as the weapon."

"That's preposterous," Laurent responded.

"I know it sounds that way, Jean-Baptiste, but hear me out. The reason they assassinated him is critical. Sternenlicht is the company that designed and deployed your command and control systems, including those used for your strategic weapons."

Laurent's brow furrowed in response to the comment. "That is classified information. How did you know that?"

"It came out in our investigation of his death."

"Go ahead," Laurent said.

"Before Schiller got the CEO job at Sternenlicht, he was the Managing Director in charge of that project. He kept in touch with the details after he became CEO. He became suspicious that the code was being compromised somehow, hacked, and shared his suspicions with one of his Lieutenants, Hans-Dieter Zimmerman, the acting CEO. Zimmerman was on the take from the Iranians and ratted him out."

"Marcus, this is preposterous!" Laurent exclaimed. "You've been reading too many novels!"

"No, I haven't. Like I said, we have incontrovertible proof that Zimmerman was bribed – 50 million euros, and we have the bank transfers to prove it. The guy is dirty."

"You actually have evidence of the bank transfers? And that evidence conclusively points to Iran?"

"Yes, but we have far more than that. Agents from Iran kidnapped my boss, Joe Barber, and tried to kill his family."

"What?" Laurent asked in a surprised and shocked tone.

"Yes." Day said. "And after they abducted him, he was taken to the Iranian Embassy here in Berlin. During his interrogation, the Savak agents essentially confirmed everything I have just said. They clearly didn't expect Joe to leave the Embassy alive."

"How do you know this? Is Barber still being held?"

"No, he's not," Day replied. "He escaped."

"How? Did the chaos from the HVAC explosion give him an opportunity to escape?" Laurent asked.

"Jean-Baptiste, he caused the explosion. Joe Barber caused the explosion as a way to get out of the embassy. It wasn't an HVAC failure. What I am telling you is that the Iranians kidnapped a U.S. citizen on German soil and renditioned him to their Berlin Embassy. We believe the truth hasn't come out because the Iranian Diplomatic Corps doesn't actually know what happened. We suspect the agents involved in Barber's kidnapping didn't survive the explosion."

"You realize how crazy this sounds? What do you expect me to do with it?"

"Jean-Baptiste, I think you are missing the point. The issue here isn't the Iranians behaving badly, or even the murder of Schiller. The issue is we believe there is a very good chance your command and control systems have been compromised. Of all people, you must understand the implications of this."

Laurent sat quietly for several seconds with a contemplative expression on his face, then pursed his lips together and slowly blew out the air in his lungs as the reality hit him. He then responded, "Yes, I do my friend. Yes, I most certainly do. I don't suppose there is any way I could convince you not to get on that flight back to the States, is there? Your cooperation would be very helpful in convincing certain individuals here of the veracity of your story."

"Not a chance, my friend," Day answered.

"That's unfortunate. And I suppose you have a backup plan if I endeavor to be a bit more 'persuasive' in asking you to stay?"

"Yes, I do."

"And I suppose I would find several aspects of that backup plan to be, how shall we say, somewhat unpleasant to me personally?"

"Yes, sorry my friend, but I'm afraid you would."

"I would have expected nothing less from a former Force Recon Marine. Go catch your plane. Can you at least provide me with whatever documentary evidence you have before you leave?"

"I will email you an encrypted file once we are well out of European Federation airspace."

"Thank you, I have some people to see," Laurent replied, then pulled his right-handed shirt sleeve back about two inches to reveal a small microphone and spoke into it, "I'm done here. Everyone stand-down," then looked at Day and shrugged his shoulders and said: "Sorry, but a man in my position has to take certain precautions."

"No problem," Day commented as he smiled at his old friend and said, "I expected as much. By the way, that thing doesn't work at the moment, it's jammed. And I have a team outside with eyes on your men just in case they tried anything. My guys, of course, are under strict orders not to use lethal force."

"You were always the planner, Marcus," Laurent said, with a slight chuckle. "Good day, my friend, and safe travels. Call me when you get back to the States."

"Will do."

Chapter 32 – The Launch

Islamic Revolutionary Guard Corps, Cyber Command, Tehran

The atmosphere in the room was tense. Everyone knew what was on the line. They were about to make history and possibly even rewrite borders in the Middle East and beyond. The Islamic Republic of Iran, Persia, was about to do the unthinkable. It had been the dream and the aspirations of the Faithful for decades. They were about to deal a death blow to the State of Israel and effectively wipe it off the map. And they would do it in a manner that would clearly lay the blame on another nation, Germany. Or so they thought. Dr. Ashkan Ghorbani, the genius of a software engineer kidnapped from a comfortable job in California on orders to deliver results or witness the painful death of his family, had left a fingerprint that would eventually point blame in the right direction. But nobody knew that today. All they knew today was they were about to remotely launch a nuclear-tipped missile from somewhere deep inside Germany at the city of Tel Aviv and set off a conflagration like the world had not seen since the Great Satan, the United States, dropped the atomic bomb on Japan. They also knew the downside of failure. They weren't told the downside in so many words, but there was no doubt that to fail meant their death and the death of their families. Several of them silently wondered if death would be the reward for success as well.

Brigadier General Garshasp Hamidi stood in the Command and Control Center of the Revolutionary Guard's Cyber Warfare Group and watched the soldiers work at their consoles. He was businesslike in his demeaner today. There was no bluster or threats in his commands. There would be plenty of time for bluster later. The men were well trained and knew their responsibilities. If all continued to go well, Hamidi was inclined to allow their last few hours on earth to be peaceful, as peaceful as one could be in the process of launching a nuclear missile at a civilian target of almost 500,000 people.

Dr. Ghorbani was seated, and other than answering the occasional question, remained mostly quiet and let his men do their jobs. A watch officer, a young captain, sat next to Ghorbani and announced, "We're in. We have control of their systems." He looked to the soldier to his right and said, "Initiate targeting software sub-routines."

"Initiating software sub-routines," the soldier responded as he tapped several keystrokes and pressed the "enter" key. The sub-routine would invade the European Federation's missile targeting software and allow the Iranians to re-target the missile to any location they wished. It was an ingenious bit of code. The code itself was scrambled and randomly distributed in small chucks throughout the host in a manner that made it all but invisible, and it didn't compromise the functionality of the base code. A separate subroutine, almost akin to digital DNA and designed to look like a benign backup command, would unscramble the code bits and reconstitute them for only as long as it took to retarget the missile. The code would then be sent back to its original state, waiting to one day be summoned again, with no one the wiser. "We're in," the soldier announced.

"Confirm target coordinates," Hamidi commanded, again in a business-like voice.

"Retargeting now," the soldier announced. "Target coordinates are 32 degrees, 6 minutes, 33.5988 seconds north; 34 degrees, 51 minutes, 19.7964 seconds east."

The Captain sitting next to him responded, "I confirm target coordinates entered as announced, and I confirm target coordinates to be downtown Tel Aviv."

"Excellent," Hamidi announced. "Prepare to begin the launch sequence."

"General, we will now authenticate the launch order," the Captain said. "Please retrieve your card."

Hamidi cracked open the plastic case then held his authorization card and read aloud the eleven-digit code. The Captain compared Hamidi's response to the code on his card, verifying they were the same. "General, we have a valid launch order."

"Prepare to launch the missile," Hamidi commanded. The Captain and another soldier at the far end of the row of consoles each retrieved their launch keys from safes then inserted them into locks. "Keys inserted and ready to rotate, General."

"Rotate keys on my command, Captain. Three, Two, One, rotate."

With that, a light on the Captain's console changed from red to green. He flipped up a plastic cover and placed his index finger on a rocker switch next to the light. "Ready to launch the missile, General."

Over 5,600 kilometers away, military officers of another nation, China, were watching Iran's actions, aware of their plans, and about to bugger things up.

Undisclosed Location, Shanghai, China

China is a nation on the rise. The progress it has made both militarily and economically since the conclusion of the cold war, to say nothing of since the days of Richard Nixon's visit half a century ago when it was all but a closed kingdom, has been remarkable. Its achievements are the result of a clear long-term objective: become the world's leading superpower in both military and economic terms by 2050. To achieve this, the nation employs several strategies. First, is the absolute control of the national government over all aspects of Chinese life. They regard this as essential to achieving their objective, and they believe there is no greater existential threat to the nation and its achievements than loosing control of the population. Second, is their relentless investment in modernizing and expanding their military. Gone are the days when the size of their population and ability to deploy the world's largest army was enough. They are obsessed with command of the seas via such modern weapons as aircraft carriers and nuclear submarines, as well as command of the skies with high-performance aircraft and pilots that rival any in the world. Third, their economic growth is driven not just by carefully-managed capitalism, but also by systematic theft of intellectual property and trade policies that are highly one-sided in their favor. Fourth, and most interesting, is their approach to global relations. One does not achieve the long-term goal of hegemony simply by building oneself up. One must also keep potential adversaries off-guard and focused on risks other than the Chinese, and at this, they are masters. Experience has taught them there is no more effective weapon for this than cyber warfare. Chinese cyber activities are deeply shrouded in mystery, and the civilized world would stand in awe and wonder if it knew their skill and breadth of impact. If the true extent of their abilities were known, nobody would be able to sleep at night. Simply put, it is their weapon of chaos.

The Third Department of the People's Liberation Army General Staff, known as 3PLA, is the Chinese equivalent of the United States National Security Agency, or NSA. There are two major differences between the two organizations, however. First, as their name would indicate, the 3PLA is part of the Chinese military and not a civilian organization like the NSA. Its employees are mostly in uniform and they serve the Chinese Communist Party, not the Chinese people. The second, and even more consequential difference, is it includes China's Cyber Warfare Command. They are the soldiers of chaos. The Cyber Command's growing remit includes espionage and the theft of technology and intellectual property, hacking the defense and command and control systems of adversaries, and the disruption of communications, power systems, and other industrial infrastructure. They even managed to hack the United States' top-secret domestic strike drone program, then take over a drone and execute the dramatic attack on the Golden Gate Bridge of three years ago, thereby exposing the program much to the embarrassment of the then U.S. Administration. The clandestine nature of their effort was so successful that, while many in the U.S. suspected the Chinese were to blame, nobody was able to prove it. Many of the scientists employed in the Cyber Warfare Command were graduates of doctoral programs in engineering and the sciences at major universities all over the world. And these bright people were noticed by the Command's recruiters by virtue of their successful work in stealing technology and intellectual property while pursuing their graduate studies.

First Lieutenant Danping Xu sat at her console and carefully watched the screen. Her hacking target for the last several months had been the new European Federation Command and Control System. Her mission was called "Operation Dove". It was approved at the highest levels of the Chinese military. She was a soldier of chaos, and she plied her trade well. As she continued to work her way ever deeper into her target's computer code, her best source of intelligence was a Chinese deep cover agent who actually worked for the company, Sternenlicht, that developed the system. The agent, a Chinese national, was a software development engineer with a Ph.D. from Cal Tech. His fluency in German and English, along with his native Mandarin made him very useful to his German employer. He was very useful to his masters in China as well; foreign language skills were viewed by the Chinese government as key enablers in the art of industrial espionage. Multilingual skills tended to open doors, and to the undiscerning, impart trust. Executives at Sternenlicht never knew that his real mission was to learn everything he could about the system's capabilities and convey the information back to 3PLA. He had worked directly for Helmut Schiller when Schiller was responsible for the project design. In the ultimate irony, the agent was the engineer responsible for design and implementation of the security protocols for the system. He had done a brilliant job, and even received a large increase in his bonus for what was considered to be visionary work. Little did they know he had also built in a back door.

Lucky for the Chinese, his skills of observation went far beyond just computer software. His boss, Herr Schiller, was a fairly transparent man who was not particularly good at hiding his emotions. He would have been a terrible poker player, the agent often thought, although he never had the opportunity to test the theory; Schiller was a man not given to trivial pursuits. The two of them continued to work together after Schiller assumed the CEO role. Schiller would often use the agent as a sounding board for ideas or concerns about the system. Then, the agent started to notice the man's odd and increasingly secretive behavior. It roused his suspicions. Schiller was behaving in an uncharacteristic way; he was becoming less open, almost secretive, and less inclined to show the agent his trust. The agent suggested that Cyber Command start monitoring Schiller's phone calls. It was through the eavesdropping that the Chinese became aware of Schiller's suspicions about Iran's infiltration of their code. As a result, the Iranians became a target of the 3PLA's interest and soon learned of the Iranian's plot.

Iran was relentlessly marching towards a nuclear weapons capability. They were slowed down by sanctions from the west, but the Chinese had no doubt they would ultimately achieve their goal, but were astonished to discover the Iranian's had found a way to takeover a nuclear missile deployed by the European Federation. An unstable, irrational adversary to their west with control of nuclear weapons was unacceptable, but even worse was their plan to attack Israel and point the blame to Germany. Nuclear war in the Middle East would not only bring global commerce to a halt, it would ignite a conflagration that could quickly spiral out of control. So, a clever plan was forged.

Danping Xu was preparing a little surprise for General Hamidi. As she monitored Iran's systems and Iran's progress towards the launch of a German missile against Isreal, she completed a series of keystrokes and pressed "enter."

Islamic Revolutionary Guard Corps, Cyber Command, Tehran

"What was that," Hamidi asked in response to a momentary flicker on his control panel.

"I don't know sir," the Captain responded.

"Let me run some quick diagnostics," Dr. Ghorbani responded.

"Do it quickly, you fool!" Hamidi now barked, as his business-like demeanor evaporated. "We are about to launch!"

"Everything looks good, General," Ghorbani announced. "I see no issues. All systems remain 'go'."

"Double check the target coordinates again before we fire the missile," Hamidi barked at Dr. Ghorbani.

The tension in the room was high. They were seconds away from launch when the screens momentarily fluttered. In a stressful environment, and under enormous stress human senses can become so focused that important words get filtered out and perceptions become selective. The Captain did not hear, "Double check the target coordinates again before w....", he only heard, "...fire the missile."

Ghorbani spoke, answering Hamidi's question, "Target coordinates are 34 degrees, 35 minutes, 2.3568 seconds north; 50 degrees, 54 minutes, 36.8100 seconds east."

"Wait, those don't sound right," Hamidi said nervously. "Dr. Ghorbani, verify those coordinates and tell me where they are!" he shouted.

Ghorbani furiously tapped on his computer, then said, "Oh my god!" he exclaimed. "That's Qom! The holy city of Qom! It has a population of over two million people! The missile's target is Iran!"

Undisclosed Location, Shanghai, China

The Chinese watch officer took two steps closer to Lieutenant Xu and asked, "Can you tell if our Iranian friends have noticed yet that the missile was retargeted?"

"I don't believe so, sir. We won't be able to confirm it until I see their launch ready indicator go back to red from green."

"I see it's still green."

"Yes sir, it's still green."

Several seconds passed as the Watch Commander and Lieutenant both became increasingly nervous. "Well, they seem to be taking their own sweet time about it, don't they, Lieutenant?"

"Yes sir, they do."

"If they are actually careless enough to launch without confirming the coordinates, I'm sure the Germans will blow that missile out of the sky before it gets one hundred feet out of its launcher."

"Yes sir, I certainly hope so. That assumption is part of our planning scenario."

"And we have the ability to send an abort signal as well, correct?"

"Yes sir, we do. It's right here," she said, pointing to another switch on her console.

Islamic Revolutionary Guard Corps, Cyber Command, Tehran

"Stand down the launch! Abort the launch!" Hamidi screamed.

The Captain passed out at his station and his head hit the console with a loud crack. He had already pushed the rocker switch to the "fire" position.

"What is going on?" Hamidi screamed, as he ran to the Captain and violently pulled him off the console, out of his chair and threw him out of the way as if he were a rag doll.

"General, we are getting launch indications!" Ghorbani said, terrified now. "The Captain must have misunderstood you and launched the missile. The switch is depressed!"

"I also confirm missile launch," one of the other soldiers said. "GPS tracking reads the missile has already reached an altitude of two miles!"

"Abort that launch!" Hamidi screamed. "Destroy that missile!"

"We can't," Ghorbani said. "We don't have that capability."

"What do you mean we don't have the capability! You told me we could abort a launch!" Hamidi screamed.

"No sir, we told you we could jam their abort signal. We never said we could create an abort signal ourselves. This is a scenario nobody ever imagined."

Undisclosed Location, Shanghai, China

"Sir, I am seeing launch indications," Lieutenant Xu announced, now sounding worried. "The missile appears to have been launched!"

The watch officer picked up another telephone headset that connected him to their satellite monitoring center. "SatCom, are you seeing indications of a missile launch in Germany?"

"Yes, Colonel, we are. Missile appears to be heading southeast. Target cannot be positively verified yet."

"I want you to stay on the line," the watch officer said. "We expect the Germans to execute the destruct command momentarily. Call it out the second you see it."

"Yes sir."

Thirty seconds passed as the phone remained silent. Finally, the watch office asked in a nervous voice, "SatCom, still nothing?"

"No Sir, the missile has reached an altitude of 35 miles and is still accelerating."

"Why haven't the Germans acted?" the watch officer shouted. "Lieutenant Xu send the abort signal now! I'm not going to wait!"

"Sending signal now, sir. Signal sent."

"SatCom, status!" the watch office shouted.

"No change, sir. Missile is still in flight. Altitude is now one hundred and fifty miles."

"You're sure you sent that signal, Lieutenant?" the watch officer now barked.

"Yes sir, I am sure!"

"What happened? Why wasn't the missile destroyed?"

"I don't know. I'm running analytics, sir."

"Hurry!" he shouted.

She then spoke words that chilled the watch commander to his bone as he realized what they meant: "Systems analytics confirms the abort signal was sent. Preliminary conclusion is our abort signal was jammed."

CIA Headquarters, Langley, Virginia

Dr. Margaret Shevchenko looked neither like a Margaret nor a Shevchenko. She was the unlikely combination of a Russian Orthodox Father, and a Baptist African American mother; "love happens, and finds a way," her parents would often tell her. She was of medium height and retained the muscular physique of a woman devoted to relentless time spent as a gym rat. In her youth she had even run several ultra-marathon races, including the brutal self-supported trek over a blistering hot north African desert called the Marathon des Sables. Men still considered her attractive, and she looked much younger than her actual age. Graduating in the top 10% of her class at West Point, she was one of the first women to get a shot at Army Ranger training. She exceled. But it was a different time, and it became quickly apparent it was not a career path that would welcome her, so she took advantage of the Army Ph.D. program and studied Middle Eastern History at the University of Michigan and Oxford. Still frustrated with the Army, she resigned her commission when her commitment expired and was quickly recruited by the C.I.A. Fifteen years later and after several close relationships with presidents from both political parties, she sat in the Director's chair.

Shevchenko and Barber had a history. She had met Barber when he was in the S.A.D., or "Special Activities Division", now called P.M.O., or "Paramilitary Operations." Barber had impressed her. He got results and his integrity struck her as above reproach. When he left government service and started his own security and intelligence firm, she often engaged his services as contract work, a practice growing in popularity. They trusted each other, and over the years they became friends and would occasionally do each other favors "off the books". He was one of few civilians whose phone calls she always returned.

Barber sat across from her in the Director's Conference Room. He had just told her everything. She sat there in stunned silence, processing what he had just said.

"You realize this is one of the craziest things I have heard since I assumed this chair, right? And I can assure you I've heard some pretty crazy things."

"I understand, Maggie. The unfortunate thing is, all of it is true."

"And you also realize that if it were anyone other than you, I'd probably have that person in irons right now."

"I get that too. I hope we can avoid that step," he said, half-joking, half serious. "What are you going to do?"

"Well, I think first I have to talk to SecDef and SecState. I think by the end of the day this must go to the President, not that I trust that witch, but I'm not about to go off the reservation. Like her or not, she's the duly elected President and I'm not."

"Fully agree," Barber replied. "And I don't trust her either."

Their conversation was interrupted by Schevchenko's intercom. It was her secretary. "Pardon me, Madam Director, but the SecDef is on the line and he says it's extremely urgent."

"Put him through," she replied, then pushed a button on the phone to silence the speaker and picked up the receiver. "Excuse me for a second, Joe."

As the Director listened, her face began to go pale. "What's your confidence level?" Barber heard her ask. "Has it made the news yet? OK, I agree. I think we should hold off on the situation room for a bit. We are likely to miss some information while in transit. Let's connect a conference call with the President, you, State, and the D.N.I." (referring to the Director of National Intelligence, the Cabinet position that oversees and coordinates all of the Nation's intelligence agencies. "That way we can at least get an early read of what's going on, then huddle in the Situation Room after that. Right," she said, "I agree. Ok, I'll have my people arrange the call for 10 minutes from now," and with that, she hung up.

"What's going on, Maggie?" Barber asked.

"We'll I would say your story just became a whole lot more credible. I want you to hang here at C.I.A. for a bit. I may want to take you to the SecDef, and maybe even the President before the workday is over."

"What the hell happened?"

"Well, it's hitting the news wires in Europe so I might as well tell you. General Forester, the 4-star who oversees StratCom, the Strategic Command, just called the SecDef and advised him that seven minutes ago there appears to have been a nuclear explosion in Northern Iran. It looks like the City of Qom was just erased. And preliminary indications are the missile originated from Germany."

"Shit," Barber exclaimed.

Undisclosed Location, Shanghai, China

The Watch Commander put his hand on Lieutenant Xu's shoulder and said: "Relax, Lieutenant. This is not the outcome we wanted, but we all knew it was possible. While the collateral damage in Iran is regrettable, it is likely far less than would have resulted from more widespread hostilities and will certainly result in less economic harm. There will be widespread condemnation of the European Federation, at least publicly, but behind closed doors I suspect many will be pleased that a pariah is punished."

Lieutenant Xu remained outwardly cool but was inwardly despondent about the human toll of her handiwork. Remaining outwardly cool and deferential in the face of exigent circumstances was the ultimate survival skill in the Chinese military. But she regarded the Watch Commander's last comment as preposterous. And Heaven help China, she thought, if the world ever discovered what really happened.

Chapter 33 – Chaos

Islamic Revolutionary Guard Corps, Tehran

General Hamidi sat in his office and waited. His 9-millimeter pistol, an Iranian knockoff of the Sig Sauer P226, sat on his desk. He had momentarily considered putting the barrel into his mouth and ending his life. He knew all too well what potential horrors could await a man guilty of his enormous failure, but he had decided to fight. He was nothing if not a survivor, and he would be ruthless in his efforts to uncover who was responsible for what happened. He had already put a bullet in the head of the young Captain who had depressed the switch that fired the missile, and was he about to do the same Dr. Ghorbani when he realized he needed the scientist's help to figure out what happened. Plenty of time to shoot him after that, he thought, and then resolved to shoot the man's family as well while he made Ghorbani watch.

His thoughts were interrupted by a knock on his door. The door opened and Major General Muhammad Bagheri stepped inside. Hamidi briefly thought about reaching for his pistol and shooting Bagheri, but he hesitated. Bagheri spoke, "The Supreme Leader would like to see you, General."

"This might be it," Hamidi thought. He pushed his chair back, picked up his pistol and placed it in its holster, then reached for his uniform jacket and put it on. Bagheri stood silently watching as he did so. Hamidi glanced at a picture of his family, the photo sitting on his desk, as he gave a tug to the bottom of his jacket to ensure it was straight. It is remarkable how monsters can be reflective and caring for their own families, especially in times of crisis, despite their otherwise brutal behavior. As he looked away from the photo, his eyes met Bagheri's. He was suddenly seized with fear. Bagheri had his pistol out and pointed at his chest. The man had gotten the drop on him, and with the momentary distraction of the family picture he hadn't noticed. The events of the last several hours had compromised his instincts, and he had let down his guard.

Bagheri finally spoke, "As I said, General Hamidi, the Supreme Leader would like to see you. As a matter of fact, the Supreme Leader would like to see you dead." With that, Bagheri raised his pistol slightly and fired two rounds into the center of Hamidi's face.

PrinSafe HQ, Palo Alto, California

Emma Clark sat in her office reading the Wall Street Journal. It was starting out as a normal day. The morning fog was rapidly burning off, and the forecast was for a sunny day with an unusually high temperature in the low 90s. The air conditioning in her office was already cranking, and she felt a slight chill on her arms thanks to the sleeveless dress she had selected. It was the classic conundrum of hot weather – the forecast led people to dress "comfortably", but to be comfortable outside usually meant freezing for those who spent most of their days inside. She reached across her massive desk and pressed the button on her intercom and asked, "Can somebody please turn the thermostat up? It's cold in here!"

She returned her focus to the Journal without allowing her attention to be diverted by her peripheral vision. She was engrossed in a multi-page article about a new financial regulatory initiative that was being considered by the Federal Reserve Bank, and she was irritated by the momentary distraction of her temperature-related discomfort. To her left was a large Bloomberg Terminal screen. Bloomberg was the news and financial markets service that had become the gold standard for information on Wall Street, private equity firms, money managers and many more. It had made Michael Bloomberg, its founder, the former bond trader, then Mayor of New York City and even a wannabe Presidential candidate, a multi-billionaire.

The screen was her personal monitor page. One of the features of the Bloomberg System it's ease in customizing. She had set up the page to monitor global stock markets, interest rates and important news stories from anywhere in the world. When market prices changed anywhere in the world, the screen would flash, and the prices were displayed in green if they rose and red if they declined. News stories would continually update as they were fed to the system. As she continued to work her way through the Journal article, her peripheral vision detected the Bloomberg screen's sudden rapid flashing and a lot of green turning to red. She glanced up from her newspaper and, as was her habit, first looked at the U.S. stock market. She was stunned. The Dow Jones Industrial Average, which had opened the morning 150 points higher, was not only red, it was down 1,768 points. Her eyes then quickly transitioned to the news stories, looking for something that would explain such a dramatic change. Her eyes moved past the financial news section and right to the list of "Top Stories." When she processed the headline at the top of the list, her blood ran cold.

Office of the Chancellor, European Federation HQ, Berlin

"What the hell did you do?" Dr. Heinrich Krúger, Chancellor of the European Federation, screamed at General Horst Brandt, Commander of the EF Airforce. "A nuclear weapon has just detonated over the City of Qom, Iran, and it was fired from German soil! Our own media, the American news services, and the BBC are all reporting there is a clear missile track from one of our military bases to where the warhead detonated over Iran! How is this possible?"

"We did nothing!" the General screamed back. "Nobody in the Air Force is responsible for launching a missile. I just personally spoke to the Field Commander in charge of the battery of mobile launchers that was the missile's origin, and nobody gave such an order. All of our systems continue to read green as if nothing has happened. The launch system itself for that battery still shows the missile is in the launch tube!" he exclaimed.

"Well, clearly it is not, is it General?" the Chancellor screamed again. "You just obliterated a city of over two million people!"

"No sir, I did not!" General Brandt responded, his voice breaking this time. "But I assure you, I will find out who did! In the meantime, we are at tremendous risk of retaliation. I don't believe Iran is capable of mounting a serious retaliation themselves, but this is the sort of bad behavior both the Americans and the English are going to want to punish. At a minimum we are at high risk of attack on our military bases, likely by American cruise missiles. I'm certain there are several of their attack submarines within firing range. I have taken our strategic forces to DefCon 2," he said, referring to the highest level of alert, short of actual war.

"You did what?" the Chancellor screamed at him again. "Are you out of your mind? What are you, some kind of present-day Curtis LeMay?" he asked, referring to the U.S. General who raised the alert status of U.S. strategic forces during the Cuban Missile Crisis without the permission of President Kennedy. "Are you mad? We cannot look aggressive right now, you fool! That action could get us bombed into oblivion! The prospects for miscalculations and mis-interpreted motives are extraordinarily high right now! Stand down those forces immediately! Use my phone! Do it now!"

"Yes sir," the General responded as he walked to the Chancellor's desk and picked up the phone to give the stand-down order.

Situation Room, White House, 2 Hours After Detonation

The tension in the room was thick, and the mood was grim. No one spoke as the senior Administration officials filed in and took their places. There were no sidebar conversations, as was usually the case at the beginning of such a meeting. The gravity of circumstances was foremost in the minds of everyone. President Einhorn sat at the head of the conference table as the last few principals took their seats.

The President spoke, with a somber voice, "General Forrester, what is the status of our forces?

"Madam President, per the National Command Authority regulations, I took our alert status to Defcon 4, or 'Double Take', on my authority prior to this meeting. I recommend you authorize DefCon 3, or 'Round House', in light of the attack on Iran being the second use of nonconventional munitions by the European Federation. We remain unable to communicate with them or otherwise determine their motive. It's the only prudent move."

"Authorized," the President responded. "Now, can you please recap for us what we know?"

"At approximately 15:00 hours Universal Standard Time, satellite monitoring systems at StratCom detected a missile launch from southern Germany with a southeast track. Seven minutes later, our systems detected a nuclear detonation over the city of Qom, Iran. According to our latest intelligence, the city had a population of over 2 million people. We estimate the explosive yield to be in the range of 3 kilotons. The European Federation did not provide us with advanced notice of the launch, and their motive is a mystery."

"Three kilotons?" the President asked. "That sounds small. The yield of the Hiroshima bomb was about 15 kilotons, wasn't it?"

"Yes, Ma'am," the General responded. "And we are puzzled by that. It is our understanding that the European Federation only deploys thermonuclear, or two-state weapons of French design with minimum yields of at least 10 kilotons, with some od their warheads producing yields far greater."

"Two-stage?" she asked.

"Yes ma'am."

"What does that mean, General?"

"Well, at the risk of being too technical, a two-stage device, or thermonuclear weapon, has two stages….."

The President cut him off. "I get the fact that a two-stage device has two stages, General," she replied with sarcasm dripping from her words. "My question is, what does It mean?"

"Yes, Ma'am, getting to that," the General responded. "If I may explain, again trying not to be too technical, the Hiroshima and Nagasaki bombs both were one stage devices that achieved their explosive force by the energy released from igniting nuclear fission. A two-stage device, or thermonuclear weapon, is essentially a nuclear bomb within a more powerful nuclear bomb. The first stage is a fission bomb. It serves as the 'spark', or trigger that ignites the second stage. When it detonates, it creates the conditions inside the containment device, the warhead's outer shell, that are necessary to achieve nuclear fusion in the second stage. Fusion is the smashing of atoms together whereas fission is the splitting of atoms apart. To ignite fusion in the second stage it has to be heated to over 100 million degrees Kelvin, that's about 180 million degrees Fahrenheit, and you have to enormously compress the nuclear material in the second stage. Chemical explosives cannot create those conditions, but a fission bomb can.

The President looked at General Weatherby, the Chairman of the Joint Chiefs, with growing irritation as General Forrester droned on with his explanation that was getting deeper and deeper "into the weeds."

"It's a much more efficient process, therefore much more energy is released. Also, the yield can be varied based on the amount of the hydrogen isotope tritium that is injected into the core of the second stage at time of detonation, and..."

President Einhorn cut him off again, "You are failing miserably at not being too technical, General! I'm not looking for a bloody physics lesson! Why the hell was the yield lower than expected? Not that it mattered much to the people who were vaporized," she snapped.

The Chairman of the Joint Chiefs spoke up. "We believe the warhead likely malfunctioned. Both stages need to work for the warhead to deliver the expected yield. Only the first stage worked. We call such a malfunction a 'fizzle'. You still get a nuclear explosion, but it's not thermonuclear. We believe this is the most likely explanation for the relatively low yield."

"Thank you General. That is clear," she said to General Weatherby, while glaring at General Forrester.

"Madam President," the Secretary of Defense, or SecDef spoke up, "it's important to understand that low is a relative term here. The destruction will still be massive, and the initial death toll could easily be in the hundreds of thousands in a city of that size. And that number is likely to go up considerably as a result of the secondary effects of radioactive fallout."

"My God," the President replied, "all those people."

"Yes Ma'am," the SecDef responded. "It's a tragedy."

The President continued, "Director Shevchenko shared a rather bizarre theory with us over the conference call that immediately preceded this meeting. Maggie, please share your theory with the group."

"With respect, Madam President, it's not just a theory, we have some very reliable evidence." For the next several minutes the Director of the C.I.A. related the story Joe Barber shared with her. At the conclusion she said, "I believe the facts are irrefutable. Iran somehow is responsible for this. We can't prove it yet, but we will."

"That's crazy," the Secretary of State replied. "Why on earth would Iran attack their own country. It doesn't make any sense."

"I agree the motive is incomprehensible, but my source is above reproach. There is no other logical conclusion. My guess is they somehow screwed up."

As the President was about to respond, she was seized with a blinding headache.

Office of the Prime Minister, 10 Downing Street, London England

"Look at the BBC," Sir Nick said. "Live pictures now, from Qom. They're horrific. Oh my God………"

As Jeremy Boren glanced at the television monitor in his office his face became white. He thought he was going to be sick.

"Krüger must be mad," Boren replied. "His motives are incomprehensible."

"I agree, sir," commented General Sir Nick Carleton, Chief of the General Staff, the English equivalent of the U.S. Chairman of the Joint Chiefs. "Have you managed to reach the American President?"

"No. I am told she is unavailable at the moment. I presume she is meeting with her principals and will return our call shortly. Nobody in Berlin is answering their phones. This business is quite the fright. I imagine it's not been this bad since the General Secretary pointed a missile at Jack Kennedy's head."

"I quite agree, sir," the General responded.

"It is essential that calm heads prevail. The risk of a miscalculation right now is extraordinarily high."

"Agreed," General Carleton replied, "but we should all remember we are closer to Germany than is Iran. We have a precise lock on the site that fired that missile. Taking it out with conventional ordinance would be a reasonable and proportional response."

"We will not fire a shot unless fired upon, is that clear?"

"Yes sir, very clear," General Carleton replied."

"I understand your concern, Sir Nick, but that is precisely the kind of thinking that will ignite a further conflagration and spiral this mess out of control."

"I Understood, sir. If this attack on Sweden didn't happen first I would be inclined to believe this is a matter isolated to The European Federation and Iran. The context of it coming on the heels of the attack on Sweden and, while not nuclear, it being nonconventional ordinance, raises the likelihood of some greater plan of aggression on the EF's part. What, and to what motive, I have no idea."

"I agree with Sir Nick, Mister Prime Minister," replied Lord David Herbert, Chief of the National Intelligence Service. "Our Signals Intelligence tell us the EF have all but put themselves on a war footing by taking their alert status to DefCon 2."

"They follow the American protocol, is that correct?" The Prime Minister asked.

"Yes sir, they do," Lord Herbert replied, "Defcon 2 is the highest alert status short of actual war. I just got off the phone with the American NSA before coming here, and they share our conclusions. The EF is at DefCon2."

"I need to talk to Einhorn and find out what the Americans are up to," Prime Minister Boren said.

"Have you tried to reach Morel?" Secretary Davies asked, referring to the French President, Gaston Morel.

"No, I haven't, but if I don't hear from Einhorn in a few minutes, he will be my next phone call."

"What is our alert status, Simon?" asked the English Prime Minister, Jeremy Boren, in a voice that betrayed the stress of the last two hours.

"Our Bikini Alert Status is 'Black Special'," reported Simon Davies, the English Defense Secretary, referring to a readiness condition that meant there was a high likeliness of an attack but no specific target.

"Do we have subs deployed in the Channel right now?" the Prime Minister asked.

"Yes, we do," Davies responded. "One attack boat, the Astute. Mister Prime Minister, I share your concern about miscalculations, but we would be derelict not to take the appropriate precautions. I have an order ready to send our submarine fleet instructing them to immediately prosecute evidence of any hostile intent. The EF has at least two boomers, nuclear missile subs, operating somewhere in the eastern part of the Channel or the southern part of the North Sea, and they could hit London with their missiles before we could even respond to their launch. If the EF appears to be about to attack English soil or any of Her Majesty's military assets, we must have a free hand to respond immediately. I ask your permission to release the order."

"Very well, release the order, but we must not escalate by accident. Make sure your officers remain extremely diligent about that."

"Of course, sir. I can assure you the lad's training will not fail them."

"Miscalculations are not the result of poor training, Simon. Miscalculations are the result of bad, albeit well-intentioned, decisions made in an environment of incomplete information, high stress, and outright fear. And they are the result of bad luck."

Chapter 34 -- Miscalculations

Aboard the English Attack Submarine HMS Astute, S119, in The English Channel

"Conn, Sonar, contact, designate sierra one. Ident as French Rubis-class nuclear attack boat; likely the Perle, S606, twelve hundred yards off starboard bow."

"Sonar, Conn, do they know we're here?"

"Conn, Sonar, unknown."

"Maneuvering, all stop," the Captain ordered. He then grabbed the 1MC microphone for the boat's main intercom system and said, "This is the Captain. All quiet. We have company, a French attack boat."

He replaced the 1MC into its holder and queried, "Sonar, Conn, this is the Captain. Do they demonstrate hostile intent?"

"Negative, Captain, but they are only making 3 knots. They are looking for us."

"So, what are you up to, my little wine-swilling friends," the Captain mused.

Aboard the French Attack Submarine, The Perle, S606, in The English Channel

"Conn, sonar, the English boat is slowing. I believe they have spotted us."

"Battle stations, torpedo!" the Captain ordered.

"Battle stations, torpedo," echoed over the MC1 Intercom system.

"Wheps," the Captain said, hailing the submarine's weapons officer.

"Wheps, Aye, Captain," the weapons officer replied.

"Lock firing solution for torpedo tubes 3 and 4." He then looked at the boat's executive officer and said, "We are at Defcon 2. If that English sub shows hostile intent, I'm going to blow her out of the water."

"Firing solutions locked, Captain; shall I open outer doors?" the weapons officer asked.

"Negative. I don't want to announce our intentions and provoke an attack. Let's wait and see if they find us. Maneuvering, 10 degrees up bubble on the diving plane, ahead slow. Let's see if we can hide above that thermocline," referring to a thin, but distinct layer of water separating the warmer water closer to the surface from the colder water below. A thermocline tends to act as a barrier to sound waves and can confuse passive sonar and mask the presence of another boat.

"Where's the L'Améthyste?" the Captain asked, referring to another Rubis-class boat patrolling off the coast of continental Europe.

"Last fix had her in the North Sea, about 50 nautical miles west of Denmark," the Navigation Officer responded.

"Ok, it's up to us," the Captain observed.

Aboard the English Attack Submarine HMS Astute, S119, in The English Channel

"Conn, Radio, Incoming Emergency Action Message." Fleet Command was transmitting a message to the submerged submarine through the ELF system, or Extreme Low Frequency. The signal is captured by a long antenna the sub trailed in the water.

"Conn, Aye." An enlisted sailor handed a printed copy of the message to the Captain. It read: TWO RUBIS-CLASS ATTACK BOATS AND ONE L'TRIOMPHANT-CLASS BALLISTIC MISSILE BOAT BELIEVED TO BE IN ENGLISH CHANNEL. IN EVENT OF DEMOSTRATED HOSTILE INTENT, PROSECUTE WITH EXTREME PREJUDICE.

The Captain showed the message to the exec and said: "This is our second EAM in thirty minutes. Let's hope the French don't bugger this up. I don't want my eulogy to include, 'started world war III'. Sonar, Conn, what's the Perle up to?"

"Conn, sonar, she's rising, sir. Slowly, but contact is rising."

"She's probably trying to hide above the thermocline," the Captain responded. "So, the 64,000-dollar question is this: does she just want to bugger off, or is she getting ready to fire and looking for a place to hide from our response? Maneuvering, 5 degrees up bubble on the diving plane. Let's follow her and see what she's up to. Exec, send a message to fleet and let them know what's going on. I want clarification of our rules of engagement. I would like explicit permission to fire preemptively if we detect them opening their torpedo outer doors."

"Aye, sir, immediately," the Executive Officer responded.

Aboard the French Attack Submarine, The Perle, S606, in The English Channel

"Conn, sonar!" the sonar operator exclaimed, "Target has turned to starboard and is starting a gradual ascent. I believe she's following us."

"I guess that confirms she knows we're here," the Captain said.

"Conn, Weapons, shall I open outer doors?"

"Negative Wheps. Not yet. Hold tight."

"Weapons, Aye."

Office of the Prime Minister, 10 Downing Street, London England

Their meeting was interrupted by a buzz on Prime Minister Boren's intercom. His secretary spoke. "Excuse me, sir, but it's the First Sea Lord, and he says it is extremely urgent."

"Put him through, Abagail."

A deep and resonate voice literally boomed over the speaker. "Pardon me, sir, but are Sir Nick and Simon still with you?"

"Yes, Tony, they are."

"Good. I'm afraid we've just received a communication from the Astute in the English Channel. They report being in a dance with a French Rubis-class attack boat."

"Is the French boat showing hostile intent?" Defense Minister Davies asked.

"Not as yet. The French intentions are unknown, and the Rubis-class has made no effort to contact the Astute. Our Captain has asked for guidance on the rules of engagement. Our instructions are to prosecute hostile intent with extreme prejudice. He would like explicit permission to fire if he detects the Rubis-class opening their outer torpedo doors. I support the request."

Aboard the English Attack Submarine HMS Astute, S119, in The English Channel

"Conn, sonar, we've lost the contact. They must be above the thermocline.

"Maneuvering," the Captain called out, "make that 15 degrees up bubble on the diving plane and increase speed to 20 knots. I don't want to lose this guy."

"Conn, radio; incoming Emergency Action Message. A sailor handed the Captain another sheet of paper. It read: RULES OF ENGAGEMENT CLARIFIED TO PERMIT PREEMPTIVE ACTION IF ATTACK DEEMED IMMINENT.

The Captain handed the second message to the XO. "The buggers are telling me it's my judgment. Bloody politicians. Ask for a yes or no and you give a bloody 'do the right thing.'"

Aboard the French Attack Submarine, The Perle, S606, in The English Channel

"Conn, Sonar, we have re-acquired the contact. We are now both above the thermocline. Contact has increased speed to 20 knots and is on collision course."

"Relax, sailor, he'll turn. He's just trying to catch up to us. Maneuvering, increase speed to 20 knots. Let's keep the distance between us constant."

Aboard the English Attack Submarine HMS Astute, S119, in The English Channel

"Sonar, Conn, contact has increased speed to 20 knots."

"Captain," the Executive Officer said, getting the Captain's attention. "I have a bad feeling about this. The EF fired on the Swedes and then the Iranians. They've remained silent, so we don't know their motive or intent. I'm afraid their remaining silent is more consistent with continued action than standing down, and we know they are at DefCon2. If this was some kind of mistake, they'd be on the horn offering an explanation."

"What's your point, XO?" the Captain asked.

"Who would they most likely attack next? It wouldn't be the Americans or the Russians, their teeth are too big."

"That would be us," the Captain observed.

"Exactly, or we would at least be very high on the list. We know there's another Rubis-class out there," he commented, unaware that their intelligence was wrong, that they were facing only one French Submarine, the Perle. "What if he's leading us into a trap?" the XO asked.

"Battle stations, torpedo!" the Captain ordered.

The Captain's command, "Battle stations, torpedo", echoed over the MC1 intercom.

"Good point, XO. Let's not take that chance. Wheps, Conn; lock firing solution for tubes 1 & 2. Prepare to open outer doors," The Captain barked.

"Conn, Weapons, firing solution locked. Standing by to open outer doors."

"Let's flush this bugger out," the Captain said. "Sonar, Conn, give that boat one active ping."

"Chief?" the sonar operator, confused by the order, asked his supervisor.

The Master Chief standing behind the sonar man smiled. "The Captain is going to flush out their intentions by announcing our presence, but in a way that should convince them we are not about to fire, at least not yet."

"How so?"

"No Captain who about to fire would announce his presence and precise location with an active ping. If it's a trap, we'll know by the reaction of the contact. It should also help us locate the other boat. Ping that boat."

"Aye, Chief. I hope we're not giving the French too much credit for rational thinking."

"You're not paid to think, sailor. You're paid to push that button. Ping the damn boat."

"Aye, Chief."

Aboard the French Attack Submarine, The Perle, S606, in The English Channel

"Active ping!" the sonar operator shouted as the sound resonated throughout the entire boat."

"He's about to fire on us!" the Captain exclaimed. "Weapons, re-confirm firing solution!"

"Fire solution confirmed!" the Weapons officer replied.

"Open outer doors!" the Captain ordered. "Radio, Conn!"

"Conn, Radio, aye!"

"If that English bastard fires on us I want you to immediately inform Fleet and the Le Viligant!" The Captain was referring to the French ballistic missile submarine, Le Viligant, S618, operating in the North Sea.

"Captain, what if he is just trying to send some kind of message?" the XO asked. "He hasn't opened his outer doors yet. If we open ours we force his hand!"

""We're at DefCon2, XO. This is not a time for nuance! Weapons, open those outer doors!"

"Opening outer torpedo doors!"

"Standby to fire tubes 3 and 4!" the Captain announced. "Fire on my mark – three, two,...."

Aboard the English Attack Submarine HMS Astute, S119, in The English Channel

"Conn, sonar, contact is opening its outer torpedo doors!"

"Wheps, open outer doors! Stand by to fire tubes 1 & 2 on my command. I'm going to blow that son of a bitch out of the water!"

Aboard the French Attack Submarine, The Perle, S606, in The English Channel

"Captain, Radio! Incoming Emergency Action Message!"

"Weapons, Captain, do not fire yet! Belay that last order! I can't believe this shit! Fleet's sense of timing is remarkable!"

"Conn, sonar, English boat is now opening their outer torpedo doors!"

"Radio, GET ME THAT MESSAGE!!!" the Captain screamed.

The radioman knocked down the boat's executive officer as he leapt forward in a panic handing the EAM to the Captain. It read: STAND DOWN FROM DEFCON2. SET CONDITIONS TO DEFCON 4. IMPERATIVE THAT NO HOSTILE INTENT SHOWN TO OTHER FORCES.

"SHIT!" the Captain screamed. "Weapons, close outer doors! Maneuvering, emergency blow! Put us on the surface! Radio, hail that English boat. I want to talk to their Captain."

Aboard the English Attack Submarine HMS Astute, S119, in The English Channel

"Conn, sonar, Captain, contact closing outer doors! It is not firing!"

"Weapons, belay that last order! Close outer doors"

"Conn, sonar, a lot of noise in the water. I think the boat is making an emergency blow! Confirmed! They are headed for the surface!"

"Thank you, dear Jesus!" the Captain exclaimed. He looked at his XO and said, "We just stuck our big toe into the gates of Hell and pulled it out again. We almost started World War III."

"Conn, Radio; the French boat is hailing us."

"What? Well, this should be interesting," the Captain remarked.

Chapter 35 – Beginnings of a Plan

Office of Lt. Gen. Jean-Baptiste Laurent, European Federation Defense Ministry, Berlin

Jean-Baptist was likely the only person in the entire European Federation who understood what had happened, or at least believed he understood. Marcus Day's comments during that strange meeting at Madame Claude's Pub now made perfect sense. The Iranians must have been behind the missile launch. But why attack their own country? That was the most puzzling piece of the mystery, and he didn't have a clue. The one thing he did know, however, was Hans-Dieter Zimmerman likely knew a great deal about what happened. The other thing he knew is he couldn't take such a wild theory to Brandt or Krüger without proof.

Laurent looked at his contact list and found the phone number, both business and cell, for Zimmerman. Their paths had crossed numerous times over the last few years, as was common for senior executives in the EF Military and their major contractors, and he had a couple of the man's business cards. He punched in the number for Zimmerman's office first, believing that would be his most likely whereabouts mid-day. His secretary answered the phone and responded that her boss was en route to the airport for a trip to France. This immediately raised Laurent's suspicions that the man was about to run. The aircraft's flight plan to France could easily be amended once airborne. Laurent asked the secretary if she would be so kind as to give him the tail number of the Sternenlicht private jet so he could contact it, and she readily complied. Executive Secretaries of high-profile military suppliers were not given to declining the requests of Lieutenants General.

Laurent's next phone call was to the EF Military Air Police. He briskly ordered the Berlin Commandant to put a hold on the aircraft's departure clearance, without explanation, and to send a vehicle directly to the tarmac and arrest Zimmerman. They were to hold Zimmerman at the airport until

Laurent arrived and took custody of the man. Laurent left his office without explanation and walked to the parking structure where his silver Porsche 911 Carrera waited for him. He estimated the sportscar would propel him to the airport in less than 20 minutes.

* * * * *

Laurent pulled up to the gate of the General Aviation section of Berlin Airport and flashed his credentials, although the sight of his uniform was likely the only thing necessary to afford him entrance. He drove past several hangers towards the Terminal Ramp of the airport's business FBO, or "Fixed Base Operator", and saw the Dassault Falcon 7X jet on the ramp with its steps deployed. At $53 million per copy, the aircraft was an impressive sight, and its almost 7,000-mile range could have taken Zimmerman virtually anywhere in the world. Laurent had no doubt that Zimmerman likely had a willing co-conspirator in the pilot, who would be well-compensated for his cooperation.

Laurent parked his car, exited and walked over to a utilitarian-looking black SUV where Zimmerman was being held. He handed the keys to his Porsche to one of the Air Police and asked him to please drive the Porsche back to the Defense Ministry garage. The man broadly smiled at the request as he accepted the keys to the 150,000-euro automobile. Laurent then walked to one of the rear doors of the SUV, opened it, and glanced inside, recognizing Zimmerman.

"Going somewhere?" Laurent asked.

"What is the meaning of this?" Zimmerman asked, almost shouting.

"Let's take a drive, Hans, and we'll discuss your question."

Laurent then asked the remaining Air Police to exit the SUV and said to the three men, "To be clear, lads, in the name of national security, this arrest did not happen, none of you saw me, and none of us were ever here, agreed?"

"We have no idea what you're even talking about, General," the Captain said, smiling, as the two other men nodded in agreement.

"Thank you, now carry on."

Laurent accepted the SUV's keys, climbed into the driver's seat and closed the door. "You and I are going to go for a little ride, Herr Zimmerman, and we are going to have a conversation. How forthright you are will determine what happens next."

"Where are you taking me?" Zimmerman demanded. "This is outrageous!"

"I know perfectly well you were not headed to France. I also have it on good authority that you are in bed with the Iranians and are somehow involved in the compromise of our command and control systems. You are going to tell me everything you know, or your life is going to become quite unpleasant."

"I have no idea what you are talking about!" Zimmerman exclaimed.

"Oh, please," Laurent responded, "don't waste my time with such a predictable response, and don't play me for a fool. I had a very interesting conversation just recently with an old colleague, Marcus Day. Marcus and his boss, a Joseph Michael Barber, I believe, had some interesting insights on the murder of Herr Schiller and, I might add, your complicity. I also understand you have recently become a very wealthy man, to the tune of about 50 million euros, expertly traced back to your new-found friends, the Iranians. I can assure you, Herr Zimmerman, you are going to tell me everything you know."

Laurent looked in the rear-view mirror at Zimmerman's face. His face was white as he remained silent.

Offices of Orion Bellicus, Rye, New York

"Hey Joe," Marcus Day said as he walked into Barber's office. "You're not going to believe this. I just got a call from Laurent. He caught Zimmerman trying to run. He's got him on ice and has offered to hand him over to us."

"Why would he hand the guy over to us? Why not hand the guy over to the EF intelligence service?"

"He said too many lawyers will get involved and he doesn't think they can afford the time. If this thing isn't resolved quicly, he believes we are looking at the risk of a large-scale conflagration, and I have to agree. The entire world is calling for Germany's head, and he doesn't trust the United States or England to show restraint, let alone Russia. Evidently the Russian Army is already amassing forces along their Western Border."

"OK, so we add to our already long list of violations of international law and do what, persuade the guy to talk?"

"He's the only lead we have right now," Day responded.

"So, where do we do this?" Barber asked. "I'm certainly not going to do it in Germany and run the risk of going afoul of their authorities. They already have a pretty long list of things they could charge me with if they had a clue what the two of us have been up to in the last couple of weeks."

"There is only one place to safely do this," Day said.

"Shetland?"

"Exactly. The most secure safe-house on the planet."

"Ok," Barber replied. "Call Laurent back and tell him we're on. We'll pick up the guy at the Berlin Airport. Let's use Net Jets instead of our plane so it's not quite so obvious who's landing on German soil. Laurent has to grease the skids for us. We'll pick up Zimmerman at the airport, fly to Edenborough, then take a chopper to the safe house."

"Got it."

"One more thing, Marc."

"Yes?"

"Once we are in international waters I'm going to call Maggie. I want her sanction on this."

"Do you think we'll get it?"

"I think there's a good chance. It will be a black op, and we will be under NOC rules," Barber said, referencing the concept of 'non-official cover', whereby agents of an intelligence service are operating in secret and are disavowed if caught, "but I don't think she has a choice. Your French friend is certainly correct about one thing – time is of the essence here. We are racing against the clock to stop things spiraling completely out of control."

"OK. And if she says no?" Day asked.

"We'll cross that bridge if we get to it," Barber replied.

Chapter 36 – Budding Clarity

Oval Office Study, Washington, D.C.

The Oval Office is largely a ceremonial space where the President of the United States greets formal dignitaries, meets with Congressional leaders or conducts other business that is enhanced by the formal grandeur of one of the most famous spaces on earth. But there is another special place in the White House, adjacent to the Oval Office, where most of the President's real work gets done. It's the President's private study. Impressive in and of itself, but in a more utilitarian way, it serves as a quiet retreat from formality, and is more conducive to the solitary work that comprises some of the duties of the chief executive. It also grants the President a rare sense of privacy.

President Sara Einhorn was in need of a little privacy at the moment. The blinding headache she experienced in the Situation Room was thankfully brief, but she had come to understand the real purpose of the headaches was a summons to an audience with her tormentor. So, she reached into her jacket pocket and retrieved a cell phone, then dialed the number for Emma Clark, the CEO of PrinSafe.

"Thank you, Sara, for returning my call," Clark said as she answered the phone.

"It wasn't a call, Emma, it was another blinding headache."

"Let's just think of it as my calling card, Madam President."

"It's not a calling card, it's a physical assault."

"But it works, doesn't it?"

The President ignored the taunt and demanded: "Was your hand in any of this business, this mess in Iran?" the President demanded.

"No, not directly anyway. We have many clients, Sara, and when they ask for our help they often don't fully disclose their intentions. Suffice it to say I am looking into it."

"We know you have a German subsidiary, CWR Industries, doing business with the European Federation's military. The C.I.A. uncovered the ownership chain that links the company back to you."

"That is correct. It's been a matter of discussion in the past, hasn't it? And thank you for not shutting us down after that mess in Sweden."

"Like I had a choice. You know that increased sanctions now are a foregone conclusion. I have no remotely credible reason for trying to block them now. If I did, I suspect the Cabinet would invoke the 25th Amendment. In all likelihood we're looking at a complete boycott, to say nothing of a military response. If your call is about blocking any response, you're out of your mind, and If you do anything to incapacitate me, that empty suit in the Vice President's chair is going to get my job. Good luck with him."

"Let's calm down, Madam President. You've done nothing, at least yet, to warrant anything so drastic. What I need from you is information. I can assure you the European Federation's recent actions are no more in our self-interest than in yours. We stand to lose billions in defense contracts and our Deutsche Franc investments are going to come under heavy pressure tomorrow morning when the Berlin stock market opens."

"What kind of information do you want?" the President asked.

"We cannot figure out the motive. Why on earth would the EF detonate a nuclear weapon on Iranian soil? It wasn't even a military target. It was a city, actually a holy city according to their religion. Given your resources, I was hoping you would have some insight."

There was a long pause as the President considered how to answer. CIA Director Shevchenko's theory about the computer hack, however far-fetched, was the only clue they had. Sharing this with the CEO of a private equity firm was about the most serious national security breach she could imagine right now. Impeachment was likely the least of the consequences she would face if she was revealed as the source. She could lie and tell Clark they didn't know anything yet, and that the EF Chancellor still wasn't returning phone calls, but she knew this would only delay the inevitable. She was quickly coming to realize she faced a binary choice – excruciating pain and possible death, or life, at least for a little while longer. She chose life.

"Sara," Clark said, "are you there? I don't need to send another calling card, do I?"

"No," the President replied. "We find the EF's motives incomprehensible; however, there is a working theory, although it's pretty far-fetched."

"I'm all ears," Clark said.

"CIA claims to be in possession of credible evidence that the EF, in fact, did not initiate the attack on Iran. The evidence points to Iran hacking into the EFs command and control systems and launching the missile themselves."

Emma Clark suddenly was overcome by a cold chill, and goose-bumps stood at attention all across her body as she realized the implication of what was just said. CWR Industries provided Iran with computer code to one of the EF's military systems. She had assumed it was for defensive purposes, but what if it wasn't. Still, what would be the motive for attacking themselves?

"Emma, my turn; are you still there?"

"Yes," Clark said. "Interesting theory, but what could possibly be their motive for attacking themselves, and a holy city at that?"

"That's what makes me a skeptic," the President said.

"Hang on a second," Clark said. She pulled out a piece of yarn and placed in on the globe sitting on her desk, with one end on Germany and the other end on Iran. She stretched it, then followed its path. The chill and the goose-bumps returned.

"Do you know, Madam President, what lies just slightly off a missiles flight path from Germany to Iran?"

"What?"

"Israel."

The President pursed her lips and blew out a full and dramatic breath as she contemplated the implications, then said, "So maybe Iran screwed up. Maybe the missile went long."

"Exactly," Clark responded.

"That still seems pretty far-fetched."

"I agree, but the theory is a lot more credible than it was 10 seconds ago. I suggest you run it to ground."

"I agree," the President responded. "I'm being called back to the situation room. No more headaches, Emma, I have to appear in control."

"Just keep me informed, Madam President," she said, then pressed "end" on her cell phone to end the call.

Dr. Emma Clark's Office, PrinSafe, Palo Alto, California

Clark spun her chair around and looked out the window. Among the many details she had not shared with the President, regarding her dealings with the Iranians, was one she found very disturbing: she was unable to reach her contact in Iran, General Hamidi. He had gone silent. Did Hamidi actually have a plan to hack into the EF command and control system and launch a nuclear missile at someone? Did his efforts fail and result in the missile hitting the wrong target? That would certainly explain his possible death. But for that to be true, he not only would need to hack the launch system, he would need to hack the missile targeting system as well. That was simply too difficult. I couldn't be done; it was impossible. Then she remembered something her old mentor, Westy Reynolds, had told her once, "What was impossible yesterday is only difficult today, and what is difficult today is actually easy tomorrow. Never think in terms of impossible; only think in terms of how, and you always will accelerate that progression. Remember, Emma, there is always a way." She had much work to do, and it suddenly occurred to her that the 500 million dollars the Iranian General paid her wasn't nearly enough.

Chapter 37 – The Video Conference

Situation Room, The White House, Washington D.C.

The large flat-panel display directly across from the President flickered momentarily, then displayed the English Prime Minister, Jeremy Boren.

"Good morning, Jeremy," the President said, then corrected herself to reflect the time difference between Washington D.C. and London, "or sorry, should I say good afternoon?"

"Good morning, Madam President. I have here with me Simon Davies, our Defense Secretary, Lord David Herbert, Chief of the Intelligence Service, and General Sir Nick Carleton, Chief of the Defense Staff."

"Welcome," the President responded.

"Sara, we nearly went to blows with the EF a couple of hours ago, and I would like Simon to brief you and your team on what happened. These are dangerous times, and I fear the risk of miscalculation remains very high."

"I agree, Jeremy. Mr. Davies, please tell us what happened."

"One of our attack submarines, on patrol in the English Channel, got into an unfortunate dance with a French boat, and we almost fired on each other. The odd thing is, at the last minute the French boat broke off the attack, surfaced and hailed our Captain. Save for the vigilance of our very talented sonar operator who correctly diagnosed the French retreat, we would have fired, and they would have undoubted responded in kind. The French Captain reported they were ordered by Fleet to break off the attack and show no hostile intent. The French Captain also said their alert status has been reduced, but he provided no other details. Our intelligence suggests the EF has reduced their alert level from DefCon 2 to DefCon 4."

"I have not been informed as yet about their reduced alert status," she said, with a stern look at the Director of the Defense Intelligence Agency, sitting several seats down the row to her left, "but that sounds like quite a story."

"Yes, and had the French conveyed that order to their boat five seconds later, it would have been too late. It was that close."

"Have you been able to reach Chancellor Krüger?" the President asked.

"No. I've tried Morel as well. Nobody's returning phone calls," Boren answered.

"Do you have any insight as to their motive?"

"No. We regard it as incomprehensible. Do you?"

"Maggie," the President responded, referring to Margaret Schevchenko, "please share with the Prime Minister what you shared with us."

Before the CIA Director could comment, the intercom buzzed. It was the NSA technician managing the video conference. He said, "Excuse me, Madam President, but the European Federation Chancellor, Heinrich Krüger is calling on this line and wishes to join the video conference."

There were several seconds of silence as everyone appeared astonished. Then the President asked, annoyed, "How did he know we were in video conference?"

"He evidently called the Oval first, ma'am, and was informed of such by your secretary."

"By all means, please put him through," the President responded.

The main flat panel display flickered again and went split screen, with the English Prime Minister on the left and the European Federation Chancellor on the right.

The English Prime Minister allowed the President to take the lead and open the conversation. She let go with "both barrels." "Good afternoon, Chancellor Krüger. We talk at last. You've had quite the last few days, haven't you? It is incomprehensible to me that you would fire a nuclear warhead at Iran, no matter how bad they are inclined to behave, and against a civilian target with a population of over 2 million people. Your actions are reprehensible and morally repugnant, and you have made your European Federation a pariah. I wish to lead off by informing you of the preliminary actions Prime Minister Boren and I have agreed to. These actions will be implemented, unilaterally effective immediately, and we intend to introduce the resolution at the Security Council tomorrow morning. We have obtained assurances of support from each of the members. The following actions will be announced, by me, later today. First, a complete boycott of any further commerce with the EF. The Russian Federation also has agreed to block any further exports of natural gas, petroleum or coal. Second, effective sundown tomorrow, we will be blockading your northern ports along the Channel and the North Sea. Third, we will introduce a petition tomorrow at the International Court at the Hague to charge you personally and senior members of your government with crimes against humanity. I emphasize that these are just the first steps. More action will follow once we achieve international consensus."

The EF Chancellor responded in a calm and business-like voice, "Madam President, my apologies for not reaching out to you earlier, but we have been intensely focused on determining the facts. I understand your initial reaction and would have expected nothing less. I hope the goodwill we intend to show over the next 24 hours will mitigate some of those actions, or at least postpone their implementation. The reason I wished to join this video conference is to provide you with the assurance that, no matter how difficult this is to believe, the European Federation was not responsible for the attack on Iran. I concede that it was one of our missiles that delivered the warhead, and I acknowledge the launch was from EF, German soil, but that missile was not fired at the direction of our National Command Authority, and we are quite certain it was not the actions of any rogue force within the EF. We have extensive systems analytics which I hope will corroborate my assurances. We would be happy to host anyone you wish from your intelligence services here in Berlin to examine them for themselves. Throughout the entire sequence of events our command and control systems showed no activity whatsoever, provided us with no warning or indication that a launch was in progress, and the system even shows the missile in to still be in its launch tube."

The President's eyes then met those of the CIA Director. Maybe there was something to Maggie's evidence after all. She hoped so.

The President continued to push, "Chancellor, how are events in Sweden connected to this mess?"

"They are not. Sweden was an isolated incident. Our aircraft responded defensively to excessively aggressive intercepts by Swedish aircraft. Once this bigger mess is dispositioned I plan to reach out to them, establish better lines of communication among our military, and discuss compensation for their loss. I understand how it may appear, but I assure you the two unfortunate incidences are unrelated."

"Chancellor Krüger, it's Jeremy Boren. I presume you are aware that one of your submarines was about to attack one of Her Majesty's subs. Fortunately, your Captain aborted the attack at the last minute and advised us that your alert status has been reduced, which both Sara and I have verified. Why did you go to a war-footing, DefCon2, in the first place. It clearly demonstrated hostile intent."

"Our military increased our alert level as a precaution, and they did so without my permission. My Generals were concerned about the possibility that you would attack our military bases, as well as the near certainty of retaliatory terrorist attacks. I recognized the provocative nature of the increased alert status and reversed the order immediately after becoming aware of it. I would ask each of you to reduce your alert levels as well. I think we all have to be sensitive to the reality that the risk of miscalculation in the current environment is extraordinarily high. I must also caution you that while we have reduced our alert level, we plan to remain vigilant about protecting our people and our military assets. I am offering you a gesture of goodwill and expect you to reciprocate. Any display of aggression on the part of either of your militaries will be met with a full-throated defense."

"Now is not the time for you to be making threats, Chancellor," the President responded, sarcastically.

"It's not a threat, Sara, it's our reality, and I don't make the comment in the spirit of bluster, I make it in the spirit of transparency, with the objective of avoiding exactly the kind of miscalculations that almost took us to blows in the English Channel."

"I think we need to excuse you now," the President responded, "and discuss your offer of inspections. Is there anything else you wish to share beforehand?"

"Yes. I assume that the international community, led by the United Nations, is planning an immediate relief response to the people in Iran. As an additional gesture of good faith and an expression of our humanity, I want you to send us the bill. That fact will remain anonymous at the moment, given the obvious complications its disclosure would cause. We will make our contribution public once we have provided uncontrivable evidence of our innocence in this matter. Now if you will excuse me, I have much work to do in the restoration of our Federation's reputation."

"Very well and thank you. Good bye Chancellor Krüger, and good luck. I would say you have a very tall mountain to climb."

"We recognize that, but I assure you, climb it we will."

Chapter 38 – The Mission

Aboard a NetJets Bombardier 5000 Aircraft, Eastbound Over the Atlantic, Flight Level 37

The aircraft was much larger and more luxurious than necessary to fly just one passenger, Joe Barber, from Westchester County Airport to Berlin, pick up Marcus Day and another passenger, then fly on to Manchester, England. From there the plan was to travel by automobile to the coast, then catch a helicopter to Heroldswick, Shetland, the northern most settlement in the Shetland Islands. The town of Heroldswick is located on a small bay in the shape of a crescent moon, with a tall hill on each side framing steep cliffs and rough waters below. The waters are reputed to be some of the best maceral fishing locations in the world. The locale had another strategic advantage. It was isolated. Tourists travelling to the Shetland Islands rarely traveled north of Lerwick, and nobody went to Heroldswick for holiday. The Orion Bellicus safe house there, a small cabin at the top of one of the hills with an expansive view of the coast, was one of the loneliest places on Earth. It was perfect.

Successful completion of the journey required intervention from at least three sources. First, General Jean-Baptiste Laurent would need to clear the NetJets aircraft into Berlin with no questions asked and arrange for an uninterrupted departure. Given present circumstances, with all commercial traffic into and out of the European Federation was on hold, if Laurent wasn't a Lieutenant General, it wouldn't be possible. As Deputy Commander of the EF Airforce, he could make a lot of very difficult things happen. Second, England would need to allow unmolested entry and exit of the plane through Manchester and then, third, Scotland would have to look the other way as a helicopter departed from the English coast towards the Shetland's northern most island. Barber was counting on his former mentor and now Director of the CIA, Margaret Shevchenko, to make the last two things happen.

Barber sat in one of the aircraft's richly upholstered leather seats. A polished mahogany folding table was deployed in front of him. Instead of the usual glass of single malt Scotch in his hand, a Macallan 25, Barber held a glass of ice water. He picked up his cell phone, sitting on the table, and dialed Marcus Day. Day answered in two rings.

"How are you feeling, pal?" Day asked.

"Pretty good, actually. I think I'm back to about 90 percent. I still wouldn't want another dance with an MMA fighter, but I'm almost there."

"That's good news. I just heard from Laurent. He's arranged our clearances into and out of Berlin. Have you talked to Maggie yet?" referring to the CIA Director. "I'd like to verify we've received clearances with the English and the Scots before we go wheels up."

"No, but she's my next call."

""I'll leave you to it, then. Call me back as soon as you talk to her. Laurent's got Zimmerman on ice in a hanger here until you arrive."

"Good. I'll call her right now."

Barber set the phone down on the table and stretched his arms out over his head, then took a long pull on the glass of ice water. As he reached for his phone again, it rang before he could pick it up. He looked at the screen and read a familiar phone number. It was Shevchenko.

"Hello Maggie," Barber answered. "I was just about to call you."

"Great minds think alike," she responded. "Listen, things have gotten very interesting here. I just came from the Situation Room and we finally connected with Krüger. He claims the EF had nothing to do with that missile launch. He said their command and control systems never indicated anything was happening, and still indicate the errant missile is in its launch tube."

"Wow," Barber exclaimed. "Did he mention the Iranians? Does he suspect them?"

"No," she responded, "he does not, but claims to be turning over Heaven and Earth to find out who's responsible."

"Listen, Maggie," Barber continued, "we've got some news too. Mark has a source, an old buddie from his U.N. days in Africa, who's very senior in the EF Military. Mark met with him two days ago and told him everything."

"Wow," she responded, "don't know what I think about that. Wished you had talked to me first."

"Hey, he judged we didn't have time, and I agree with him."

"OK, good point, as usual."

"Anyway, the guy, Marc's contact, wanted to talk to the acting CEO of Sternenlicht, the firm that designed the command and control system, a guy named Zimmerman."

"I'm familiar with him. An arrogant SOB, if I remember correctly."

"Yeah, that's our guy. Anyway, when he called the guy's office, turns out he was headed to the airport, supposedly for a business trip. Long story short, the guy was trying to run. Marc's contact intercepted him and is holding him at the Berlin Airport."

"What, exactly, are you planning to do?"

"We're going to take him to our most secure safehouse."

"The one in Shetland?"

"How did you know that?"

"I'm the Director of the CIA, Joe. I know everything."

"OK, maybe it's not as safe as I thought."

"We digress. What's your plan, and what do you need from me?"

"We're going to have a 'conversation' with the guy in Scotland. And when we find out who's responsible for this, we, make that I, am going after him. What I need from you is clearance from the English for a flight into Manchester, and clearances from both the English and the Scots for a helicopter ride from the east coast of England to Heroldswick."

"Why do you want to land in England? Why not fly directly to Scotland? That way I only have to get State to grease on customs service," referring to the U.S. State Department,."

"First, there's no airport in the Shetlands with a runway long enough for this jet, and second it's way too high profile. Nobody ever flies a plane this big to the Shetlands."

"Ok, I get it. Well, at least you don't want much. OK, I'll take care of it, but there are two conditions."

"What are they?" Barber asked.

"To avoid breaking a whole lot of laws, you are going to be working for us, under your normal contractor purchase order. We're going to call it 'security work' which is technically correct, if a bit of a stretch. That means you're 'Non-Official Cover', or 'NOC'. If you're caught or in any way captured...'

"Yeah, yeah," Barber interrupted, "the Secretary will disavow any knowledge of my actions. I've seen 'Mission Impossible'."

"OK, good, but I felt a need to be clear." she said. "Anyway, the second condition is you are going to stay within the rails of previously approved enhanced interrogation techniques, and you are not going to permanently injure this guy in any way, agreed?"

"Agreed to both, although I may scare him a bit."

"Scare him all you want, but if he's seriously injured your immunity is off. Sorry, but that's the world we live in. I'm going to execute a Presidential Finding to cover this."

"What do you mean, 'execute a Presidential Finding?'."

"I have a blank one in my safe for just such an occasion. All I have to do is fill in a few names and facts. It's already signed by Einhorn."

"Wow, such a thing exists?" Barber asked.

"Only one, Joe, only one, and to be used only in exigent circumstances. I would say, 'pulling back from the brink of global thermonuclear war' probably qualifies."

"You're the best, Maggie," Barber said.

"Just be careful out there."

"Will do, Sergeant Easterhouse," he said in reference to the old Hill Street Blues character.

Chapter 39 – The Beginnings of a Noose

Offices of the European Federation Defense Ministry, Berlin

Lieutenant General Jean-Baptiste Laurent walked purposefully towards the office of his boss, General Horst Brandt. Laurent had left Zimmerman with the three Air Police Officers at the airport and instructed them to release the man into the custody of two men who would confirm their identity with a code word, and not to interfere as the three then boarded a NetJets aircraft to depart. The Air Police were told it was a national security matter and they were forbidden from revealing anything about the detention of Zimmerman or his departure without Laurent's expressed permission.

As Laurent walked towards Brandt's office, he questioned how much he should reveal to his boss. Laurent knew that Brandt was close to Zimmerman and spent a lot of time at Sternenlicht while the command and control system was being developed. His boss also knew Emma Clark, the CEO of CWR Industries' parent company, PrinSafe. He had no reason to believe Brandt was complicit in what happened, but the coincidences were too many for him to take Brandt fully into his confidence. He also was quite certain that if Zimmerman had been able to get in touch with Brandt, it would soon be Laurent in custody no longer Zimmerman. On the other hand, Laurent was now in possession of material information regarding what happened, and as a senior military commander he couldn't just sit on it. He had a responsibility to his chain of command. As he reached for the handle to Brandt's office door, he made his decision. He would tell his boss most of what he knew, but he would hold back details about handing over Zimmerman to the two Americans and about what really happened at the Iranian Embassy, including Barber's abduction.

General Horst Brandt, Commander of the European Federation Air Force, including the Strategic Rocket Forces from which the hacked missile was launched, sat at his ornate desk and stared at the French General sitting across from him as Laurent weaved his fantastic tale. The more Brandt listened, the more his stomach started to churn. The number of coincidences and connected dots were starting to add up. He had done nothing wrong, he kept telling himself. But what of his sins of omission? He had the lead on the command and control system. He knew Emma Clark personally. His phone log would show a dozen or more calls to her. He never thought to hide them. Worse yet, he had asked her, just recently, to personally intervene with the U.S. Government to kill the sanctions that were about to be placed on their key supplier, CWR Industries, and he had even bragged to Laurent about it. How did he miss the signs? Did he want that rail gun breakthrough so badly that he ignored the potential security breaches that must have been occurring? Was this supplier, CWR Industries, somehow complicit in what happened? His head was spinning. And this French General, did he suspect him in any way? Was he being totally open with him? Was he holding anything back? Brandt was struggling with an emotion that was completely absent for the most of his life. He was insecure.

"Mon General, I believe the only appropriate course of action is to have our security forces take up residence at the offices of Sternenlicht and CWR Industries, and to do it today. We don't know how widespread their involvement may be, and I'm hoping not very much, but I regard it as an unescapable conclusion that there are, at a minimum, individuals in both companies who must have been involved. There is a high risk they may be destroying evidence and we must move quickly to protect it."

Brandt now started recalling all of his meetings at both companies. His office diary who have a detailed record of them. Should he destroy them, he wondered. No, that would be stupid. No better way to quickly raise suspicions than to start destroying evidence. It wouldn't work anyway, the office diaries at both of the companies would also show the meetings. His mind began to think in terms of worst-case outcomes. An image flashed through his consciousness of him being led away from his office in handcuffs.

He imagined sitting in a jail cell. At least the EF didn't allow capital punishment, he thought. His mind was racing so quickly to evaluate his personal risk that he was struggling to listen to Laurent speak. "STOP," he silently screamed at himself. "You're not going to survive this by losing control of yourself. Get a grip!" he thought, and finally began to regain his composure when his intercom buzzed. It was his secretary.

"Excuse me, General, but the Minister of Defense is on the line."

"Thank you," he responded. "Jean-Baptiste, hold that thought for a minute."

"Yes, sir," the General said crisply.

The Minister of Defense spoke, "General Brandt, I need to inform you that on the orders of the Chancellor, our national security forces have raided the offices of both Sternenlicht and CWR Industries. Both companies will be instructed to continue to provide whatever vital services are needed, and we will need the assistance of your staff to identify that, but we are securing all written and electronic documentation of their activities for the last two years. The Chancellor is in possession of intelligence that suggests our command and control systems have been compromised, although we have no idea by whom. It is the most logical explanation of what happened I have yet to hear. You are to provide the resources and all necessary cooperation that is needed."

"Of course, Minister."

"We are going to find whoever did this to us, to the Iranians, and we are going to blast them into hell," the Defense Minister said. "I am to be advised of any material insight achieved the moment it happens, is that clear?"

"Yes, Minister, very clear."

"Thank you. Now if you will excuse me, I have much work to do."

"Well," General Laurent said, "this theory got their attention a lot more quickly than I imagined. I know the Chancellor talked to the American

President and the English PM this morning. My guess is he heard something from one of them."

"What could they possibly know about a hack of our systems?" Brandt asked.

"I think you underestimate their capabilities, mon-General," Laurent replied. "We may have beat them on rail-gun develoment, but nobody is better at intelligence than the Americans, except maybe the Chinese," he mused.

General Brandt's heart was now racing, his face slightly flushed and a couple of beads of sweat popped on his forehead in spite of the generous air conditioning feeding his office. Laurent noticed.

"Are you OK, Horst?" he asked, sufficiently concerned that he took the unusual step of addressing Brandt by his first name.

"Yes, I'm fine. My breakfast hasn't set well with me this morning," he proffered as an excuse. "My wife keeps telling me to cut back on the sausages, but you know, after all, I am a German."

"Of course," Laurent replied, without smiling or acknowledging the joke. His boss's behavior was odd, he thought. "I will leave you to your indigestion, sir."

"Thank you," and with that Brandt watched the Frenchman rise from his chair and walk out the door.

"I've got to regain command of my emotions," the General scolded himself. But then he thought about agents from the EF Security Service arriving at the offices of Sternenlicht and CWR Industries and imagined them combing through phone logs and meeting diaries. "Should I call Emma," he asked himself. "Yes, of course, how could he do less." He picked up the receiver on his phone and punched in the two numbers, but quickly put it down as he realized what a colossal mistake that would be, creating a record of a phone call from his office to an American CEO connected with a defense supplier under suspicion less than five minutes from receiving a phone call from the Defense Minister advising him of the pending raid. "HE HAD DONE NOTHING WRONG," he told himself again. But he was making mistakes, and if he kept doing so he would quickly become a suspect, innocent or not. But was he really innocent? What had he missed? No, what had he deliberately overlooked? That was the real question, and it was a question that would continue to haunt him as the imaginary noose he now felt around his neck began to tighten.

Chapter 40 – Haroldswick

Haroldswick, Shetland Islands, Scotland

Their travel to Scotland was uneventful, thanks largely to the efforts of the American and British governments, and General Laurent. The NetJets aircraft was in and out of Berlin with their human cargo, Herr Zimmerman, without raising any red flags, and was subsequently passed through English passport control without incident. Barber called a last minute audible and decided to land the Helicopter in Gutcher, Shetland on the Island of Yell, and then travel by boat to Haroldswick. It was his first visit to the remote safehouse. Marcus Day, who had been there before, reminded him that people normally traveled to the northern most Shetland Island by ferry or private boat, and that the arrival of a helicopter would raise as many questions as a private jet. Quietly slipping into the harbor in a fishing boat, however, would appear entirely normal. Zimmerman was kept quiet and compliant throughout most of the trip with death threats while, not real, were nevertheless quite convincing. The tactic was aided by a modest dose of the drug Versed, which had the added benefit of ensuring he didn't remember much of anything about his travels.

Two words best describe Heroldsick: Isolated and stark. The first thing one notices upon arriving on the island is there are no trees. Visitors who ask why are quickly given a description of Shetland winters and told there is an average of ten storms each season with flat-line winds that average over 100 miles per hour for over 10 hours. It's an experience beyond the imagination of most people, and there are no trees capable of surviving such a climate. However, it is not a land without beauty. Travel north of the town proper into the country side and one is reminded of the astronaut Edwin "Buzz" Aldrin's description of the moonscape: "magnificent desolation."

The safehouse itself was a one-story, non-descript building built of grey cinder blocks and a glass-reinforced plastic roof. The materials were stout and provided the resilience needed to stand up to the relentless Shetland winter climate. Access to the house was via a long, unpaved path just off the hill, overlooking the bay. The exterior of the house had a vibe that matched that of the island – stark and non-descript. There was nothing about it that was noteworthy. Passers-by would regard it as nothing more than shelter, likely for an old mackerel fisherman living out his last days, as Thoreau famously said, "in quiet desperation", or perhaps transient fishermen looking for a place to lay their heads after a time at sea. The important thing was it drew little attention. It wasn't designed that way, that was just the way things were in Haorldswick. It had two small bedrooms, a kitchen, a living room, a bathroom and a small attached one-car garage.

Barber carefully idled the vessel up to the local dock and secured the 37-foot deep-V hulled fishing boat that had provided their transportation from Gutcher. Marcus Day hopped off the boat and walked towards a local fenced yard where locals rented storage space in exchange for an annual fee. The yard stored boats during winter, and a few automobiles owned by the fishermen while they were out to sea plying their trade. Day elicited a few stares as he walked away from the dock; people were not used to seeing many black men in Haroldsick. But eventually he was ignored, as his large size and a chiseled body suggested more of a lifetime of hard labor at sea than a threat. For a Summer day it was chilly, as a northern wind gusting to 30-40 miles an hour whipped though the valley that cradled the small town.

Day walked up to the yard's gate and unlocked the Master padlock with his key, the same one provided to each resident who rented space. As he walked into the yard and looked to his left, he saw their automobile about 50 yards away, just where he had left it. The vehicle, a 2001 Volvo S40 sedan, looked filthy and weathered. The Shetland climate was hard on an automobile, especially ones kept outside. But Day had a contract with a local garage to periodically check on it and top off the battery's charge, so while it looked like crap, he was confident it would run. He climbed in, started the motor, then hit the windshield washer to swipe off several months of dirt. He slowly exited the lot, then headed back towards the pier to pick up Barber and their "guest."

Transporting Zimmerman to the safehouse was a challenge. Barber and Day knew they couldn't just walk him to the car, put him in the back seat and drive away. That would require Zimmerman to remain conscious, and that provided too many opportunities for something to go wrong. The two men looked around the boat for something big enough to hold him and found a large, zippered equipment bag in the forward locker. Day cut a breathing hole in the bag, sedated Zimmerman again and stuffed him into it. They carried the bag to the Volvo and placed him length-wise into the trunk. With half the backseat folded down he fit, although he would not enjoy a comfortable ride if the sedation wore off.

Drugs affect people in different ways. Some are more resilient than others and require a higher dose to deliver the required impact. But Marcus Day was cautious with how much of the sedative he gave Zimmerman. He didn't want the guy to sleep the day away. He and Barber were anxious to begin working on him.

Zimmerman sprung to consciousness as one of the Volvo's wheels hit a large pothole on Beach Road while en route to the safehouse. The jolt threw him several inches into the air causing his head to hit the inside of the trunk lid. He then came down hard and torqued his back as the vehicle swerved sharply immediately after the initial collision, forcing his body to twist inside the tight space in an unnatural way. As his brain processed the pain, he lay there for several seconds not recognizing where he was or remembering anything thing that happened to him after he was forced onto a private jet in Berlin. He then recognized the smell of dank wool and realized his head was covered with some kind of hood. As the mental fog slowly began to lift, it became apparent he was in the trunk of a vehicle. His breathing was labored and felt barely sufficient to keep him alive. As he reflexively lifted his head, he noticed resistance to his movement by a fabric of some sort and concluded he must also be trapped inside some kind of a bag. He momentarily panicked, thinking it was a body bag, and cried out, but then remembered he was still breathing, albeit with difficulty, so it had to be something else. He remembered being detained at the airport by the EF military, then remembered who he was and what he had done. As the realization flooded his consciousness he became seized by fear. Where was he? Who had abducted him? What were they going to do? Bile rose in his throat as his mind quickly inventoried the kinds of abuse to which he was about to be subjected. Why had he done it, he scolded himself. He was already wealthy along with the power and prestige of being CEO of a prominent European Federation military contractor. He had thrown it all away on the altar of greed. He then thought of the people, the hundreds of thousands of people whose lives had ended in the nuclear conflagration enabled by his hand, and the hundreds of thousands more whose lives would horribly ebb away in the coming weeks and months. But most of all he thought about himself. He saw no way he could escape accountability. Realizing that, he was seized again, not by fear, but by a terror he found almost unimaginable.

"Sounds like our cargo is coming to," Barber observed in response to the sounds of Zimmerman thrashing in the back, then crying out.

"I gave him a light dose of the sedative," Day responded. "I didn't want us sitting around the safehouse waiting for him to wake up."

"Good thinking," Barber responded.

It took them about 15 minutes to get to the private access road. The sound of gravel crunching under the tires was prominent as they approached the house. As Barber pulled up to the garage door, Day jumped out and opened it, then Barber pulled the vehicle inside. It was unlikely that leaving the Volvo in the driveway would raise the curiosity of any passers-by, but why take the risk? The lower their profile while there, the better, they reasoned.

After closing the garage door, they opened the Volvo's trunk and pulled out the bag containing Zimmerman, who was now fully awake. They were not gentle about it, and he cried out in pain at the rough handling.

"Be quiet," Day commanded in his best authoritarian voice, and Zimmerman complied.

The two men dragged the bag to one of the rear bedrooms, opened it, and roughly pulled Zimmerman out, still wearing the hood over his head, then shoved him into a plastic chair.

"Where the hell am I?" Zimmerman demanded, hood still over his head. "What do you intend to do with me?"

The first question was Zimmerman's tepid attempt at bluster, which was immediately negated by the second. The guy was obviously terrified and likely to offer up the details of his involvement quickly, Barber thought. This might be easier than he thought.

"Where you are isn't important," Barber responded. "What I intend to do with you is up to you. It's going to be very important for you to remember that over the next several hours. Let's begin with a re-introduction," he said as he roughly yanked the hood off of Zimmerman's head.

"So, it's you," Zimmerman observed. "I thought I recognized your voice. You and your partner over there," referring to Day, "are the ones who forced me on the plane in Berlin. You have no idea the trouble you are in. The two of you are guilty of kidnapping and torture...."

Barber cut him off. "Actually, we haven't started the torture part yet, but we've got some dandy plans if you don't cooperate."

Zimmerman was visibly shaken at Barber's comment. As a German CEO he was used to being treated with great deference and respect. This was an entirely new experience for him, and he didn't know how to process it. He made a feeble attempt at bluster again: "I am in charge of a very important defense contractor, and the Federation will be looking for me. You will not get away with this!" he exclaimed.

"Well, your right about one thing, Hans, they certainly are looking for you. Allow me to cut through the crap and level-set this discussion for you."

"Level-set?" Zimmerman asked, confused.

"Sorry, an American figure of speech. It means bring you up to speed, get all of us on the same page, or make sure you know what I know so we can have a productive conversation."

Zimmerman did not respond to the explanation. He looked worried again.

"First, you will remember that it was Laurent, not us, who detained you at the Berlin airport. You should ask yourself why that is the case. Second, we couldn't have departed Federation airspace, especially under present circumstances, without Federation clearance. You should ask yourself why we received it. Third, even if we did manage to get out of Federation airspace, Allied Air Forces would certainly have intercepted and detained us, yet that didn't happen. You should ask yourself why that didn't happen. And fourth, we could never have made it to this place without being cleared though local passport control, which we were. So, here's the deal. We know you were the one who fingered Schiller to the Iranians. That makes you complicit in his death. We also know that you were paid 50 million Euros by the Iranians for something, and it's safe to assume it wasn't for your stellar counsel."

"That's preposterous!" Zimmerman exclaimed.

"Hans," Barber said, condescendingly, using his given name, "we have all the details of the bank transfers to your account, including the bank wire identification numbers, so don't waste my time by denying it. Now, as I was saying, we have you cold, pal. Laurent suspected you were running when he called your office to see where you were. By the way, I would say you should ensure your secretary is more discrete about revealing your whereabouts in the future, but you're never going to have a secretary again, so it's a moot point, isn't it? General Laurent is aware of far more than you realize, thanks likely to the information my colleague here, Marc, shared with him about the Iranian's attempt to murder me and my family, and I am quite confident he has already provided the information to his superiors, including the Chancellor. So, you're right about another thing – I'm certain the Federation is looking for you, but not for the reasons you think."

Zimmerman sat in the chair silently, not responding.

"Also, by the way," Barber continued, "I'm sure you heard about that tragic explosion at the Iranian Embassy?"

"Yes," Zimmerman replied.

"Well, it wasn't an HVAC malfunction," he replied. "Ok, to be fair, I guess it was actually an HVAC malfunction, but it wasn't the result of a faulty system. I blew the thing up. It was how I managed to get away from your Iranian friends after being kidnapped by them. Seems they believed I figured out a few too many things. And since my captors never expected me to leave their embassy alive, they were quite open with me during their initial interrogation. So, don't try and lie to me. The consequences will be quite painful."

"So, if you know everything already, why you need me?" Zimmerman asked, trying to regain a bit of his defiance.

"What we don't know yet is the exact nature of what it was you gave them that was worth 50 million Euros, and you're going to tell us that. Was it the keys to your strategic weapons command and control systems? I also know, by the way, the Schiller was suspicious of that, and that's why you had him killed."

"You're mad!" Zimmerman exclaimed.

"I don't think so. He would be alive today if he hadn't shared his suspicions with someone, and he wouldn't have done so with somebody of junior rank. There's a short list of candidates he likely talked to, and your bank account and attempt to run point the finger directly at you."

"That's preposterous!" He exclaimed. "Helmut was my friend, my mentor, I would never do anything to hurt him. It's simply not in my nature, and I don't know anything about 50 million Euros!"

Barber ignored his denials. "And what makes absolutely no sense is why we don't know Iran would target one of your missiles against one of their own cities, and the Holy City of Qom, no less. I'm especially interested in the answer to that question. Care to shed some light on it?"

"I have no earthly idea," Zimmerman replied.

"We'll I have a theory," Barber replied. "Want to hear it?"

"I'm all ears," Zimmerman answered.

"I think it was a mistake. I suspect they intended a different target. What to guess where?"

"All of this is preposterous!" Zimmerman exclaimed.

"No, not so much," Barber replied. "Geography is an interesting discipline, isn't it?" Barber asked.

"What's your point?" Zimmerman fired back, actually summoning a bit of irritation in his voice.

"If you take a string and stretch it from the launch site to Qom, Iran, guess what you find?"

"What?" Zimmerman asked.

"Israel," Barber answered.

Zimmerman looked stunned. The expression on his face betrayed the fact his mind was obviously in hyperdrive. "That's crazy!" he responded.

"Is it? Think about it. What a perfect plan for the Iranians if they managed to pull it off. Destroy an arch enemy and point the finger towards the Germans."

"The two of you are crazy!" he shouted. "I have no idea what you are talking about!"

"This is about to get very unpleasant, Hans. We're going to give you a few minutes to contemplate your fate before we continue our little conversation," Barber said as he placed the dank woolen hood back over the man's head.

Barber and Day walked out of the room, closed the door, then walked into the small living room at the front of the house.

"Do you believe him?" Day asked.

"Yes and no," Barber replied. "He obviously knows a lot more than he's telling us. He certainly knows what the Iranian's did; even if they didn't tell him their plans, which I'm sure they didn't, he could easily guess based on the information he gave them. But I'm very doubtful he has any clue as to why it was an Iranian city that was hit."

"I think that's right," Day responded. "He's not going to tell us anything right now unless you start cutting his fingers off with pruning shears. Margaret would not be happy about that. So, do we soften him up a bit before you do your magic?"

"Yes. The room's soundproof, so let's keep him up all night and keep him in a little sensory overload. He's not a strong man, at least not mentally, so I suspect about 12-16 hours of it should have him singing like a canary."

"What do you have in mind?" Day asked.

"We'll start an IV drip with caffeine to keep him awake. We won't tell him what it is, which should freak him out a bit."

"And the sensory overload?"

"You know, Marcus, my favorite. We put Barbara Striesand's "The Way We Were" on a continuous loop and play it at 80 decibels."

"You are one mean SOB, man. I think pruning his fingers would be more merciful," Day said with a chuckle. "Why only 80 decibels?"

"We're going to be pumping this into the room for 12-16 hours, I don't want him deaf when we're done. He needs to be able to hear my questions. And by the way, I'm not into mercy right now."

"Roger that. Neither am I. You and I can each take a 4-hour watch after it gets dark. We need to finish this business and get the intel to Maggie by mid-morning tomorrow at the latest. We need to have a real sense of urgency here."

"Agreed," Barber replied. "Hopefully earlier than that. We should look in on him every hour, and if he appears to be breaking early, we'll start."

"Sounds like a plan. I'll go prep the IV."

"Thanks. I'll fire up the sound system."

As Barber and Day set out to their individual tasks, little did they realize there would soon encounter a very nasty surprise.

Chapter 41 – A Plea for Help

Tehran, the Islamic Republic of Iran

A thick cloud of smoke lingered over the city and nearly blocked out the sun. Flames could be seen engulfing a number of buildings across the horizon as rioters plied their craft. Even the Milad Tower, an architectural marvel dominating Tehran's western skyline, was not spared as flames could be seen pouring out towards the top of the Tower's twelve-story head, perched more than a thousand feet over the city. Students and other young people were taunting soldiers by shouting obscenities as they threw rocks and bottles indiscriminately, often hitting as many of their own as they were their opponents. The city was descending into chaos as the crowds all but ignored the barrage of tear gas lofted into their midst and kept moving relentlessly forward. The scene repeated itself in major cities across the country, including Mashhad, Isfahan and Karaj as well as others. It was a nation about to be sucked into the vortex of anarchy as an angry and restive population reacted to the attack on Qom. Then the soldiers started shooting, and then things began to change.

Iran was a nation ripe for a revolution. A progressively younger population aching for a better life and greater freedom had grown tired of being ruled by the "bearded old men" as the religious ruling class had come to be called. The aged mullahs that dominated the nation's halls of power had failed to deliver the promises of the Revolution. The nation was weary from years of suffering under the sanctions and dismal economic growth in spite of the its vast wealth trapped in oil reserves. The average citizen had difficulty understanding their leaders' "end game". It was difficult to see the promised pot of gold at the end of the rainbow in compensation for all of the suffering. Even the devout had come to long for a more peaceful practice of their religion and better relations with the West. Few of its citizens, other than the aging mullahs themselves, had any experience with life before the Revolution.

The old slogans of yesteryear held little sway. Previous revolts had been swiftly put down. But when the holy city of Qom was vaporized by a nuclear weapon from the West, or so they thought, massive riots sprung up all over the country. Tehran was now a city under martial law. Anyone who challenged the Government's authority was summarily shot. The Supreme Leader himself ordered the military to be unyielding and merciless in their efforts to quell the civil unrest. Even with their savage tactics they had struggled to regain control. But as the population realized there was no limit to what the Mullah's were willing to do to enforce their will, the government was slowly beginning to regain the upper hand. Against this background, a handful of individuals within the Supreme Leader's inner circle possessed a troubling truth. They knew the destruction of Qom was by their hand, not the Germans'. They knew the fate that awaited them if the truth became known, and that terrified them.

The Supreme Leader knew that success was not guaranteed. A contingency plan was developed in case the project failed in some catastrophic way. A special contingent of Revolutionary Guard soldiers provided security for the complex housing everyone involved in Project Allah's Sword. The late General Hamidi had always assumed the soldiers reported to him. The ruse was reinforced by their day-to-day interactions. But in reality, their chain of command went directly to the Supreme Leader himself. As the plan was implemented, the Supreme Leader's first order was the execution of General Hamidi, and he indulged General Bagheri that pleasure. His second order was to the Commander of the Guard troops. The Commander was to implement the broader contingency plan. He was to instruct his soldiers to walk through the offices and shoot everyone.

The only person to escape was Dr. Ashkan Ghorbani, the genius mathematician whose skills brought the Project to completion. The moment the Iranian city was hit, Gharbani was certain he had only minutes, if not seconds, to live as he expected to be the next target of Hamidi's rage. But somehow, he had been gifted a reprieve. When Hamidi stormed out of the launch control center, inexplicably ignoring him, Ghorbani ran from the building under cover of the ensuing chaos and headed towards his vehicle. By the time the Revolutionary Guard soldiers were methodically killing all of his co-workers, Ghorbani was in his car speeding out of the city. It would be days before the Supreme Leader and his inner circle would become aware of his escape.

But they had another, even bigger problem. They had paid 50 million euros to purchase vital intelligence about the European Federation's Command and Control software from Hans-Dieter Zimmerman, the acting CEO of Sternenlicht. Zimmerman no doubt by now had accurately guessed it was Iran that was responsible for the launch, and he could potentially finger them. Worse yet, there was a risk that he could produce their digital fingerprint on the hack to prove it. General Bagheri swiftly ordered Zimmerman's execution, but was stunned when he was told that Zimmerman was on the run and hold up in a remote part of the Northern Shetland Islands. They knew where he was because he had been injected with a micro GPS tracking device when given a recent vaccination. The Sternenlicht corporate physician was an Iranian agent who, like Erich Farhang, was a deep plant who lived his life waiting for a request from his home country to one day render it a service. The request came, and the service was injecting the device into Zimmerman's shoulder under the guise of it being a mandatory vaccine for all senior executives. Zimmerman had complained at the time about the unusual pain the vaccination caused and questioned why it required such a large needle, but quickly dismissed his concerns as his day was subsequently met with the myriad of distractions typical for top management. The device actively tracked Zimmerman's travel from Berlin to England to the Shetland Islands with great precision. It pinpointed his location in Heroldswick to within an error of only 2 meters.

Being in Heroldswick, Scotland put Zimmerman out of Iran's reach. They couldn't send agents there without sticking out like a sore thumb and it was too far away for a viable military operation. They had never planned for such a contingency, as the Shetland Islands were about the last place on earth Iran ever expected to go. But there was someone to whom they could turn.

The Russian Federation had been working to foster the Islamic Republic as a client nation since the days of the Soviet Union. Russian President Vladimir Putin relished poking a stick in the eye of the United States by providing Iran with arms and nuclear technology. The Supreme Leader himself called Putin and asked for help. As the call progressed, however, it became clear to Putin that the Supreme Leader was holding back something very important. Putin was quickly developing a very good idea of what is was.

"Good morning, your Excellency," the Russian President said. "If you are calling to inquire about the status of our relief aid, I can assure you our initial provisions will arrive shortly. Our aircraft should be taking to the air as we speak. I trust the security situation in Tehran remains stable enough for our planes to land."

"Thank you, my friend," the Supreme Leader responded to Putin. "Yes. I have placed the entire country under martial law, and the rioting is now confined to small areas that are quickly being quieted."

"That is good to hear. As we discussed, we will unload the provisions on airport property, and I will leave it to your Transportation Ministry to see to it they get to your people."

"Of course. And thank you again for your generosity. These are trying times."

"Yes, Your Excellency, they certainly are."

"We have another request, Mr. President," the Supreme Leader said to Putin, "and it's an important one."

"How may we be of additional service, my friend?" Putin responded.

"If I may be completely transparent, there is an individual that we most urgently need eliminated."

"Of course, Your Excellency. You may consider him already dead. Who is he and what has he done to deserve such a fate? And if I may also be transparent, as is the pleasure among friends, how is it you find yourself in need of our help. This is an area in which I regard your agents as quite skilled."

"Thank you, my friend," the Supreme Leader said, as he prepared to convey a carefully-crafted lie. "He is an agent of the European Federation Intelligence Service, masquerading as an executive of one of their important military suppliers. We believe he acquired important details of our military defense systems which aided the Federation in their attack on our most holy city of Qom. This knowledge of our systems must die with him, and as quickly as possible."

"What is the name of this agent and the military supplier you reference?" Putin asked.

"Sternenlicht is the supplier and Hans-Dieter Zimmerman is their CEO," the Supreme Leader responded. The answer got Putin's attention.

"And how is it you need our help in this matter?" Putin asked.

"We have it on good authority that he has fled the European Federation and is hiding on one of the northern islands of Scottish Shetland. This puts him beyond our reach. We know you have many agents deployed in both England and Scotland and were hoping you would be willing to help."

"Of course, my friend," Putin responded. "As I have already said, you may consider him dead. I presume you have accurate information as to his present location?"

"Yes, we do. We have exact GPS coordinates."

"Excellent," Putin said, wondering how their intelligence could be so good. "I will have our intelligence service task a satellite to take pictures. I see no reason why this cannot be completed within 24-48 hours. I will call you when I get confirmation the task is complete."

"Thank you, President Putin. Your friendship means a great deal to us."

"And likewise, Your Excellency. Now allow me to bid you farewell and go do some work. I hope to call you shortly." With that, Putin ended the call. Suddenly he was highly motivated to help.

Putin was many things: ambitious, egotistical, cold, calculating, brutal and even sadistic. One thing he was not, however, was unintelligent. The man was strategically brilliant and could even be charming when it suited his purposes. People who underestimated him because they disliked him or didn't like what he was doing did so at their great peril. He also had a remarkable sixth sense. He could see through people's motives with ease. He could also detect the truth like a bloodhound could smell a bleeding rabbit ten feet away. The Supreme Leader had just handed him a gift of staggering potential, and the doddering old fool had no idea. Russia had been trying to penetrate Sternenlicht for over two years, without success. A Russian asset inside the company could steal valuable technology on the Federation's portable rail gun that could accelerate Russia's development of the weapon by years. It could also give them insights into the Federation's strategic weapons command and control systems and potential ways to defeat it. And there was something else. Putin was suspicious himself that Iran was somehow involved in the launch of the nuclear weapon, and that the attack on Qom was caused by a colossal mistake. Why else would it be so important to the Supreme Leader to want Zimmerman killed if it wasn't to keep him from somehow revealing such a truth. It's the only thing that made sense. Being in possession of such knowledge would give Russia tremendous leverage over the Iranians and a strategic advantage over the West as the present crisis played out. This executive, Zimmerman, was a treasure trove of information.

The assistance the Iranians were about to receive would be very different from what the Supreme Leader was expecting. Vladimir Putin had no intention of killing Zimmerman. Zimmerman's continued health had just become a matter of urgent importance. No, he wasn't going to kill him. He was going to capture him.

* * * * *

The Supreme Leader sat back in his chair and waited. Waiting was difficult, because he knew if he was waiting, he was vulnerable. He was vulnerable to exposure of the truth. His contingency plan was a good one. It was good to have friends like the Russians to do his bidding in Scotland. On further reflection, he realized they were far from his friends. But they were opportunists with shared interests. For the time being, that was enough. But the hair on the back of his neck stood up as he reminded himself his contingency plan had a gaping hole. Iran had paid 500 million dollars to that infidel woman in California for the final piece of code they needed to retarget the missile. Did she double-cross him, he wondered? Somebody certainly did. It made sense. In fact, he could think of nobody else who had a credible motive. There must have been some part of the code that overrode their instructions and insured the missile would hit Iran instead of Israel. He burned with rage as he reflected on that. The contingency plan would not be complete until that woman was dead, along with her employees who wrote the code. Killing the employees at CWR Industries in Germany would be easy. The nation was seized by chaos and they had plenty of agents in place to do it. General Bagheri could arrange it. He would call the General right away and so order it. Killing the woman would be much more difficult. He certainly had agents in the United States, the Great Satan, who could kill her. But it would be difficult to do it quickly. It would take planning and care to dispose of her in a manner that didn't point the finger back at them. And he had to kill the woman first before killing the employees in Germany. If they were killed first, she would quickly know about it and then take measures for her safety that could put her beyond their reach.

So, the Supreme Leader continued to sit in his chair and wait, and think, and worry.

Chapter 42 – Preparing for the Assault

The North Sea, 0200 Universal Standard Time, 25 Nautical Miles Northwest of Haroldswick

The clear night sky was brilliantly lit with a panorama of stars that would have been breathtaking had there been anyone to see it, but the open waters of the North Sea were very lonely. A brisk wind of 20 knots hailing from the north churned the saltwater into ten-foot seas with periodic gusts tearing the wave crests into foaming cauldrons of white-caps. Surface conditions made navigation not just uncomfortable but dangerous for all but the largest and most stout of vessels, such as warships or freight carriers stretching in length of a thousand feet or more. The water temperature of 50 degrees would bring the onset of hypothermia in a matter of minutes to those unfortunate enough to find themselves immersed in it, unprotected. Unconsciousness, then death would soon follow in less than half an hour. Ideal conditions were luxuries rarely afforded elite special forces headed downrange, so on this night the team and the vessel would forge ahead towards their appointed task, regardless of the challenges.

The Russian Federation submarine Severodvinsk was an attack boat of the fourth-generation Yasen-class, launched on December 30, 2013. Commissioned for the Northern Fleet, it hailed out of the submarine base in Murmansk, a closed city at the top of the world on Russia's northern coast. The 140-meter boat glided 30 meters beneath the surface, deep enough to avoid any turbulence from the churn on the water's surface. That was about to change.

"Sonar, conn. Report surface contacts," the Severodvinsk's Captain queried.

"Conn, sonar. Negative, Captain. Surface is clear."

"Make all preparations for surfacing," the Captain ordered.

"Making all preparations for surfacing," came the reply.

"Blow all main ballast tanks. Ten degree up bubble."

"Blowing main ballast tanks. Making ten-degree up bubble," the order was confirmed.

"Rig for rough seas," the Captain ordered.

"Rigging for rough seas."

As the boat broke the surface, its hull immediately yielded to the heavy swells, pitching the boat back and forth and making conditions below miserable for its compliment of 64 officers and crew. The Captain ordered the helm to bring the boat about, into the wind, steering it directly into the path of the waves to restore some measure of its lateral stability. The seas made things even tougher for the team of special operators who were preparing to depart on a secret mission.

Covert operations launched from a Russian submarine normally are conducted by the Army's Special Operations Force, or "SOF" soldiers, often referred to by their old moniker, Spetsnaz. This night, however, was different. This night required more than the skills of special operators. It also required absolute anonymity. More importantly, it required plausible deniability for the man who had ordered the men downrange. Sometimes during special operations missions "shit happens", and Vladimir Putin had to be 100% certain there was no possibility that the capture or killing of the soldiers could point back to him.

A very special cadre of soldiers fit the bill perfectly: the employees of a Russian private paramilitary company named the Wagner Group. Wagner was a Russian version of Blackwater, the company used by the United States Defense Department that came to notoriety during the Iraq war. The Wagner Group was named after the German composer loved by Adolf Hitler, Richard Wagner, and its leadership retained much of the culture of the Third Reich's SS. It's CEO, Lt. Colonel Dimitri Utkin, was a former Spetsnaz Brigade Commander with a reputation for savagery almost without equal. His name struck fear into the hearts of ISIS leadership during his time in Syria, where he served before leaving the Russian Army and forming Wagner.

This night, four Wagner operators would be deployed from the submarine and travel by inflatable boat to the Northern Shetland Island of Unst. Their mission: abduct Hans-Dieter Zimmerman and return him to the sub, then escort him back to Russia and deliver him to a GRU interrogation cell housed in the basement of the Russian Federation Ministry of Defense. The men did not wear uniforms. Each had backpacks that contained 4 kilos of cocaine so, if killed or captured, they would pass as Russian mafia attempting to infiltrate the Shetland drug trade.

The Wagner team leader climbed up the ladder inside the submarine's sail, or tower-like structure on the top of the boat, to the observation deck and joined the Captain, who was scanning the horizon with a pair of powerful binoculars. The boat, now being steered into the wind, was riding up the peak of each wave then crashing into the trough on the other side as if it were a giant a roller coaster. Both men braced themselves against the motion.

"Thoughts?" the Captain asked the Wagner team leader.

"Way too dangerous to try and deploy from the deck, Captain. We are barely able to remain standing here on the observation deck. I think we need to submerge and deploy from underwater. That way we can tether the team together with the equipment before rising to the surface to ensure nothing gets lost."

"My instructions are to provide you with whatever support you need. So, if that's what you need, then that's what we will do. I assume your team is ready?"

"Yes, Captain. We just need to move the men and equipment to the pressure lock. We should be able to do that and be ready to deploy with 20 minutes."

"Very well," the Captain said. "Then get below and see to it."

"Yes, sir," replied the team leader, as he opened the hatch and descended back into the boat's sail.

The Captain took one final scan of the horizon. "Rig for dive, clearing the bridge," he said as he descended into the bowels of the boat, closed the water-tight hatch and took his place in the control room.

"Rigged for dive, Captain," the Diving Officer replied.

"Make your depth fifty feet," the Captain ordered.

"Open all main vents. Flood negative. Five degree down bubble," the Diving Officer announced.

The words "Dive, dive, dive," then echoed throughout the boat on the 1MC main intercom and an alarm sounded as the boat gracefully slipped beneath the waves.

"Approaching depth of 50 feet, Captain," the Diving Officer announced.

"All stop and hover at 50 feet," the Captain ordered.

"Commencing hover at 50 feet," the Diving Officer replied.

The Captain then hailed the Wagner team leader on a private channel. "Are you ready?" he asked.

"Yes, captain, we are ready."

"Deploy at your discretion."

The four men switched on their rebreathers, then the team leader pressed a button in the inside of the pressure lock to signal they were ready. Heated wetsuits protected the men for the frigid water that began filling the chamber. Once full, the watertight hatch above them was opened and the men, tethered together with their equipment, floated gently out of the submarine and into the open water. The team leader deployed a nitrogen capsule in a small floatation device to gently lift everything to the surface. Luck was with them, as once they broke the surface they noticed the winds must have calmed slightly and the waves, although still probably eight feet, were now farther apart, allowing for a more manageable roll on the surface instead of the nasty churn he had witnessed from the sub's observation deck. He then fired a much larger nitrogen capsule that inflated a nine-foot Russian version of a CRRC, or Combat Rubber Raiding Craft, equipped with a 55hp muffled outboard motor that would propel them to their destination. The four men climbed on board the inflated craft and opened the single case that held their weapons and portable GPS device. Their firepower was limited to 4 Glock 19s, a nine mm pistol with fifteen round magazines, and 4 Israeli Uzis. The Uzis were more for show, as it was the preferred weapon of the Russian drug trade and would help corroborate their cover story, if captured. They weren't anticipating much resistance on this mission. But they were in for a surprise in the names of Barber and Day. Once situated, the team leader fired up the outboard motor, checked the heading on the water-proof GPS device, then started the 50-mile journey towards a small inlet about a mile and a half from Zimmerman's position.

Chapter 43 – An Unpleasant Surprise

Orion Bellicus Safehouse, Heroldswick, The Shetland Islands, Scotland

Marcus Day walked out the back door of the safehouse and looked out over the barren landscape. How could a place be so beautiful and so desolate at the same time? The smell of fish and salt air wafted up from the harbor below. He could hear the faint sound of Barbra Streisand's "The Way We Were" playing from the soundproof room that held Zimmerma,n and he wondered how the man was holding up. He would check on him when his watch was over, right before he woke up Barber. Day glanced at his watch, confirming there remained 90 minutes before the two of them were to switch. He was growing sleepy. There wasn't a lot to do in the middle of the night in a safehouse at the top of the world. Then he heard something.

A man hardened in combat develops certain instincts not given to those who have never faced that crucible. That is, at least anyone who survived the crucible and remained alive. He wasn't sure what triggered it. Perhaps the cracking of a twig. But with the lack of trees he knew there couldn't be any twigs. Perhaps the movement of a rock? Maybe that was it. He wasn't sure, the hair standing on the back of his neck told him it was definitely something. And in this particular place there wasn't supposed to be a "something". He went back into the house and retrieved a pair of infrared, or "night vision", binoculars. They were a combination of binoculars and an infrared flashlight that would illuminate anything that radiated heat, like a man. As he walked back out the door and scanned the horizon, he noticed something. It was far away and difficult to identify, but it was moving. Perhaps a sheep, he thought, that had wandered away from its usual sleeping place. He zoomed the binoculars and continued to scan with a growing sense of urgency. Sheep didn't tend to wander away in the middle of the night. Then he saw it. It was small, almost indiscernible, but he knew what it was. It was an arm. Somebody was out there.

Day immediately went back into the house and woke Barber. "Hey Joe, wake up. We've got company," he said in a half whisper.

"What?" Joe replied, appearing confused.

"I said we've got company. Somebody is out there, and they are approaching the house from the meadow behind us."

"There's nothing behind this house for miles, Marc. It's just open land."

"Exactly," Day replied. "Get your pants on, grab your infrared glass and follow me out back again."

Barber rolled out of bed, slipped his denims back on and retrieved his own infrared binoculars and followed Day out the back door. Both men put the glass to their eyes and scanned the horizon. What they saw was disturbing.

"Wow," Barber said. "I count three figures. They appear to be headed towards the house."

"They're about 50 yards closer than when I first saw them, and it's actually four figures now."

"Can you tell if they're armed?"

"No, not with infrared," Day answered. "And they're still too far away to make out that detail with night vision," referring to a different technology that magnified the ambient light to make objects easier to see.

"They won't be too far away for very long," Barber observed. "I'm going to grab two sets of NVGs. Go grab the two Weatherby 300 mags from the gun safe and a couple of Sig 10s," referring to the high-power hunting rifles and the Sig Sauer 10 mm pistols. "And grab suppressors for each of them."

"Roger that," Day replied as they both went back into the house. "What about Zimmerman?"

"Leave him be for the moment. If those are really bad guys out there, I suspect it's Zimmerman they're after and not us."

"That's got to be right," Day replied. "But how did they know he was here? We've been here less than a day. How in the world did they track the guy here? Even if whoever 'they' are had an asset inside CIA, MI6 or Scotland Yard I don't see how they could have pointed this location so quickly. All you told Maggie is we were going to Shetland. You didn't give her the location of this safehouse."

The two men stared at each other for several seconds then spontaneously came to the same realization. "GPS!" Barber shouted. "They must have somehow implanted Zimmerman with a GPS chip."

The two men ran to the room holding Zimmerman. Day turned off the music while Barber ripped off the man's shirt and started looking him over closely for any scar that might betray where a GPS device was planted.

"What are you doing?" Zimmerman screamed.

"Did anyone implant you with a GPS device?" Barber asked.

"What are you talking about?" Zimmerman responded. "You're mad! Of course not!"

"Joe, look at this!" Day exclaimed. "There's a reddened bump on his left outside shoulder."

"What is this?" Barber demanded of Zimmerman.

"It's just a flu shot! You're crazy!" he protested.

Barber pulled a Zero Tolerance D460 folding knife with a four-and-a-half-inch blade from his pocket, flipped the blade open and dug the point into Zimmerman's shoulder. The man screamed in pain.

"Shut up and be still!" Barber demanded. With a couple of twists, he dug out a small metallic looking device and held it up to the light. "I don't know exactly what this is, but it sure isn't something that belongs in a man's arm. This has to be a micro tracking device." Barber placed it on a table, pulled the suppressed Glock from his waistband, positioned the barrel right over the device and pulled the trigger. "There. Not anymore. Leave this clown here and let's get back out and see what's going on."

The two men, now wearing night vision goggles and fully armed, exited the back door and looked through their binoculars again.

"They're armed, all right," Day commented. "So much for them being a bunch of blokes out for a stroll."

"Yep, looks like some kind of small automatic like a Mac 10 or Uzi. I can't see pistols, but you can bet they have them as well."

"I just saw one of them retrieve something from his belt."

"Yeah, I didn't catch that but I'm looking at him now. Can you see what it is?"

"Nope, but my guess is it's his sidearm."

"That's got to be right."

"Hey Joe, the guys seem to have stopped moving."

Barber smiled. "They've lost the GPS signal. They're trying to reacquire. They still know the general direction, but they can no longer pinpoint which house. That should buy us a little time."

"Good work, partner. Now how about maybe we flank these clowns and capture one of them. I've got a couple of questions I'd like to ask."

"Sounds like a capital idea, Marc. You take the right flank; I'll take the left."

"Roger that."

Barber and Day quickly walked about 10 meters to each side of the safehouse, about 25 meters behind it and took watch positions. It felt eerily reminiscent to each of the men of their earlier lives as snipers. Both had to resist the temptation to zero in on a target and pull the trigger. The four Wagner operators drew ever closer to the safehouse, now walking almost right in between where Barber and Day.

"I can see them pretty clearly now, Marc. Four military-aged males in what appears to be black night combat gear, and they're each carrying some kind of automatic weapon."

"Wadda ya think?" Day asked.

"They've walked right into our field of fire. I say we put two of them down. That makes the odds a lot more reasonable and still gives us two targets to choose for an abduction."

"Any preference as to which one?"

"Look at the second guy back, closer to you."

"Ok."

"He just sent a bunch of hand signals to the three others and they've started to move again. My guess he's got command of this little siorée. He's the one I'd like to nab."

"Got it. The two in front have just gotten closer together and are starting to move ahead of the others. I'm going to circle around and come up on the six of the two in back, and when I give you the signal you drop the two in front. Let's try as best we can not to kill the guy who's in charge."

"Roger that."

Barber started crawling on the ground away from the safehouse to position himself behind the two Wagner men in the rear. His earpiece crackled again with the voice of Marcus Day.

"Hey, the two in front are starting to accelerate their pace and our leader is staying put. I think he's assigned them to make the initial assault on the house, then the two in reserve will join once they think the place is secure. Do you want me to pop them? I've only got about 10 seconds to act or they will be on the house. They may have lost the GPS signal, but they appear to have guessed correctly which place. They are heading right towards it."

"Can you wait till they are almost at the back door? I want the leader to think they've made it to the house. That might give us a few extra seconds before he realizes they've been compromised. I'm less than 10 yards behind them now and I'd like to be no more than about 10 feet so I can pounce on them before they realize what's happened."

"Yes. I'll be firing in about 5 seconds."

It's a fallacy perpetuated by the movies and TV shows that a firearm "silencer" actually silences the sound of a bullet. It certainly reduces the noise, but to a well-trained ear, it's unmistakable, sounding like a distinct "thwack". And then there's also the problem of the sonic boom created by a high-powered round like one fired from a weapon like a Weatherby 300 magnum rifle. The Wagner team leader understood instantly what he just heard. He and the other man immediately put their binoculars to their faces, momentarily focusing on their colleagues at the house and ignoring everything else, as they tried to process what had just happened. They weren't expecting resistance. It was just what Barber was counting on. He quietly moved up on the fourth man, laying on the ground and peering through his binoculars, and slit his throat with the same knife he used to dig the GPS device out of Zimmerman. The team leader was about 3 yards in front of them, still looking at his downed men, when Barber hammered him on the side of his skull with the butt of his Sig in a blow intended to knock the man out but not kill him.

Barber and Day secured the Wagner team leader in the room with Zimmerman, then dragged the three dead men to a cliff and pushed them off. It would be a case the Shetland Police would never solve, but there was no way they would tie it to them.

"Hey Joe, did you notice what's in these back packs?"

"No."

"It's cocaine. What's up with that?"

"I have no earthly idea. These guys are pros. No way are they cocaine smugglers. Why would they be assaulting our safehouse if that were the case?"

"Right. Maybe it was something to throw the police off if they got caught."

"Possibly. Not our problem right now."

The Wagner team leader sat in a chair next to Zimmerman and slowly came to. Day threw a bucket of cold water at his head that completed the process. The man's eyes slowly came into focus as Barber stared into his face.

"So, here's the deal, pal," Barber said. "I suspect you came for our friend here," pointing to Zimmerman, "but you got us instead. You're going to tell us who you are and why you are here, or I'm going to fillet you like one of those mackerels this place seems to be famous for."

The Wagner man just sat there, mute. Wagner men didn't talk. Ever. Then Barber leaned into the man's ear so Zimmerman couldn't hear them. "Here's the real deal. I'm not sure I care much whether or not you talk. It's our friend here I really want to talk. And I think if he sits here and sees what I do to you, it's going to loosen up his tongue quite a bit. Wouldn't you agree?

The man's wrists were zip-tied behind his back and his torso was duct-taped to the back of the chair. His feet, however, were not secured. It was an uncharacteristic oversight on Barber's part. He was tired, and men who are tired sometimes make mistakes. As Barber finished his taunt, his mouth still in the Wagner man's ear, the man launched himself upwards, spun the chair around violently and slammed its legs into Barber's knees, sending him to the floor, writhing in pain. It bought the assailant a few precious seconds before Barber could recover. He was swift and sure in his movements, thanks to relentless training, and a few seconds was all he needed. The Wagner man kept a small, flat-head jewelers screwdriver in a sleeve in the back of his pants for just such a contingency. He retrieved the device with his right thumb and forefinger, then twisted his wrists violently until he could get the end of the screwdriver into the zip tie's small, rectangular locking mechanism. The plastic band tore into his flesh as he did so, slicing him like a kitchen knife. Fortunately ,it missed the radial artery, so the bleeding was superficial. He depressed the tip of the screwdriver against the tiny tongue inside the locking mechanism and pushed it down until it was free of the row of plastic teeth that held the strap in place. He then pulled the strap out, and with his now free hands moved his right arm around to the front and pulled off the duct tape holding him in the chair. By this point Barber was on all fours trying to get up, but the Wagner man was now standing. He kicked Barber hard in the ribs, exactly where he had been injured just a few days ago, and sent him to the floor again on his stomach. Before Barber could recover, the Wagner man picked the spent zip tie off the floor and secured Barber's hands behind his back. He then grabbed the roll of duct-tape that was just used to restrain him and fashioned a makeshift rope between Barber's hands and his neck. Barber's restrained arms were arched slightly behind his back, creating a tension that would choke him if he didn't strain to keep his arms lifted. The arrangement was highly effective at immobilizing him, and the Wagner man figured Barber had about 10 minutes before fatigue would set in, his arms would relax, and the choking would begin involuntarily. Marcus Day was outside making sure there were no tell-tale signs of the three men killed and didn't hear a thing, thanks, in part, to the room's soundproofing.

Having secured Barber, the Wagner man turned his attention to Zimmerman. No way was he going to give up on his mission to kidnap him, as long as he had breath. Not seeing any rags nearby, he fashioned a ball out of the duct tape and put it in the Zimmerman's mouth. He then wrapped the duct tape three times around the man's head, over his mouth. Zimmerman would be miserable, but he would remain quiet. He retrieved a small knife from the inside of his boot and cut the man loose from the chair. He then grabbed him by the neck of his shirt collar and forcefully shoved him towards the door.

"Make a sound and you're a dead man," the Wagner man said. It wasn't true, of course, he knew he would be dead if he didn't deliver the man back to Russia alive. Zimmerman couldn't betray any secrets if he were dead. But Zimmerman didn't know that, and the Wagner man knew that civilians sucked into the vortex of his business usually were as compliant as sheep.

The Wagner man yanked Zimmerman to his side then slowly opened the door and looked into the hall. Nobody was there. "Excellent," he thought, as he pulled Zimmerman behind him and slowly exited the room. The two men moved in tandem out of the house and across the field in the direction of the small cove where the assault team had hidden the inflatable boat. He was aware now that Barber and Day had night vision equipment, including infrared, so it was essential to make it across the 500 meters that stood between the house and the downward slope of the hill before the big black man discovered they were gone, or Barber and Day would be able to see the two of them bugging out. The Wagner man was quite confident that if he was sighted, it would be through the scope of the rifle that took down his three teammates.

Zimmerman was a man in his late 50s and, like so many businessmen his age, wasn't in particularly good cardio-vascular condition. Consequently, he was seriously slowing the Wagner man down.

"Move your ass or I'm going to cut something of yours off," he chastised Zimmerman in a whispered voice. It lit a fire under the out-of-shape German executive for a few yards, but the initial adrenaline boost quickly faded and they once again slowed to a crawl. As the Wagner man roughly pulled Zimmerman along, he heard a muted "thwack", and an instant later felt a searing pain in his left calf. He looked for cover, but there was none. This was the Northern Shetland Islands and they were just two guys crawling on a rock in the middle of the night with nowhere to hide. Survival instincts kicked in and he reflexively reached for the side arm he usually carried on the right side of his combat belt, but then realized he was no longer armed. He had been relieved of that comfort blanket when he was initially captured. He tried to get up on all fours to speed up his crawl. Maybe there was still time to get over that rise before it was game over. But as he moved, he realized his tibia was broken. Must have been from the bullet. He had been shot in the leg. But why the leg, he wondered? Why not just shoot him center mass and end it? Then it occurred to him, they wanted him alive. Then he heard footsteps running towards their location.

Chapter 44 – A Call for Help

Orion Bellicus Safehouse, Heroldswick, The Shetland Islands, Scotland

The Wagner man once again found himself in the same chair as before, in the same room, but this time he was only wearing his boxers. Arms and legs were tightly duct-taped to the chair, along with his torso, but this time his two captors appeared to have used twice as much tape. The pain in his leg was excruciating, but not as bad as the pain of being dragged over 200 meters back to the house from the spot where Marcus Day sent a 300-magnum hardball round into his leg.

"So here's the deal, asshole," Day said. "You're going to tell me who you are and who you work for or I'm going to start cutting off body parts, and you're not going to like where I start. Actually, I think I'll let my friend here do it," he said, referring to Joe Barber, who was standing next to him looking a little worse for the wear. "He has a little score to settle with you, doesn't he? We know you're Russian, that's obvious. The lettering on the GPS receiver in your 'go bag' is Cyrillic. You should really be more careful about that. Leaving such obvious clues is sloppy. Are you Spetsnaz? Private contractor? Who sent you?"

The man sat mute.

"Joe, be my guest," Day said, making a show of handing Barber a pair of pruning shears.

"Wait!" the Wagner man exclaimed in heavily Russian-accented English. There are some threats even the strongest of men have difficulty ignoring. "I don't know who sent us. I mean," he quickly continued, realizing his mistake, "I mean yes, we are Russian, but we are not told who gives the orders. The only thing I was told is they came from very high up."

"How high up?" Day asked.

"From the very highest up, that is what we were told."

"OK, we know how you found Zimmerman. He had a GPS device implanted in his shoulder. We found it. But how did you get here? We are in the middle of nowhere. You couldn't have come through the harbor without creating suspicion."

The man sat mute again for several seconds.

"I'm starting to get impatient again. Joe, grab those pruners."

"Wait!" the man exclaimed again, this time with resignation in his voice. "My team was launched off shore by a submarine. We came in by inflatable boat."

Barber and Day looked at each other, faces betraying a sense of great concern. "What happens when you and your team don't show up?"

"We were to rendezvous no later than 12 hours after launch."

"With Zimmerman?"

"Yes, with Zimmerman."

"So, what happens when you don't show up?"

"A man like me is not given those details. But I did hear the Captain talk about some kind of contingency plan."

Barber and Day looked at each other again, this time with the look of mutual recognition.

"They're not going to let this guy go. They're going to send another team of some sort to ensure they clean up the mess," Barber said.

"I think you're right," Day responded.

"We can't fight the whole Russian army, Marc."

"No, we can't" Day responded. "I think you better call Shevchenko, like right now."

"I think you're right."

* * * * *

Fawn Lake Gated Community, Spotsylvania Courthouse, Virginia

Margaret Schevchenko, CIA Director, sipped her Manhattan cocktail on the veranda of the Fawn Lake Harbor Club Restaurant as she gazed at the lake and the peaceful scene of a boater enjoying the last leisurely cruise of the day at sunset. The Bartender at the Harbor Club could mix an excellent Manhattan, and she enjoyed it martini-style, straight, with an up-trade to Woodford Reserve bourbon instead of the standard Maker's Mark. She was a fan of the Manhattan, and of bourbon in particular, and guests at her lakefront home would occasionally be treated to the martini made with Pappy Van Winkle Bourbon, which she secured from a private wholesaler at the modest price of $3,500 per 750 ml bottle. Fawn Lake was a gated community about 90 minutes south of DC, just off the I-95 corridor. The stretch of Interstate 95 between the Nation's Capital and Richmond was, statistically, the most dangerous stretch of highway in the county. There were still many members of the Government's Senior Executive Service who braved the gauntlet every day to avoid the absurd real estate prices and congestion of the DC bedroom communities like Arlington or Alexandria, and the CIA Director was one of them. And besides, her job came with a driver, so her commute every day was a productive one.

Shevchenko sat at her table with several friends and enjoyed the conversation among a fairly eclectic group, which included a cardiologist, a retired 4-star Admiral and a partner in a major DC law firm, including their spouses. Her converation with the group was interrupted as she felt the buzz of her cell phone in her jacket pocket. She looked at the screen. It was Joe Barber.

"Sorry, but please excuse me for a minute. I need to take this call." Everyone knew what she did for a living, and the interruption was hardly regarded as unusual.

She pressed the touch screen to accept the call and said, "Hang on a second. I need to walk to a place where I can talk." She walked down towards the lakefront out of earshot of her dinner partners and took Barber off hold. "What's up, Joe?"

"I'm calling on the scrambled satellite phone, Maggie. You need to get to a secure line. ASAP. We need to talk."

"OK, I'll get to my study at home. I have a secure Agency line there."

"OK, but you need to do it right now, and get there quickly. I have some information that is extremely time-critical," Barber replied.

"Alright, Barber. I call you back in 5."

"Go, Maggie, and now. I'm not kidding."

Shevchenko walked back to her table and offered her regrets, then briskly walked to her car. She was home in less than 5 minutes. She parked her car in the garage, walked through the kitchen and down a hallway towards her study, entered it, locked the door and then threw a switch that essentially turned the room into a giant Faraday cage, making it impossible for anyone to monitor anything said inside the four walls. She lifted the receiver from a call director on her desk, punched in a 10-digit code she had committed to memory, then heard a dial tone. She punched in Barber's satellite phone number, which she also knew by heart. He answered on the first ring.

"OK, Joe, what's up? Have you learned anything from Zimmerman yet?"

"No. Listen carefully. We were just softening him up when the safehouse was hit by an assault team of four men who, get this, were transported here by a Russian sub. They knew exactly where Zimmerman was, Maggie. They had implanted the guy with a GPS locator. Marc and I managed to put down 3 of them and got the fourth guy to talk. We're pretty sure he was the team leader."

"Let me guess, you used the old 'You're not going to like where I start line', right?"

"Yeah, but listen, the guy told us there is a back-up plan. They are going to send someone else, and I expect fairly soon, to clean up the mess.

And get this, the guy told us his orders came from the highest level of the Russian government. I think this Zimmerman guy has got to be a treasure-trove of intel for them to send an assault team to Scotland."

"And you didn't get anything meaningful out of Zimmerman yet?"

"No, we didn't have time, and we certainly don't have time now, and I don't have the kind of resources we are going to need to get the guy out of here before the Russians return. You've got to arrange an extract ASAP."

"OK, I've got an agency chopper in Aberdeen I can order to pull the 3 of you. He can be there in about 90 minutes."

"You'll take care of the diplomatic stuff?"

"I'm going to call my contact at Scotland Yard, but screw the rest of the diplomatic niceties right now. That helicopter is going to be airborne in 20 minutes, diplomatic clearance or not."

"Where are we headed?" Barber asked.

"I can't tell you that. And sorry, I'm going to have to put a hood over you and Marc as well as Zimmerman. Cooperate with the crew, alright?"

"OK," Barber replied. "It's nice to be trusted."

"Just deal with it, Joe. This is the way it has to be."

"Got it."

"We'll take over the interrogation of Zimmerman. Sounds like we need whatever it is he knows quickly."

"How does that play out, Maggie?"

"It can't be on U.S. soil, for legal reasons. I can tell you that much about where you're heading."

"Tell me something I don't already know. Do you have an interrogator in mind?"

"Yes."

"Can you tell me who he is?"

"It's not a he, it's a she.

"Is she Agency?"

"No, she's contract. It's the way it has to be."

"You're not talking about who I think you are talking about, are you?"

"Yes, I probably am. It's Donna Riley."

"Oh my god," Barber responded. "Zimmerman's toast. I hear that woman has a higher body count than Chris Kyle," Barber said, referring to the Navy SEAL of American Sniper fame. "You are serious, aren't you?"

"Deadly."

Chapter 45 – The Inquisition

The Yacht "Stormy Seas", CIA Floating Safehouse, International Waters, The North Sea

She was 110 feet in length but, other than her impressive size, looked entirely ordinary. The hull was laid in 1954, and the yacht appeared to the casual observer well-worn and not particularly well-maintained. Faint but visible signs of rust appeared above the waterline. Her silhouette suggested old, even utilitarian. Nothing about the yacht suggested wealth or gravitas, except perhaps from a bygone era.

But her appearance belied what lay beneath. Underneath the rough skin was a pair of Volvo Penta 2000 hp turbocharged engines capable of propelling her at 45 knots. The helm was rigged with marine electronics and navigation systems that rivaled a modern warship, and the flip of a switch from the bridge would open aft deck doors and elevate two Exocet missile pods and a 50-caliber rotary cannon capable of spitting depleted uranium ammunition at a rate of 1500 rounds a minute. Forward of the bridge was a long flat surface that appeared to be a sundeck, but really served as a helicopter landing pad. She had a Liberian registry, and hailed from Bergen, Norway where she spent most of her life hiding in plain sight.

The small black helicopter flew 50 feet off the surface of the North Sea as it headed for the Stormy Seas. As the chopper arrived at the yacht, it slowed down and came to a hover just off the forward deck. Fortunately, the stiff north winds of the previous night had quieted to a gentle breeze providing conditions that permitted a landing on the yacht instead of disgorging their passengers by rope. The bird's skids gently made contact, and the pilot reduced the throttle to idle as four passengers egressed. Once the passengers were clear of the swirling rotor, the pilot advanced the throttle, pulled the collective upwards, pushed the control stick forward and, with sufficient rudder pressure to keep the bird's nose pointed straight, lifted the aircraft off the deck and flew back towards the horizon from whence it came. Joe Barber, Marc Day, Hans-Dieter Zimmerman and the Wagner team leader were quickly ushered below deck.

Two rather tall and muscular-looking men took control of Zimmerman and the Wagner man as Barber and Day were ushered into the yacht's main salon down a short flight of steps just forward to the bridge. As they entered the salon, two people, both standing, were waiting for them. The man, about five-foot eight and medium build, appeared to be in his early 50s. He proffered his hand and said, "I'm Kirk Wihlelm."

Barber and Day both shook his hand, then Barber commented, "So let me guess; you're Special Activities Division," referring to the CIA's paramilitary arm.

"We don't call it that anymore," the man responded. I'm formerly SAC/SOG, but now with NCS. Humint."

"Of course," Barber replied, somewhat irritated by the guy correcting him. "Typical Agency type," he thought. He then replied, with precision, "Special Activities Center/Special Operations Group. Now National Clandestine Service gathering human intelligence. The Farm certainly loves its acronyms, doesn't it?"

"Yes, we do," the Agency man replied. "Gives the millennials in HR something to do: think up acronyms."

Barber smiled as his initial negative impression of the man suddenly turned positive at the millennials reference.

The woman was about five-foot five with medium dark hair and looked to be in her later 30s, although her age was hard to tell. She looked fit, but not particularly imposing at first glance. As Barber sized her up, he noticed the definition in her arms and shoulders, more like a person addicted to CrossFit than distance running. His next thought was to wonder how many necks she had snapped before transferring from Special Activities Division to becoming an interrogator. Rumor had it the number was pretty high, although there was talk that much of that body count was actually interrogation targets who failed to cooperate. "I'm Donna Riley," she said, also proffering her hand, first to Day, then to Barber.

"So, I meet the legend," Barber said. "Your reputation precedes you."

"We're just here to do a job, so let's get on with it," she said, without smiling.

"Works for us," Day responded for the both of them.

"Good," she said. "We're going to concentrate on Zimmerman. He's the one with the information we really need. It's been, how shall I say, 'reinforced on me', how time-critical this information is, so I'm not going to waste time on the Russian until we're done with our German friend. First, a few ground rules. I am running this show. If I want your opinion, I'll give it to you. Do not interrupt me unless you have important information you believe I need. I don't need advice on how to run an interrogation. Second, I may do some things that you will regard as unpleasant. After studying Zimmerman's bio, he strikes me as soft, so I'm hoping I don't have to resort to much of that, but if I do, don't get in my way. I'll hurt you if you do, and that's not an idle threat. That goes for you too, big guy," she said to Marcus Day. "You're a big dude, but taking down big dudes is a hobby of mine. Are we clear?"

Day just smiled.

"As far as I'm concerned, the two of you are civilians, at least until this job is completed."

"Got it," Barber said.

"Ok, Let's get to work," she said.

The four of them walked down another short flight of steps and into a stateroom. In the middle of the room a chair was bolted to the floor instead of the normal bed. Zimmerman was seated in the chair with arms and legs restrained by ample amounts of duct tape. A large strip of duct tape also was wrapped around his forehead several times restraining his head backwards in what was obviously an uncomfortable position.

"It's a little tight," Riley said, referring to the close quarters. "Kirk, you're not needed in here right now, so go get a beer or whatever."

"See ya. Have fun, Donna Marie," he said.

She then looked at Barber and Day. "One of you can stay. Two of you keeps this room too tight."

"He's all yours, Joe," Day said as he walked out of the room. Barber backed up a few steps and leaned against the wall, waiting for the show to begin.

"What's your name?" she asked Zimmerman. He remained silent.

"I asked you for your name. What's your name?" she asked again.

"You know perfectly well what my name is," Zimmerman responded.

She walked over to a table and picked up what appeared to be a bottle of rubbing alcohol. Returning to Zimmerman, she grabbed his left pinkie finger and poured a small amount of the liquid on it, making sure the finger was coated from its tip to the first knuckle, but nowhere else. She then retrieved a Zippo lighter from her pocket, flicked the case open, spun the wheel and ignited a small flame. She reached the lighter over towards his hand and lit the finger, allowing the flame to burn until all the alcohol was consumed. Zimmerman screamed. He was shocked by more than just the intense pain. As he saw the threat begin to unfold, he knew right away what she poured on him was alcohol; he could tell from the smell. But his mind processed it as a warning, not as an immediate threat. It was part of the game, designed to intimidate, he told himself; she wouldn't actually do it. The fact that she lit his finger immediately was difficult for his brain to process, and it delivered three important results: it confirmed she wasn't bluffing, it confirmed she wasn't operating under a civilized set of rules, and most importantly, it reinforced the importance of answering her questions quickly. The entire exercise was designed to speed up the interrogation process.

"Shut up," she said, authoritatively. "Stop acting like a baby. That was just a little wake up. I haven't started to inflict pain yet. Let's try this one more time. I'll target the ring finger on that hand next, and if you disappoint me I'm going to break it first and then light it. Now, tell me your name."

"Zimmerman," he said. "Hans-Dieter Zimmerman."

"Excellent. We're making progress. Now, what is your job?"

"I am acting Chief Executive of Sternenlicht."

"Good boy. What is Sternenlicht's business?" she asked.

"We are a defense contractor to the European Federation."

"What is your involvement with the Iranians?" she asked.

"We are expanding our commercial and defense relationships with the Iranians. In the process, we cooperate on issues of mutual interest."

His face turned white as he saw her walk back to the table and pick up a small container that looked like Vaseline. She walked back to him, pulled the lid off the small tub of the jelly-like substance then spread a generous amount over his ring finger. Before he could process the fact that she had finished that task, she quickly grabbed the finger, placing her thumb on its side where it was attached to his hand. With her index and middle fingers bracing the other side, she moved it slowly to the side until it reached a position unintended by nature. Doing it slowly, instead of a quick snap, was so much more effective. It gave the subject time to think about what was happening and magnified the pain of the break. The action yielded a snapping noise that even made Barber a bit squeamish. As Zimmerman screamed, she retrieved the lighter again and lit the Vaseline that coated his now broken finger.

"I always use Vaseline the second time because it burns slower and creates more damage to the flesh," she said, taunting him. "Also, it's viscosity allows me to coat the finger with a far greater amount of fuel than is possible with just alcohol." She let the finger burn several more seconds then retrieved a small bucket of slightly melted ice from the table and positioned his hand in it, deadening the pain

"You can't very well tell me much if you're screaming, can you?" she asked. "This is just the easy stuff, by the way. I'm going to start asking you the important questions now, and because time is of the essence, I will need to use far more serious measures from here on if you don't cooperate. Do you believe me?" The second exercise, the one he had just endured, was designed to reinforce her intention to escalate. It worked.

"Yes," he said, sobbing.

"Good. Now, I want you to start telling me everything you did for the Iranians, everything you gave them for that 50 million Euros they paid you. And here's something for you to think about as you start. If you don't really impress me, as a matter of fact, if you don't really knock my socks off, you're not going to like where I put that Vaseline next," she said as she removed the bucket of melted ice and dumped it on the floor. She then handed Barber a knife and said, "Cut out the front of his pants and underwear, and be careful not to damage anything. That's my job."

Riley put on a rubber glove, then stood and watched with a tub of Vaseline in her other hand as Barber walked towards Zimmerman with the knife. As Barber slit the first piece of clothing just to the right of Zimmerman's crotch, he started singing like a canary.

Chapter 46 – Revelations

Situation Room, The White House, Washington D.C.

President Sara Einhorn waited several extra minutes in her private study before getting up to walk to the Situation Room. She had an iron-clad rule of always being the last person to arrive at a meeting, except when she conducted business in her normal power base of the Oval Office or the private study adjacent to it. People waited for her. She didn't wait for people. Anyone who broke the rule and arrived after her would feel the blistering thrust of her wrath. She regarded fear as her most effective management tool, and her inner circle would often refer to her style as 'management by random acts of violence', always doing so, of course, behind her back.

She looked at her watch and concluded enough time had passed to ensure a proper arrival. She got up from her desk, grabbed the briefing folder that sat in front of her and started the walk down the hall towards the elevator leading to the White House basement and the storied meeting place. Completing her journey, she opened the door and was pleased to see that everyone was seated and waiting. She enjoyed making people wait. It gave her a sense of control. She sat down without saying a word.

As she settled into her place at the head of the conference table, she opened her briefing book and looked at the contents. She was doing it just for effect, as a way of ignoring the people in the room. It was another way of projecting her power and her sense of self-importance, and to reinforce the lack of same for everyone else. But behind the non-verbal bluster she was seized with a terrible sense of fear. Would she be subjected again to another blinding headache in front of her entire inner circle by her tormentor from the West Coast, Emma Clark? Would it force her to behave in a way that would cause some in the room to doubt her stability? Would some fate worse that a headache befall her at the hands of that crazy woman, her puppet master? At the moment, she felt anything but powerful and in control, but she was a master at illusion and kept up the act.

"Why are we here?" the President asked, without looking up.

CIA Director Margaret Shevchenko spoke, "Madam President, in the past couple of hours we have come upon important information regarding events of the last several days, and it is important that you and the senior leadership team be brought fully up to speed."

"So, am I the last person to be made aware of this information?" she asked, sarcastically, still looking down at her folder, flipping a page.

"No Ma'am. I am the only one in the room presently in possession of it. I felt it important to share it with everyone at once and not waste time with pre-briefings."

"Go ahead," the President said, finally looking up.

"In the last several hours the Agency has come into possession of critical information regarding events of the last several days, including clarity around responsible actors, methods, and motives."

Carleton Epsy III, the Secretary of State, cut her off and asked in an authoritative voice, "Just exactly how did YOU come upon such information?"

"We interviewed one of the principals," she said.

"And exactly how do you define 'interview', Margaret?" he asked in an accusatory voice, louder than necessary, emphasizing her full first name instead of the "Maggie" she preferred.

"Shut up, Carl," the President barked. "Let her finish. This is a briefing, not an inquisition." The President could be blistering in her criticisms of her staff, even Cabinet Officers, but usually reserved such direct admonishments for smaller settings. The Secretary of State looked shocked at her rebuke in front of people he largely regarded as his lessors.

"As I was saying," Shevchenko continued, looking directly at the Secretary of State, "we arranged an off-site interview with Hans-Dieter Zimmerman, the acting Chief Executive of Sternenlicht. There are two very important points of context for what I am about to share. First, Sternenlicht is the European Federation defense contractor, German actually, that developed the command and control system for the Federation's strategic weapons. Second, our people obtained irrefutable proof that Zimmerman was paid 50 million Euros by the Iranians for something. We now know what that something was and how it played into recent events." Shevchenko paused a moment, for effect.

It worked. An eerie quiet hung over the room. Everyone sitting around the table seemed to be on the edge of their chair, intensely focused on what the CIA Director would say next. Even the Secretary of State appeared nonplussed. The President and Shevchenko's eyes met. The President spoke. "Go on, Margaret. You certainly have our attention."

Shevchenko continued, "Zimmerman confirmed that Iran successfully hacked into the Federation's strategic weapons command and control system. You should all remember the name Helmut Schiller, the late CEO of Sternenlicht. The system was his pet project and he became suspicious. That's why he was assassinated, and it was by the Iranians. They were fearful of exposure."

"Mother of God," said General John Weatherby, Chairman of the Joint Chiefs, as he reflected on the implications of what he just heard.

"Anyway," the CIA Director continued, "Zimmerman was paid the 50 million Euros to help the Iranians speed up their efforts and get through a couple of roadblocks. They were evidently in a hurry."

"He actually provided them with code?" asked Burt Hagenlocker, the Secretary of Defense, astonished.

"Yes, he actually provided them with code."

"That's treason isn't it?" asked General Weatherby. "My God, was he aware of their intentions?"

"He claims not," the CIA Director responded, "but that's still unclear. Anyway, the Iranians developed a virus that laid dormant in the Federation's systems. Now this is the real scary part: the virus provided them with much more than access to data or the ability to impede functionality. It provided them with remote launch capability. They not only penetrated the EF's strategic weapons systems, they developed the ability to remotely deploy them." She paused again, allowing a few seconds for what she just revealed to sink in.

"You mean they actually developed the ability to remotely launch another country's nuclear missiles?" General Weatherby asked.

"Yes, General, that's exactly what I mean."

"That's impossible!" the Secretary of Defense exclaimed. "Those systems are hardened, and fail-safe firewalled!"

"Well it would appear, Burt, that your belief on that point may be a bit flawed," Shevchenko said, sarcastically.

"Their fail-safes are modelled on ours," the Chairman of the Joint Chiefs said. "That was one of Germany's selling points on safety when they moved some of the nukes from France into their territory."

"Yes, they are," said Radek Malecek, the National Security Advisor. "I suggest we all pause a second and reflect on exactly what that means."

"It means our systems are potentially vulnerable as well," the Secretary of Defense said.

"Precisely," Malecek responded.

There were several more seconds of contemplative silence as a grim mood descended over the room. "Ok, Maggie, but those missiles are pre-programmed for their targets. I think we've all just learned that the art of the possible is far more frightening than any of us imagined, but remotely retargeting a missile is vastly more difficult that hacking into the command and control systems. Why would they fire a missile not knowing where it was headed?"

"I think that's where the story gets even more interesting," Shevchenko said. Zimmerman claims the Iranians figured out a way to remotely retarget."

"That's incomprehensible!" exclaimed the Chairman of the Joint Chiefs

"But why attack their own country? Especially the holy city of Qom?" asked the Secretary of Defense. "That just doesn't make sense."

"Our source, Zimmerman, didn't have an answer to that. We have a couple of working theories, however."

"Which are?" the President asked.

"They screwed up. It was a mistake. If you look at the flight path of the missile something really stands out."

"Israel," said the National Security Advisor.

"Exactly," Shevchenko replied. "Their retargeting capability may not have been as good as they thought, and the missile may have just gone long. It's not exactly like you can test the retargeting capability before the fact."

"And your other working theory?" the President asked.

"A scarier one. There's another state actor involved. The hackers themselves were hacked."

"Who?" the President asked, astonished.

"We believe there are only four countries that could have a cyber capability that sophisticated: Russia, China, Japan, and maybe India. You can dismiss Japan and India right off the bat. What would be their motive?"

"Russia?" the Secretary of State asked.

"Possible, but I don't think so," Shevchenko replied. "They tried to kidnap Zimmerman from one of our safehouses. Working theory is, having seen what happened, they wanted him for the technology themselves. Why would they want to kidnap Zimmerman if they already had it? And by the way, it was no ordinary mission. He was being held in a safe house in one of the northern Shetland Islands. They actually launched an assault team from a submarine in the North Sea to capture him."

"So, that leaves China," the President said.

"They're certainly the prime suspect."

"Good luck proving it," the Secretary of State said.

"I know," replied Shevchenko, "but we're going to try."

General John Weatherby, Chairman of the Joint Chiefs, spoke up, "Madam President, I'm not sure how to even process this information. Its implications are far greater than what's happened between Germany and Iran. If the information Dr. Shevchenko just shared is correct, every nuclear arsenal presently deployed is potentially vulnerable, and not just ours. What's next? India fires at Pakistan, or vice versa? Somebody fires our missiles? Somebody fires Russia's missiles? How do we even secure our own arsenal?"

"I agree with John," the Secretary of Defense said. "We need a strategy on how to deal with this. Taking our entire strategic deterrent offline would be massively destabilizing."

The President spoke up. "OK, I want Burt, John, Carl and Radek to stay back and talk this through. Let's reconvene back here in the situation room in two hours and discuss where we're at. Maggie, go back to your people and see what else they have or can find out. I need options, people. Get to work," the President said as she stood and walked out of the room.

Chapter 47 – Conversations

White House Executive Wing, Washington, D.C.

The President walked alone from the Situation Room back towards her private study. She told her Chief of Staff to go back to his office, that she needed time alone to think. As she walked into the outer office of the Oval suite, she told her secretary to clear her calendar for the rest of the afternoon and hold any phone calls that were not from a Head of State, the SecDef or the Chairman of the Joint Chiefs. She proceeded through the Oval to the President's Private Study, closed the door, then sat down at her desk. She was uncharacteristically reflective. She thought about her road to the Presidency. She reflected on her motives, her ambitions, the high she got from the power of the job. She loved the power, and more than anything else loved to "lord it over" people in a manner that could turn the most confident person into a mere child in the face of her raw aggression. But for a brief moment, she almost had a twinge of regret. The circumstances she faced were arguably the most serious any President had faced in the history of the Republic. The gravity of the situation didn't escape her. She had no delusions about her lack of moral character. She knew exactly what she was, and most of the time she was damned proud of it. But this was different. She had the capacity to grasp what was at stake, and it didn't just frighten her, it saddened her. What was her fate, her karma, that placed her in this job at this moment in time? Wouldn't the world be a much better place if there was someone else in this job right now: a man or a woman of true character and not the ruthless opportunist consumed by the ambition she knew was her true character.

But this feeling didn't last. All people occasionally experience doubt, she told herself. Her parents were devoutly religious. Her father was a missionary. They experienced doubt. She knew her mother occasionally wondered whether their faith was just a big hoax. But both her parents died with a faith stronger than that of their youth. It's what they were; it defined them. She had followed a different path. Her religion was power, and it began to ascend again after its momentary stumble. Mean-reversion to what you really are, she told herself, then growth to the next level. The moment of self-doubt quickly faded as her survival instincts and ambitions once again enveloped her like a warm blanket. She was stronger now after having been tempered in the momentary fire of self-doubt. She had a destiny to fulfill, and she would forge ahead to fulfill it, the world be damned. But first, she had a phone call to make.

Offices of PrinSafe, Palo Alto

Just shy of three thousand miles to the West, Emma Clark sat in her office and pushed "end" on the private, encrypted cell phone she had in her hand. To say the news she just received was unsettling would be a colossal understatement. Her contact at CWR Industries had just advised her the Iranians were in the process of eliminating anyone with knowledge of Iran's involvement in the missile launch and Zimmerman was likely abducted by the Americans, putting him out of reach. Hamidi was dead, as was the entire launch team. The mathematician she had helped the Iranians abduct in California was nowhere to be found, but they were looking for him. The implications were clear. She herself was one of the biggest loose ends, and they would soon be coming for her. Suddenly the $500 million dollars she received for providing CWR's assistance in developing the missile retargeting software didn't seem nearly enough.

As she contemplated her options, she knew there was only one way to save herself. She had to "out" the Iranians. They were covering their tracks to ensure nobody discovered they fired the missile. If that became public knowledge there would no longer be a reason to go after her, and the Iranians would be occupied with far more urgent matters, like survival. She knew exactly what to do. This nitwit in the Whitehouse was still useful after all, she thought. She would provide President Einhorn with irrefutable evidence of what happened and CWR Industries' involvement. She realized that in doing so she would be throwing the subsidiary under the bus, but sometimes that was the price of business.

President's Private Study, White House, Washington, D.C.

The President retrieved her private cell phone from her suit jacket and dialed the West Coast number. Clark answered on the first ring.

"Hello, Sara. I was just about to call you."

"Thanks for not delivering your customary heads-up," the President said, referring to the headaches that were induced by Emma Clark by activating the cranial implant nestled in the President's brain.

"Let's not focus on unpleasant matters right now, Madam President," Clark said. "I would actually like to offer you help. We have a mutual interest in seeing this thing contained, cauterized."

"Mutual interest?" the President almost shouted into the phone. "So, your company did somehow have a hand in this! That's why your wanted me to hold off those sanctions! I thought it was just about your profits, the money!"

"I had no idea what they were really up to, Sara," she lied, " and it was about the money, at least initially. But it's no longer about money. It's now about putting an end to an existential threat and focusing on damage control. We are both going to survive this if we keep our heads."

"It's unravelling, Emma," the President said. "CIA has Zimmerman. Apparently the guy is spilling his guts about helping the Iranians hacking the European Federation's Command and Control systems. He's admitted to his complicity in all of it. And worse yet, he's fingered your sub, CWR Industries, as the ones who helped the Iranians with the missile retargeting software. But that's not the worst of it."

"So, what's worse?" Clark asked.

"Think about it. A nuclear power's weapons system, a nuclear-tipped missile, was not only fired by another nation-state, it was done without the owner even knowing about it until the thing was in the air. That means everyone's Command and Control systems is potentially vulnerable. That is going to become public knowledge very soon, and when it does it will create an ugly faceoff among every nuclear power on the planet. Everyone will be scared to death that they might be next. This was no ordinary hack. The threat of a full-scale nuclear exchange is as high now as it was during Cuba, if not even higher. I thought half the people in the Situation Room were going to have a heart attack when that implication became clear."

Clark leaned back in her chair and allowed several seconds to pass before responding. This was going to be easier than she thought. Her plan had been to give the President information on CWR Industries that would document their giving Iran the code needed to retarget the missiles. But it wasn't necessary now. The President already had that information thanks to Zimmerman. Her only remaining task now was to frame a small group of Iranian employees of CWR for working with Iran so it would be viewed as a rogue operation and not something that could be tied back to PrinSafe or her. This was about to blow up in the Iranian's faces and they would no longer have a need to silence her. She was in the clear! Her thoughts were interrupted by the President's voice.

"Emma? Are you still there?"

"Yes, I'm still here, and sorry, that was quite a lot to digest. I want to look into the issues with CWR Industries in Germany. It's incomprehensible to me that the executive management of that company would do something so reckless," she lied. "I need 24 hours to figure out what happened. I know we have a number of Iranian nationals working there, writing computer code and I suspect it must have been a rogue operation of some sort, but I'll get to the bottom of it."

"The EF authorities are going to want to raid that company the moment they find out what happened, and I'll have no earthly excuse to ask them to wait. Right now, we only have Zimmerman's word about what happened. Everybody is going to want proof. Not only proof that the systems were hacked, but proof the Iranian's actually launched the missile, and remember those are two different things. The fact the Iranians developed the capability doesn't prove they actually used it. And Iran could argue that Germany launched that missile as punishment after discovering Iran's hack. It's not that crazy a theory. "

"You are to take no action on CRW for 24 hours, Madam President. That's not negotiable. Am I clear on that point?"

President Einhorn bristled at Emma Clark's comments, and especially the way they were conveyed as almost a command. "I can't promise that, Emma. The Principals are meeting in the Situation Room again in less than two hours to discuss our action plan and giving the Federation everything we know is going to be the first item on the list. I will face major pushback on if I try to withhold something."

"You're the President. Put your big girl shoes on and just do it. You can give them everything but CWR, and I'll greenlight you to give them CWR sometime tomorrow."

Einhorn's face flushed at being talked to like some kind of middle manager. She was furious. Her rage turned to fear at Emma Clark's next comment.

"And don't forget, Madam President, that I am capable of proving some highly effective pushback myself. And my pushback is much more painful, potentially even deadly. There will be no giving the European Federation any information on CWR Industries until I give you clearance sometime tomorrow. Period."

Several seconds of silence followed Clark's last comment. She finally broke the silence. "Sara, are you still there?"

"Yes, I'm here."

"OK, let me go to work. And don't worry, I'll give you CWR tomorrow with a bow tied around it. Just be patient for a little while longer. Good luck getting through the day. I'll say you're going to need it."

The President pushed "end" on her private cell phone and placed the device back insider her suit jacket. She then hung her head a bit and braced it with her hands, elbows on the desk. Her headache returned, and it was splitting, but at least it was of organic origin and not a gift from the West Coast. She reflected on the conversation. Her previous bluster was now gone. She no longer thought of ambitions and destiny. She thought about survival. It then occurred to her that in her candor she had just revealed the highest of classified information to a private citizen. That was not only an impeachable offence, it was also a felony. As a matter of fact, it was likely treason. "How did things come to this," she asked herself from the depths of her sudden-onset depression, as she continued to hold her head in her hands.

Offices of PrinSafe, Palo Alto

Emma Clark sat at her desk and thought about the phone call. She knew exactly what to do. There was a template for surgically removing a problem from any part of the PrinSafe empire. With a few tweaks to the template, one of her Lieutenants would have several CWR employees, Iranian nationals, abducted and put on a plane to Iran where they would face certain death, despite them having nothing to do with the missile retargeting code, of course, but that didn't matter. They provided credible scapegoats. Problem solved. She then thought about the President. Einhorn was losing it. She was becoming less useful by the day. In fact, she was becoming a liability. Clark was seriously starting to wonder how long she should keep her around.

Chapter 48 – Another Mission

The Yacht "Stormy Seas", CIA Floating Safehouse, International Waters, The North Sea

Barber stood in the Yacht's bridge and looked out over the horizon. As the vessel churned through the saltwater at 30 knots, the seas presented only a moderate chop, enough to make the ride interesting but not enough to make it uncomfortable. A mid-afternoon sun brightened the partly cloudy sky and seemed to corroborate the satellite report of improving weather for the remainder of the day.

Barber looked at his watch, a Rolex Submariner in all-stainless steel; rugged, accurate, and perfect for a mission downrange or wearing with a tux. Checking the time, he confirmed it was just a few minutes before his next scheduled call with the CIA Director, Margaret Shevchenko. It had been a good day. The interrogation of Zimmerman had yielded a treasure-trove of information, and they were through with him. But now, what to do with the guy? Barber knew there would be enormous fallout if it ever became public knowledge that the United States had kidnapped and renditioned a German national then tortured him. Two of the guy's fingers were severally burned and one of them was broken as well. Torture was indisputable; likely against the law even with Presidential authorization, and Barber was skeptical they had it. So, the guy needed to be "dispositioned" in some manner. The Agency certainly would have a plan. He was hoping the phone call from Shevchenko in a couple of minutes would clarify things.

Marcus Day bounded up the ladder from the main cabin to the bridge. "So, what's up partner? Aren't we about ready for that phone call?"

"Yes. She's should be calling anytime now. How are things below?"

"Riley bandaged the guy's burnt fingers but he's still in a lot of pain., I hate to think of what she might have done if the he hadn't talked."

"She would have done whatever was necessary," Barber replied. "The woman's a real pro, Mark. She seemed to approach the task like it was a science. She knew just exactly how much to do and at how fast to do it to loosen the guy's tongue. And she's no sadist. I didn't see any evidence that she was enjoying it. She just did what she had to do, and it worked. Legend has it they keep her on retainer for just a circumstance like this."

"I wonder if anyone else does?" Day replied.

"That's a really interesting question, and I guarantee we'll never get the answer, but I suspect the answer is yes."

"Right. Not enough work from just the good ole U S of A to keep her employed full time," Day responded, "at least anymore, now that the rules have changed."

"Something like that," Barber said.

"You know what's weird?" Day asked. "Our female grim reaper downstairs just injected Zimmerman with another GPS device, this time into his butt."

"Why would she do that?" Barber asked.

"I asked her. All she said was one word, 'orders'."

"That doesn't make sense," Barber responded. Why plant a GPS device in him when we have the guy in our custody. We already know where he is."

Barber was interrupted by the ring of the satellite phone. "Hello, Maggie," Barber said as he pressed "Accept" on the phone's touch-screen.

"Again, Joe, great work," the CIA Director said.

"Well, the heavy lifting was done by that female Torquemada you sent," he said, referring to Tomás de Torquemada, the 15th century Dominican monk who ran the Spanish Inquisition.

"But we wouldn't know anything if you hadn't gotten the guy out of Germany and successfully fought off a Russian assault team," she replied.

"Yeah, ok, thanks again, but what are we going to do with this clown now?" Barber asked.

"We're going to kill two birds with one stone."

"Not sure I like the sound of that, especially the 'kill' part, but I'm listening."

"First," the CIA Director responded, "the guy's a threat. We know the Russians tried to kidnap him for what he knows. They want the technology, and we can't let that happen."

"Roger that!" Barber exclaimed. "So, you're asking us, er, to, ah, make the problem go away?" Barber asked in a thinly veiled reference to them killing the guy.

"No, not exactly. Our other objective, or other 'bird' to use my analogy, is we want to bolster the evidence of Iran's complicity in all of this."

"OK, now I'm really confused. I don't follow you. How do we do that?"

"We're going to have a SEAL team insert him into Iran. We have an asset in the Revolutionary Guard who will ensure a patrol 'stumbles' on him. Our asset will provide us with conclusive evidence they have him, and we'll be able to corroborate it with a GPS device I had implanted in the guy."

"Ah, so that's why Riley stuck a needle in his butt."

"Exactly. And a fairly large-scale needle at that. We then float the story that he defected to Iran. Iran will execute him, of course. They'll be convinced he was responsible for the software's malfunction and the missile hitting Qom. So, there it is. Two objectives accomplished. Two birds, one stone."

"Got it, and very clever. Where do Marc and I come in."

"Just you. I want you to get him to the 5th fleet. The three of you will be helicoptered back to Scotland. We'll fly Marcus back the States, but I'll have an Agency plane standing by to take you and Zimmerman to Bahrain. SEAL Team 2 will take over Zimmerman from there."

"Did you say I'm going to the Bahrain as well?" Barber asked, a bit confused.

"Just a stop off. You're going to Afghanistan."

"Afghanistan? Why am I going to Afghanistan?" Barber asked, stunned.

"The Orion Bellicus contract with Agency just got extended," she answered, somewhat tongue in cheek. "I have another job for you."

"Oh great," Barber said, "I can hardly wait to hear about it."

"You're going to have to be a little patient; I have to confirm something first. We'll talk once you're in Bahrain. Pleasant travels. I need to go. I'm due in the Situation Room in about 5," she said, then disconnected the call.

Barber put the phone back into his pocket, then turned to Day. "You're not going to believe this, Marc."

Chapter 49 – Plans

Situation Room, The White House, Washington D.C.

Waiting for this meeting had been the longest two hours of her life, President Einhorn thought, as she walked into the Situation Room and took her place at the head of the table. She knew this was likely the most consequential meeting of her Presidency. If the decisions they were about to make didn't put recent events on a path to resolution, the consequences could be unimaginable. Failure meant far more than continued chaos; it potentially meant all-out nuclear war. Once word got out that a nation's nuclear arsenal was compromised, every member of the nuclear club would fear theirs was compromised as well. Paranoia would trump reason. Each would fear they had no choice but to act or face annihilation. Each would go to the highest level of military alert. Each would have their strategic weapons systems on a hair-trigger. The risk of a mistake or miscalculation would be extraordinarily high. Whether from fear, miscalculation, or mistake, someone would undoubtedly act, and the moment the first missile left its silo, an unstoppable sequence of events would commence. She looked around the conference table and surveyed the faces. These were good people, she conceded. Smart people. She hoped the collective intelligence in the room would have the answers, but she was far from certain of it.

But Sara Einhorn, President of the United States, was still Sara Einhorn, and a different emotion also consumed her. She didn't want hundreds of millions of people to die, more importantly, she didn't want to die. She remembered Emma Clark's warning about preventing the shutdown of CWR Industries before tomorrow. She had no doubt that if she wasn't successful, Clark would make good on her threat and trigger the device in her head that would cause a deadly aneurism. Preventing that outcome was more important to her than saving the world. What was the point of saving the world, she reflected, if she couldn't be part of it? She very much wanted the outcome of this meeting to accomplish both, but she was at peace with the realization that the latter was far more important to her than the former. It was the way she was wired.

Several people in the room shuffled anxiously as they waited for her to speak. She took careful notice of the nervous body language, believing it was a sign of weakness. She also noticed that three of the attendees sat quietly, looking calm and even slightly annoyed at her non-verbal theatrics. These three, The Secretary of Defense, The Chairman of the Joint Chiefs, and the CIA Director, were both the problem and the solution. They were a problem because they were not intimidated by her and they let her know it through a body language that conveyed strength, not weakness. They were the solution because, if there was any hope in dealing with the present mess, she knew the only workable ideas would come from them. The President then noticed the CIA Director was doing more than just sitting calmly. Margaret Shevchenko's eyes seemed to be boring holes into her. It made the President uncomfortable. Time to reassert control, she thought.

The President finally spoke. "OK, you've had two hours. Where are we, and what are we going to do?"

Carleton Espy III, the Secretary of State, cleared his throat nervously and began to speak. "Madam President, the one thing we are all agreed on is the absolute need for transparency. We must provide our intelligence on Iran's complicity to each nuclear power. It is essential that we hold nothing back."

Almost everyone around the conference table nodded their heads in agreement. This was the first and easiest point the group had agreed on, along with the decision to allow the Secretary of State to lead off the discussion with the point. The Secretary of State, however, a man who loved the sound of his own voice, then proceeded to shoot himself in the foot.

"State recommends we call a joint meeting of the United Nations General Assembly for the purpose of presenting the intelligence."

Burt Hagenlocker, the Secretary of Defense, almost came out of his chair. "Oh, for Heaven's sake, Carl, that's a complete waste of time. We don't have the luxury of diplomatic niceties right now, and that group couldn't even come to a consensus that the world is round or that the oceans are wet. Besides, we don't have the time. Madam President, you need to call everyone today. A conference call would be the best and quickest way to convey the intelligence. It has to include the European Federation."

General John Weatherby spoke next and reinforced his boss's points. "I agree. Defense Intelligence has confirmed that Russia and China are at their highest level of strategic weapons readiness. We don't know conclusively about India or Pakistan yet, but you can bet that are too. If there's going to be a near-term miscalculation I think India or Pakistan are the most likely candidates. We have to get credible intelligence into everyone's hands as quickly as possible."

"Sorry, Carl," the President responded, looking at the Secretary of State, "but I agree that taking this to the UN is a stupid idea. If I am reading circumstances correctly, we're all on the razor's edge and nobody has a clue what the next move is or who's going to make it."

"That's correct, Madam President," General Weatherby interjected.

"And," the President continued, "we can follow up quickly with a meeting of the Security Council to 'check the UN box'."

"Precisely," Secretary Hagenlocker said.

"Ok, we're agreed on a conference call," the President continued, "and we do bilateral calls for any of the nuclear powers that balk at being on the phone with potential adversaries. I'm agreed that we'll give them everything we have. But that still doesn't solve the problem of convincing everyone the remote launch software may still be in the wrong hands."

"Madam President," CIA Director Shevchenko said, "Secretary Hagenlocker, General Weatherby and I have put a plan in motion, subject to your approval, of course, that addresses that."

The President looked sternly at Shevchenko and replied, "What do you mean you have put a plan in place, subject to my approval? If it's already in place, how is it still subject to anything?"

"What I mean, Madam President," the CIA Director said, "is that we are in process of deploying assets to the appropriate theaters. We haven't launched the actual missions yet. May I continue?"

"Yes, by all means," the President replied sarcastically.

"Our idea rests on three things. First, and the easiest, we must provide the EF Ministry of Defense with the intelligence we have on the complicity of the company, CRW Industries, in helping Iran with the remote missile launch and retargeting code. It is essential that they act quickly, raid the place and lock down all evidence. Every minute we wait increases the risk of the company destroying vital evidence."

The President visibly grimaced at the suggestion. This was exactly what she hoped to avoid. She regained her composure and said, "Go ahead."

"Second, we have a SEAL Team 2 standing by on the George Washington to insert Zimmerman into Iran. Our asset in-country will provide undeniable evidence of his presence, and we will plant a highly credible cover story that implies he was abducted by Iranian agents in Germany and renditioned back to Iran."

"And how does that explain Iran launching a missile on itself?" the President asked.

"The cover story implies he was abducted on suspicion of altering the retargeting software, and that the original target was Israel. This, plus the evidence we get from a raid on CWR Industries, should provide incontrovertible proof that Iran was responsible for the launch."

"It's not fool-proof, Madam President, but it's a good plan," the Secretary of Defense responded. "All we have to do is create suspicion. This plan does that in spades. Every good ruse has an element of truth, and this one has a double-advantage. Most of the cover story is probably what actually happened, and people are going to want to believe Iran is responsible. It just 'rings true'."

"And how is it we convince everyone, including ourselves, that somebody else doesn't have this code?"

"There's a short and a long-term answer to that," the Defense Secretary responded. "Maggie, please share your short-term answer."

The CIA Director spoke. "This is my third point. We've had a major breakthrough. Apparently ,the scientist who headed the project was a former professor at Berkeley who was kidnapped two years ago and sent to Iran to oversee its development. He did so under threat of death. He apparently escaped in all of the confusion following the destruction of Qom and somehow got his hands on a satellite phone. It was a Motorola, U.S. manufacture, and it has a GPS chip in it. We know exactly where he is."

"How the hell did the Islamic Republic of Iran get its hands on a Motorola satellite phone?" asked Secretary of State Espy. "Is the company violating the sanctions?"

"Shut up, Carl," the President admonished again. " They probably got it from the Germans, and we've got a few more important things to focus on now than the provenance of a Satellite phone. Go ahead Maggie."

"Anyway," the CIA Director continued, "the guy called his old Department Chair at Berkeley and asked for help. The Department chair happens to be a friend of mine, and he called me immediately. I've got a contract asset in route to Afghanistan as we speak, and John has agreed to have the Army insert him in-country by helicopter. I want to get this scientist out. He can answer a lot of questions and will likely be able to confirm that Iran is the only one with the code, at least for now. And since he's the guy who developed it, he's the best person to help us defeat it."

"Are you kidding, Maggie?" the Secretary of State asked, astonished. "We can't put an U.S. Army Team in Iran to kidnap someone, then rendition him back to the States. I'd hate to have to explain that to the U.N.!" he exclaimed.

"Oh, for Pete's sake, Carl, get some backbone," the President responded. "Do it, Maggie, and do it quickly. How far in country does the chopper have to penetrate? No matter how stealthy the helicopeter is, Tehran is a city of over 9 million people. That's an awful lot of eyes potentially looking up."

"We're not taking the asset all the way to Tehran," General Waverly responded. "We are going to insert him about 75 miles to the east of the rendezvous point, which is about 300 miles into the country. We will fly about 100 feet above the deck to avoid radar, and on a flight path that keeps us off populated terrain. The bird will be very quiet and painted black. It will also carry in an old motorcycle, something that will look appropriate for the area and not raise suspicions. The asset will travel by motorcycle the rest of the way and pick up the scientist, then back to the exfil, or pickup."

"Good. Now what's the long-term issue you made reference to, Burt?" the President asked, looking now at the Secretary of Defense.

The Secretary of Defense spoke. "It's important to realize what's happened here. We can't uninvent the technology. The ability to hack into a Command and Control system and remotely deploy weapons has been created. We can't undo it. We can develop measures to mitigate the risk, but that only buys time. The problem is, no matter how many safeguards we have, at the end of the day Command and Control systems are nothing more than a series of pipes that manage the flow of electrons. There will always be a way to re-configure the pipes to do whatever you want to do. That, in essence, is what a cyber-hack is. So, the 'short answer' is, there is no workable long-term answer. I'm afraid this is just like that early morning at 5:30 A.M. on July 16, 1945 when the first atomic bomb was detonated. Once a breakthrough is successfully tested, there is no putting the Genie back into the bottle. We have crossed the Rubicon."

"My, aren't you a bundle of optimism," the President responded, sarcastically. But this wasn't the issue that was really on her mind. She was worried about what she was going to do to push back on the plan to raid CWR Industries.

Chapter 50 – The Mission

Forward Operating Base Lagman, Afghanistan

Barber strapped himself into the UH-60 Blackhawk helicopter as the Army pilot spooled up the rotor and punched the GPS coordinates into aircraft's NAV system. He would have preferred something not quite as large for better stealth, but range was an issue with smaller birds, and this baby could fly 1,200 miles without refueling. The Army pilot pulled the collective up and gently pushed the stick forward, lifting them into the air. A slight application of pressure on the left rudder swung the nose around to the Northwest, and they were then headed towards Iran. It was a moonless, cloudy night and the sky was jet-black, providing ideal conditions for a covert flight into the country. They would be flying low to the ground, at an altitude of only about 100 feet, to avoid detection by radar. Their flight path would keep them away from any population center for as long as possible. The engine was heavily muffled and would be almost quiet. The aircraft itself was painted flat black to render it invisible in the night sky. Stealth was critical to mission success.

The ride was rough. Afghanistan was not a flat terrain, and the pilot was constantly banking the bird left and right, then taking it up then down as he hugged the terrain. The vibration of the motor and modest ground turbulence constantly transmitted themselves through the airframe, the aircraft's uncomfortable seat, then through Barber's body. His ribs hurt in response to the continuous micro-assaults. He was not fully healed from several recent altercations, and on more than one occasion, in route to this mission, he told himself he was getting too old for this. But for every moment of doubt, he kept hearing the little voice in his ear reminding him that the only easy day was yesterday, and that he didn't have to like it, he just had to do it. "Just remember," the Master Chief had told him when he left the Navy, "there may be former SEALS, but there are no ex-SEALS. Live the code every day of your life." Those words seemed to grip him every time he thought it might be time to scale back.

Barber was under no illusions about his prospects for success. The mission was a difficult one. The consequences were high. The pilot would deliver Barber to a remote area about 75 miles east of Tehran. A beat-up looking but well-maintained motorcycle was in the cargo hold. The bike would carry him to the rendezvous point closer to the city, then take him and his "package" back to the exfil point where the helicopter would be waiting to fly back to Afghanistan. A thousand things could go wrong from the minute they penetrated Iranian airspace. But he wouldn't have agreed to go if he didn't think he could do it. He had no issues with the difficult, just the impossible. The difficult and the dangerous for him was a way of life. It's what he did. It was his job.

"Thirty klicks to the LZ, about 10 minutes," Barber heard the pilot announce through the headset. "Roger that," Barber responded. He took inventory of his "kit", the nickname given to the equipment he carried on the mission. It included a portable Garman GPS device, a satellite phone, three bottles of water, half a dozen Snickers bars, a Zero Tolerance CF562 folding tactical knife, and a Sig P226 9mm suppressed pistol with 4 extra magazines. He was offered a HK 7 sub-machine gun by the Master Sergeant who geared him up, but he declined it. "Too difficult to conceal," he had commented. "Besides, if I get into a firefight where I need more than my Sig, I've already lost," he reasoned. The Sergeant had simply smiled at the response, and his opinion of Barber went way up.

"OK, partner, I can sit you down basically anywhere," the pilot said. "How about that clearing up ahead. That will put you about five miles southeast of the city of Lasjerd, right off highway 81."

"That works," Barber said, looking at his GPS. "That's about a 50-minute ride to the rendezvous point just south of the city of Aradan. And that's at the speed limit, which I doubt they'll be patrolling. I'm sure I can get there much faster than that."

The Blackhawk flared into a hover as the landing gear deployed, then gently settled to the ground. Almost before Barber could unstrap himself and climb out of his seat, the Crew Chief had the motorcycle out of the cargo bay and on the ground. Barber threw his leg over the bike, worked the kick-starter, and his ride came to life. He mounted the portable GPS on a bracket installed on the top of the handlebars, kicked the transmission into first gear, worked the throttle , then clutch, then quickly sped off to the northwest towards highway 81. By the time he had the motorcycle moving, the Blackhawk was already airborne and headed east, where it would sit just inside the Afghan border and wait for confirmation that Barber had "the package", the scientist, and was headed back to the rendezvous location.

The terrain between the landing point and the highway was rough, but he only had to endure it for a few minutes before reaching the highway. Everything was dead quiet. No signs of life anywhere. If there had been Iranian Revolutionary Guard troops deployed in this part of the country they would have been moved to Qom to deal with the carnage or to Tehran to suppress the riots. As Barber reached Highway 81, there was no sign of life, no vehicle headlights anywhere. He slowly rode the bike up onto the pavement and then accelerated towards his quarry.

Things were quiet for about 5 minutes, but then he thought he heard something over the engine noise of the motorcycle. Suddenly a small reflection of light appeared in his side view mirror and caught his attention. He twisted his head around to look. It was a vehicle of some sort, but he couldn't make out what kind. However, one thing that was obvious, it was moving fast. As he kept glancing into the side view mirror a shape began to form. His blood suddenly ran cold as he realized that something that big undoubtedly meant military. Options raced through his mind. Should he head off the road and hide until it passed. Not a wise choice, he concluded, in the event the vehicle had spotted him. That was a big risk, as he knew that a sizable military vehicle travelling fast at night in the middle of nowhere would likely have some kind of night vision capability. If he bugged off the road it would raise their suspicions. Should he speed up and try and outrun them? He didn't like that idea either. He wasn't sure he even could, and, stressing the bike's engine risked a mechanical problem. It wasn't like there was a nearby mechanic he could call to fix it. After exhausting several other options, he concluded the best course of action was what his gut had told him the moment he recognized that image for what it likely was. He had to maintain his present course and speed and pray they didn't pull him off and question him. The moment he had to open his mouth and answer a question, he knew he was done. He just continued to hope and pray that their speed was evidence they were in route to something more important than him, and he would be ignored.

He could now make out the image clearly in the side view mirror. It was a large armored troop carrier. This was not good, he thought. The sound was almost deafening now. Brave men accomplish dangerous tasks not because they lack fear, but because they overcome it. Barber's heart was now beating out of his chest. He wasn't just afraid, he was terrified. Thoughts of his wife and children flashed through his mind as the massive vehicle closed in on his small motorcycle. His heart was beating so hard the bike was almost difficult to control. As he continued to glance in the mirror, it appeared as though the vehicle took up the entire width of the highway. Maybe they would try and run him over, he thought, as the APC relentlessly continued to close the gap. He wouldn't let them do that, of course. He would drive off the road and hope for the best.

The last few seconds of the encounter seemed to shift into slow motion. Barber stopped thinking as the lizard part of his brain and the desire to survive that was encoded into the DNA of all living things took over. The vehicle was still not drifting to the side to pass him. The distance was now about ten feet, then eight, then five, then………

Barber suddenly swerved the bike to the left and drove off of the road. He hit the back break hard to quickly slow down and reduce the risk of hitting obstacles like rocks or bushes or any other number of things that could send him flying into the air and landing with a damaged bike and damaged body. As he regained control, then came to a stop, he looked up and saw the back of the armored personnel carrier as it continued speeding down the road, moving away from him. They would have run him over, he realized, like a bug, had he not made his last-minute move. And it wasn't because they had any particular desire to kill him. He just didn't matter. He wasn't worth the inconvenience of a momentary swerve to the right to pass him unharmed. It was the essence of the Iranian Revolutionary Guard Corp's ethos. They were important. Their mission was important. Others were not.

As the post-traumatic stress surge of adrenaline flooded his arteries, his arms and hands shook noticeably as he twisted the handlebars to the right and engaged the clutch to get the motorcycle back onto the highway. He had survived his first in-country encounter with the Iranians, at least for now. It wouldn't be his last.

Chapter 51 – The Raid

Corporate Headquarters, CWR Industries, Berlin

German workers are often creatures of precise habits. If the prescribed lunch hour is noon to 1 PM, at precisely noon they stop whatever they were doing, no matter how important, and proceed to the Company cafeteria. If the workday ended at 5 PM, at 5:01 they would be in route to whatever transportation they used to get home. The executive offices would occasionally remain occupied after hours, but that represented a small percentage of the work force. Relying on these long-established habits, the German Federal Police waited until nightfall to launch their raid, thinking the premises would be mostly empty. They would be surprised.

Numerous middle management and professional staff were busy purging files and destroying records. They were told all the Company's intellectual property records had been digitized and then encrypted, and the purge was to get rid of paper records that were much more vulnerable to theft. Most of them had no idea of the real reason behind what they were doing. They had just begun the process of attempting to destroy evidence of how CWR Industries aided and abetted Iran in their pursuit of taking control of the European Federation's strategic weapons systems. They would fail.

The raid began with the Federal Police sending in a "point team" secure the doors of the building with chains and padlocks, except the main entrance at the front. Locking the potential points of exit was necessary to prevent anyone escaping with important evidence. Once the doors were secured, the assault team would use a battering-ram to break open the front door and enter the building. Their objective was a large walk-in safe on the top floor, adjacent to the Chief Executive's Office. It was where the records were kept on their development of the missile re-targeting software. Zimmerman had given up the location during his interrogation, and it was provided to the Federation's Ministry of Intelligence by the American C.I.A.

The sounds of breaking glass and shards hitting the floor echoed through the building's lobby. A dozen Federal Police officers, weapons drawn, stormed through the lobby and up the stair wall. Fortunately for them, the building was not large and only had three floors.

The Chief Executive Officer of CWR Industries stood in his office and spun the dial on the safe to the last number in the combination, then moved the safe handle upward to open a large, six-inch thick door. He heard the noise from downstairs. He wasn't certain what it was, but he knew it wasn't good. It imparted a sense of urgency to his actions. As he used both hands to quickly push the heavy door out of the way he shouted at one of his assistants to lock his office suite outer door. Three other men in the room looked at him, confused. They weren't in on the secret and no idea of what he was trying to get to and destroy . He moved quickly into the safe and towards one of its inner locked drawers. The surge of adrenaline messed with his fine motor skills and caused him to fumble with the set of keys he just retrieved from his pocket. He finally found the correct one, but as he tried to insert it, wouldn't penetrate the lock, and he realized he was trying to force the key into the lock upside down.

The CEO was sweating now as his actions changed from a sense of urgency to a sense of desperation. The consequences of failure had been made very clear to him by his masters back in Palo Alto, California. As he continued to fumble to turn the key right side up, he heard the outer door to the executive suite burst open along with the sound of breaking glass. A man with an authoritative voice loudly ordered everyone to immediately stop what they were doing and raise their hands in plain sight. He was so close, he thought. He finally positioned the key correctly and unlocked the drawer. Just seconds now and the most damning evidence would be destroyed. He reached his hand inside the drawer and felt the portable, solid-state hard-drive containing the incriminating code. There was a thermite-based incendiary flair attached to the device as part of their standard security protocol. All he had to do was press a button and two seconds later it would ignite. The drive would be beyond salvage.

As he raised his hand to place it in the drawer and reach for the button, he heard the same authoritative voice shout out, “Stop! Move away from the drawer immediately!” He turned his head around and saw a large Federal Police Officer with weapon drawn and pointed at him. This was a circumstance he had never experienced before, and it was frightening. The lizard part of his brain over-rode his conscious intentions and he froze. It wasn’t in his makeup to proceed with the cold efficiency of a professional. He regained his purpose and resumed the upward move of his hand towards the drawer. Two shots rang out. One hit his wrist, rendering useless for the task. The other hit him in the knee, dropping him to the floor and making it impossible to raise the other hand high enough to complete the task. The police were under strict instructions to take him alive. /

President’s Private Study, White House, Washington, D.C.

It was unusual for President Einhorn to stay in the Executive Wing of the White House past dinner time. She much preferred the quite of her study in the First Family residential area that occupied the third floor of the building. But this was an unusual day, and she craved privacy more than just quiet as she contemplated her next course of action. She was alone, other than the Secret Service Personal Protection Detail. She could tell them to leave her alone far easier than she could her family. And the agents wouldn’t get their feelings hurt. If they did, of course, she didn’t care.

She had been successful so far in holding off the raid on CWR Industries. In another 15 hours she would satisfy Emma Clark’s demand. She just had to keep the hounds at bay for a little longer and hopefully she would be past the risk of Clark’s retribution. It hadn’t been easy. Both the Secretary of Defense and the Chairman of the Joint Chiefs had pushed back hard, especially the General. But in the end she had prevailed, or so it seemed.

"Too early to share everything with the European Federation," she argued, and as President it was her decision. The General had left the meeting almost in a huff, but she knew he would follow orders and keep his mouth shut. It's what four-star generals did, she thought, at least those who wanted to keep their jobs. But she hadn't figured the potential actions of Joseph Michael Barber into her calculus.

Her thoughts were interrupted by the ring of the phone sitting atop her private study's desk. She was irritated by the interruption. Everyone knew she was normally in the private residence by now, so who could possibly be calling? She lifted the receiver and answered by simply saying "What?"

"Madam President, this is Margaret Shevchenko. Sorry for the interruption, but I have some news you need to hear."

"What is it?" she said, with the tone of fatigue in her voice as she rubbed her left temple with her free hand."

"I just received a call from the European Federation's Minister of Intelligence, my counterpart."

"And?" the President asked, irritably.

"Two hours ago, German Federal Police conducted a raid on the corporate offices of CWR Industries in Berlin. I am told employees of the company were in the process of destroying records when the police arrived, but fortunately only in the early stages of the process. Evidently the Police collected quite a bit, including several hard drives that were in a large closet-sized safe next to the Chairman's office."

The President's face flushed bright red on a combination of rage and existential fear. She responded in a voice dripping with cold fury, "I thought I gave strict instructions that the Federation was not to be given our intelligence on CWR for at least 24 hours. Who at C.I.A. disobeyed my direct order?"

"Yes, Ma'am, you did," Shevchenko replied. "C.I.A. didn't give them anything," she said, stretching the truth. "They did this all on their own. I would point out that it was common knowledge that CWR was an important sub-contractor to Sternenlicht. They must have decided to do this on that suspicion. Evidently they also raided Sternenlicht."

"What did they find?" the President asked.

"I don't know yet. They have an army of lawyers and digital forensics analysts examining what they found. But the good news is they are tripping all over themselves to be transparent and have promised to share everything. They agreed to make me the point of contact."

The President's head was spinning. She was in trouble, and she was certain of it. She had a pounding headache, not from the cranial implant but from raw stress, and her heart was about to pound out of her chest. Several seconds passed without her saying a word.

"Madam President, are you still there?"

"Yes," she replied.

"We should pull the crisis group together again by mid-morning. I am fairly confident I will have a preliminary analysis of the intelligence by then."

"Yes, of course," were the only words the President could think to say.

"I understand your reasons for wanting to wait," Shevchenko said, "but this is really good news. I think we are very close to getting a lot of questions answered."

"Yes, of course," the President repeated. "Thank you Margaret. I need to go."

"Yes, Ma'am. Have a pleasant evening."

"You as well." The President hung up. It was going to be anything but a pleasant evening, she thought. She had heard the word picture, "the noose was tightening" many times. She now had a far better understanding of what it meant.

Director's Office, 7th Floor, Central Intelligence Agency, Langley, Virginia

Director Margaret Shevchenko placed the phone back into its cradle and looked across her desk into the face of the man sitting opposite of her. Federal Bureau of Investigation Executive Assistant Director for National Security, Donald L. Benson, stared back at her with a face that was ashen white.

"Tell me what you heard, Don."

"What I heard, Maggie, was a person seized with fear."

"Exactly," the Director said. "She's hiding something."

"Yes, she is," Benson replied.

"I've had this suspicion for several days now," Shevchenko continued. "Actually, I've had it ever since she killed England's push for more sanctions, which was some time before this whole mess started. What do your instincts tell you, Don?"

"That's a real problem, Maggie. My instincts tell me complicity of some kind, although it's hard to imagine a motive, and we don't have a shred of real evidence. Has any other members of the crisis committee expressed anything?"

"Off the record, SecDef is pretty twitchy. Waverly hasn't said a word, and he would die on the hill of the chain of command before he would accuse his Commander and Chief of anything without solid evidence."

"As should we all, Maggie."

"I agree. Like I said to the President, we are going to know a whole lot more real soon."

"I don't like it, but I'll think through a worst-case plan for the right process just if the intel uncovers anything actionable," Benson replied.

"Good. That's all I ask," Shevchenko said.

"So, Maggie, exactly how did the Europeans get ahold of what you learned by interrogating this Zimmerman guy?"

"Well, I was honest when I said it didn't come from me, from C.I.A. Our contract guy, Joe Barber, shared it with his partner, a guy named Marcus Day. Day is a friend of General Jean-Baptiste Laurent, the Vice Commander of the EF Air Force. Day called Laurent. Day felt he owed it to the guy, since Laurent helped us get our hands on Zimmerman and get him out of the country. I found all of this out after the fact, of course."

"Of course," Director Benson replied.

Offices of PrinSafe, Palo Alto California

She had ordered the evidence purge the minute she discovered the C.I.A. had captured Zimmerman. She hoped it was soon enough. An unfamiliar emotion was enveloping her, and it seemed to become more powerful every day. Things seemed to be spiraling out of control. It felt like every problem she solved was quickly followed by two more. Or maybe it was like that "smack the gopher" game, where slaying one antagonist immediately brought life to another. She possessed a remarkable mind, but cognitive intelligence was not the same thing as a strategic mindset. Applying one's intellect to solve a difficult math or engineering problem was not the same thing as seeing and managing the broad interdependencies of a grand vision. She was every bit as smart as her late mentor, Westy Reynolds, in the cognitive sense, but had he exceeded her in the "vision thing", she wondered? This was no time for self-doubt, she reminded herself. Self-doubt didn't solve anything. Refocus, she admonished, lest you start feeling sorry for yourself. Work the problem. Nobody is better at doing this than you. Her thoughts were interrupted by the buzz of her private cell phone. She looked at the number. It was blocked.

"Hello," she simply said.

"Emma, this is Horst Brandt," a familiar voice replied. General Horst Brandt was the Commander of the European Federation Air Force.

"General Brandt. What time is it there?"

"Very late, but I have urgent news."

"It seems a lot of people have been telling me that lately. What is it?"

"I have just been briefed that German Federal Police raided the corporate offices of CWR Industries a little over two hours ago. Apparently the Americans have floated the theory that they are somehow complicit in the breach of our command and control system. WE both know, of course, that this is preposterous. But I am very concerned they will find the work they did for us on Project Dart, the rail gun. The police evidently have retrieved documentation on much of their classified work. Knowledge of their involvement was limited to only a handful of people to ensure that nobody could know an American firm helped us develop the weapons system. Are you aware of the raid? Can you tell me how vulnerable we are?"

Clark sat in stunned disbelief, mouth literally open, trying to process what the General had just said.

"Emma, are you still there? Were you aware of this?"

"Yes, I'm here, and unfortunately, no, this is the first I've heard of the raid."

"I assume your subsidiary has robust precautions in place to protect such sensitive information?"

"Yes, General, they do. Highly confidential information is stored on solid state hard drives kept in a safe, and there is an incendiary device attached to each drive to ensure it can be destroyed before it gets into the wrong hands."

"I am told that several such drives were recovered intact, and from a large safe. I am also told that the CEO of the company is in custody. So, let me ask my question again, Ms. Clark. Are the data secure?"

Clark was horrified. This was the worst news she could have received. She sat there in her office chair, a toxic mix of boiling rage and existential fear. "Yes, the data should be secure," she lied.

"Should be secure or are secure?" the General responded in a condescending tone.

"I am confident in our procedures, General," she lied again. "Let me see what I can find out."

"Very well and thank you. Please call me back as soon as you know anything definitive."

"Yes, of course. Good day, General. I need to go to work. And I suggest you go to bed."

She placed her hand in her suit jacket and retrieved the cell phone that was the controller for the cranial implant. Her first instinct was to put an end to Sara Einhorn there and then. But she realized it would be indulging her rage of the moment, and that wasn't smart. "The one thing I am going to do," she told herself, "is call that bitch right now."

Chapter 52 – The Mission, Part 2

Highway 41, Approaching the City of Aradan, Iran

He could see the lights of the city as he approached it on Iranian Highway 41. The GPS device attached to the motorcycle's handlebar indicated he was about 10 minutes away from Dr. Ashkan Ghorbani, the U.S.-trained mathematician, who was the unwilling mastermind behind the cyber hack of the European Federation's Command and Control systems. After the scary encounter with the Iranian troop carrier, there had been almost no traffic. The balance of the journey had been uneventful, but Barber knew this would not last. On the list of the 500 hardest things do to, penetrating Iranian territory by over 350 miles and bringing a scientist back to the rendezvous point with a U.S Blackhawk helicopter, ranked 1st.

As traffic became more congested, Barber had to slow the motorcycle down. He wore a helmet with a plastic bubble that covered his face. He had grown a heavy beard, which also helped make him fit in and be less noticeable. Most men in Iran wore beards. As he rode the bike, he was careful to look straight ahead and limit the opportunity for a straight-on look. He made several slightly aggressive moves in and out among traffic. He was briefed that Iranians were almost reckless on their motorcycles, and a subdued rider would stand out. It elicited the ubiquitous honks of automobile horns, but that just seemed to his actions to be in context of a country under extreme duress.

The GPS now had him just two minutes from his target. As he looked at the readout, the blinking light representing Ghorbani's location seemed to be several meters south of the highway. It was also moving towards Barber, suggesting the man was walking. The scientist must have placed some distance between himself and the surrounding mass of humanity, Barber reasoned.

One minute away now, only 50 meters. Barber turned the bike sharply to the left, gunned the throttle and in another aggressive move, drove off the highway and in the direction of his quarry. A beat-up looking Iranian Saipa Tiba automobile blasted its horn as Barber made the move, but nobody else seemed to care. The horn sounded like something that belonged more on a Tiny Tikes play-car than on something that transported adults.

Now only 10 meters away. The blinking light on his GPS was still moving in his direction. Barber slowed the bike to a crawl and surveyed the crowd. It was chaos. The people seemed to make up two very distinct factions. The first was an angry mob congregated around local police, taunting them, with several of the protestors throwing rocks at the police, the symbol of the government that had failed them. Revolutionary Guard soldiers stood back at the ready with hands on their automatic weapons, but not yet joining the fray.

The second was a mass of people, mostly women, children and old men who were moving, on foot, away from the chaos, headed east, with heads mostly down. Their expressions were not of rage but of resignation. Several were crying. That made sense, Barber thought. Their country was in crisis. Many of them likely suffered personal loss as a result of what was happening. They were depressed and wandering almost without purpose.

But then he noticed someone who stood out, a man not neatly fitting into either faction. A man whose head was level and scanning the scene around him. He seemed to be looking for something. Or maybe looking for someone. The man had a satchel hanging over his right shoulder, in contrast to most people who walked only with the clothes on their back. Perhaps that satchel held his possessions. It was as if he was planning to go somewhere.

Barber looked at the GPS again. The distance between them was about right. He turned towards the man and approached him with a speed that was just enough to keep the bike vertical. He pulled up alongside the man and stopped, placing his left leg on the ground for support and tilting the handlebars towards the man as he stopped. The two of them stood there and stared at each other for several seconds. Barber kept his hands on the motorcycle's throttle and clutch, prepared for a quick exit if things went south. This was the most dangerous part of the mission. If he had approached the wrong man, he would quickly be made when the man stared into his faceplate and recognized that he was not an Iranian. He stood there, heart beating out of his chest and waited for the man to respond in some way. Finally, to his enormous relief, the man nodded his head, slightly. There was a code-question Barber was to ask for positive identification. Ghorbani's contact in the States, the Chair of the Math Department at Berkeley, had given it to him. Barber asked the question.

"What's your favorite movie?"

The man responded, "A Man for All Seasons," the last movie a Muslim would cite as a favorite.

The man smiled slightly and started to make a move towards the bike to climb on.

"Wait," Barber commanded in a calm but authoritative tone. "I'm a cautious man. I have another question."

The man now looked frightened, almost as if he were about to run. Before the man could move, Barber asked, "Where's the math department at Berkeley located?" It was his own question. He had looked it up. It was something the man should know, and if he couldn't answer the question then their plan had somehow been compromised.

The man smiled, then said, "970 Evans Hall."

Barber just nodded and said, "Get on," as he handed him a helmet with a built-in microphone so they could communicate.

Barber noticed one of the Revolutionary Guards was staring in their direction as the man began to mount the motorcycle on the saddle behind him.. Barber tried not to look, but years away from actual combat had caused his tradecraft to atrophy, and he involuntarily looked back at the soldier.

Their eyes locked. The soldier started walking briskly towards the motorcycle and appeared to be shouting at them. He then saw the soldier raise the automatic weapon from its rest position across his chest and point it in their direction. The soldier's brisk walk turned into a run, then a sprint. It was an extraordinarily dangerous circumstance, because if Barber yielded to the "fight or flight" response and rocketed the bike away from the soldier, it would draw the attention of others. He had to walk a fine line by riding away quickly enough to escape the risk but not so quickly as to draw others into pursuit.

"Hold on," he said to the Ghorbani, on the back of the bike. Just when he was about to accelerate away and pray the soldier would not be so reckless as to fire his weapon with so many civilians around, he heard an automatic weapon start to fire. Barber was now terrified. His first instinct was he was hit. It had to be, there was no way that soldier could have missed as close as he was. He didn't feel anything, but he knew that when shot in combat the shock that immediately sets in delays the sensation of being wounded for a few seconds. But he also sensed that everything was still working. His arms and legs responded to his commands, and the bike was still accelerating away from the scene, so it hadn't been hit either. He was confused but stayed focused on his task of getting away. Then he heard Ghorbani speak into his headphones.

"Somebody threw a small rock and hit the soldier in the head. He turned and started firing into the crowd. We need to get away quickly. The Revolutionary Guard are going to start shooting everyone in sight."

Barber could hear screams coming from the crowd. He knew that nobody would be looking at the two of them now. After riding about 300 yards to the east, he slowed the bike down and looked for a gap in the highway's westbound traffic, then weaved in between two stopped vehicles to cross the westbound lane. Several cars honked their horns as he did so, and one of the drivers shook his fist at Barber as he crossed directly in front of him.

As he got across the westbound lane, he eased the motorcycle onto the sparsely populated eastbound lane and accelerated back towards the rendezvous point with the Blackhawk. All he had to do now was put a few kilometers between him and the angry soldiers and the most difficult part of the mission was behind him, he told himself. He would soon find that thought to be an illusion.

Chapter 53 – The Phone Call

President's Private Study, White House, Washington, D.C.

President Einhorn opened the bottom drawer on the left-hand side of her desk and pulled out a bottle of Scotch whiskey and a Waterford Crystal tumbler. She poured about 3 ounces of the amber liquid into the glass and drank the entire thing in three painful gulps. The liquid badly burned the back of her throat as it went down, and she immediately admonished herself for such a dumb move. She was hoping to calm her nerves, although she knew full well an alcohol buzz would not change her circumstances.

She tried to steel herself from the coming fallout from the raid on CWR Industries. There would be nothing in the evidence the Germans retrieved that would directly implicate her, but the evidence would make her look bad, especially for pushing back on England's proposal for increased sanctions and for holding off on the raid itself. She would argue a forceful defense of her actions the next time the crisis group met, then concede things had changed and agree to more forceful action. She was superb at tiptoeing through political landmines. There was one landmine, however, she had no idea how to navigate -- Emma Clark.

Her thoughts were interrupted by the buzz of her private cell phone. She retrieved it from her jacket pocket, looked at the screen and recognized the number immediately. She froze. Her heart started to beat out of her chest as her fight or flight response arose in full bloom from the out-sized flush of adrenaline suddenly coursing through her veins. This was a call she was dreading. This was a call she knew would be coming. This was a call she wasn't even persuaded she would survive, thanks to the cranial implant resting in her head, waiting to be summoned to its dreadful task, her personal sword of Damocles. This was a call from Emma Clark.

"Hello, Emma," the President said.

"Hello, Madam President," Clark replied, in an oddly calm voice. The President expected the woman to open the conversation by screaming at her. Then she realized that she was spared the blinding headache that was Clark's normal calling card. "I assume you are aware of the raid?"

"Yes, I was briefed by C.I.A. a short time ago," she replied, stretching the truth a bit. It had actually been several hours since Director Shevchenko had called her, but she didn't want Clark to think she had deliberately withheld the information. "I want you to know I had nothing to do with the timing of the raid. I gave strict instructions to hold off until tomorrow. The Germans made the decision themselves, evidently based on intelligence they independently obtained."

"I am aware of that," Clark replied. "You apparently don't have as much clout as I thought you did."

"Apparently not," the President replied.

"Have you been told what the Germans may have found?"

"No, not yet. I am to be briefed sometime tomorrow, hopefully by mid-morning."

"Ok, here's how you're going to redeem yourself," Clark said, ominously.

"How is that?" the President asked.

"You are going to call me tomorrow no later than noon, Eastern Daylight time, and you are going to tell me everything you know. Is that clear?"

"Very. What if I am still being briefed at noon?"

"Step out and send me a text. And you better have a good reason for not meeting my noon deadline. Is that also clear?"

"Very," the President replied.

"I'll talk to you tomorrow, Madam President," Clark said, "and have a pleasant evening."

The President hit "end" on her cell phone and placed it back into her pocket. She then waited, terrified. She waited for the blinding headache she knew would be Clark's retribution for not holding off the raid. It would be the ideal way for that crazed woman to reinforce her point. "That's what I would do," the President thought to herself. But the headache didn't come, and as time passed her heartrate slowly started to return to its normal elevated rate. She would survive this night. That was clear. Would she survive another? That was far from clear.

Offices of PrinSafe, Palo Alto, California

Clark opened the top middle drawer of her desk, and placed the phone inside, then relocked it. At that moment she was the least sure of herself as she had been in years. This was unfamiliar territory, emotionally. What troubled her even more was she knew she would go to bed that way. She was relieved she hadn't given in to her emotions and killed the President when she first learned of the raid. Einhorn was her only early source of intelligence on what evidence the Germans may have discovered, short of potentially reading it on her arrest warrant. Getting that intel quickly was crucial to her reaction plan and survival. However, one thing was clear to her, the President's usefulness would soon come to an end.

And this clown, Barber, was becoming a thorn in her side. Westy had tried to kill him three years ago after he outed the clandestine surveillance program her company, Prinsafe, had supported through their subsidiaries QuarkSpin and General Aviation Services. But he failed, then backed off when he concluded the guy was harmless and killing him would create more problems that it would solve. And more than a decade earlier he tried to take him out in the Middle East before PrinSafe was even started. One thing was now clear to her. She had to do something about this guy.

Chapter 54 – The Mission, Part 3

They had been riding east for about 30 minutes, and the farther they rode the lighter the traffic became. Ghorbani had been silent since Barber got the motorcycle onto the eastbound lane of the highway, and he appreciated that. He was finally starting to breathe a little easier and indulged the thought that the two of them might make it out of Iran after all. Only about 20 minutes to go and they should be at the rendezvous point.

Suddenly numerous red and yellow lights started flashing ahead in the distance.

"What is that?" Barber asked reflexively, not necessarily intending to draw Ghorbani into a conversation.

"It looks like they have set up a road block. It also appears that they are covering both the east and westbound lanes of the highway."

"Oh crap," Barber responded, as he shut off his headlight.

"That won't do you any good, my friend," Ghorbani said. "I'm sure they've already seen us, and besides, they will have night vision equipment. All you will accomplish is to make them suspicious."

"I don't look like a Persian and I don't speak a word of Farsi," Barber said. "There is no way that I'm going to get through that roadblock. Unless you have a better idea, I'm going to pull off the pavement and head north for a few klicks in the hope they won't think we're interesting enough to follow."

"They don't think that way," Ghorbani responded. "Those guys are just sitting there, bored. They love to hunt. They will want to satisfy their curiosity. Capturing someone who tried to evade a road block will please their officers."

"Like I said, unless you have a better idea, I don't think we have a choice."

Barber slowed the bike down and pulled off the highway, then started a slow track north. His plan was to get a couple of kilometers north of the highway, then resume the eastward route over rough terrain. That would slow him down, but it was better than getting caught, he reasoned. He did a quick mental calculation and concluded the detour would slightly more than double his remaining travel time. Instead of being 20 minutes to rendezvous, they were now more like 45, assuming no other issues arose.

After several minutes travelling north, they resumed their eastwardly course. The terrain was rougher than he thought. He left the headlight off so soldier's efforts to track them wouldn't be too easy, but it made him worry about damaging the bike by hitting something in the dark, moonless night. He glanced into the sideview mirror and saw a flicker of light.

"I think we've got company," he said through the headphones.

"I think you're right," Ghorbani responded. "My guess is they are following us with night vision gear."

"Do you know what type of vehicle it might be?" Barber asked.

"They would use an all-terrain vehicle of some sort to drive me places through the desert. It's nowhere near as good as what the American Army uses, but it's a whole lot better, and faster over this kind of ground than this motorcycle."

Barber looked into the sideview mirror again. The lights of the vehicle were getting larger as they quickly closed the gap. He realized there was no chance of avoiding a confrontation. Looking around for someplace to hide, he noticed a small hill about 200 meters to their left which appeared to be covered with knee-high grass. The height of the grass was difficult to discern in the darkness, but it was better concealment compared to where they were, out in the open. Barber pointed the bike towards the hill. As he did so, he heard Ghorbani through the headset.

"You know they can see us heading towards that hill," the scientist said.

"Yes, I know that. This isn't my first rodeo. Unless you have a constructive suggestion, kindly stay quiet." Admonished, the scientist didn't respond.

The bike climbed the crest of the hill, just over to the other side. Barber spoke into the headset again, "Get off, and lay down in the grass." Ghorbani complied without comment. Barber laid the motorcycle on its side and did same. He pulled his backpack off, unzipped it, then reached inside and retrieved two items. The first was a pair of night vision binoculars for both ambient and infrared light. The second was the Glock and two magazines.

"Are you going to try and shoot them?" Ghorbani asked, as he noticed the Glock.

"No, not right away anyway. A handgun at this range is useless as a sniper weapon. We're going to see what these clowns are up to first, then I'll decide what to do."

Barber then laid down in the tall grass next to Ghorbani, placed the binoculars to his face and looked at the approaching vehicle. He then handed the glasses to Ghorbani and said, "Take a look at that vehicle and tell me who you think it is."

"Bad news," Ghorbani said, looking through the binoculars.

"What?" Barber asked.

"As I feared. They're Revolutionary Guard soldiers," he answered.

"That's great," Barber replied, sarcastically. "That means they'll have automatic weapons and sniper rifles. The sniper rifles will likely be equipped with night vision scopes."

"What do we do?" Ghorbani asked, sounding very frightened.

"First of all, stay calm and be quiet. My assignment is to get you out of here alive, and that's what I plan to do, but you're going to have to cooperate. You can't panic on me, got it?"

"Got it," Ghorbani replied.

"Just remember I'm your best, no I'm your only hope out of here, so do everything I say exactly like I tell you and you'll be fine. Panic on me and you'll get both of us killed."

"OK," Ghorbani replied. "So, what are we going to do?"

"One step at a time, my friend. And remember, these guys have no idea it's you and me up here. They don't know they are pursuing high-value targets. They probably think they're chasing a couple of scared goat-herders and looking for a little amusement. They will assume we're unarmed. That will give us the advantage of surprise."

"Good thinking. Do we stay right here?"

"No," Barber answered. "First, they can't see us behind this hill's rise, so we are going to move about a hundred yards to the east from where they saw us drive up. That will give us the opportunity to flank them if they climb up the hill."

"Are you going to drag the motorcycle?" Ghorbani asked.

Barber was amused that the scientist assumed he would drag it by himself if necessary. "No," he replied. "We'll leave the bike here for now. We can retrieve it later."

"OK."

"Follow my lead and do what I do. We have to crawl on our bellies. Do not get up on all fours or they'll see you."

"Ok."

The two men crawled for what seemed like several minutes to get a couple of hundred yards away from where they climbed the hill. They could hear the sound of the vehicle clearly now. They heard it stop. The driver killed the engine, then the sounds of opening and closing doors. They heard muffled voices. The soldiers were talking to each other. Then footsteps crunching on ground vegetation. Barber increased the zoom on the binoculars and their tactical situation came more clearly into view. Three soldiers were at the base of the hill. He scanned back towards the vehicle, and saw a fourth standing by it, automatic weapon at the ready. He looked back at the three, who had taken a few steps up the hill, then stopped. They were not armed with automatic weapons. In fact, they didn't even have their side-arms drawn. That confirmed his suspicions that these guys were just in pursuit for sport, thinking they were tracking a couple of locals.

One of the soldiers at the base of the hill was holding what looked like a megaphone of some sort. He raised it to his mouth, then started to speak.

"What is he saying?" Barber asked.

"He's telling us they know we're here and demanding we show ourselves. He says they just need to ask us a few questions, and they don't intend to harm us if we cooperate. He now said he'll let us go if we just answer a few questions."

"Do you have any idea how these guys operate?" Barber asked.

"Yes, I do," Ghorbani replied. "They will initially act nice as they ask their questions, but as soon as they are done they will force us to our knees and put a bullet in the back of our heads. That is life in Iran right now, my friend. The Government is terrified of losing control, and they should be."

Barber continued to observe the men as they walked several additional steps up the hill. Their sidearms were still secured in their waist-level holsters. Barber turned to Ghorbani and said, "I want you to stay right here and remain absolutely quiet. They don't know where we are right now, so you'll be safe. I'm going to belly-crawl down this hill a bit and towards them. The only way we are going to get out of this is if I engage them. With the element of surprise, I'm confident I can get at least two of them down before they realize what's happening."

"You said the one by the vehicle has a machine gun. What are you going to do about him?" Ghorbani asked.

"One step at a time, my friend, one step at a time. I haven't figured that one out yet, but I'll think of something."

Barber began the slow and careful process of moving diagonally down the hill and back towards the soldiers. He held the frame of the Glock in his right hand as he moved in a crab crawl. Holding the pistol by its frame wouldn't allow him to immediately raise and fire it, but it was far better than placing it back into his backpack. He had clipped the folding tactical knife inside his left waist band, which would allow for a rapid cross-body draw and deployment if things came to a close-quarters altercation. His face was buried in the grass as he moved, so he stopped every 10 or 20 meters to survey the men. One of them was about a third of the way up the hill, his sidearm now in his hand. One of the men continued to talk through the megaphone, but without Ghorbani next to him to translate, Barber had no idea what he was saying.

The soldier with the automatic weapon was the biggest risk. Barber's strategy was to first take out the guy by the vehicle. Problem was he had to get close enough. A handgun was not the ideal weapon to go up against a guy who could throw back a lot of larger caliber ammunition at a rapid rate. The likelihood of missing the target went up exponentially at a range beyond 20 or 30 yards, He couldn't afford to miss. His shot would announce his location. If the soldier was still standing, Barber would soon face a return fuselage he would not survive.

He looked at the soldier again through the binoculars and increased the zoom. The man was wearing a jacket. That was bad news, he thought, because there was no way to verify whether the man was wearing a bullet-proof vest. His first shot would have to make a head shot. Easy to do with a rifle but much more difficult with a pistol. It was the hand he was dealt, so he would play it the best he could.

He continued to crawl, managing to get to about 15 yards from where he and Ghorbani had originally started up the hill and about 10 yards from where the car was parked. If he got any further down the hill, the grass wouldn't be tall enough to hide him. Let's think, he told himself. Ten yards up and fifteen yards downrange. Barber, trained in the art of the sniper, was schooled in geometry. He remembered the Pythagorean theorem: "A squared + B squared = C squared; 225 + 100 = 335. The square root of 335 was about 18. He was about 18 yards from the soldier with the automatic weapon standing by the vehicle. That was close enough. He should be able to make the shot.

He picked up the suppressed Glock and rested the butt of the handle on the ground as he took aim at the man. He would fire three shots, he decided, to maximize a fatal hit. One to the head and the others to center mass. Even if he missed the kill-shot to the head the other two would at least knock the guy down. He would have to immediately turn the weapon and fire on the man standing at the base of the hill in case he heard the shots. That would be two down. Much better odds, he thought to himself.

He was used to firing a handgun standing, in what is called the Weaver position, body angled towards the target and the left hand supporting the weapon from the bottom. This was different, and nothing like taking a sniper shot with a rifle. But he didn't have a rifle. He had to work with what he had, and he had to make what he had work.

He lay in the grass, the pistol pointed downrange, and began to slow his breathing and heartrate. He gradually increased pressure on the trigger, instinctively waiting for the split-second between heartbeats when his pulse would be dormant and not affect his fine motor skills. The moment came. The pistol fired and reported its discharge with the sound of "thwack". Then all Hell broke loose.

Chapter 55 – The Mission, Part 4

Eastern Iran, Two kilometers North of Highway 41, About 15 Miles from Rendezvous Point

The soldier standing by the vehicle went down immediately after the shot. But the pistol jammed. There could be no second shot, or third shot. "Shit!" Barber thought to himself. Glocks don't jam! They can eat almost any kind of ammunition. That was one of their selling points. But he knew that brass casings re-loaded too many times could develop a small crimp or bulge that would hang up in the pistol ejection mechanism and the slide would freeze, rendering the weapon useless. Had they given him ammunition that had been reloaded too many times? He reflexively wondered if it was the consequence of tight military budgets and cost saving measures. He had checked the pistol carefully before departing, but he hadn't looked at the ammunition. That was a mistake he would never make again, provided he was given another "again".

The sound of the pistol's one and only discharge had echoed through the still night. The other soldiers heard it. They immediately shifted their relaxed focus on likely goat-herders to the serious business of reacting to an armed threat.

Barber slammed the heel of his hand into the back of the Glock's slide several times to try and free it, but to no avail. Still lying down, he laid the pistol on the ground and withdrew the folding tactical knife from his waistband. With the flick of his thumb he deployed the blade. He recalled the tired phrase from too many old movies, "Never bring a knife to a gunfight", but again knew he had to work with what he had. Three soldiers were still standing, walking slowly in his direction while scanning the tall grass with flashlights, trying to find the source of the shot. The flashlight beam was arching back and forth about five meters from him now. He was outnumbered by three men with working pistols and all he had was a knife. So, this was how it was going to end, he thought to himself. Well at least he would take one of these clowns with him.

He sprang from the grass and launched himself at the soldier closest to him, hoping the element of surprise would allow him to stab or disarm the man before the soldier was able to process the threat. As he sprung, he heard two shots ring out. In his peripheral vision he noticed two of the solders to his target's right go down. Had they been shot? He quickly refocused on the man looming in front of him. He couldn't allow himself to be distracted. In hand to hand combat, distraction meant death. His target was not as disciplined. The soldier was in the process of sweeping his right arm upwards to bring his pistol to bear when he heard the gunshots, and the noise caused him to hesitate. Barber continued the upward thrust of his body, swinging the knife towards the man's right wrist in the hope of stopping its momentum and inflicting a fatal arterial wound. He missed the wrist but managed to slice a deep wound into the man's thumb. The blade carved off a large portion of flesh as it continued its sweeping momentum past the injured thumb and scraping the side of the pistol frame. The man cried out in pain and dropped the gun. Three Revolutionary Guard soldiers had been killed, but this last one was far from out of the fight.

Barber saw a long blade suddenly appear in the man's left hand. It looked more like a bayonet than a knife. The solider had retrieved it from a sheath on his leg. He thrust the weapon at Barber's mid-section, missing, but put a gash in Barber's arm as he swept back the double-edged weapon from its initial parry. Barber stumbled backwards, surprised by the wound. He stopped his backwards momentum by bracing his body with a rearward plant of his left leg. The soldier faked a lunge with the bayonet, forcing Barber to raise his other arm to block the man's wrist. As he did so, the solder grabbed Barber's shirt sleeve with his left hand and pulled him towards the knife as he started another upward thrust of the blade. Barber spun his torso and shifted to the side, dodging the knife again, then hit the soldier with a hard upper-cut directly under the front of the man's chin. He was pretty sure he had broken the man's jaw. The man screamed again but didn't go down. Quickly ignoring the pain, the soldier responded by delivering a knee to Barber's gut, forcing him backwards and knocking the wind out of him. Before Barber could steady himself, the soldier swept a leg behind his left knee and knocked him to the ground and onto his back. Things then appeared to shift into slow motion. Barber looked up at the ominous figure towering over him, bayonet raised towards the night sky at the top if its arc, ready to begin a fatal plunge. He stared into the man's eyes looking for the sign that the weapon was about to come down. Timing was everything. He would quickly roll right to avoid the plunging blade, grab the man's ankles, then pull his feet out from under him forcing him to the ground. If he executed the move a second too soon, his assailant could adjust. A second too late, and he wouldn't move his body out of the way in time.

As he stared into the man's eyes, his focus was distracted by the sound of another gunshot. The soldier's eyes rolled slightly upwards in his head, and he fell to the ground. Barber quickly grabbed the bayonet and leapt to his feet, ready to attack whoever fired the shot. As he stood up, he was stunned. There stood Ghorbani, a small caliber pistol in his hand.

"You're armed!" Barber exclaimed.

"Yes," the scientist replied. "I tried to shoot all of the other soldiers, but I missed the one that attacked you. Once the two of you got into that fight I wasn't confident I wouldn't accidently hit you instead if I took another shot, so I waited until you were out of the way."

"Out of the way, like when he put me on the ground," Barber replied.

"Yes," Ghorbani answered.

"Under the circumstances I guess I won't get mad at you for not telling me you were armed," Barber said, trying to force back a smile. "Thank you. Now let's get back up the hill and retrieve that bike. We should get to the helicopter in less than 20 minutes, assuming we don't encounter any more company."

"How bad is your arm?" Ghorbani asked.

"He didn't hit an artery, so I'll be fine. I've got a bandage I'll wrap it with before we start moving."

"Ok. You know we could take that Revolutionary Guard vehicle," Ghorbani observed. "It would be easier to steer with a wounded arm than a motorcycle, and I could even drive."

"Ha," Barber laughed. "Thanks, but I don't want to take a hellfire missile on our nose from that Blackhawk as we approach it. We'll do just fine on the motorcycle, and that's what the Army Rangers will be looking for."

"Good point," Ghorbani said.

The two men retrieved the motorcycle, fired it up and continued their journey east. At about four kilometers from the rendezvous point, a tiny black dot materialized on the horizon. As they got closer, the dot began to elongate and eventually took the shape of a helicopter. From a little more than one kilometer away, Barber could see the helicopter's rotor start to spin. Its crew of Army Rangers had seen them approach and was preparing for a quick departure. Barber and the scientist dropped the bike, quickly climbed on board, then strapped themselves into seats in the open cargo bay as the bird lifted into the air. It was over, almost at least.

Barber was a thankful man. As he sat there silently, he took inventory of his experiences over the last couple of weeks, including at least three close encounters with death. It had all started as the result of a routine executive protection contract for Orion Bellicus. The sequence of events that unfolded from that contract was mind-blowing. He said a silent prayer of thanks for still being alive. He resolved to lose about 20 pounds and spend a lot more time in his weight room when he got home. He had been good enough to survive the recent encounters, but, he told himself, it was like the Toby Keith song – "I'm Not as Good as I Once Was". He hurt all over, and he knew he might not be so lucky the next time. His partner, Marcus, and his wife, Diana, would tell him to delegate more and leave the altercations to the younger members of his team. He knew that was a non-starter. As he sat in the Blackhawk and surveyed the Iranian countryside, he couldn't imagine sitting behind a desk and not doing this. It was in his blood. He had almost died, but he felt very much alive. Sitting there and soaking up his moment of "survivor's high", he was blissfully unaware that he would soon face the crucible again.

The helicopter ride to the east, out of Iranian airspace, was uneventful. The Iranians had more important matters consuming their attention, and nobody in their military was paying attention to the Iran/Afghan border.

Chapter 56– Growing Clarity

Situation Room, The White House, Washington D.C.

Margaret Shevchenko walked into the storied meeting room and took her place at the conference table to the left of the President's chair. Sitting next to her was a new attendee to the crisis group, Donald L. Benson, Executive Assistant Director of the F.B.I. for National Security. She had invited him, and the President would not be happy about it. Einhorn was very proscriptive about who attended the meeting. She had a special dislike for the F.B.I., an organization she regarded as "deep state" and a constant thorn in her side, especially the Bureau's executive suite. Her concerns were not without merit, to paraphrase the old saying, "Just because I'm paranoid, doesn't mean everybody isn't out to get me". But Shevchenko knew Benson was the consummate "straight shooter", the Agency's one true "Boy Scout". She trusted him. It was fortunate, Shevchenko thought, that the F.B.I.'s Director was testifying before Congress at the moment. The President really hated the Director; one of his Lieutenant's, the Executive Assistant Director, would be less threatening and easier for her to simply ignore. She would introduce him to the President and defend his presence based on one of the more troubling revelations she was about to reveal: a potential domestic connection to the Iran's hack of the EF's weapons systems. She, of course, had another reason for Benson to be there. That reason she would keep to herself, at least for now.

Over the next several minutes, the attendees filed into the Situation Room and took their seats. Several stared into or texted on smart phones while others sat with open leather folders appearing to read briefs of some sort. Four of the attendees, however, sat with hands folded in front of them and waited for a President, who was always late. They were the Secretary of Defense, Chairman of the Joint Chiefs, Shevchenko and Benson. They indulged no distractions waiting for her arrival. Each was singularly focused on thinking about what was about to be shared, and what their roles would be in fulfilling their pledge to "Preserve, protect and defend the Constitution of the United States against all enemies, foreign and domestic".

The President finally entered the room and sat down at her customary place at the head of the conference table. She scanned the attendees to confirm all the necessary individuals were there, then paused when her eyes met Benson, sitting next to Shevchenko.

"Who are you?" she asked, coldly. It was a telling comment, as she had met with him on several previous occasions and as recently as two weeks ago. Telling, also because her momentary amnesia sprung more from her complete indifference to anyone she regarded as unimportant than it did from difficulty in remembering names.

Shevchenko answered the question. "Madam President, this is Donald Benson, the Executive Assistant Director of the F.B.I. for National Security. He is here at my invitation. His presence is important because our interrogation of Zimmerman has disclosed a potential domestic link to recent events. As you are aware, the Director is testifying on the Hill this morning. These issues are Director Benson's remit; and I likely would have chosen to invite him anyway."

The President's blood ran cold at the words, "domestic link". Who had Zimmerman given up, she wondered, horrified? She regained her composure and responded, "I assume Director Fields is aware?" she asked, referring to Emit Fields, the Director of the F.B.I."

"Yes, Ma'am," Benson replied.

"Good," the President responded. "Ok, Maggie, we're all dying to hear what you've got."

Shevchenko began to speak. "First, Zimmerman put up little resistance and was extraordinarily forthcoming. He confirmed many of our suspicions. Iran did indeed hack into the European Federation's strategic weapons Command and Control systems. The late C.E.O. of the company that designed it, Sternenlicht, became suspicious, informed Zimmerman, and Zimmerman gave him up to the Iranians who executed him. We don't know yet the details of why the missile hit Qom, but I can also report that about 4 hours ago we successfully extracted from Iran the scientist responsible for the hack. He is being interrogated as we speak, and I am told he is also being extraordinarily forthcoming."

The President tried to mask the sound of her swallowing hard at the revelations. She hoped she was successful. She was not, and what she didn't know was both Shevchenko and Benson were taking detailed mental notes on her reaction to everything said, and they would be comparing their observations as soon as the meeting concluded. It was actually the reason Benson was there.

"This scientist, does he have a name?" the President asked.

"Ashkan Ghorbani," Shevchenko replied.

"How can we believe a word this guy says," the President responded, realizing she had sounded too defensive. "He oversaw the murder of hundreds of thousands of people. The man is a monster."

"We don't believe he has any incentive to lie, Madam President. He was kidnapped from his home in California and forced to work in Iran under penalty of death for both himself and his family. We believe he's telling the truth, and the best polygraphist we have confirms that judgment."

Benson carefully watched the President during the exchange. Her hands were trembling. It was slight and would likely be missed by most in the room, but Benson noticed it. Her reactions didn't make sense. She should be delighted at the growing clarity about recent events. But she wasn't; she was upset. His years of experience at interrogating suspects in the field led him to a disturbing but irrefutable conclusion: the woman was indeed hiding something.

Shevchenko continued, "And now the most troubling thing of all. Zimmerman believes there was a domestic connection to the hack. We don't have evidence yet, but we're close. The Germans are interrogating the C.E.O. of CWR Industries who was arrested in the raid. The N.S.A. is in the process of breaking the encryption on several hard drives that were recovered. They expect results by the end of the day. The scientist, Dr. Ghorbani, should have information on this as well, and I expect to hear from my interrogator within a few hours."

The President's face was ashen. Most in the room thought she was aghast at the incomprehensible thought of a U.S. company's involvement. Shevchenko and Benson had other suspicions.

"Don will share what the F.B.I.' is doing to try and nail this down. Don?"

Benson spoke, "We want solid evidence before going to the F.I.S.A court," he said, referring to the Federal Intelligence Surveillance Act court, the judicial body which had to approve domestic surveillance. "We doubt that information garnered from foreign nationals, some of which was admittedly obtained under enhanced interrogation, will suffice. Our accounting forensics team is attempting to untangle the provenance of CWR Industries and confirm or deny the domestic connection. Their ownership structure is extraordinarily complex, but we are getting close. If we can confirm a U.S. link, I think we can make a good case for an F.B.I. raid on their domestic connection."

"That's astonishing!" exclaimed Burt Hagenlocker, the Secretary of Defense.

"If there really is a domestic connection to this, I'd gladly put a missile down their throats myself," replied General Weatherby, the Joint Chief's Chairman.

"Easy, General," Hagenlocker said as he placed his hand on the General's forearm, forcing back a smile.

"Relax, Burt, I was only kidding."

"I know that, but I'm not sure the President does," the SecDef replied.

"I was just kidding, of course, Ma'am. Just the gut reaction of a gruff old man," he said with a smile. The President didn't respond.

Shevchenko took control of the meeting again. "That's what we have for now, Madam President, at least definitively. I expect to have more by later today. I suggest we meet early evening. If there are any major revelations before then, I will call you."

"All right," she responded. "Is there anything from anyone else?" The room remained mute. "Let's reconvene at 7 PM, unless Margaret calls us together earlier."

The President looked at her watch. It was 11:30. She had to get out of that room and back to her study to make a phone call. She hoped she would still be alive at 7 PM to attend the meeting.

Offices of PrinSafe, Palo Alto California

Emma Clark pressed "end" on her cell phone to terminate the call from the President. Things were unravelling, and she fought back the welling up of yet another emotion rare to her, a sense of helplessness. For the first time in her life she didn't know what to do. She actually thought about running. She had access to a small jet that could take her anywhere in the world. She had financial resources that would allow her to live with means. Running would make her safe, but it would also deny her of the thing she craved most, power. If she ran she would be a nobody. Just another rich person hiding from the past, but always looking over her shoulder.

She admonished herself again for her indulgence in self-pity. She would fight. She would keep the President alive as long as Sara Einhorn remained useful. That wouldn't be much longer, she was convinced, but killing the President now would be nothing more than the indulgence of her temper. It would deprive her of valuable information, and that would be foolish. There was another target, she realized, that could just as easily assuage that blood lust: Joe Barber. She would buy a contract on him immediately.

She steeled herself for the gauntlet she was to face the next several days. “Think with your brain, not with your glands,” she admonished herself. She was, as many had called her, “the consummate fixer”, and she would fix this. It’s what she did. What she didn’t do was run or give up. If it was her fate to be overwhelmed by circumstances, she would take out as many of her adversaries as possible in the process. But being overwhelmed was not in her plans. Her plan was to prevail, to triumph.

“Now, how to I take out this Barber character?” she wondered, and then began to devise a plan.

Chapter 57 – Fallout

Office of the Chancellor, European Federation, Berlin, Germany

The fallout from recent events, to use an unfortunate word, was horrific. It seemed as though every civilized nation on earth had completely isolated the European Federation after the missile launch. Foreign embassies, so recently the center of growing diplomatic and commercial activity, now stood mostly empty. Ambassadors and embassy staff were recalled on a wholesale basis. The Port of Hamburg, Germany's busiest, was now a ghost town. Just one month ago, it had been the scene of cargo ships lined up offshore waiting to be unloaded, and similar vessels trying to navigate the congested traffic as they headed outbound, loaded with German and French goods. German and French manufacturing had come to a halt as their global suppliers stopped shipping them parts. Of course, because even if they could build their manufactured goods, nobody would buy them. The Russians had cut off the flow of natural gas and petroleum. Iran, which one month ago had been an important client state, would not send them a drop of oil even if they could. French wine sat unwanted in hot warehouses as energy shortages forced air conditioning systems to sit idle. Federation financial markets were in chaos, and economic activity was collapsing as incomes and savings suddenly vanished. There were food shortages. The public was angry and confused. The military had gone back to high alert. It was a toxic and dangerous mix.

Dr. Heinrich Krüger, Chancellor, faced challenges he never imagined. Circumstances felt like they were spiraling out of control. Individual crises seemed to approach a critical mass and feed on each other. Two of them had his particular attention this morning. Several of his Generals were becoming restive and impatient to act, and the President of France was making noise about dissolving the Federation. At the moment, he was a lot more worried about the first.

Krüger had a bitter argument with General Horst Brandt, the Commander of the European Federation Air Force, about confessing to the Americans the motives for firing the rail gun at the Swedish Air Base. They had fired the weapon to demonstrate they developed the technology and deployed it. It was not part of some bigger military move on the part of the Federation against the rest of the European Continent, as the Americans had feared. After the missile launch, Krüger argued, it was critical to ensure that the rest of the world understood their limited motives. Otherwise, the Federation risked a potentially catastrophic retaliation. They had to be transparent in everything, or it would be assumed that they were transparent in nothing. Brandt was nearly apoplectic at the suggestion and fought it bitterly. Krüger overruled him.

Then the unfortunate happened. The Commander of the Federation military, Brandt's boss, died suddenly of a heart attack. By Federation law, Brandt was elevated to acting Commander, putting him in charge of all military forces. One of the first things he did was raise the alert level back to DefCon 2, one step short of actual war. And he did it publicly. It was important, he argued, to "send a message" that the Federation would not tolerate a military attack. This time it was Krüger's turn for apoplexy, arguing Brandt's unauthorized action had increased the risk of an attack, not diminished it. Krüger ordered him to reduce the alert status back to where it was. Brandt was smart enough not to be overtly insubordinate and refuse a direct order; he simply ignored the Chancellor and refused to act. Krüger summoned the Minister of Defense to a meeting in his office and demanded he bring Brandt with him.

Krüger stood behind his desk, facing the window, waiting for the two men to arrive. The weather matched his mood, gloomy. He steeled himself for the coming task. Display an iron will and authority, he told himself, but not anger or arrogance. This would be like a pack of dogs, he mused. The alpha male needed to demonstrate calm but decisive leadership and broker no dissent.

His intercom buzzed, and his secretary announced the men had arrived for his next meeting. "Send them in," he responded.

Krüger stayed standing behind his desk as he waited for his door to open. He would have his Defense Minister and General Brandt sit directly across from him as a way to reinforce his authority. As the door opened, he was surprised to see four men walk into his office. Besides Brandt and the Minister of Defense, the Foreign Minister and Minister of Justice were there. His defenses went to high alert, but he maintained his composure and exhibited no signs of surprise or displeasure.

"Good morning, Gentlemen. Let's sit over here at the conference table," he said, gesturing his hand towards the table. The five men sat down.

Krüger took immediate command of the meeting. His first task was to take the General down a notch. "General Brandt, I have instructed you to reduce our alert level back to where it was before recent events. I am not going to reiterate the arguments. You made your case and I overruled you, as is my prerogative. President Morel," he said, referring to Gaston Morel, the President of France, "agrees with me. Yet I am told no such action has been taken. What is your explanation for the delay?"

"Chancellor Krüger," Brandt replied, "we remain extremely concerned that the allies are planning a retaliatory strike on our strategic facilities. We continue to believe that only a clear demonstration of resolve will prevent such a strike. To reduce our alert level at this time would appear weak and invite it. We cannot place the citizens of Germany at such risk."

Krüger was seething with rage as he noticed several things about Brandt's response. First, he didn't provide reasons for delay, he provided reasons for refusal. He had ignored a direct order from the Chancellor who, under the Federation Constitution, was his Commander in Chief. Second, he used the pronoun "we" in the presence of three of the Federation's senior cabinet members. What was the implications of that? Were they in agreement and there to support Brandt's view? Third, he referred to "citizens of Germany", not "citizens of the Federation", excluding everyone in France. This man was mad.

Krüger fought back a welling up of rage and continued with a measured voice. "General, we have had this discussion before. I have taken your counsel, but I have come to a different conclusion. I have ordered you to reduce the alert level, and you are to do it now. I have a conference call with the American President in two hours. It is essential that our alert level be reduced in a highly public manner before I make that call. You are to pick up that phone in front of you and do it while we all listen. Do I make myself clear?"

There was a long, silent pause while the men sitting around the table exchanged glances. Finally, General Brandt spoke, "Chancellor, I'm afraid I can't do that."

Krüger was stunned at such a blatant act of insubordination. He looked at the Defense Minister and asked, "What is the meaning of this?"

The Defense Minister now spoke. "Mr. Chancellor, we all had hoped matters would not come to this. We very much wanted to see you come to your senses and make the proper decision. Sadly, you have not. It is my unfortunate duty to advise you that we are prepared to invoke Article 14."

The European Federation Constitution established a couple of principles. First, it formalized a hierarchy among Federation Cabinet positions that elevated five posts to a senior status. The five posts were the Foreign Minister, the Minister of Defense, the Minister of Justice, the Minister of Finance, and the Minister of the Interior. Second it established the provision that a majority vote of the seniors could remove the Chancellor from office. Krüger looked around the room and suddenly realized that three of the five seniors were sitting at his conference table. They had not only threatened it, they had done it.

The Defense Minister retrieved a cell phone from his pocket, punched in a speed dial code, and after several seconds simply said, "Do it." He then looked at the Chancellor and continued to speak, "I have just ordered the arrest of the Vice Chancellor for complicity in your failure to adequately defend our citizens. By law of succession, the Chancellorship will now default to me until a new election can be called."

Krüger was so upset and filled with rage that he was shaking. "This is a coup!" he shouted, as he got up from the table and walked to the intercom on his desk to buzz his secretary. "Frau Helger, call in my personal protection detail immediately!" he shouted into the phone. He then looked at the four men sitting around the table, looking calm.

"They are already here, Herr Krüger," his secretary said over the intercom. He immediately noticed she referred to him as "Herr Krüger" and not "Herr Chancellor."

The door opened and four Federal Policemen entered his office. They were not his usual protection detail. "Herr Krüger, I regret to inform you that you are under arrest."

"This is outrageous!" he shouted, as he was led out of what had been, up to five minutes ago, his office. "You all are mad!"

The office door remained open after Krüger was led out. The secretary stuck her head in and announced, "President Morel of France is on the line."

"I'll take the call," announced the Minister of Defense, now the Acting Chancellor.

Chapter 58 – Bad News

Offices of PrinSafe, Palo Alto California

Emma Clark looked at her watch. It read 8:50 Pacific Daylight time, which was 11:50 Eastern Daylight time. The President had ten minutes left to call her or she would have to somehow make good on her threat. She wouldn't kill the woman, at least not yet, but she would give her one hell of a headache. She retrieved her private cell phone from her jacket pocket, laid it on her desk, and waited.

Three minutes later it buzzed. She looked at the number on the screen. It was the President of the United States.

"Good morning, Madam President," Clark said. "You made it in under the wire. Congratulations."

"Don't say congratulations yet," the President replied. "You're not going to like what I have to say."

"What did you learn?" Clark asked, avoiding the bluster and sounding worried instead.

"The N.S.A. is helping decrypt the hard drives and expect to be successful before the end of the day. Whatever is on those drives will be known in a matter of hours. The C.E.O. of CWR is being interrogated by the Germans. I haven't been told anything specific yet, other than he's cooperating. Turns out the Federation actually has an extradition treaty with Iran. They've threatened to send him there if he doesn't tell them everything. The guy is supposedly scared to death. Unlike the Federation, which prohibits capital punishment, being sent to Iran certainly means death by torture. Whatever that guy knows, we're going to know as well by the end of the day."

"Shit!" Clark exclaimed, cutting her off.

"That's not the worst," the President said.

"What?" replied Clark.

"The C.I.A. has brought in the F.B.I. on, guess what, suspicions of a domestic link. If you weren't successful on covering your tracks, fingers will be pointing at Palo Alto within 24 hours, at the latest. Did you manage to cover your tracks, Emma?" the President asked.

"I don't know. I can't get any information out of Germany now. Nobody's answering their phones."

"They undoubtedly confiscated all of the employee's cell phones," the President replied.

"You're probably right."

"We are looking at worst case, Emma. There's no point in "giving me CWR with a bow on it" as you described it, because the Germans and C.I.A. are going to have everything within 24 hours anyway. The F.B.I. has forensic accountants looking at CWR's provenance, and they believe they can establish a connection within the next 24 hours. That will tie the company directly to you. Imagine the headlines. Even if you were successful in planting fake evidence, that it was the actions of a small group of rogue CWR employees, that will do little to deflect blaming the United States for being complicit in this mess. If they can tie it to you, you'll be charged with treason."

Clark remained silent as she processed the President's last comment.

"Emma, are you still there?"

"Yes. What happens next? When does your crisis group reconvene?"

"Seven PM this evening, unless C.I.A. learns something earlier."

"Ok, Sara, same rules as before. You are to call me the minute you learn anything important, but no later than 9 PM your time. Understood?"

"Yes," the President replied.

"Good. I have to go," Clark responded.

"Emma," the President said, voice breaking.

"What?"

"Where do I stand? This device in my head?"

"Just do what I ask, Madam President," Clark said, coldly, as she ended the call.

Clark placed her cell phone back on her desk and rubbed her temples. "Keep it together," she admonished herself as she reflected on the call. "Work the problem, one problem at a time." For the first time in her professional career, she didn't know what she was going to do next. She had to clear her head and focus. Barber, she thought. Maybe I can clear my head by ending that clown. She picked up her cell phone again and placed a call.

Chapter 59 – A Turn of Events

Situation Room, The White House, Washington D.C.

Director Shevchenko called the crisis group back together at 3:30 that afternoon. She briefed the group that the digital wizards at the N.S.A. just broke the encryption on the hard drives obtained in the raid, much faster than anticipated. The drives were yielding a treasure trove of information. The most stunning revelation was they contained computer code that was designed to alter a missile's targeting instructions, and clearly had been tailored to work with the European Federation Strategic Weapons Command and Control System. It was the smoking gun. The group was stunned. A German company had aided and abetted another nation in taking control of their nuclear weapons. It was treason of the highest order. The President's reaction was odd, though, Shevchenko thought. She didn't look angry. She looked worried.

During the meeting, F.B.I. Director Benson was interrupted by the silent buzz of his phone. He pulled it out of his pocket and looked at the screen. It was the Special Agent responsible for the investigation into the provenance of CWR Industries. Benson said, "Excuse me, but I need to step outside and take this. I think I may have some incoming intelligence on the potential domestic link."

"Go ahead, of course," the President said, as the worried expression on her face seemed to deepen.

Benson stepped just outside the Situation Room and answered the call. The Special Agent began to speak. "The ownership structure looked like a pile of spaghetti, but we were able to find an undeniable link to a Hedge Fund located in Palo Alto, California. It's called, PrinSafe. Its CEO is a woman named Emma Clark. I've heard that name before, so we looked it up. She's a big high-value donations bundler, Silicon Valley, Private Equity, Hollywood and the like. She works both sides of the aisle, but about 75 percent of her donations go to Democrats, with the biggest recipient being the President."

"That's not all that unusual in and of itself," Benson replied. "We need to find out if PrinSafe is directly involved in any way in CWR's operations. The CWR guys are trying so spin a story that their work was with just a small group of rogue Iranian employees, Iranian citizens, and they had no idea what they were up to."

"And I've got a bridge in Brooklyn I'd like to sell you," the agent replied.

"Exactly," Benson said. "I'm going to take this into the Situation Room ask if N.S.A. can pull the metadata on Clark's phone calls to see if any went outside of the U.S."

The National Security Agency, N.S.A., no longer routinely turned cell phones into passive monitoring devices as it had done several years ago under Project Sparrow, but it kept the "big data" collection process. A record of all telephonic communications to and from the 25 most populated cities in the country was kept in a data base, updated continuously. To stay within the letter of the law, they didn't keep recordings of actual conversations, but captured what was called the "metadata" -- the time, duration, and the owner of record of each end of the conversation.

Director Benson took his revelations into the Situation Room, and all the people around the conference table strongly supported the recommendation to evaluate PrinSafe and its Chief Executive more closely. All but one. Shevchenko and Benson both thought it odd that the President had approved the recommendation by silent assent and seemed far from enthusiastic about it. Their suspicions were mounting with every meeting.

Once the approval was obtained, N.S.A. retrieved the records of all of Clark's calls over the last three months, including every signal coming out of her office, whether she was the owner of record or not. As the recipient phone numbers for her calls were analyzed, a pattern became clear. She made numerous calls to the Oval Office. Clark was frequently talking to the President of the United States. This in and of itself was not noteworthy – Clark was, after all, a major bundler for Einhorn's campaigns. But the context of the calls revealed two problems: it wasn't a fundraising season, and the frequency of calls over the last several weeks had gone way up. As Shevchenko and Benson reviewed the summary from N.S.A., they kept asking themselves, "Why would the President make time for her now, in the middle of the biggest global crisis since Cuba? What could Clark have that could be so important?" It didn't make sense. Or did it? Both of them were skirting on the edge of suspecting the unthinkable.

Two more revelations proved even more disturbing. There were incoming calls to Emma Clark herself from the European Federation Defense Ministry and, worst of all, there had been a call from Tehran.

Director's Office, 7th Floor, Central Intelligence Agency, Langley, Virginia, 9 PM EDT

It was late for the C.I.A. Director to be in her office, but there was no way she was going home anytime soon, and she had already resigned herself to sleeping in her office tonight. Fortunately, there was a small suite adjacent to the office with a bed and bathroom. She was engrossed in reading the interrogation transcript when there was a knock on the door. She had been altered by security that a visitor was on the way and had cleared him. "Come on in," she said. Director Benson of the F.B.I. opened the door and entered the office. She got up from her desk and walked over to the sitting area, gesturing for him to take a seat.

"This is quite a lot to process, Don," she observed.

"Yes it is, Maggie. The question is what do we do next? We can't exactly interrogate the President."

"Right," Shevchenko replied. "Let alone enough to discuss the 25th Amendment."

"I was wondering about that," Benson said.

"Have you talked to the Attorney General?" Shevchenko asked.

"About the 25th Amendment?"

"Good grief no! About our suspicions regarding Einhorn's behavior."

"No. I don't know what I'd say at this point. 'She looks suspicious?'," Benson replied. "That certainly won't fly. And besides, I don't think he was crazy about us going to the N.S.A. for those phone records. I'm not exactly on his good side right now. He's been a stickler for following the privacy guidelines after the Project Sparrow mess."

"As he should," Shevchenko replied. "I agree we need something more concrete. What about this Clark woman? Can you get a wiretap approved based on that metadata analysis?"

"Yes, I'm sure I can. We're at the FISA court right now, as a matter of fact," Benson said, referring to the specialized courts established by the post 9/11 Federal Intelligence Security Act, which allows intercept of phone calls between foreign agents and U.S. citizens if there is probable cause for establishing a crime or terrorist threat.

"Have the Europeans completed their look at those hard drives?" Benson asked.

"Not hardly," the C.I.A. Director replied. "They contained two terabytes each. It's going to take days, if not weeks, to examine all the data. Their focus, understandably, has been proving their assertion that they were hacked, and that nobody from the Federation launched that missile."

"They've got proof positive now, don't they?" Benson answered.

"Yes, but they are going to continue to try and bolster the evidence as much as they can, which is understandable. Are you keeping a journal of your observations about the President?"

"Of course," Benson replied.

"So am I. At the moment I think that's about the best we can do."

Their conversation was interrupted by the ring of the telephone on the C.I.A. Director's desk. She got up from the sofa, walked over to her desk, reached across and picked up the receiver.

Standing there, phone to ear, she suddenly had a pained expression on her face, went ramrod straight, then said, "Dear God!"

Benson stood up and took several steps towards her, stopped and asked, "What's the matter? What is it?"

Shevchenko turned towards him as she placed the phone back in its cradle. "That was the Secret Service. The President of the United States is dead."

"What?" Benson exclaimed. "How? What happened?"

"A massive stroke," the C.I.A. Director replied.

Chapter 60 – A New President

Situation Room, The White House, Washington D.C.

Charles "Boomer" Ellison was an unlikely person to find himself President of the United States. The son of a wealthy steel heiress, he was born and raised in Connecticut, educated at Phillips Exeter Academy, Yale, then Harvard Law, following his father to each of the schools, whether he wanted to or not. He was given the nickname "Boomer" by his classmates at Exeter. It was not a sign of respect.

He walked out of Yale with a C+ average. His admission to law school was nevertheless fast-tracked, which tends to happen when one's parents endow the school with an executive education wing. He never made law review at Harvard, but private tutors, costing over $100,000 over three years of legal studies, at least helped facilitate passing grades. Each tutor was required to sign a non-disclosure agreement as insurance against his future political viability.

After Harvard Law, he practiced at the prestigious firm of Covington and Burling for three years on a partner track, having passed the Connecticut Bar on his third attempt. Having failed to distinguish himself, he was relegated to the lesser track of "career associate", where he spent the next thirteen years doing little more that legal research. His lack of intellectual gravitas, however, was oddly paired with an outsized personality and a high amount of what some call "emotional intelligence". The guy knew how to work a room. He became obsessed with politics, and it was there he found his true calling.

He was elected to the U.S. Congress, a place he was smart enough to realize, in its present incarnation at least, lauded form over substance. He never sponsored an important piece of legislation and missed half of his assigned committee meetings, but the lad could really deliver a speech. He was good at reading his base and championed their every whim, though he himself had few, if any, core beliefs. His oratory skills garnered him a national stage and following. Hollywood loved him and flooded him with campaign contributions. After three terms as a U.S. Congressman, ambition fueled by an outsized ego and hubris, led him to launch a Presidential campaign.

As a Presidential candidate, he was an embarrassment to the party establishment. Among younger voters, however, he developed a passionate, though small, following. Many took to calling him by his nickname, "Boomer", which he didn't discourage. He never managed to elevate himself over 5% in national polls, but then a strange thing happened. During a bitterly contested party convention, he emerged as the "safe" compromise for the Vice President slot on the national ticket. He was "the young guy who hadn't lived long enough yet to acquire much baggage". Sara Einhorn didn't want another fight, and nobody really cared about who was number two on the ticket. Then came that fateful day when the President was found unresponsive, slumped over her desk in the President's private study. Fifteen minutes later Charles "Boomer" Ellison was sworn in as President of the United States. And it happened in the middle of the biggest crisis the Country had experienced since Russia planted missiles in Cuba.

Boomer Ellison, President of the United States for two hours, walked into a packed Situation Room and took his place at the head of the table. He invited several members of his personal staff, most of them from the Office of the Vice President. He scanned the room, almost as if wondering what he was supposed to do or say and broadcast a vibe that suggested he was a man very much in circumstances way over his head. He was burdened by more than just his own evident mediocrity -- President Einhorn hated him. Unlike most Presidents, she refused to include him in critical meetings. This was his first time in the Situation Room. He was, of course, routinely briefed about the ongoing crisis, but none of his intel was from sources with first-hand knowledge. His briefings were relegated to the lesser staff of cabinet officers who had the information second or third hand, at best.

Secretary of Defense Burt Hagenlocker broke the awkward silence and said, "Welcome, Mr. President. I am sure I can speak for all of the senior staff in this room when I say our hearts and prayers are with you as you take on the mantle of leadership under such tragic circumstances. If I may offer a suggestion, we have found these meetings more productive when we keep them small. I would like to recommend we excuse the extra members of your staff, at least for now." What Hagenlocker didn't say, but thought, was his certainty that several of the new invitees didn't even have the security clearance to hear what was about to be said, let alone the knowledge or judgment to offer constructive suggestions.

"Thank you for your kind remarks," Ellison said. "I want my people to stay."

It was an interesting comment, Hagenlocker observed, referring to the new invitees as "my people", as though the others in the room were not.

"So, what's going on?" the President asked. Several people in the room involuntarily exchanged glances, aghast at the casual and uninformed comment.

It was an odd way to start the meeting, C.I.A. Director Shevchenko thought, and an odd question for the new President to ask. She took command and answered.

"Mr. President, it is the task of the senior staff in this room, under your leadership, to review late-breaking intelligence and agree on a response. That is why we are here. There have been important developments in the last several hours that are very troubling. Given that, I believe it would be most helpful if I started off by briefing you and the rest of the crisis group on what those developments are, and we can proceed from there. Is that acceptable to you, sir?" she asked, feigning a deference she didn't feel.

"OK," the President said.

"C.I.A. believes there is solid intelligence that there has been, in effect, a military coup in the European Federation. Chancellor Krüger and the

Vice Chancellor have been removed from office under Article 14 of their Charter. It's similar to our 25th amendment. If two-thirds of a select group of senior cabinet members agree, the Chancellor can be removed."

One of President Ellison's young staffers interrupted her and asked, "If they invoked this Article 14 thing, then how can it be a military coup?"

The President looked nonplussed and remained quiet at the comment.

Shevchenko remained expressionless and looked at the President as she answered the staffer's question. "As I said, it was 'in effect' a military coup. I didn't say it WAS a military coup. There are several attributes of what happened that lead us to the conclusion. Both State and Defense agree. First, the Chancellor was not removed for issues of mental competence. The evidence, which I will share in greater detail in a minute, suggests he was removed for purposes of differences over military policy, or, more accurately, over differences about the appropriate Federation military POSTURE under present circumstances. Second, the Vice Chancellor was also removed. Third, they were both arrested and detained. Detention is not provided for in Article 14, absent formal charges. Charges were not filed. And finally, General Horst Brandt, the Commander of all of their military forces, was appointed acting Chancellor."

The young staffer interrupted her again, "Tell us about this guy Brandt." Another example of inexperience, and arrogance, Shevchenko thought – the guy didn't ask a question, he gave a directive, and to someone way above his pay grade.

SecDef Hagenlocker locked eyes with the young staffer and said in a commanding voice, "Hold your questions and allow the Director to finish her brief." He continued staring into the young man's eyes after finishing his rebuke. The staffer was the first to break the stare. He then looked at the President, who slightly shrugged his shoulders then gave a discreet nod of his head to signal the staffer to comply.

"I don't think there is any other possible way to interpret their sudden change in leadership. If it walks, talks and smells like a military coup, it's a military coup. The most disturbing thing I have to share," Shevchenko continued, "is the Federation has raised their alert status to DefCon 2. That was not the path that Krüger promised us. He was explicit in promising their intent to maintain a low military profile to avoid any appearance of hostile intent. And nobody from the Federation, let alone their new Chancellor, Brandt, has reached out to us to explain the recent series of events."

Secretary of Defense Hagenlocker then spoke, "And the real concern, Mr. President, is what this potentially says about their propensity for hostile action: the fact that Brandt hasn't called you to reassure us they have no such intentions. That's a very bad sign"

"In addition," Shevchenko said, "Russia has responded by raising their military alert status. We don't have as good an intel on China and the North Koreans, but prudence demands we assume the same from them."

"There's another dynamic here we need to focus on," said General Weatherly, the Chairman of the Joint Chiefs. "The Federation is aware that we just had a change in leadership as well, with the death of the President. They may also be wondering why we haven't called them. The potential for misinterpretations and miscalculations right now is enormous. We are operating in an information vacuum, which is the most dangerous of circumstances. We, the United States, need to take the lead in communication and keeping everyone calm and on the same page."

"Mr. President," Secretary of State Carleton Epsy added, "it is essential that you call Acting Chancellor Brandt immediately and inquire as to his intentions."

"Absolutely sir," Director Shevchenko added her voice to the exhortations, "and you should do it now. From here, in the situation room. You should call him now."

Everybody was aghast as the young staffer started to speak again and add his voice to the comments. "Mr. President, I agree that reaching out to Brandt could be a good thing. But, you've been President for the sum total of two hours. First impressions are very important. We don't have a communication strategy for this. There's no script. This will be your first call to a head of state, and in the middle of a crisis no less. It could do your Presidency significant harm to reach out before you're ready. I suggest we get together a small working group and craft some talking points. I'd be happy to lead it for you. We could pull something together fairly quickly and have you ready by tomorrow morning."

"That's a good point," President Ellison said.

Secretary of Defense Burt Hagenlocker looked like his head was about to explode. He took a deep breath, steadied himself, and began to speak. "With respect sir, it's a terrible idea. We don't have time to put to put together a study group. This needs to be done now, not tomorrow morning. You don't need a script. You just need to call the guy and ask, 'What the hell are you up to?', and we play it from there."

Under his breath General Weatherby added, in an inaudible whisper, "and get a pair."

Hagenlocker then looked at the young staffer and said, "Not another word from you." He knew he was taking a big risk with the admonishment of the President's aide, but he didn't care. Whatever the President's inward reaction, he remained quiet.

There was a silent, awkward, pause as the people in the room processed the exchange. Maggie Shevchenko had an image flash across her consciousness of a small poodle barking at a pack of pit bulls. She forced back a smile. She didn't know this young staffer. The kid probably went to Harvard or Yale and spent his entire life being told how smart he was. He hadn't grasped yet his new reality. He had been thrown into a pond with tier-one alphas, both male and female. It would be interesting to see, she thought, it he could grasp that, then learn and adapt. She gave it about a 30% probability.

"Mr. President, let's call Chancellor Brandt now, please," Shevchenko said. "Time is of the essence." This time the young staffer kept his mouth shut.

Chapter 61 – Confrontations

Office of the Chancellor, European Federation, Berlin, Germany

"Power corrupts, and absolute power corrupts absolutely." The phrase is often attributed to the twentieth-century sage of international relations, Henry Kissinger. But it was actually first expressed by the nineteenth-century British politician, Lord Acton, who consolidated the concepts of several previous writers into its more recognized and pithy form. The insightful nature of the observation was, at the moment, very much on display.

Acting Chancellor Horst Brandt was 'feeling his oats' as he sat at the head of the conference table in his new office. There was a slight smile on his face as he thought about the former occupant sitting in a jail cell, just several blocks away, in the offices of the German Federal Police. The guy deserved it, he thought. He was weak, and these were times for displays of strength, not weakness. Brandt had no particular animosity towards the Vice-Chancellor, who was 'next in line' under Article 14, but he knew the man to be a protégé of Chancellor Krüger. Brandt wasn't willing to take the risk that one weak man would succeed another, so the Vice-Chancellor had to go as well. He thought about what he was going to do with them. Problem was, as long as they remained alive, they were a threat. They didn't get elected by being unpopular, and alive they could mount a defense. They had to die. Maybe they would suffer an unfortunate accident. Perhaps they would be discovered after having hung themselves in their cells. There were many possibilities for dealing with such "inconveniences", he mused, as the smile returned. That was tomorrow's problem. There were more important priorities today.

The senior cabinet members flanked Brandt at the table as they discussed a communication strategy about what just happened. It was necessary to calm Federation citizens and assure them recent steps were lawful and undertaken to ensure their security. That would be relatively easy, they agreed. It was also necessary to convey a sense of strength and resolve to world leaders so that nobody would be tempted to take advantage of the present chaos. That task was more difficult. Their biggest concern wasn't the Americans. Everyone agreed they were more bark than bite, and early intelligence on the new President suggested he was even weaker than Einhorn. They were terrified, however, about the Russians.

Russia was mobilizing troops on their western border. Nobody was much concerned about a missile strike now. A ground invasion appeared to be the far greater risk. The EF's fancy new rail gun was only deployed on a half-dozen jets, and while that was enough to scare the Swedes, it was hardly enough to repel a large-scale invasion. They had played their cards too soon. If the weapon had been widely deployed across their entire air force, they would be invulnerable. In attacking Sweden, however, they had given up the element of surprise and the Russians would be looking for their new toy. And six jets would not be that difficult to shoot down. The sobering truth was it was useless against the Russian threat.

Their discussions were interrupted as Brandt's secretary walked through the open door of his office and announced the President of the United States was on the phone. The men looked at each other with various degrees of surprise. Brandt responded, "It is good that he is coming to us first. Let's take the call and see what the new President has to say. I would like to take the measure of the man."

Brandt told his secretary to transfer the call to his office. They all waited for a few seconds until the light appeared on the phone in the middle of the conference table. Brandt then pressed the button to activate the call and put it on speaker. "Hello Mr. President. Our condolences for your loss of President Einhorn. I have been meaning to call you, but as I am sure you are aware, we have been a bit busy the last 24 hours."

"Good morning, General Brandt, and thank you."

Brandt bristled and replied, "As I am sure you know, Mr. President, it's no longer General Brandt, it's now Chancellor Brandt."

Situation Room, The White House, Washington D.C.

The President hit the mute button and looked at his senior staff with an expression that telegraphed the question, 'How should I respond?'

"Ignore the comment, Mr. President," Secretary of Defense Hagenlocker counseled, "He's probably just a bit miffed at what he sees as a slight for you not referring to him as Chancellor. I would just get to the point."

The President unmuted the phone and asked, "So, what the hell are you all up to over there?"

Several people in the situation room cringed at the comment. Hagenlocker's face flushed. "Was this guy that dense?", he asked himself. Hagenlocker had used that phase with the President in the previous meeting to convey the substance of what they needed to know. It was a figure of speech. It wasn't intended to be a literal question. Grasp of nuance was obviously not one of the new President's strengths.

"I'm not sure I understand your question, Mr. President. Would you care to be more specific?" Brandt asked.

"What's happened to Chancellor Krüger?" the President clarified.

There was a long pause on the other end of the phone. Chancellor Brandt then answered, "Mr. President, we have constitutional processes just as you do. I can assure you those processes were followed. We decided a change of leadership was necessary to effectively deal with what we acknowledge is an existential crisis for the European Federation. The Federation appreciates the continued support of your country as we establish the facts and make it clear to the world that the Federation was not responsible for the missile attack on Iran. We can expect your continued support, can we not?"

Shevchenko motioned for the President to hit the mute button again, then said, “Burt, I suggest you frame the proper question for the President.”

“Mr. President,” Burt Hagenlocker responded, “with respect you’ve asked Brandt the wrong question. Brandt is the Chancellor. How he got to the Chancellorship our biggest concern at the moment. We need to know why they raised their alert status, and in such a visible way. You need to ask him why he did that. We can address Krüger later.”

Ellison unmuted the phone, then spoke, “Ok, Chancellor Krüger, that’s a fair point, and yes, we all want to understand exactly how that missile was launched and are continuing to work towards that end. That is not the reason for my call, however. We were surprised, no concerned would be a better way to put it, to see you raise your military alert status. We had an agreement with your predecessor to, militarily, keep a low profile to avoid miscalculations. Why did you raise your alter status? Nothing has changed to warrant that, at least as far as we are aware.”

Hagenlocker grinned and gave the President a thumbs up, then whispered, “perfect.” Several others in the room followed with the same gesture. The President smiled.

“We believe it is necessary to demonstrate our resolve to protect our citizens, Mr. President, and to ensure nobody is tempted to take advantage of the present chaos.”

Hagenlocker furiously wrote out a question on a legal pad and scooted it across the desk to the President.

President Ellison asked it verbatim, “Our concern is that it is more likely to signal an increased likelihood of hostile intent on your part. Your citizens are not safer because of your action, they are at greater risk.”

“We have debated that very point extensively among ourselves, Mr. President, and we respectfully disagree. I might also point out that, unlike you, we are not separated from the physical presence of our adversaries by an ocean. As we speak several divisions of the Russian army have been deployed to their western border. We are not that worried about you. We are worried about them. Russia needs to know, needs to fear, that there will be grave consequences for launching a ground assault."

It was the Secretary of State, Carl Epsy's turn to quickly scribble a question on a legal pad and slide it across the table. The President read it verbatim as well, "We implore you, Chancellor, to reduce your alert level back to where it was. If you do not, I fear you will be misunderstood, and your county could experience grave consequences."

Brandt replied, "That is not going to happen, Mr. President. We are quite firm in our decision to remain at a higher state of readiness. It is our solemn duty to our citizens. However, I offer you my personal word that the Federation does not contemplate any form of preemptive military action, and least of all against you. You have been most helpful to us over recent days. We will act only in a defensive manner. If, however, it becomes necessary, I can also assure you that we will do so, as I believe you put it, using all necessary means. If there are no other topics to discuss, I must go now. Again, our best wishes for you personally as you assume your country's mantle of leadership. Good day, Mr. President." The line went dead.

"Well, that went well," Hagenlocker commented, sarcastically.

"I told you we needed more preparation for this," the young staffer said, with a feigned tone of authority in his voice. "This accomplished nothing because we weren't ready."

"I disagree," General Weatherby responded. "We went on record with our displeasure, Brandt understood that, and we have a reasonable assurance of no imminent hostile intent. I don't like their escalation, but let's be honest with ourselves, if we had an adversary massing troops that close to our border we'd do exactly the same thing. Put yourselves in their shoes."

"I agree, John," Director Shevchenko replied. "The only way we are going to de-escalate this is by offering conclusive evidence of Iran's hack into their systems. We are very close on that."

"Great," the President responded. "Let's make that our top priority. Margaret, please keep me up to date on where you stand."

"Of course, Mr. President," she replied, fighting back the urge to add, "it's my job."

The young staffer then spoke up, "Maybe I could act as a liaison between you and the C.I.A.," he said, speaking to the President but looking at Director Shevchenko.

"Great idea," the President said.

Shevchenko ignored the young staffer's stare and inwardly bristled at the exchange. There was no way, of course, that she was going to indulge the young man's grab for power. And the President indulging such a suggestion said far more about Charles "Boomer" Ellison than it did about the young staffer, who could arguably be forgiven for not knowing better.

"Maybe we should meet back here sometime tomorrow," the President added.

"We should meet again a lot sooner than that," Secretary of Defense Hagenlocker responded. "Maggie, why don't you call the meeting as soon as you have something new to share."

"Will do," she responded.

* * * * *

As the meeting concluded, everyone shuffled out of the Situation Room and headed back to their individual offices. Shevchenko headed down the hall and towards the exit door where a driver would be waiting to take her back to Langley. As she approached the door, the young staffer, now out of breath from running, caught up to her and said, "Hey Maggie, I'll have the White House call your secretary and schedule some time for us to meet tomorrow. I'd be happy to come down to Langley, of course, unless you already have business at the White House."

Shevchenko paused her walk and looked at the young man. Some parts of her job were more fun than others, she mused, and this was about to be one of those times. She suppressed a smile as she cleared her throat and prepared for her performance, then replied in a cold and authoritative voice, "It's Director Shevchenko, sonny, and if I ever see you within ten miles of Langley, I'm going to cut your nuts off."

As she turned to continue out the door, the young staffer just stood there with his mouth open wide enough to accommodate both of his feet. He was smart, and perhaps he'd learn, she thought. Lessons like the one he just received could help, buts he still only gave him a 30% chance.

A broad smile crossed her face as she approached the waiting car. "Good meeting, I see," her driver said.

"Rough meeting, actually, but it did end on a positive note."

Chapter 62 – The Worst She Could Imagine

Offices of PrinSafe, Palo Alto California

Information is power. Recognition of that reality is one of the things that drove the success of the private equity firm, PrinSafe. Emma Clark, its Chief Executive, was schooled in that principle at the feet of her mentor, Charles "Westy" Reynolds, from the moment she became his protégé. They craved it, even lusted after it, and they didn't care how they obtained it. Insider trading laws, intellectual property rights, and other legal impediments only applied to those not clever enough to circumvent them, or so they believed. Obtaining access to whatever critical information they needed was part of their tradecraft, and they plied it brilliantly. It revealed their best ideas, provided actionable intelligence on their competitors, and clarified the optimum timing of their investments. Their intellect was the engine of their wealth, but critical information was the fuel that powered it. Occasionally, the right information, provided at the right time, could literally save their lives.

Sara Einhorn was not the only source of information Emma Clark had in the U.S. government, although the President of the United States was arguably a pretty good one. Sometimes it was more useful to have access to information much further down the food chain where it could be acted on before it reached the President's desk. Otherwise, it might be too late to effectively use it. This was especially true for information percolating up through the bowels of the Executive Branch's "alphabet agencies" like the N.S.A., F.B.I. or C.I.A. Clark was very resourceful at placing former employees within those agencies in positions that provided access to all kinds of useful, even classified, information. In return, they were paid handsome bonuses by PrinSafe in BitCoin, the "crypto currency" that was untraceable.

Several of her best software engineers made their way into the employment of the N.S.A. Fortunately for her, one such former employee found himself working on F.B.I.'s request to pull and analyze the metadata from phone calls to and from her PrinSafe office. She was about to receive a call from that man, and it would shake her to her core.

It began with a text from an unrecognizable phone number. The text contained only three words: "Wolverine Protocol One". It was code, and she recognized it immediately. "Wolverine" identified the caller. It confirmed he was her former employee working for the N.S.A. "Protocol One" meant the information was extremely valuable and too sensitive for the call to be made in the normal manner. It directed Clark to drive at least 25 miles from her office, purchase a local burner phone, then text the number back to the source and await his call. The 25-mile distance was designed to place Clark outside the range of the N.S.A.'s monitoring of metadata in the San Francisco area. That ensured their phone call would not be intercepted. Protocol One had never before been used. She was simultaneously annoyed and frightened. Annoyed, because a 25-mile round trip this morning was not in her plans. Frightened, because Protocol One confirmed the gravity of the information. She was about to get the worst news she could imagine.

She got into her Mercedes and drove down highway CA-85 towards the city of Alamitos. It was 24.4 miles from her office, but she decided that was far enough. The day was gloomy, which matched her mood. Intermittent rain pelted the windshield and slowed traffic. What was it about California drivers, she wondered, that required shaving five miles an hour off the speed limit whenever the pavement got a little wet? It was irritating. Heavier than normal traffic made it impossible for her to weave around the slower vehicles. Her frustration level was growing as a 30-minute trip was quickly turning into something much longer. Was this a bad omen, she wondered, but quickly dismissed the thought. She was many things, but superstitious was not one of them.

Finally arriving at Alamitos, she found a local Rite-Aid drugstore and purchased a pre-paid burner phone for $50. She then drove around trying to find a place to make the call; someplace where she would appear inconspicuous. As she drove down Santa Theresa Blvd, an In-and-Out Burger Restaurant appeared on her right. It had an outside seating area, and only one of the tables was occupied. Perfect, she thought. She pulled into their parking lot, entered the restaurant, and ordered a cheeseburger with fries. After being handed her food, she walked outside and sat down at one of the several picnic-style tables that was empty. She wasn't hungry, but she forced herself to take a bite of the burger to bolster an appearance of normalcy. This was it. Her stomach was in knots. She was terrified. These were feelings and emotions that were mostly foreign to her, yet here she sat experiencing them. How did this happen, she wondered? How had she gone wrong? What mistakes had she made? What would Westy do in this situation? That last question was silly, she realized, because he never found himself in this position. This was it. Whatever sensitive information was about to be shared during this phone call, she had to receive it. She steeled herself.

After forcing down a couple of French fries, she retrieved the burner phone from her purse, turned it on, then waited for it to come to life. She opened the SMS text app, entered the phone number of the incoming text, then, on the message line, typed the number of her burner phone. In less than 60 seconds, her phone rang.

"Hello," she said. "Wolverine?"

"Ident please," replied the voice on the other end of the line. Protocol One required her to give a password, a movie name, to positively identify her as Emma Clark before the caller would provide the information.

"La La Land," she replied.

"And you?" she asked.

"The Martian," the voice replied.

"We are confirmed," she said.

"Hello, Emma,"

"Hello Wolverine. What do you have for me?"

"You've been made," the voice said.

It was about 87 degrees and muggy in Alamitos, but her arms instantly burst out in goose bumps. She could feel the hair stand up on the back of her neck. Her throat constricted and she found it difficult to breathe. Her stomach felt like it sank all the way to her seat and her heart was pounding so hard she could feel her pulse in her neck. She steeled herself again and simply said, "Details please," although she already knew what they were.

"The N.S.A. pulled metadata from your last 3 months of phone calls. I was on the project with three other analysts. The request came in from the F.B.I."

"What did they find?" she interrupted.

"The data showed a big spike in your calls to Einhorn's private cell phone, but that's not the worst. It also showed a call to you from the European Federation Defense Ministry.."

"Shit!" she said, interrupting his report.

"You need to let me finish. That's not the worst. It also shows a couple of phone calls from Iran, and that's what really has them animated. The F.B.I. must have taken the findings to the F.I.S.A. court, because two hours ago we got a request to provide them manuscripts of the phone calls themselves."

"I thought you didn't record the actual calls, just the metadata."

"That's what everybody thinks," he replied. "The calls are recorded, but they're not recorded."

"What does that mean?" Clark asked.

"We have a secret facility at Naval Air Station Keflavik, Iceland. It's manned by Icelandic nationals. Their job is limited to monitoring systems and reporting problems. It's fully automated and they have no idea what is going on there. Evidently some clever lawyers at Justice wrote a memo that says it technically doesn't violate the law, since it's not on U.S. soil and no U.S. citizen touches it. It falls under F.I.S.A. as well, and they must have approved a warrant because we are compiling transcripts of calls as we speak."

"Why am I just hearing about this now?" she asked, with a quiet voice but one that was filled with unmistakable anger.

"Because until one hour ago I had no idea it existed either. It's not exactly like they would be inclined to share that all the way down the food chain to me. As far as I can tell, this is the first time we've used it. This will completely open your kimono, Emma. I would guess that in less than six hours they are going to know everything."

"Have you read any of the transcripts?" she asked.

"Yes."

"And?" she asked.

"You know what's in those phone calls. I've only read the transcripts for about 5 percent of them, but they're pretty damning. The F.B.I. guys are kicking around the "T" word, and even a couple of our analysts said it. Treason. You were that obvious. And before you interrupt me again, I need to tell you the F.B.I. is in the process of getting a warrant for your arrest. You need to get out of Dodge, and right now."

He was right. She'd been made, and the news was the worst she could imagine. "I agree," she responded. "I'm going to get out of the country and lay low for a while. I'll figure something out."

"Good luck," he said, "I'm sure you will."

"Thanks. You've certainly earned you bonus today."

It was terrible news, but she collected her wits and remembered she had a plan. She would charter a jet under a false identity and get out of the country. She couldn't travel now under her own name. The F.B.I. would have a BOLO out on her, which meant "be on the lookout", essentially an "All-Points Bulletin." If she tried to flee using routine transportation she would certainly be detained. She owned a home in the mountains in Argentina. That would do just fine for now. She was still reeling from the phone call but remembered a line from one of her favorite movies, The Thomas Crown Affair, when Pierce Brosnan tells Rene Russo, "Fugitives with means. All the difference in the world". It made her smile. She was getting her bearings back. She would survive this.

But first, there was something she had to do. There was a detail to clean up in the States before she took flight. This clown, this Joe Barber, was the thorn in her side. He had connected way too many dots and put her in this predicament. He had to go. No mercy this time. She punched another familiar number into the burner phone. When the call connected the man on the other line simply said, "What?" She gave him her code name. He acknowledged with a code name of his own. Their identities were verified. They could now close the deal.

"Let loose the dogs," she said.

"Acknowledged," he confirmed. "I want 72 hours to consummate."

"I'll give you 48," she countered.

"Fifty percent premium then," he said.

"Agreed," she acknowledged. "I'll wire 50% today, the other 50% once I receive confirmation the contract has been completed."

"We are agreed on terms," he said. "Consider it done," then he disconnected the call.

Clark then punched in the number for NetJets. Argentina should be beautiful this time of year, she thought.

Chapter 63 – Another Attack

Barber Residence, 200 Locust Ave, Rye, New York

Barber stood in the en suite of his bedroom and looked at himself in the mirror. It was one of those "truth moments" when middle-aged men are forced to channel the inner truth of the Toby Keith song, "I'm not as good as I once was". It wasn't pretty, he had to admit, but it would do. At least for the first time in several days he felt a bit better than he looked. The pain in his ribs, courtesy of multiple altercations over the last couple of weeks, was finally starting to subside, although he still popped four Advil, 800 milligrams in total, as an insurance policy. But at least this time he left the Vicodin in the drawer.

Running down the steps, around the corner and into the kitchen, he grabbed a set of car keys off one of the multiple hooks just to the side of the door leading to the garage. The keys were to a brand-new Mustang Shelby GT500, 760 horsepower with 625-foot pounds of torque. He also owned a high-end Porsche, a 911 Carrera 4S, which was more than twice the price of the Mustang. The Porsche was a marvel of precision, almost like a piece of jewelry on wheels, but the Mustang exuded a rare combination of raw power and beauty. He needed raw today. He entered the garage and just stood there, looking at the beast, bright blue with a black racing stripe down its middle. It made him instantly feel better. Driving a car like that was one of the subtle ways he defined himself. It made him feel alive.

Barber climbed into the beast, hit the garage door opener and fired up the engine. The engine's deep rumble reverberated throughout the garage. The engine was specially tuned to sound that way, and some of the noise was deliberately channeled into the vehicle's interior to enhance the driving experience. He revved the engine a couple of times, soaking up the sound, and loved it. He pulled out of his driveway, headed west on Locust until he hit North street, turned left, then headed towards Orion Bellicus headquarters.

In the Parked Car on North Street

The warm sun beat on his face through the open window and caused him to perspire. He sat in the car and waited. He didn't have a lot of time. Ordinarily he would have preferred to do extensive research on a target, then observe him for several days before attempting to engage. But he had a short fuse. It had to be completed only 48 hours from the phone call, which occurred about 30 hours ago. If it didn't happen today, he would forgo a 50% bonus. That wasn't going to happen.

He looked at the photos in his target package. He had checked vehicle registration records and had a license number and photo of each vehicle his subject owned. He guessed the man would either be driving the Porsche or the Mustang this morning. Those cars seemed to best fit his profile. Not the Lincoln Navigator; that was likely the preferred ride of the guy's wife. Between the Porsche and the Mustang, he guessed Mustang. It was the newest of the two.

He took a sip of his coffee and scanned the area. He was very disciplined in the way he observed his environment. The viewing area was divided into eight equal parts, and he focused on each area for about 2 seconds, moving from right to left. Any slower and he could miss something in the next area, any faster and he could miss something in the area he was scanning. Area 1, woman walking down sidewalk to his right with baby in push-chair; they call them strollers here in the states, he reminded himself. Area 2, man locking bicycle to rack outside of local Starbucks, also to the right. Area 3, older man and woman getting out of parked car 10 meters ahead, engaged in what appeared to be an argument of modest intensity, not drawing attention. Area 4, motorcycle 5 meters ahead, having just passed on the left. And so on, and so on.

As he scanned, he placed his coffee into the console cupholder then proceeded to multitask using his right hand to verify the availability of his weapons. A Heckler and Koch VP9 Tactical pistol with a 15-round magazine sat on his lap, under a large hat to mask it. It was his weapon of choice. It was beautifully engineered, almost like a piece of jewelry, relatively lightweight at 27 ounces, and very accurate for a handgun, owing in part to the small extension of the barrel out the front of the slide. No safety, just point and squeeze the trigger. Chambered in 9mm, it would eat any brand of ammunition, and it never jammed. He also had an H&K SP5K machine pistol as a backup. It wasn't to use on his target, it would be overkill for that, and automatic weapons fire would bring the police quickly. But it was a great insurance policy if he got into trouble. He kept the SP5K under his seat, and reflexively stretched his arm down to feel it to ensure it was there. He picked up the VP9 and felt its grip. The feel was reassuring. The Germans really knew how to engineer a firearm, he thought.

His senses detected a faint noise down the street. It was the sound of an engine, but it stood out from the rest of the traffic. It was deep and throaty and louder than a car engine should be. Not like the sound of a failing muffler, but more like something powerful and finely tuned. He recognized it. It was the sound of a Ford Mustang, but somehow different, more powerful. He looked in his rearview mirror. About two hundred meters back he could make out the hood. It was Blue. Pay dirt. His instincts had been correct. It was a deep blue Mustang and its driver was undoubtedly his target, Joseph Barber.

As the vehicle approached to 125 meters he could now make out a wide, black racing strip down the middle of the vehicle. He looked at the picture of Barber in his folder and burned the image in his head. He had to make a positive identification before pulling the trigger. He placed his car into drive, holding firm the brake, the vehicle now at the ready. His left hand reflexively tightened on the steering wheel, anticipating that the vehicle was about to move, then eased the brake pressure a bit and allowed himself to slowly creep forward. His right hand closed around the grip of the H & K pistol. He was ready.

Mustang Shelby GT500, Headed South on North Street, 125 Yards Behind the Assassin

Barber had the radio tuned to Sirius "Radio Classics", listening to a 1952 episode of the drama, "Yours Truly, Johnny Dollar". It was more than a bit dated by today's standards, but he found the old radio dramas had a charm lacking in much of contemporary entertainment. He reached over and turned on the heated seat, even though it was Summer and the vehicle's air conditioning was cranking full blast. You could fry and egg on the heated seat, he would joke, but the warmth helped loosen his back.

He felt fairly relaxed for the first time in several weeks. But as he drove, he nevertheless scanned the area. His internal threat-detection radar was never completely off. Something still nagged him. There were three recent attempts on his life, and he was unconvinced there wasn't someone out there who regarded him as unfinished business. As he scanned, he saw nothing unusual. It was going to be an uneventful drive, he convinced himself. And besides, this was a highly unlikely place for an attack.

He switched the radio channel to local weather. Hot and humid. Thanks, Captain Obvious, he thought, as he looked at the temperature gauge that read 94 degrees. Pollen-count high. Yup, he thought, as he remembered sneezing several times since first walking into his garage.

His mind drifted to the "to-do" list. Item number one was seeing Marcus. He hoped his partner would have some inside information on what was going on in Europe now, from his friend General Laurent. There were about a dozen items tied for number 2.

Assassin's Vehicle

The deep blue Mustang was now only about five car lengths behind him. Things were unfolding quickly. The driver was becoming more prominent in his sight-picture. "That's him!" he said. Positive ID! As the

Mustang passed he pulled out of the parking space and quickly drifted two lanes over so he could approach Barber from the left, while accelerating to match the Mustang's speed.

He scanned the upcoming area. He would be firing from left to right, so it was important to try and make sure there were no civilians on the right-hand sidewalk. A block and a half ahead of him he found his spot, then accelerated again to close the distance to his target.

He momentarily pulled ahead of the Mustang by about 2 meters, then slowed ever so slightly to allow his target to come back to him. It only took about five seconds. Barber slowly started to pass. The assassin had the right window of his vehicle down to provide an unencumbered shot. The two vehicles finally closed to where they were next to each other and Barber was directly to his right. He lifted the H&K VP9 suppressed pistol and fired once, directly at Barber's temple. Professionals don't do "spray and pray". They mark their quarry, then fire a single, carefully placed shot. He did so then accelerated away from the Mustang as fast as he could without drawing unwanted attention, all the while looking in his rear-view mirror to confirm a successful shot, of which he was certain.

Mustang Shelby GT500, Headed South on North Street, Even with Assassin's Vehicle

Barber was finally becoming engrossed enough in the radio drama that he stopped thinking about his to do list. Suddenly he was overtaken by a violent sneeze, about the sixth or seventh in the last fifteen minutes. As he sneezed, his head snapped several inches forward in a normal reaction.

It took at least two or three seconds for Barber to process what had just happened. There had just been a loud sound, one that he recognized but could not yet place. He also thought he heard the sound of glass breaking, which didn't make any sense as his windshield was fully in tack without any sign of damage. He felt a burning sensation at the back of his neck and reached back to feel it. It felt wet. He pulled his hand back around and looked at it. It was covered with blood. He then looked to his right and saw a what appeared to be a bullet hole in the passenger-side window, then looked to his left and saw the same. He had been shot! He quickly took inventory. He felt fine, save for that burning sensation at the back of his neck. There was no other pain, and everything worked. He was ok. The sneeze must have caused the shot to miss. He slowed down and pulled over to the curb.

Assassin's Vehicle

The assassin looked in his rear-view mirror. He would have expected the Mustang to have swerved and lost control by now. That is, if the shot was successful. Could he have missed?

He had to verify. There were no parallel streets to North Street that would allow him to inconspicuously backtrack, so he did the only thing he could do. He made a U-turn and headed back towards the Mustang.

Mustang Shelby GT500

As Barber looked up, he saw a vehicle make a U-turn. His threat-detection radar flashed red. He hadn't noticed the vehicle before, but it had to be the source of the attack. Nobody made U-turns on North Street. He put the Mustang in gear and hit the accelerator, launching himself from his parking spot at the curb. He could hear people screaming. Charge towards the source of the threat, he told himself. It gave you the highest probability of survival.

Assassin's Vehicle

The assassin saw the Mustang launch away from the curb and start accelerating quickly towards him. That confirmed the attack had failed. Even if Barber had been hit, it obviously wasn't grave, as he was still fully in control of his car. The assassin was stunned. He never missed. It wasn't even a difficult shot. It didn't make sense.

It was like he had swatted a hornet and missed. He was no longer the sole aggressor with the benefit of surprise. He also was now a target. Two alpha predators squared off against each other. When that happened, he knew, things would get messy real fast. He was no longer thinking about the 50% bonus, he was thinking about survival.

As the Mustang barreled towards him he pulled the H&K SP5K machine pistol out from under his seat. With his right hand holding the steering wheel, he held the firearm out the window with his left hand and started shooting at the Mustang that was headed directly towards him and closing the distance fast. It was difficult to hold the weapon steady as he fired. The barrel moved around in an unsteady hand. He emptied the clip and hoped one of the shots found its mark.

Mustang Shelby GT500

The Mustang's windshield suddenly exploded from the relentless spray of lead from the SP5K. Barber ducked down and brought the vehicle to a stop. Fortunately, the assassin was not skilled at shooting with his non-dominant hand, and most of the shots went high as the barrel of the weapon naturally climbed in reaction to the automatic fire. But Barber was unarmed, thanks to the rigid firearms regulations of New York State. Then, he realized he actually did have a weapon. He was armed with horsepower and speed. The shooting had stopped. The assassin must be either reloading or trying to assess whether he got lucky and Barber was dead. He had just been handed a brief window of opportunity to counterattack and he quickly prepared to do so with a vengeance.

Barber could now hear police sirens. That meant the assassin could not stay on scene much longer or his ability to escape would vanish. He had to put this guy out of the fight before he got away to try again. Barber cautiously looked up over the dashboard and noticed the assassin's vehicle had stopped in the street in a slightly cocked position. That provided a closing angle to the driver's side. Barber sat up, put the Mustang in gear again and punched the accelerator, pointing the nose of the car directly at the driver's side door. Tires smoked and the engine screamed as the Mustang raced towards the other vehicle like a missile launched from the wing of a jet. The Mustang's left front corner made first contact as it rammed its target. There was a sickening sound of compressing sheet metal as the vehicle turned clockwise and formed a perfect "T" with the Mustang, The assassin's car was pushed sideways several feet into a light pole, compressing its other side. Barber's airbag deployed, rendering him unconscious but likely saving him from serious injury. The next thing he remembered was waking up in the emergency room of St. Vincent's Hospital. His first words were, "How's the car?"

Chapter 64 – To the Brink

European Federation Defense Ministry, offices of General Jean-Baptiste Laurent, Deputy Commander, Federation Air Force

General Jean-Baptiste Laurent punched the final digit of the code into the key pad then pressed the "send" button. He then looked at the aide standing in front of his desk and barked, "Confirm the order was received."

The aide picked up a handset from its cradle in the briefcase and spoke into it, "Confirm receipt of order alpha, charlie, oscar twenty-one X-ray." After a two second pause, he looked up at the General and said, "General, receipt of the order is confirmed."

Exactly seven minutes later, five French-built Dassault-Rafale fighter jets, with afterburners glowing, were lifting off runway 21 at Büchel Airbase in Germany headed towards Evreux-Fauville Air Base in northern France. They were the five jets in the Federation Air Force equipped with the newly developed rail gun. They were going home.

Office of the Chancellor, European Federation, Berlin, Germany

Diplomatic pressure was mounting rapidly on the European Federation to clarify their intensions regarding their high level of military alert. Tension with their neighbors, to say nothing of the United States, was so strained it was like a pressure cooker about to blow, and the Federation's political leadership was feeling increasingly isolated. All of the nuclear powers had responded in kind and were at their highest level of military readiness. Yet Brandt refused to provide assurances other than The Federation would only act defensively, whatever that meant. Chancellor Brandt was frustrated. This was not the way things were supposed to play out. He was signaling strength, not aggression. He was protecting his citizens against what he feared might be a pre-emptive strike. Why couldn't those idiots see that? Russia was massing troops on their western border. The United States and

England were making threats. He reluctantly realized the Americans had been correct, that Federation citizens weren't safer, they were at greater risk.

He struggled to come up with an exit strategy. Reducing his military readiness level was out of the question. It would make him look weak, and worse yet, would invalidate the reasons for invoking Article 14 and removing Chancellor Krüger. That could result in him being the one sitting in a Federal Police prison. He was a man in way over his head. He sat there, stomach churning, trying to think of a face-saving answer. Underestimating the reaction of other nations to raising the Federation military alert status wasn't the only miscalculation he made. He was about to learn of another one.

His thoughts were interrupted by his secretary, as she walked into his office and announced, "The French President is on the phone, sir."

"Great, that's just what I needed right now, that pompous ass nipping at my flanks," he thought, then regained his composure and said, politely, "Thanks, please transfer the call."

"President Morel, good afternoon. These are busy times," Brandt said, signaling the call was not welcome, much to the French President's annoyance. "What can I do for you?"

"This is an official call, General Brandt."

Brandt took notice of being called "General" and not "Chancellor." It was a deliberate slight.

"What is on your mind, Gaston?" he asked, referring to the French President by his first name, intentionally signaling that he now regarded the man as his peer, not his superior, as had been the case when Brandt was Commander of the Federation Air Force.

"I am calling to give you formal notice that we are invoking Article 15 of the European Federation Constitution."

Brandt sat there in stunned silence. Article 15 was the provision for a member state to withdraw. Since, at present, there was only two-member states, it meant that France was acting to dissolve the European Federation.

"I am sorry, President Morel, I fear I may not have heard you correctly. Would you repeat that please?"

"Yes," Morel replied. "I said we are invoking Article 15. The French Republic is giving notice that we are withdrawing from the Federation. In addition, we are demanding immediate return of all of our strategic military assets, with immediate effect. The French Military will no longer acknowledge your orders."

"Are you mad!" Brandt screamed into the phone.

"No General, I am not mad. Your recent actions have placed every citizen of the Federation at catastrophic risk. We cannot stand by while you take us to the brink of nuclear annihilation. I am holding a press conference in fifteen minutes to announce our actions. We are taking these actions to protect the French people. I will leave it to the German people to do what they will with you."

"You are out of your mind!" he screamed again. "You are throwing away a grand vision and years of work!"

"No, General Brandt, you are throwing those things away."

"I will not stand for this!" Brandt replied. He took a deep breath and regained his composure. He realized that screaming at the French President was not going to be productive. He forced himself to calm down and regain his command voice. "President Morel, we will not return command of your strategic weapons to you, at least until such time as you and I can meet and discuss a more appropriate and diplomatic resolution to our differences. In the meantime, any uniformed French soldier who does not obey orders will be arrested in accordance with the Federation's Uniform Military Code of Conduct."

"Then you are going to have to arrest a great number of French men and women, General Brandt. As for our nuclear weapons physically under your control, now would be the appropriate time for me to reveal to you that they were all equipped with a failsafe device before being moved to German soil. The devices have been remotely locked down, rendering the weapons inoperative. We will be aware if you attempt to tamper with them, so I suggest you do not. I suggest the two of us cooperate in effecting a de-escalation."

Brandt was stunned. He attempted to hold back his rage but was failing. "I'll tell you how I'll de-escalate, you pompous, wine-swilling ass! I'm going to sortie a couple of Rafales equipped with the rail guns and pay a visit to a few of your air bases. That should improve your cooperation!"

"I regret that we have come to this point, General Brandt. I did not expect you to react in such a reckless manner to what I said. I am afraid your behavior reinforces our decision. As to your threat, I can assure you that will be quite impossible. The former Federation Rafales equipped with the rail gun technology are in French air space as we speak, headed to one of our bases. They are now fully under French control."

"What?" Brandt screaming into the phone again. "Under whose orders?"

"Good day, General," the French President replied, then disconnected the call.

Brandt was standing now, clutching the telephone's receiver so hard his knuckles were white. He slammed the phone back into its cradle, and yelled out across his office to his secretary, "Get me General Laurent!"

Chapter 65 – At the Precipice

Aboard the English Attack Submarine HMS Astute, S119, in The English Channel

"Conn, Radio!" announced the excited voice of a sailor over the MC1, or Main Circuit 1, the boat's public address system.

"Radio, Conn, aye" replied the Submarine's Executive Officer, the watch officer on duty.

"Sir, we are being hailed by a French Submarine, the Pearle," said the boat's radio man.

"Get the Captain to the Conn!" shouted the Executive Officer.

"Aye, sir," said the Chief of the Boat, who picked up a handset to call the Captain's cabin.

"Sonar, Conn, where are they, and why the hell am I hearing about a Federation attack boat's presence for the first time from *their* Captain?" the Astute's Captain shouted in an angry voice.

"Conn, sonar. Designate target Sierra One. The Pearle is 1,500 meters aft and travelling at a 30-degree angle to our course at 20 knots. They must have been in our baffles, sir. The boat just started cavitating . They just changed direction and increased speed."

"They're announcing their presence," the Captain observed. "But why? I'm not taking chances! Weapons, Conn. Prepare tubes 2 and 4, lock firing solutions, keep outer doors closed for now."

"Weapons, Aye."

"Put the Pearle through," the Exec said as he removed a handset from its cradle mounted next his watch station.

"Conn, Radio, the call is patched."

"Sonar, Conn. Ping this guy! I want him to know we are serious! One ping only."

"Conn, Sonar, Aye. Engaging active sonar. Firing one ping."

He pressed the mute button and said, "This should be interesting," then unmuted the handset and said, "This is the Executive Officer of Her Majesty's submarine, Astute. Identify yourself and declare intentions."

The Executive Officer listened intently as a heavily French-accented voice began speaking in the earpiece.

"HMS Astute, this is the Captain of the French Submarine Pearle. I have been instructed to contact you and report that this vessel is now under the command of French President Gaston Morel. We are no longer under the command of the European Federation and will not acknowledge their orders. We represent no threat and have been ordered to surface and return to France. Our alert status has been lowered to DefCon 4. We are further instructed to no longer regard British or American forces as potential hostiles."

"What the hell is going on?" the Executive Officer demanded.

"I do not know anything more than what I just revealed to you," replied the French Captain. "That, sir, I am certain, is presently a topic of discussion among our respective National Command Authorities."

"Very well," the British Captain replied. "Proceed as indicated. The Astute will stand down from Alert 1 as soon as we confirm you are at a distance of 20,000 meters."

"Very well, Captain, and thank you. We wish you well as our respective commands sort out this mess."

It had all happened very quickly, and was essentially over by the time the Captain made it to the Conn. For a second time a British sub had almost fired a shot in anger. The Exec shuttered at the thought. He would have been perfectly in his right to fire on the French boat. It was a logical conclusion that the Pearle, appearing suddenly out of nowhere, was demonstrating hostile intent. The French Captain had made a mistake by announcing his presence so suddenly, and especially while behind the Astute in what any submarine Commander would regard as an ideal firing position. But the British Officer had hesitated and decided to answer the other submarines hail, hoping it wasn't a trap. The next time, the next Captain, from either side, he thought, might not show the same hesitation. That was the problem with brinksmanship. You quickly lose control of events, and mistakes are made with potentially catastrophic consequences.

As the Captain made it to the Command Station, he shouted an order, "Dive Officer, bring her up to antenna depth. We need to report this to Fleet immediately." He then offered a question everyone found chilling. "Ok, so the French have pulled back. But what about the damn Germans?"

Situation Room, The White House, Washington D.C.

President Ellison sat in his normal place at the head of the conference table. Unlike the new President's first meeting in the Situation Room, he was no longer flanked by his two sycophants from the Office of the Vice President. Director Shevchenko had told both SecDef Hagenlocker and General Weatherby about her confrontation in the hall with the young aide she had dressed down as "Sonny". All three had gotten a huge laugh at the encounter and started referring to the two of them as "Sonny 1" and "Sonny 2". Ellison was now flanked by SecState Epsy to his right and Hagenlocker to his left. General Weatherby, the Joint Chief's Chairman, sat to the right of Hagenlocker, and Shevchenko sat next to him. Perhaps the young President was learning, she mused. No, reality check, that's probably too much to hope for.

"Carl," the President began, directing his comments to Secretary of State Carleton Epsy, "please share with the team what you just told me."

The Secretary of State spoke. "One hour ago, we received notice from the Office of French President Morel that he wishes to phone the President about a matter of great importance. We have arranged to have the call piped in here, and it is scheduled to begin in 15 minutes. We also understand, from the British Ambassador to the United States, that Prime Minister Boren has received a similar request and President Morel intends to call him as soon as his call to us is complete. Our best guest is there has been some sort of rift between Germany and France."

"Thoughts, people?" the President asked.

"Well, that's both good and bad," SecDef Hagenlocker responded. "On the one hand, that will clearly weaken the European Federation, and could even signal its demise. France could be contemplating anything from a public protest, a lack of agreement with the recent military coup, all the way to a formal withdrawal under Article 15 of their charter. The bad news, and I'm afraid in the short term it could be very bad news indeed, is what it does to further de-stabilize Germany and how they might respond. My fear is it creates a greater risk of a German miscalculation and some sort of rash action."

"C.I.A. agrees with that analysis, Mr. President," Shevchenko replied. "We fear in the short-term this is very de-stabilizing."

The conversation was interrupted by a buzz on the conference intercom. The Situation Room's communications technician announced, "President Morel of France is on the line. He apparently decided not to wait the declared 15 minutes."

"Put him through," the President replied.

In a couple of seconds, the French President appeared on the large video screen. He began speaking to the group in English. "Good day and thank you for helping arrange this call. The French people have found recent events to be very troubling. We categorically reject the assertion that the European Federation is responsible for the missile attack on Iran, and believe you are in possession of evidence that will prove that. I ask you to make that publicly available as quickly as possible so we may put this issue behind us and so we can find and prosecute whoever is guilty in this horrific matter. Having said that, France cannot stand by and accept the recent actions of Federation political leaders, which we regard as essentially a military coup. Consequently, just his morning I telephoned acting Chancellor Brandt to provide formal notice of the withdrawal of the Republic of France from the Federation under the provisions of Article 15. Since there are presently only two members of the Federation, our action will bring it to an end. In addition, as Commander in Chief of the French military, I have ordered all French forces to obey orders from the French National Command Authority. I have ordered the Federation to return French assets to French soil, including our strategic arsenals. The French military alert status has been reduced to DefCon 4, and we have instructed all of our forces to no longer regard United States or British military forces as potentially hostile. Much work remains to be done to consummate the withdrawal of France from the Federation, but we believe it is important that you understand our resumption of sole authority over our military is effective immediately."

There were several seconds of silence as the group processed what the French President had just said. Finally, the President spoke.

"How did the German's take it?" the President asked. "And how do you think they will respond?"

"General Brandt did not take it well, as you might imagine. But we are also convinced that General Brandt does not speak for the German people. We believe in the long term this will be well-received."

"Have they agreed to repatriate your strategic weapons?" General Weatherby asked.

"No, they have not. Whatever was portable, such as our aircraft and naval vessels, are being moved as we speak, and the Germans have not yet interfered. Repatriation of our strategic weapons I expect to be more problematic."

"Are they still able to deploy them?" Weatherby asked.

"My Generals tell me no. All nuclear weapons have remote lock-down devices that should have de-activated them."

"Should have?" Weatherby asked.

"Nothing in life is certain, is it, General? We believe there is a very low probability that the weapons can be detonated, but control systems are nothing more than sophisticated plumbing systems for electrons. If you can find a clever plumber to rearrange the pipes, you can redirect those electrons to go wherever you need them to reactive systems. No matter what your scientists tell you, no system is truly fail-safe."

"And there are a lot of clever plumbers out there," Weatherby observed.

"Yes, there are," Morel responded. "I doubt clever enough, at least today, but one never knows."

"And in the short-term?" President Ellison asked. "My second question, how do you think they will respond in the short-term?"

"I do not know, Mr. President. We had no other moral choice than to invoke Article 15, but this is clearly destabilizing. Russian troops are massing on their eastern border, and while I don't believe even Putin is crazy enough to launch an invasion, I do know the Russians are very wary right now and their response is unpredictable. I suspect the massing of troops is just for show, but a strategic action on their part is not out of the question."

The last comment made everyone in the Situation Room shutter.

SecDef Hagenlocker then spoke up. "Mr. President," he said, addressing the French President but locking eyes with President Ellison, "under the circumstances do you remain comfortable with an alert status of only DefCon 4?"

"To be clear," the French President replied, "our alert status is bifurcated. We are at DefCon 4 with the rest of the world, including Russia, and are reaching out to each country to reassure. We have instructed our military forces to regard all German forces as if we were at DefCon 2."

General Weatherby scribbled on a legal pad and slid it in front of SecDef Hagenlocker. It read, "What could possibly go wrong?!?," followed by the word "BOOM!"

The conversation was interrupted again by a buzz on the Situation Room's intercom. The President muted the call, and the communications technician announced, "Mr. President, Prime Minister Boren is on the line. He says it's urgent."

"Tell him to hold, briefly, please."

The President unmuted the call. "Good luck, President Morel. These are dangerous times. Is there anything else?"

"No, Mr. President, and thank you. I actually have to go. I have many more of these phone calls to make. Godspeed."

"Godspeed to you as well, Mr. President." The call to the French President was disconnected, then Ellison said, "Please put the Prime Minister through."

"President Ellison," the Prime Minister said, as he appeared on the video screen.

"Jeremy," the President replied.

"Mr. President, one of our subs in the Channel was just hailed by a French attack boat and informed they had been placed back under the sole command of the French National Command Authority. The French Captain was sloppy about how he made his presence known, and our sub Commander almost blew him out of the water. We almost came to blows with the French!" he exclaimed. "Fortunately, our man hesitated, and that hesitation saved the day. The situation is becoming very unstable."

That, the new President thought, along with his entire senior staff sitting in the Situation Room, was the understatement of the day.

"General Weatherby," the President said, locking eyes with the Chairman of the Joint Chiefs, "what are our plans if Germany does something rash? I want options!" he commanded.

Shevchenko was not a woman given to emotions, but the comment made her blood run cold. "This is madness," she thought. Major powers on both sides of the Atlantic were suffering from new and unstable leadership, seemingly incapable of contemplating the strategic implications of their actions. She stared at the young President as General Weatherby sat mute, and thought, “This young Turk is taking us right to the precipice, and he doesn’t have a clue.”

Chapter 66– Of Iron, Gold, and Running Out of Time

Undisclosed Location, Shanghai, China

The General Staff of the People's Liberation Army was made up of the senior leaders of the Chinese military. It was the General Staff that approved the project to hack into the Command and Control systems of both Iran and the European Federation. It was code-named "Operation Dove". Its objective was to create chaos in the Middle East, Europe and the United States, and to heighten divisions and mistrust among the nations to their west. It had worked brilliantly, although not quite in the manner they anticipated.

Iran had remotely launched a nuclear missile from Germany, believing it was headed towards Israel. China's cyber warfare group had hacked into Iran's systems and retargeted the missile to Iran's holy city of Qom. But the missile was never supposed to reach its target. The missile was supposed to be destroyed by the Germans as soon as the errant launch was detected. The idea was to make Iranians believe they had been double-crossed by the Germans and thereby drive a wedge between the two nations. The point was to stop their growing alliance, an alliance that China regarded as dangerous to China's security interests in the region. It was also supposed to drive a wedge between the European Federation and the rest of the West. It was an opportune time, given the growing world-wide suspicions about German ambitions.

But the game changed when the missile cleared its launcher and took flight. Germany, inexplicably, hadn't destroyed the missile after confirming the errant launch. China was in possession of faulty intelligence that convinced them the Germans had a fail-safe missile-destruct mechanism. What China didn't know, until it was too late, was that the Iranians had disabled that safeguard as part of their hacking efforts. Iran wanted to make sure the missile destroyed their arch-nemesis, Israel, and that Germany was saddled with the blame.

The loss of so many lives in Qom was unfortunate, but the People's Liberation Army General Staff regarded it as acceptable collateral damage. China's strategic objectives, after all, had been largely achieved. The European Federation was collapsing. Iran was on the brink of civil war, and it would be a long time before Iran would acquire a nuclear weapon. Chaos reigned among China's adversaries.

As events continued to unfold, however, they realized there could be too much of a good thing. They wanted chaos, and they achieved it. But they didn't want a global conflagration, and events seemed to be quickly spiraling in that direction. There was already a radioactive cloud drifting towards their Western provinces from the warhead's detonation over Qom. It would be largely dissipated by the time it arrived at major population centers, but a global conflagration would multiply it many-fold. That would plunge China as well into chaos and civil war. Losing control of the population was the one thing that kept the leaders of the Chinese Communist Party up at night. They regarded it as an existential risk. It was now time to cauterize the wound.

This would be accomplished by a clandestine effort to plant incriminating evidence of Iran's culpability. Iran would be conclusively shown to be responsible for the missile launch with an intended target of Israel. And there would be incontrovertible evidence, albeit false, that it was Iran's incompetence, a mistake in their targeting code, that caused the missile to over fly its target and hit Qom. Once Iran was unmasked as the culprit, the world's nuclear powers could step back from the brink, or so the Chinese hoped, and the risk of a global war would subside.

But they would also take out an insurance policy, just in case. China raised the alert level of their strategic forces to the U.S. equivalent of DefCon 2, one step short of war. And they announced a no-fly zone over the South China Sea and the Taiwan Straits with a promise of strict enforcement. So, the entire world stood at the brink of war, with the strategic weapons of every nuclear power at a hair-trigger. Suspicion and mistrust were ascendant. What could possibly go wrong?

Undisclosed Location, Shanghai, China, Cyber Warfare Command

The Commanding General of China's Cyber Warfare Command, Third Department, People's Liberation Army, stood pensively over the shoulder of First Lieutenant Danping Xu as she typed a series of commands on her keyboard. After a flurry of activity, she paused and looked up at the Commander and said, "The package is ready, sir. Shall I proceed?"

"How does it feel, Lieutenant," the General asked, "to potentially have the fate of the entire world at the tip of your index finger right now?"

She replied with an old Chinese proverb and said, *"If luck is absent, gold turn into iron, but let luck be with you and iron becomes gold."*

The General smiled. "Well, said, Lieutenant, very well said. Let us pray for gold today."

"The code is flawless, sir," she replied. "it will deliver the information we wish. How our adversaries respond, however, well, that I fear, is beyond our control."

"Indeed, it is, Lieutenant. Execute the command."

And with that, she depressed the "enter" key with her right index finger.

"Command is executed, sir."

The "Package", as the General described it, was several pieces of computer code that were transmitted and uploaded into the European Federation's Command and Control backup system as Lieutenant Xu's hit her final keystroke. One piece of code was a replica of the hacking software that allowed Iran to temporarily take control of the EF weapons system and launch the missile. It was tagged with a digital fingerprint -- an IP address that would conclusively trace it back to the Iranian Cyber Warfare Command. Another piece of code was a replica of the retargeting software that was developed with the help of the German supplier, CWR Industries, with one key difference. It was altered to show a flaw. The code would include the precise targeting coordinates for Tel Aviv, Israel, but would also contain a mistake that would cause the missile to overfly Israel, wobble its course slightly and land in Iran when it ran out of fuel. The third piece of code was a replica of the sub-routine designed to erase all three pieces immediately after the missile launch. It contained several errors that would cause it to fail, but its existence would provide conclusive evidence of Iran's attempt to cover their tracks.

The European Federation's backup and audit database kept a record of every command entered into the system. It included the names and status of authorized personnel, changes in alert levels, authorizations received from the National Command Authority, up to and including warhead arming commands, and launch orders. Most importantly, it also kept a meticulous record of all warhead targeting instructions as well as any changes made to the software itself. The "Package" would insert additional records into that backup system. Federation Military Intelligence, under the Command of General Jean-Baptiste Laurent, would find the errant code during their third review of the backup databases. They initially would be puzzled as to why they had missed it during the first two reviews. But it would provide conclusive, undeniable evidence of Iran's intention to attack Israel and their responsibility for the missile launch itself. Iran's digital fingerprints on the affair would be undeniable, and their angry and restive population on the brink of civil war would not be inclined to give the nation's leadership the benefit of the doubt.

Iron, the Chinese hoped, would soon turn to gold. But the world still stood at the brink, and the world was running out of time.

Chapter 67 -- Coincidences

European Defense Ministry, Berlin, Germany

General Jean-Baptiste Laurent was a man impaled on the horns of a dilemma. French President Morel had ordered him to return to Paris and no longer regard himself as an officer of the European Federation Defense Force. Laurent had argued with his President that, as one of the few remaining voices of restraint, pulling him out now would be counterproductive and potentially dangerous. Acting Chancellor Brandt was isolated among a small group of confidants, and his behavior was becoming increasingly unpredictable. His presence was needed, Laurent argued, to prevent the man from doing something crazy, and crazy was the order of the day. The two men had settled on a compromise. He could stay in Berlin temporarily, as a "transition advisor" to the new government as it worked through the Federation's dissolution and the messy details of separating the German and French militaries from their former unified command. He could stay for perhaps as much as several weeks, if necessary. But French President Morel made it clear that, if circumstances deteriorated further, there would be no appeal against the next recall.

Laurent had another reason he wanted to stay. He was in the middle of a third review of the EF Command and Control backup systems, trying to determine if they had missed something. He had a team of French military cyber specialists looking at every line of code. They knew they had been hacked. The intel from the raid on CWR Industries had all but confirmed it, but the evidence was circumstantial. It proved they were developing the capability, but it didn't prove they had used it. Iran would continue to deny culpability until presented with incontrovertible evidence that they actually had penetrated EF systems. That evidence had to be there somewhere, he kept telling himself. It was inconceivable to him they could get inside EF systems and not leave any digital fingerprints whatsoever. He wouldn't rest until his team found them. And he knew that once he surrendered his credentials and left Berlin, he would be permanently locked out of the EF defense systems and unable to do further investigative work.

Acting Chancellor Brandt remained furious with Laurent about not being told the French nuclear warheads had lock-out codes installed before they were transferred to Germain soil. Laurent had pushed back by telling him it was an arrangement worked out between the two heads of state, Morel and Krüger, of which he too had been kept in the dark. It temporarily satiated Brandt's rage, but the Acting Chancellor now regarded Laurent with contempt. Laurent didn't care. He had only two objectives – comb every line of code in their system to make absolutely certain no incriminating evidence was missed and keep the mad man, presently occupying the Chancellor's office, from doing anything reckless.

Laurent's thoughts were interrupted by the ring of his phone. He picked up the receiver and heard the voice of a young female French Army Lieutenant, the officer overseeing the digital forensic analysts who were combing the archives of the EF Command and Control Backup systems.

"General Laurent, you need to get down here immediately!" she exclaimed.

"What have you found?" he asked, reacting to the urgency in her voice suggesting it was something very important.

"Just get here quickly sir, please."

"I'll be right there," he said, then quickly exited his office and headed to the computer facility with a newfound sense of urgency.

It took about fifteen minutes for the Lieutenant to explain their process and review the findings. The Chinese had done a magnificent job of planting the evidence. Laurent was astonished at what they had found. It was a "smoking gun", as the Americans would say.

"How did we miss this during the first two reviews?" he asked.

"I don't know, sir," she responded. "I've checked all of our logbooks and the sign-offs. I signed off on these particular reviews myself. It's almost as if the evidence appeared out of thin air."

"So, are you suggesting it may have been planted?" he asked, thinking the same thing himself.

"We've checked everything, sir. There have been no security breaches, so that rules out third-party interference. There are no external ports on the backup systems, so nobody could have done it from the inside either by, for example, inserting a USB keyfob and downloading fake data. Besides, these computers have almost the same level of security as the weapons they control. We even use the 'two-person rule'; nobody is allowed to enter the server room alone. There must be two, so collusion would have been necessary if the servers had data input ports."

"What about the closed-circuit cameras?" he asked. "Anything suspicious from reviewing the footage?"

"We haven't reviewed the footage, sir. You are talking about at least a week of 24/7 recording, and we don't have the time. Besides, like I said, I think it's a very low probability that it was an inside job."

"You're right," Laurent replied. "What troubles me is it's almost like we've been handed a gift."

"Exactly what I thought, sir."

"OK, so this puts a bow on it in a way that is almost impossible for Iran to deny. I won't 'look a gift horse in the mouth', as the Americans would say. I need to get this information this to the right people as quickly as possible."

"General Brandt?" she asked.

"No, not the Acting Chancellor. At least not yet."

"Then may I ask who, sir?"

"It's better if you don't know, Lieutenant."

"I understand, sir."

"One more thing," Laurent said. "Under no circumstances are you to speak of these matters to anyone outside this room. Neither you nor any of your people are to mention it. If asked, just lie. You are all to play dumb. You've found nothing, understood?"

"Yes sir."

"Lieutenant, I need you to do something very unusual and to trust me. Can you do that?" he asked.

She looked at him skeptically. "What is that, sir?"

"I need you to put this information on a USB key, right now, and give it to me."

Several seconds passed as the two French officers looked at each other. Laurent thought he could detect the slight presence of perspiration on her forehead.

"Yes sir," she finally responded, as she turned to complete the task just asked of her. After several seconds, she handed him the small device. It was a USB key equipped with two "male" jacks – the standard USP jack and an Apple "Lightening" jack. The "Lightening" jack allowed it to be used with an iPad or iPhone. Laurent placed the device in his pocket and turned to leave. As he approached the door he paused, turned, and looking at the young Lieutenant said, "This sudden discovery was most convenient, wasn't it, Lieutenant?"

"Yes, sir, it certainly was."

"I don't believe in coincidences, Lieutenant, do you?"

"No, sir, I do not."

"On the other hand, neither will I turn down the equivalent of a winning lottery ticket," he said.

"I just hope, sir, there's enough time left to cash it in," she said, in a sobering voice.

"So do I," he said, then walked out the door.

Laurent headed towards his vehicle instead of his office. He needed to make a couple of phone calls, he needed to make them quickly, and he needed to make them in private. First he would call his old friend, Marcus Day, and tell him what he just learned, then transmit a copy of the digital file he had just received. Day would know how to get the information to the Director of the U.S. Central Intelligence Agency. Next, he would call the French President, Gaston Morel, and tell him. Then and only then would he approach Brandt with the news. That should be an interesting conversation, he thought, as he walked out the door and headed towards his car.

It was a beautiful day. As he walked outside the sun was shining, there was a gentle breeze and the temperature was a mild 74 degrees. It was the kind of day that could really lift a man's spirits were it not for the enormous weight Laurent felt upon his shoulders. It seemed as if the entire world was going mad. As he walked up to his vehicle, he felt almost depressed. If he knew how his next 24 hours were about to unfold, he would have felt a great deal worse.

Chapter 68 – Another Mission

Director's Office, 7th Floor, Central Intelligence Agency, Langley, Virginia

The three of them sat at the conference table across from the Director's expansive desk. Classical music, a Mozart violin concerto, played softly through the built-in sound system. A laptop computer sat in front of Director Shevchenko; a USB key plugged into one of the ports on its side. All three remained silent as the Director slowly and deliberately read the contents of a file on the laptop's screen. It was the "Executive Summary of Findings", prepared by the young French Lieutenant who worked for General Laurent. It laid out the evidence of Iranian duplicity the French had found in the European Federation Command and Control backup and audit systems. Attached to it was a copy of the actual code uploaded to the system that allowed Iran to retarget and launch the missile with the nuclear warhead that destroyed the city of Qom, Iran. After about ten minutes, she had enough.

She looked up from the screen and glanced at Joe Barber, then Marcus Day, then spoke, "This is powerful stuff, if it's true. Problem is, it also strikes me as pretty convenient. How do we know it's not manufactured?"

Day answered, "Their systems have a very disciplined audit trail. Federation backup systems keep a record of all changes in the Command and Control System Computer Code. The record includes a date and time stamp of when the change is made and a digital fingerprint that identifies the source. The time stamp on the rogue code was approximately two hours before we detected missile launch. Laurent assures me there is no way to backdate the time stamp without a separate hack, which would also have been recorded by the backup system. The digital fingerprint itself is comprised of two pieces. The first is an approval code, a unique 8-digit alpha numeric sequence that is random, changed daily, and resident in the system itself. It authenticates that the software change has been approved. The system checks the code contained in the new software against the day's authorization code already resident in the system, and if the two don't match, the new software doesn't get uploaded and an alarm is sounded."

"But if the EF controls the code," Shevchenko interrupted, "doesn't that give the EF the ability to plant evidence?"

"No, it doesn't. Nobody knows the code. The codes are generated inside the system. No human touches the code, and nobody sees the code until 24 hours after the change, unless two don't match and an alarm is sounded. It's not like somebody can look it up and enter it on a keyboard. And bear with me, the second part of the digital fingerprint also rules out planted evidence."

"What's that?" she asked.

"The second piece of the digital fingerprint is the identity of the source of the software change – where it came from. It's the IP address, in other words the internet address, of the source. It's an audit trail requirement, so it has to be there. If the field is blank, the software won't upload. But here's the point. The source code can't be input by whomever is making the change – the system must read it automatically from the source. That's the only way the field gets populated. And the system will only accept a software upload If there is both a correct authorization code and a legitimate source IP address."

"Ok, but I'm still confused about something. You told me the EF systems generate the approval codes, and it's automatic, there's no human intervention."

"Correct."

"So how, then, would the Iranian's get ahold of the daily code? If they uploaded this software into the Federation system through a computer hack, how did they get a correct authorization code into the digital fingerprint? Wouldn't the system reject it?"

"Exactly the right questions, Maggie," Barber chimed in. "Guess who designed the security system for software changes?"

"Oh my God," she exclaimed, as it dawned on her. "CWR Industries."

"Exactly," Day replied.

"Ok, that's compelling, but forgive me guys, this still seems just a bit too convenient. Why would the Iranians be so sloppy and leave bread crumbs?"

"They wouldn't," Day answered. "I guess you stopped reading before you got to the last couple of pages of General Laurent's 'Summary of Findings' document, right?"

"Correct. What did I miss?"

"There was another piece of software they found that had nothing to do with launching or retargeting the missile."

"What was that?" she asked

"It was software code designed to erase any evidence of the Iranian's presence in the EF Command and Control system," Day responded. "That rogue code was supposed to digitally 'blow itself up', if you'll forgive the unfortunate phrase. It was supposed to erase itself immediately after it confirmed a missile launch."

"You mean nobody was supposed to see the rogue software Laurent discovered?" Shevchenko asked.

"That's correct," Day answered. "All of it was supposed to disappear like a vapor in a hurricane."

"Then what happened? Laurent obviously found it, and we just looked at it."

"You're not going to believe this," Day said, forcing back a smile.

"What?" she asked.

"There was a typo in that piece of the code. It didn't work. The rogue software, therefore, was never erased. That part of the uploaded software didn't execute."

Shevchenko looked back and forth at Barber and Day, then took a deep cleansing breath, blowing it out slowly for effect, as she shook her head in bewilderment at what she was just told. "So, hundreds of millions of dollars of sophisticated computer equipment, along with countless hours of work by what, no doubt, are some of the brightest hacker minds on the planet, and Iran's plan to attack Israel is foiled, and they get caught with their pants down, by human error?"

"Yes," Barber answered. "If it really was an error."

"What is that supposed to mean?" Shevchenko asked, surprised by the comment.

"Well, no, I don't think Iran deliberately attacked itself. But I have suspicions that there is much more to this mystery than meets the eye."

"Yeah, I have the same suspicion. But let's keep a lid on it until we have solid evidence. Raising conspiracy theories prematurely is just going to make people skeptical."

"I completely agree," Barber replied.

Shevchenko looked at Marcus Day and said, "Give us a minute, will you Marc?"

"Yes, Ma'am," Day replied, then stood up and walked out of the office, leaving Shevchenko and Barber alone.

"So, how are you doing, Joe? Another attempt on your life means someone regards you as unfinished business. Are the police looking into it?"

"I'm OK, Maggie, thanks for asking. Yeah, the police are investigating. A shootout in downtown Rye, New York tends to get a lot of attention. It was a pro, though, so they'll never find anything."

"We know who's behind it," she said.

Barber was stunned, and just stared at her in disbelief for several seconds. "What did you just say?"

"I said we know who's behind it."

"Would you care to share that information? Who is he?" he asked, in a tone that was one part seriousness and one part irritation.

"Who is *she*," Shevchenko corrected. "It's a she. Her name is Emma Clark. She's the Chief Executive Officer of a private equity firm on the west coast. Big player on the Hill – owns half the politicians inside the Beltway."

"How did you find out?" Barber asked.

"That's above your paygrade," the Director answered.

"Where is she?" Barber asked.

"That's the problem. We planned to arrest her yesterday, but she's disappeared, or so she thinks. She's hiding at an estate she owns in Mendoza, Argentina."

"Why are you telling me this? Arrest her for what?"

"Suspicion of treason. Here's the thing, if we rendition an American citizen from Argentina and put her on trial here, well, things could get very messy."

"What are you asking me to do?"

"I'm not asking you to do anything. I'm suggesting we have aligned objectives at the moment."

"Why does a private equity executive want me dead, and how do you know it's her?"

"As to how we know, Joseph, you know I can't tell you that. But I can assure you we know. I can also tell you that she, or more accurately a colleague of hers, was behind the attempts on your life three years ago when you got sucked into that Project Sparrow disaster. And I have reason to believe the same former colleague was responsible for the attempt on your life in Qatar more than a decade ago, although the evidence is not as conclusive on that one, at least not yet."

"Who is the former colleague?"

"He's dead, so his name is not important."

Barber just sat there and stared at his former mentor. His head was spinning. She walked over to a wall, opened a safe, and retrieved a large sealed envelope. She walked back to the conference table and laid it down in front of him.

"This envelope contains information you may find interesting, and dare I say, useful. It also contains enough cash for a first-class round-trip airline ticket to Buenos Aire along with miscellaneous expenses. I don't suggest you travel in your company plane. I wouldn't travel under your real name, either. You'll find an alternate passport in that envelope as well. Walk out of here with that envelope and you have my sanction to prosecute our mutual interests as you see fit. No questions asked. Or leave it on the table. No harm, no foul."

Barber sat at the conference table and stared at the envelope for several seconds. He then picked it up, stood, turned and started to walk out the door. Just before he passed through the now open doorway, he turned, and paused. "Thanks, Maggie."

"Be careful, my friend."

Day was standing in Shevchenko's outer office, talking to her secretary. As Barber walked past him, he simply said, "Let's go." He remained quiet for the first minute or two as they walked towards the elevator to take them back to the lobby.

Day asked, "What's up, partner? You're awfully quiet."

"You're not going to believe it," Barber answered.

"Believe what?" Day asked.

"We're headed to Argentina. Buenos Aires. And you're going to need one of your alternate passports."

"What?"

Chapter 69 – Spiraling Out of Control

Oval Office, The White House, Washington D.C.

President Ellison was afraid. Events seemed to be spiraling out of control and he didn't know what to do. Over the few short days he had been President, meetings in the Situation Room had become his nightmare. He was insightful enough to realize that everyone the room was likely smarter than he, to say nothing of being more experienced. It made him feel very small, even vulnerable. It felt like every time he opened his mouth he was challenged. He was certain that at least one or two of cabinet-level people in the room had rolled their eyes at something he had said. He was President of the United States, the most powerful person on Earth, yet he felt like every time he walked into that damn room he was getting a performance review. He had taken keen notice of how cabinet officers reacted to President Einhorn before she died. Some treated her with respect. Others hated her, but still treated the office she held with respect. Some faked respect out of fear. But it was clear to him that nobody in that room respected him, let alone feared him. It made him angry, and he decided to do something about it. He only wished he knew what, but he determined to look for the opportunity. He stood up from the Resolute Desk and picked up his leather folder as he prepared to go to the Situation Room for the next crisis meeting. His eyes surveyed the majesty of the Oval Office, and he reminded himself that this was now *his* space. He was President of the United States, and he was going to make sure every one of those pompous asses in that meeting knew it.

Situation Room, The White House, Washington D.C.

"What do we have, people," the President asked in his best command voice.

"Mr. President," Dr. Margaret Shevchenko replied, "we just received very important intelligence from French military officers still in Berlin and……"

The President cut her off. "Why are French officers still in Berlin. Morel told us all French forces were recalled."

Shevchenko took a breath and fought back the irritation in her voice. "That's correct, sir. There is still a small cohort of French military there to manage the transition to separate command structures as well as to complete the digital forensics review of the Federation computer systems. As I was about to say, the forensics review found rogue computer code buried deep inside their Command and Control systems. It provides conclusive and incontrovertible proof that Iran hacked into their systems and launched the missile. As you know, the evidence we received in the raid on CWR Industries only demonstrated that Iran had the capability. This new evidence proves they actually did it. It is as good as a smoking gun."

President Ellison looked at SecDef Hagenlocker and said, "If it's really a smoking gun, we must respond. We must attack Iran. Do we have a plan for that?"

"For an attack on Iran?" General Weatherby, the Chairman of the Joint Chiefs, asked, incredulously.

"I asked the Secretary, General," Ellison snapped. "Burt, do we have a plan?"

There was an uncomfortable pause as several of the attendees looked at each other with expressions of disbelief. SecDef Hagenlocker broke the silence and said, "No, Mr. President, we do not have a plan for a retaliatory attack on Iran. First, we, the United States, are not a principal in the conflict. Iran and the European Federation are. Or, more accurately, at this point Iran and Germany are. Germany is hardly going to conduct a military strike on Iran when Iran is in the middle of dealing with nuclear holocaust, one that Germany still stands accused of perpetrating. Striking Iran under such circumstances would make a pariah out of any country that did it, especially Germany. The role of the United States in all of this must be to de-escalate, not to punish."

President Ellison's face was now flushed from equal parts anger and embarrassment. He was spared from having to immediately respond to the SecDef's comments by an interruption from the Situation Room's media coordinator. "Mr. President, Prime Minister Boren of England is on the line and is asking to be patched into the meeting. He says it's urgent."

"Put him through," the President responded, with a feeling of relief. In just a few seconds the Prime Minister's face appeared on the large screen at the end of the conference table.

The President spoke, "Jeremy, tell us what's going on."

"Mr. President, thanks for taking my call. You will recall our recent conversation when I advised you that one of our subs was hailed by a French submarine and told they had been instructed to no longer regard English or American Forces as hostile?"

"Yes, of course," the President answered. "What's happened?"

"Apparently the Germans are taking a different tack. One of their destroyers in the Channel just depth-charged the same English submarine, the Astute. Fortunately, our Captain kept his cool and made the decision not to fire, then escaped."

"Have you talked to General Brandt?" the Secretary of Defense asked, drawing a stern look from the President for stepping in front of him.

"I have tried, but he is not returning our calls. Has the United States has not been attacked by German forces as of yet?"

"No, Jeremy, we have not," Ellison answered. "But if we are, I am not sure I am comfortable with showing the same restraint."

"Mr. President, I strongly urge you to do so. The situation in Germany is very fluid right now. We remain convinced that Brandt's actions don't represent the will of the German people or even much of his military. It is important that we do not escalate."

"It's also important that we show resolve, don't you agree? In fact, I think you and I need to make a joint statement that an attack on any member of the Western Alliance will be regarded as an attack on the United States and England and will be responded with all necessary means."

The Prime Minister looked stunned. "I believe that would be exceedingly unwise, Mr. President, and potentially back us into a corner."

Shevchenko knew somebody had to "bell the cat" and get the President to start thinking with his brain and not his glands. She decided to take control of the meeting, whatever the consequences. She said, "Mr. Prime Minister, you raise some good points worthy of consideration. Give us some time here to more fully discuss our position, and we can then call you back."

The English Prime Minister fought back a slight smile, relieved that a "calm head" had pulled this new and inexperienced President back from a foolish decision. "That sounds like an excellent idea, Madam Director. Let's be deliberate in our thinking. We can't afford to bugger this up to a fare-thee-well. Mr. President, I'll leave you with your team. In the mean-time, we are agreed that both of us will maintain cool heads. Talk to you soon." The screen went blank. As the Prime Minister ended the call, he couldn't help but wonder what kind of wrath Margaret Shevchenko was about to experience from the new President. One thing he knew for certain, however; in a one-on-one against Margaret Shevchenko, Charles "Boomer" Ellison was hopelessly outmatched.

Office of the Chancellor, European Federation, Berlin, Germany

Acting Chancellor of the European Federation, Horst Brandt, felt the pressure of walls that were increasingly closing in on him. His inner circle was growing smaller. He had just digested the news that his Minister of Justice, a cabinet position comparable to the Attorney General of the United States, was having second thoughts about the legality of invoking Article 15, the removal of EF Chancellor Zimmerman from office and replacing him with Brandt. The man had been one of Brandt's supporters, albeit a seemingly reluctant one, but now was morphing into a potential adversary. And he wasn't Brandt's most serious challenge.

The Chancellor of Germany was making the argument that the EF would soon dissolve because of France's withdrawal. It would no longer exist. After all, he argued, a Federation must have at least two members to be a Federation. Consequently, the position Brandt held, Chancellor of the EF, would also soon no longer exist. It was imperative, the German Chancellor argued, they begin transition immediately and that all decisions going forward be made by the German Chancellor, not the EF Chancellor. Brandt was furious. He argued the French withdrawal was illegal, or at a minimum could not be legally finalized until the Article 14 process for member secession was certified as complete. He was determined to put this arrogant rival for power in his place, and he was determined to foil France's withdrawal.

Brandt was increasingly angry, short-tempered and unpredictable. Other heads of state, from the United States, England, Russia and other nations didn't trust him. This was the geopolitical background, temperamental leaders who didn't trust each other, as the world edged ever closer to the brink of a new global war.

Situation Room, The White House, Washington D.C.

"What the hell was that!?" President Ellison screamed at Director Shevchenko. "How dare you cut off my conversation with the English Prime Minister! I'm the President, not you!"

Everyone else in the room remained calm at the outburst. Shevchenko all but expected it, and she didn't care. She looked at the President and began to speak to him in a calm and measured voice. "We are your team, Mr. President. We are all here to help you. I know Jeremy Boren and I know his temper. My intention was to spare you from a display of it. It would have been counterproductive. I defused the situation and bought us time for a measured response." It was mostly a lie, at least the part of protecting the new President from Boren's temper, but she thought it sounded good. She continued. "Joint statements of the nature you just suggested have potentially enormous consequences, and I think it's important to remember Burt's comment from a few minutes ago. We are not a principal in this conflict. Neither the EF or Germany has even threatened the United States at this point. It's prudent to be wary, but not aggressive. A statement such as the one you just voiced would be viewed as an escalation, and it could make us a principal in the conflict. We must remain a neutral third party as long as is possible to retain our ability to mediate and de-escalate."

"Well said, Margaret," SecState Epsyy commented.

"Very well said," commented General Weatherby.

President Ellison's face remained red, but not as flushed as two minutes ago. He responded, "Ok, but I want to retain the option of my joint statement as a fall back plan." It was a face-saving comment, and everyone in the room let it pass without comment, although a few took note of his contradiction – *"my"* and *"joint* statement".

Chapter 70 – A Profile in Courage

En Route to the Office of the Chancellor, European Federation, Berlin, Germany

As General Jean-Baptiste Laurent walked through the lobby of the EF Chancellery he steeled himself. He knew he was walking towards what was likely the most consequential moment of his professional career. He did not know what the outcome would be, but knew that, whatever happened, he would be faithful to the oath he swore so many years ago as a cadet on the plain of The École spéciale militaire de Saint-Cyr, the French military academy. Duty, Honor, Country were not the exclusive values of the Americans.

He had a carefully laid-out plan, but as he had learned early and often during the fog of war, plans seldom survive first contact with the enemy. He hated to think in those terms about this meeting, to think of the Acting Chancellor as his enemy. General Horst Brandt was a man he had once respected, a former mentor, almost at times a friend, and a senior leader of a nation he still considered an ally. But there was no other way to characterize what he was about to do. He was entering a battlefield to engage the enemy. He was about to cross the line of departure. He prayed he could defeat the enemy with the power of his words, but he wasn't sure.

Laurent had asked for an audience with the Chancellor and his senior cabinet members under the guise of presenting the recently discovered evidence of Iran's complicity in the missile launch. Briefing them on the information was his duty as a senior military leader, and he knew they would be very interested in it. The subject matter would guarantee an audience, otherwise he knew that Brandt wouldn't give him the time of day. Once he got in front of the group, however, his real mission was to challenge them on their aggressive military posture. It was pushing the world to the brink of a global conflagration. He would argue that the incontrovertible evidence against Iran gave them license to pull back from the brink. He prayed that the more rational voices of Brandt's cabinet ministers would prevail. If that didn't happen, he had a plan B.

General Jean-Baptiste Laurent walked up to the security checkpoint and presented his credentials. He looked resplendent in his full-dress uniform, bedecked with nine rows of ribbons and even the ceremonial officer's sidearm on his hip, under a leather holster polished to the shine of a mirror. Everyone recognized him. He was one of the top 5 senior officers in the EF military and extremely popular for his unique combination of an outsized sense of humor and absolute serenity under stress. There were about ten people in the security line being processed for entry into the inner sanctum of the building. His position, however, provided him with certain advantages. He was ushered around the metal detector and walked through a gate into the secure area without being scanned. The leather briefcase handcuffed to his wrist was not disturbed. The security officer saluted him as he walked past the checkpoint and headed to the bank of elevators that would take him up to the office of the Chancellor. The salute was not required in the security lounge. It was offered voluntarily as a show of respect, and the look on the security officer's face spoke volumes. The man was sad.

As Laurent rode up the private elevator, he steeled himself. This was no time for self-doubt. As the elevator reached the top floor, there was a quiet chime as the doors opened. Laurent stepped out and surveyed the surroundings. The doors to the Chancellor's office suite were directly in front of him. He walked up to the security desk where an armed guard stood, saluted him, then waved him in. As he walked past the guard, he heard the guard whisper *"Geh mitt Gott, General",* or "Go with God, General".

Office of the Chancellor, European Federation, Berlin, Germany

"General Laurent, come in," Brandt said, coldly, as he saw the Frenchman enter his office. "Please join us."

Laurent entered the office and took the open seat next to Brandt's position at the head of the conference table.

"I am told General Laurent is a now 'transition officer', pending his recall to France. Tell me, General Laurent, what exactly is a transition officer?"

Laurent ignored the question, which was clearly intended as an insult.

"So, what sort of evidence do you have for us, my French General," Brandt asked in a patronizing tone. "Tell us quickly please, before you run back home, where I am sure your presence is much needed. Do you know, gentlemen," he said, now addressing the other men in the room, "how many Frenchmen it takes to defend Paris? Nobody knows! It's never been done!" he laughed heartily at the overt insult of a tired joke. Laurent sat stone-faced, unfazed by the slight, while the rest of the men in the room remained silent and shifted uncomfortably in their chairs. "OK, tell us what you have."

Laurent unlocked the briefcase from his wrist, opened it, retrieved several copies of the Summary of Findings document prepared by his staff and passed them around the table. He then proceeded to take the next several minutes going through the key points that proved Iran had taken over their weapons systems and launched a missile intending to hit Tel Aviv, Israel. The men around the table, including Brandt himself, sat stunned and silent as Laurent presented what was now clear evidence. He was initially encouraged by their reaction, although the encouragement would quickly fade for reasons he had not anticipated.

Laurent continued, "As you can see, the digital forensic evidence establishes Iran's actions beyond any shadow of a doubt. It is essential that we make this public immediately and use it to justify reducing our military alert level. This is the only way we can stop the rapidly escalating tensions between ourselves, Russia, and the West. I am very confident this information is already in the hands of the Americans," he said, without revealing that he was the one to leak it. "If they announce these findings before we do, and we have not already reduced our alert status, our adversaries will certainly conclude we harbor hostile intentions. They will regard no other conclusion as plausible, and we would conclude exactly the same thing if our roles were reversed. We have an opportunity to pull the world back from the brink of unimaginable destruction. We must take it, and we must take it now."

There were several seconds of silence as Laurent surveyed the faces of the men around the conference table. They were difficult to read, except for the minister of defense who was shaking his head affirmatively. The man was the second most influential person to Brandt, and Laurent's spirits started to soar in anticipation of a potential breakthrough. But the terrible timing of an unforeseen event was about to send the meeting terribly off the rails.

At the same moment, a little over 4,000 miles to the west, the same unforeseen event was about to cause tensions to soar in in the White House Situation Room.

Situation Room, The White House, Washington D.C.

Ongoing conversations were interrupted by the abrupt voice of the Situation Room's audio technician. "Excuse me sir, I have an emergency call coming in from COMSUBLANT," the acronym for the Commander, Submarine Force Atlantic.

President Ellison looked at General Weatherby, the Joint Chiefs Chairman, as Weatherby said, "Put him through."

The image of a three-star Navy Admiral in fatigues immediately appeared on the large screen TV at the end of the conference table. The call originated from COMBSUBLANT's garrison at the Naval Support Activity, Hampton Roads, Virginia.

The Admiral spoke, "Excuse me sir, but we just received a flash traffic message from the fast-attack sub Virginia. They are being pursued by a European Federation sub, of German origin. Our skipper believes the boat is showing hostile intent. It appears to have opened its outer torpedo doors and is pinging the Virginia with active sonar. The skipper is asking for clarification of the rules of engagement."

"The Virginia?" the President asked.

"Yes sir. It's one of our nuclear-powered fast attack boats, submarines, operating in the English Channel," replied the Admiral.

"If that German sub so much as twitches we should blow it out of the water," the President said.

"Wait a minute, Mr. President!" Burt Hagenlocker responded. "It sounds to me like it's just trying to chase us out of its area of operations. Pinging our boat with active sonar gives us an exact fix on their location. Firing at us would be an act of suicide. Even if they get lucky with a shot, it wouldn't be before we fired back."

"That's correct, Mr. President," the three-star replied.

"So, what do you want to do?" asked the President.

SecDef Hagenlocker interjected, "We need to be the cooler head, here, Mr. President. We should not give the Virginia's skipper clearance to fire unless he is fired upon."

"I agree," responded the three-star. "I'd go a step further. I'd like to order the Virginia out of the Channel. The Federation, or Germans, or whoever the hell is in command of that boat, is just trying to flex their muscles and put on a show. Let them. There is only a downside, and likely uncontrolled escalation, if we allow our boat to engage."

"I don't like running," the President replied.

"We're not running, Mr. President," responded SecDef. "That German boat is no match for the Virginia, and they know it. We are taking the high road and walking away from a useless fight. It's the right decision. Our Captain should be authorized to fire only if fired upon and told to do everything he can to de-escalate."

"I agree, Mr. President," replied the three-star Admiral. "In fact, the Captain began a course out of the Channel before he got to antenna depth to contact us."

Hagenlocker wrote a quick note on the legal pad in front of him and slid it over for Director Shevchenko to see. It read, "Our 30-something Navy Commander is more of an adult than his CNC."

"OK," the President said, "But I don't like it."

The President of the United States had been talked down by the grownups in the room. Several thousand miles to the east, the acting Chancellor of the European Federation, and older and more stubborn man, was about to confront the same pushback and put up a more forceful argument.

Office of the Chancellor, European Federation, Berlin, Germany

Their conversation was interrupted by the buzz of the intercom on the conference table. Brandt leaned across and pushed a button to open the line. "Yes?" he asked.

"Sir, Admiral Schmidt is on the line. He said it is an emergency and that it is imperative I interrupt."

"Put him through," said an irritated Brandt.

"Sir, one of our submarines, the U-32, is being engaged by an American Boat, we believe Virginia Class. The Captain has asked for clarification on the rules of engagement. He has the American boat under chase and wishes permission to fire."

"Arrogant Americans," Brandt said in disgust. "They think they can strut around the Atlantic and our Channel as if it were their own private lake, while their poodle Jeremy Boren does nothing to stop them. We need to teach them a lesson."

The hair stood up on the back of Laurent's neck, and for the first time in as long as he could remember he was genuinely afraid. The other men around the table displayed varying levels of concern.

The Minister of Defense was the first to speak, pleading, "Herr Chancellor, we must not escalate. We must de-escalate."

Laurent felt a momentary sense of relief and was grateful the man had the courage to speak up. His relief was short lived.

"Shut up!" Brandt boomed. "I need cabinet ministers with steel for spines, not sponges!," then said, "Admiral, blow that American submarine out of the water!"

Laurent could no longer hold back. "Belay that order, Admiral! General Brandt, you do not have the authority to issue such an order!"

Brandt looked at Laurent in disbelief. He was astonished at the direct challenge. "The hell I don't," he screamed.

"No sir, you do not!" Laurent fired back, not relenting. "The moment France gave notice of its withdrawal from the European Federation, the Federation ceased to exist. As a result, the positions and authority of each of you in this room no longer exist. That order can only be given by Chancellor of Germany! Admiral, you are to ignore that order!"

"General Brandt," the Admiral replied in a calm and unemotional voice, deliberately using Brandt's military title and not the title of Chancellor, "I'm afraid I find General Laurent's arguments compelling. At a minimum, I am going to have to seek clarity from the German Ministry of Defense before acting on orders of such potential gravity."

Brandt looked like he was about to explode. "Guard!" he screamed. "In here immediately! Place this spineless Frenchman under arrest and escort him out of the building!" He then looked at his Minister of Defense and said, "If this spineless Admiral will not follow my direct order, put me through at once to the Captain of that submarine!"

Events then began to play out in what seemed like slow motion. In his peripheral vision, he could see the guard enter the office. It was the same man who met him at the security station as he walked in. He noticed the officer's sidearm remained in its holster. He remembered the man's sad look, and his comment, "Go with God, General." A profound sense of calm enveloped him, like a warm blanket. It was a moment of clarity like he had never felt. Odd, he thought, as he was convinced he was about to experience his last few moments on Earth. He knew what he had to do.

He heard Brandt continue to scream, but this time he could not make out the words. They were muffled, almost sounding like they came from the opposite end of a long tunnel. He discretely reached under the table and carefully pulled open the flap to the holster of his sidearm. The Minister of Defense was sitting next to him, and Laurent could see the man watch what he was doing. Yet the Minister sat silently. As he began to retrieve the pistol it was odd, he thought, that he didn't seem to need to be in a hurry. He was actually relaxed. His actions were slow, fluid, and deliberate. He raised the pistol above the table and pointed it at Brandt, his former mentor. Laurent felt neither fear nor anger, only sadness. He saw Brandt's facial expressions begin to change as the man noticed the firearm. Brandt's eyes grew wide and his face began to contort as the lizard part of his brain processed what was increasingly obvious a threat. Laurent leveled the sidearm, steadied his right hand, and fired three rounds into Brandt's chest.

It was over. Laurent continued to sit, as he processed the fact that for the moment he still seemed to be alive, unless, of course, shock was blocking the signals getting to his brain of a mortal wound to himself.

Then he noticed it. The guard's sidearm was still in its holster.

Chapter 71 – Emma

La Casa de le Emma, Uspallata, Argentina

Depart Mendoza, Argentina and drive south on Highway 40 to Highway 7, then travel west, then north, and in about 2 hours and forty-five minutes you find yourself in the quaint town of Uspallata, elevation 6,700 feet, on the eastern approach to the Andes Mountains, population 3,400. It is far off the beaten path of anyone interested in Argentine wine country and almost never visited by tourists. It also is an excellent place to hide, or so she thought.

On the outskirts of the town, largely hidden by the rugged terrain, lies a large mansion of about 9,000 square feet. The locals call it "La Casa de le Emma", or "Emma's house" in English. It is the home, the South American safe house, of Emma Clark.

Clark stood outside on the veranda and soaked up a view of the Andes that was breathtaking. Although she had left a Summer in the Bay area that felt like Hell's Front Porch, it was winter in Argentina and the temperature was about 40 degrees, made tolerable by her Canada Goose down jacket and the large propane-fueled fire pit she was standing next to. Her tenure as CEO of PrinSafe proved far shorter than she had imagined. That was a disappointment, but she was happy to be enjoying her large estate, complete with an impressive Argentine wine cellar, and not sitting in some jail as the guest of the U.S. authorities. She would lay low for a while, she decided, as long as it took for things to settle down and the world to turn the page on recent disasters, then plan her next move. Perhaps Southern Europe, she thought. Italy could be a lovely place to live for a person of means. Perhaps even somewhere in South America. One thing was certain – there would be a next move. She learned at the feet of her mentor, Westy Reynolds, that resilience was as essential an element of success as intelligence. Living out her life in quiet isolation, no matter how comfortable, would be a fate almost as bad as death.

She reached down to the side of the firepit and turned the knob to shut off the gas. Time to go inside. She would have her cook prepare a medium-rare ribeye and open a bottle of Catana Zapata Estiba Reservada Agrelo, a superb red blend with a local price tag of over $500 a bottle. She had a contract with the vineyard for a minimum of five cases a year, ten times the normal customer allocation.

She walked through the living room and towards an intercom speaker mounted on the wall. She pressed the call button, and hailed María, her chef de le casa. There was no answer. Odd, she thought. She then called out María's name. Again, no answer. She walked into the kitchen and looked. It was dark. The lights were turned off. Odd, she thought again. She could have sworn she saw the lights on in the kitchen before going outside, and even heard the clatter of pots and pans, presumably María getting ready to prepare the evening meal. She briefly wondered if this was her cook's day off, then remembered it was Friday. Her cook worked Monday through Friday. She then remembered she had fixed her breakfast.

Somewhere buried deep inside the lizard part of Emma Clark's brain her threat-detection instincts were starting to gradually fire. She was neither worried nor afraid, but somewhere in her gut a tiny sense of unease was starting to take hold. She walked across the expansive space and approached one of the front windows of the estate. She glanced out and looked at the circular drive where her cook normally parked her car. It was gone. She must have left early for some reason, Clark concluded. She would have to talk to her about that on Monday. It was rude to leave early without saying anything. But she felt a modest sense of relief at solving the mystery and resolved to go into her study to retrieve the phone number of the local restaurant and order a hot meal for delivery to the estate. After ordering the food, she would open the Catana Zapata herself and enjoy a glass while she waited.

As she walked towards her study she noticed it was dark. That was odd, she thought, as she distinctly remembered turning on the lights when she got home about an hour ago. As she got closer to the open doors of the study, she felt a growing sense of apprehension. This was silly, she admonished herself. She had never been uneasy about living alone, and the estate was in the middle of nowhere. There hadn't been a violent crime anywhere near Uspallata for as long as anyone could remember. Get a grip.

After taking several more steps, the front of the large partner's desk came into view. Then she saw it. The hair stood up on the back of her neck. She could feel goosebumps engulf her forearms. She stopped. Then she stared. Sitting there on a silver serving tray, in plain view, towards the front of the desk, was an open bottle of the Catana Zapata, with a Rabbit wine opener laying on its side next to the bottle and two wine glasses with full pours. There had been several strange observations over the last few minutes, most of which had reasonable explanations. But she knew full well that the $500 bottle of wine had not been there when she left the study a while ago, and she had certainly not opened and poured two glasses of it.

She took a few more steps towards the open doors, more slowly now. In seconds she had an unobstructed view of a dark figure sitting in her chair behind the desk.

"Please, come in," the man said, as he picked up one of the wineglasses himself then motioned her towards a chair across the desk from him. "And please, have a seat."

Her heart felt like it was beating out of her chest. She was so consumed with fear that her legs barely obeyed her brain's instructions to move. As she approached the chair, she noticed it was moved closer to the desk. As she sat down, her eyes strained to make out the face of the figure in front of her. He swirled the liquid in the glass a few times then took a sip.

"I certainly must complement you on your cellar. I have a few bottles of this myself, but nowhere near your inventory. Please, join me," he said as he gestured towards the other wine glass that was directly in front of her.

She picked up the glass. It remained in her peripheral vision as she kept an intense focus on the face in front of her. She then took a sip, and the man took another sip as well. Then it came to her. She realized who he was. "So, it's you?" she asked, as a rhetorical question.

"Joseph Michael Barber, at your service, Dr. Clark, in spite of numerous efforts on your part to accelerate my demise."

She didn't bother denying his accusation. She immediately knew anyone smart enough to find her, get past her security, then be in the house the last hour and a half she was here without being noticed was too smart to believe any lame denials. But now she was as curious as she was afraid. She took a long drink of the wine, hoping the alcohol would calm her nerves.

"I have to ask," she said, "how did you get past my security, and where is my staff?"

"Getting past your security was easy, given we had a complete set of plans and all electrical schematics for this estate."

She looked astonished. "How did you manage that?"

"We live in a digital world, Dr. Clark. You should know that better than almost anyone. My digital forensics lab in Rye hacked the records of the construction company that built this place. We figured that newer building plans would be in digital format, CadCam and all that stuff. We were correct. I can practically tell you where every nail is in this estate. The security systems themselves were disabled remotely, also from Rye. As for your staff, we sent them all emails from your private account, also hacked, informing them that you would be out of the country for an extended period and that their services would not be required until early Summer, although I had to talk to your cook directly, as she was thinking about your dinner." He raised his wine glass and took another sip. "Please, don't let it go to waste. It's been breathing for over an hour and has opened up nicely. It would be a crime to let it go to waste." She took another large sip as well, praying the alcohol would soon take effect.

"How did you find me?" she asked in bewilderment.

"That took a few more extra resources, but I have some colleagues who have very impressive resources."

"C.I.A.?" she asked.

"I can neither confirm nor deny," Barber said with a broad smile.

"F.B.I.?"

He didn't answer.

"But please, how? I really have to know."

"You place too much stock in your own intelligence, Dr. Clark. You have a fatal flaw. You are predisposed to underestimate potential adversaries."

"What?" she asked.

"Ok, the moment we confirmed your hands were dirty in all of this, agents from the F.B.I. San Francisco Field Office were watching your every move. You thought you were staying one step ahead of us. We were actually always one step ahead of you. Your outsized ego couldn't imagine anything else. And the pilot of the NetJet you used; he was one of ours, switched at the last minute. I'll concede the trail went slightly cold for a bit when you immediately left Mendoza after landing to head up here. But really Dr. Clark, La Casa de le Emma? Do you know how many women are named Emma in the Mendoza Province? Exactly one. Very disappointing. If you had just been a little more creative, we may never have found this place, or at least not anytime soon." Barber then took another long pull on the wine, emptying his glass. "Please, finish your wine. We need to take a little walk."

Her emotions were a mix of terror and resignation. She emptied her glass, set it down on the desk, and started to follow Barber out the door of the study.

"Where are we going?" she asked.

"We are going to take a little walk down to your panic room. I've made a few modifications I'd like you to see."

She was now shaking as she followed Barber across the living room to a bookcase, where he pushed a button to reveal a stairway downstairs. As the two of them walked down the staircase and into the room, she was on the verge of tears, and the bluster was gone. As she looked around the room she noticed it was stark. Most of the furniture had been removed. There was only a bed, a small table and one chair.

"What have you done here?" she asked, her voice breaking. "What are you going to do with me?"

"You have provisions for about 2 months, although you will have to eat the food cold. I've disabled the stove."

"You intend to lock me in here, don't you?"

"That's part of the plan."

Her spirits began to soar. She had a plan "B" if the doors to the panic room wouldn't open. Maybe she had outsmarted him after all. She maintained a dour countenance so as not to reveal her new-found hope.

"And in case you are thinking about your backup plan, we've disabled the explosive bolts in the door hinges. They won't work. I'm afraid you'll be stuck in here. And I'm afraid that after I lock you in, we plan to weld the doors shut as an additional insurance policy against your escape."

"So, you do plan to kill me?" she asked, "By starving me to death."

"Kill you? Why Dr. Clark, I already have," Barber said, but this time without the smile.

"What? What do you mean?"

"In a most elegant fashion," he replied.

"I don't understand," she replied, her voice now breaking.

"The wine, Dr. Clark, the wine?"

"What? You've poisoned me?"

"Well, technically I guess the answer to that question would be yes, but not in a conventional sense."

"Just tell me, you bastard!" she now screamed.

"I've taken a page out of your playbook."

"What?" she asked.

He retrieved a device from his pocket, slightly larger than a cell phone, and tossed to her.

"What is this?" she asked.

"Turn it on and hold it next to your wine glass," he said.

She turned it over, found the on switch, depressed it, and before she could even get it next to her wine glass it started rapidly clicking."

"What!" she exclaimed with a renewed look of horror on her face.

"It's a Geiger counter. It's measuring the decay of the Polonium 210 you ingested a few minutes ago."

"You bastard!" she screamed again.

"Now, now, Dr. Clark, we've learned you are experienced in its use, right?" he queried, referring to three years prior when she gave it to her boss so she could assume the Chief Executive position of PrinSafe. "I've given you a slightly smaller dose than you used to cook the insides of your former mentor. Don't worry, the dose is quite lethal, but it should take a bit longer to complete its work. Our best estimate is 4-6 weeks. I wanted to give you some extra time to think about your recent contributions to mankind. We've tried to remove everything in here that you could use to take your own life, but I suspect a person as creative as you could still find a way. But here's what I predict. Despite knowing the certain outcome, you are going to want to try and figure a way out of here, and maybe believe I dialed the dose down enough that you might recover from it. But by the time you finally come to the realization it's hopeless, you won't have the strength left to do anything."

"How could you do this?" she sobbed.

"Believe me, I've asked myself that question many times over the last week. Truth is, thinking about all the innocent people in Iran you helped barbeque, it actually wasn't all that hard. If it's any consolation, I am sure I will have some very bad dreams about this day."

Barber walked out of the panic room and shut the door. Marcus Day emerged from the shadows, pulled a portable welding torch out of a bag, fired it up, and began to seal the door. When finished, the two of them left the house and waited for a C.I.A. helicopter to pick them up and deliver them to the airport in Mendoza, where their waiting jet would fly them back home.

Epilogue

Barber walked out a side door of La Casa de le Emma and headed towards the front lawn. He expected the helicopter to arrive in about 10 minutes. As he rounded the corner, he was suddenly stopped in his tracks by an image he couldn't believe. It was Clark! How had she gotten out? He noticed she had an iron bar in her hand and was swinging it like a baseball bat towards his mid-section. As the makeshift weapon made solid contact with Barber's side, he buckled over in excruciating pain, but managed to stay on his feet. He saw her raise the iron bar again and commence another arc that would likely land a blow to his head this time. With that piece of metal, he was certain the strike would be fatal. Where the hell was Day? He tried to cry out for help, but his voice wouldn't respond. His mind shifted into automatic. He closed the distance between the two of them and wrapped his arms around her torso, trying to hold the two of them tightly together. It was a technique he was relentlessly trained to use both in the Navy SEALs and C.I.A. It was counterintuitive, but the highest probability of survival came from running towards danger, not away from it. The problem was his arms seemed weak, incapable of controlling her. His sudden lunge managed to throw off the trajectory of her strike, but in his peripheral vision he could see her cock her arm upwards again to ready another blow. He wasn't strong enough to stop her this time, and he could feel his legs begin to give out as everything now shifted into slow-motion. "So, this is what it feels like when a man is about to die," he thought, as the metal bar reached its apex and began a downward arc.

Then he remembered. He still had one trick left, a final desperate gesture that had saved his life once before in the woods three years ago. As his legs were failing him and forcing him ever closer to the ground, his head became level with hers. He opened his mouth as wide as he could, turned towards her neck and savagely sunk his teeth into her brachial artery. An arterial spray of blood covered his face as Clark's heart pumped the life out of her. Their eyes met. But she was smiling. What the......? He didn't understand the smile. Why on earth was she smiling? He was stunned as she began to speak in a low but very clear voice.

"Got you, asshole," she said, her eyes locked on his. "You just swallowed a good amount of my blood, laced with the Polonium 210 you intended for me alone. Welcome to the walking dead. See you in hell, real soon."

Barber closed his eyes. He saw his life flash before him. "How could things end this way?" he thought. The blow to the head would have been far better. At least it would have been quick. Was he now condemned to weeks of horrific pain as the Polonium cooked his insides while his loved ones watched, he wondered? He opened his eyes again. He sensed he was now horizontal, laying down. He must have fallen to the ground. Then suddenly he sat up. He could feel his heart beating hard and fast. The strength in his arms had returned. He looked around. His vision was fuzzy, but he could tell the environment was pleasant, even comfortable. Was he in Heaven? Then he started to recognize things. He noticed a TV hanging on a wall in front of him. He looked to his right and saw a large dresser. He was in his bedroom, back in Rye, New York! His wife, Diana, was lying next to him! It had been a dream, or more accurately another nightmare. It was a new one, but the most horrific part had been fueled by the old one that still tortured him from time to time. Now there were two. As he sat there, he wondered how often this new one would visit. It was the cost of survival, he concluded, and he would pay it. He would deal with it the same way he dealt with the other.

As he lay in bed and gradually became fully awake, he realized it had been six weeks since the fateful trip to Argentina. He was very much glad to be alive and in his own bed. He wondered if Clark was still alive. He doubted it. His bluster about weakening the dose of Polonium to extend its effects had been just that, more bluster than fact. He had said it to Clark to terrify her, and it had worked. She was likely dead now, rotting in that panic room and unlikely to be discovered for several months. The half-life of Polonium was only 138 days, so the room would be relatively safe by the time she was found.

He quietly slipped out of the bedroom, leaving his wife asleep, and went downstairs to make a cup of coffee. After making the coffee he retrieved the New York Times from his front porch and went into his office and turned on the TV news. He chose the BBC, hoping to hear more about how things were settling down in Europe. They were reporting on the weather, so he picked up the paper and began to read the lead story, displayed on the paper's right-hand column "above the fold". The Times headline read, in large bold font:

The European Federation, Once Seen as the Successor to the Failed European Union, is Officially Dissolved as France and Germany Partner with the United States, England and Other Nations to Begin the Work of Forging a New World Order

The right-hand column featured a story on Iran:

Riots in Iran Subside as Provisional Government is Established

Riots throughout Iran have finally begun to subside as a new provisional government is established and the formerly closed nation opens its borders to facilitate delivery of international aide. The Provisional Government has renounced the former regime's nuclear ambitions and has offered unfettered access to the nuclear weapons inspectors of the United Nations.

At least 20 nations are now actively engaged in providing medical services to the victims of the nuclear explosion over Qom, along with charitable organizations including The Red Cross, The Red Crescent, Catholic World

Charity, The Salvation Army and Samaritan's Purse. The relief arm of the United Nations is coordinating the delivery of food and clothing. In an unexpected move, the Government of Saudi Arabia has offered technical support to bring Iran's petroleum industry back on line to renew an important source of national income.

The Provisional Government has promised to honor the nation's Islamic institutions and culture but has announced Iran will no longer be governed as a theocracy. The position of Supreme Leader has been abolished, and new elections are promised as soon as order is restored. Mass demonstrations of support for the Provisional Government have begun to spontaneously spring up in several major cities.

"Maybe something good will come from this mess," Barber thought, but the price struck him as way too high.

He had much to be thankful for, he realized. He had survived multiple attempts on his life, and his body was finally almost fully healed. Most of all, he was thankful that there was nobody out there still trying to kill him. That is, at least so he thought..........

The End

(but stay tuned!)

Soli Deo Gloria

Acknowledgements

Many people have contributed to the successful completion of this novel, both directly and indirectly. First and foremost, I wish to thank my wife, Edith K. Tosh, without whose love, support, patience and humor this book would not have been written.

Much thanks are due to many dear friends in our new community of Fawn Lake, Virginia, for their extraordinarily positive response to my premier novel, "The Orion Affair", and strong encouragement to write a sequel. They would ask me about the sequel's status and exhort me to "get it done" virtually every time our paths crossed. Their encouragement helped fuel my ambitions.

Special thanks are again due my editors. Long-time friend and crack legal secretary, Sandy Horning, my former boss at Ford Motor Company, James Keefer, and my cousin and retired English teacher, Loretta Hitchcock, all contributed greatly to making this a much better product. Any mistakes that remain are strictly mine.

Inspiration for the scenes in the Shetland Islands came from my travels there in August 2018. I was moved by the stark and desolate beauty of the place and thought, "What a great location for a safe house!"

Brilliant and talented artist, Brandi Doane McCann, at e-Book Cover Designs, is responsible for the cover art on both Command and Control and my premier novel, The Orion Affair. Her work perfectly captured the imagery I wanted, and she was a delight to work with.

Finally, I wish to thank the many authors whose novels have thrilled me over the years, including such masters as the late Robert Ludlum, the late Tom Clancy, Brad Thor, the late Vince Flynn, David Baldacci, Daniel Silva, Mark Greaney, and Ben Coes to name just a few. They have been no small part of my inspiration to dare and imagine that I could craft compelling stories of my own.

Enjoyed "Command and Control"?

Check out "The Orion Affair", the premier novel by Dennis A. Tosh, also available at Amazon.com

*Praise for the Orion Affair**

"This book kept me on the edge of my seat. Could not put it down. What a plot!"

"This was the best work of fiction I have read in years. The character development, rich storytelling and the pace of the work was just fantastic. I can't wait for the next book!"

"It kept me guessing right to the last page."

"Could not put it down. A great combination of political intrigue and overreach combined with exciting military action. Realistic scenarios of government surveillance."

"Had many late nights because I didn't want to put it away. Can't wait for the next!"

"A real page turner – keeps the reader on the edge of your seat!"

"This book kept me on the edge of my seat. Could not put it down!"

***Amazon verified purchasers**

Made in the USA
Monee, IL
07 January 2020

20009618R00289